A Young B
sets out to
stirring "Ra

A Proud Southern Lady
has her secret life stripped bare in William Faulkner's
startling tale, "A Rose for Emily"

A Faithful Wife
has her first lesson in infidelity in Kate Chopin's "A
Respectable Woman"

A Pregnant Woman
reassures her lover in a display of grace under
the pressure of an imminent abortion in Ernest
Hemingway's terse "Hills Like White Elephants"

Two Very Different Women
lock in a ruinous conflict spurred by jealousy and
frustration in Jessamyn West's poignant "The
Condemned Librarian"

**These are but five of the thirty unforgettably
revealing stories that come together to form—**

The Experience of the American Woman

BARBARA H. SOLOMON is Professor of English at Iona
College in New Rochelle, N.Y. She is the editor of the
Signet Classic editions of *The Awakening and Selected
Stories of Kate Chopin,* and *Selected Stories of Mary
Wilkins Freeman and Sarah Orne Jewett.* Solomon has also
edited *American Wives: Thirty Short Stories by Women*
and *American Families: 28 Short Stories,* available in
Mentor editions

The Experience of the American Woman: 30 Stories

Edited by
Barbara H. Solomon

A MENTOR BOOK

MENTOR
Published by the Penguin Group
Penguin Books USA Inc., 375 Hudson Street,
New York, New York 10014, U.S.A.
Penguin Books Ltd, 27 Wrights Lane,
London W8 5TZ, England
Penguin Books Australia Ltd, Ringwood,
Victoria, Australia
Penguin Books Canada Ltd, 10 Alcorn Avenue,
Toronto, Ontario, Canada M4V 3B2
Penguin Books (N.Z.) Ltd, 182–190 Wairau Road,
Auckland 10, New Zealand

Penguin Books Ltd, Registered Offices:
Harmondsworth, Middlesex, England

EX

First Mentor Printing, June, 1978
15 14 13 12 11 10 9 8 7

Acknowledgments

Anderson, Sherwood: "Mother." From WINESBURG, OHIO by Sherwood Anderson. Copyright 1919 by B. W. Huebsch. Copyright renewed 1947 by Eleanor Copenhaver Anderson. Reprinted by permission of The Viking Press.

Bambara, Toni Cade: "Raymond's Run." Copyright © 1970 by Toni Cade Bambara. Reprinted from GORILLA, MY LOVE by Toni Cade Bambara, by permission of Random House, Inc.

Canfield, Dorothy: "Sex Education." Copyright 1945 by Dorothy Canfield Fisher; renewed 1973 by Sarah Fisher Scott. Reprinted from A HARVEST OF STORIES by Dorothy Canfield by permission of Harcourt Brace Jovanovich, Inc.

Childress, Alice: "The Pocketbook Game." From LIKE ONE OF THE FAMILY, copyright © 1956, by Alice Childress. Reprinted by permission.

Dreiser, Theodore: "The Second Choice." From FREE, AND OTHER STORIES, copyright 1918, renewed 1946 by Mrs. Theodore Dreiser. Used by permission of the Dreiser Trust, Harold Dies, trustee.

Elliott, George P.: "Sandra." Reprinted by permission of Georges Borchardt, Inc. Copyright © 1967 by George P. Elliott.

Faulkner, William: "A Rose for Emily." Copyright 1930 and renewed 1958 by William Faulkner. Reprinted from COLLECTED STORIES OF WILLIAM FAULKNER, by permission of Random House, Inc.

Greenberg, Joanne: "Gloss on a Decision of the Council of Nicaea." From SUMMERING by Joanne Greenberg. Copyright © 1961, 1963, 1964, 1966 by Joanne Greenberg. Reprinted by permission of Holt, Rinehart and Winston, Publishers.

Hemingway, Ernest: "Hills Like White Elephants." Copyright 1927 Charles Scribner's Sons. Reprinted by permission of Charles Scribner's Sons from MEN WITHOUT WOMEN by Ernest Hemingway.

Hunter, Kristin: "Debut." Copyright 1968 by Kristin Hunter, reprinted by permission of Harold Matson Co., Inc.

Jaffe, Rona: "Rima the Bird Girl." Copyright 1960, 1962, 1963, 1964, 1965 by Rona Jaffe. Reprinted by permisison of Simon and Schuster, Inc.

The following page constitutes an extention of this copyright page.

REGISTERED TRADEMARK—MARCA REGISTRADA

Library of Congress Catalog Card Number: 77-95345

Printed in the United States of America

For Nancy and Jennifer—
and their favorite magician, Stanley

Acknowledgments

I would like to express my appreciation to Constance Ayers Denne of Baruch College, Katherine Usher Henderson of the College of New Rochelle, and Pat O'Sullivan for their continued encouragement and warm friendship. For his judicious reading of my manuscript, I would like to thank Michael Palma of the Department of English of Iona College. At the College, a great deal of assistance was offered by Barbara Beauzethier of Ryan Library, Mary A. Bruno and the staff of the Secretarial Services Center, and Thomas Matamoros, English Department Student Assistant. To Iona College, I am indebted for a research and writing grant for the summer of 1977.

Contents

Introduction

The thirty stories of this volume portray varied aspects of the experience of American women. Representative of the work of some of the country's finest writers—both female and male—these portraits reveal the widely differing lives women have led and the ways in which we have typically thought about women over the last hundred years.

Much about the American woman has been unique, from the special value she acquired in a frontier nation in which there were often few women to become the wives and partners in toil of isolated settlers to her modern position as the occupant of a technically advanced, luxurious, middle-class house which is the envy of people around the globe. Yet not until a revitalized feminist consciousness emerged about a decade ago did women gauge the extent to which they had been mythologized in literature and maligned in life. When they began to examine the ideals created for them to live by and to see how thoroughly their experience and emotions repudiated the easy generalizations made about them, women individually and in groups made a commitment to gain true self-knowledge and to mint a clear, truthful image of their selves to replace that counterfeit currency, the coined stereotypes, which had so long been passed about.

When women examined the literature in which they had been accustomed to find their models, they were shocked to find that in many of their most treasured volumes they were depicted as mere stereotypes, or bit players, unimportant creatures except as they related to male characters. The literary and interdisciplinary approaches of these new feminist critics were varied and revitalizing. For example, Cynthia Griffin Wolff skillfully analyzed some of these literary stereotypes, such as the virtuous woman, the sensuous woman, the liberated woman, and the American girl, tracing the underlying political and economic theories about women which

1

were current at the time the female portraits were created.[1] In *The Troublesome Helpmate: A History of Misogyny* (1966), Katharine M. Rogers focused attention on the extensive number of literary works in which fear and hatred of women motivate much of the male characters' behavior.[2] A book with a somewhat different perspective, Mary Ellman's *Thinking About Women* (1968), pointed out the extent to which literature by women has been treated with condescension by critics who practice a form of sexual discrimination, considering women's writing in a separate category rather than as part of the mainstream of American literature.[3] And, in the course of substituting females for males in descriptions of a series of familiar plots, Joanna Russ demonstrated the kinds of plot limitations on female characters we had always unconsciously accepted. Among her "revised" plots were: "Two strong women battle for supremacy in the early West" and "A young girl in Minnesota finds her womanhood by killing a bear."[4]

As a result of the feminist dedication to reevaluating literary materials and seeking valid portraits of women's lives, numerous female writers, either entirely neglected like Kate Chopin or insufficiently valued like Edith Wharton, received some of the attention and appreciation they had earned through their extraordinary talent. Long-forgotten tales such as Charlotte Perkins Gilman's "The Yellow Wallpaper" and works such as Sarah Orne Jewett's *The Country of the Pointed Firs* began to be recognized as American treasures which had too long lain dusty and unregarded in our attics. Many valuable collections of women's writing began to appear and these anthologies have helped to provide some redress of an outrageous and ludicrous situation in which women authors were often entirely absent or represented by one or two entries in anthologies which claimed to fully represent the American literary scene. It seems apparent that we must reconsider not only the female perspective in the writing of fiction but also the variety of roles played by women characters in our literature.

Perhaps a few words explaining the informing principles behind my selection of the stories of this volume would be helpful here. First, I chose to include the work of male authors because it is imperative that we reexamine their contributions to our American literary heritage in a new context of feminist awareness. No male writer was chosen to act as a whipping boy, but insofar as I could, I sought to present the writer through his best and often most typical work.

The stories are all literature and not propaganda for any particular political bias. They reflect the ways important American writers have been thinking and writing about women, not necessarily the ways we would like to see women portrayed in our literature. Surprisingly, some of the early stories, such as those by Anne Warner and Edith Wharton, reveal very contemporary attitudes. The roots of today's feminist consciousness have been quietly nourished in such unexpected places as the sparsely populated, rocky hillsides of nineteenth-century New England and the formal gardens of a wealthy New York society woman.

Next, it might be well to take up here the optimistic or pessimistic viewpoints dramatized in these stories, many of which chronicle the disillusionment or despair of women. Certainly, to a large extent, American literature suggests that women are sufferers and victims. But do they suffer and fail because of their sex? In my comments on the stories, I emphasize the purely feminine situations which lead to painful existences and unfulfilled lives.

Finally, I would like to remark on the following seven categories I have employed for the purposes of a brief description of each story: Female–Male Encounters, Women Among Women, Insights and Identities, Women and Madness, Courtships, Married Women, and Women with Children. These divisions are admittedly artificial and in many instances arbitrary. For example, a story in which a woman gains insight, such as Wharton's "Souls Belated," might be equally well described as a "Female–Male Encounter." Rona Jaffe's "Rima the Bird Girl" is a story of identity—or lack of one—as much as it is a story of courtship. Nevertheless, as imperfect as the following section arrangements may be, they are still useful for noting themes and patterns of organization crucial to a contemporary consciousness of American women's literary roles.

Female–Male Encounters

A considerable number of these stories capture a significant aspect of a relationship between a woman and a man.

Several dramatize the unbridgeable gulf between the masculine and feminine perspective or experience. For example, biological identity is an inextricable part of the dilemma of the pregnant women in the stories by Ernest Hemingway and William Carlos Williams. Both the authors and male readers may sympathize greatly with the female characters, but they know that they will never need to face the physical reality of carrying an unwanted child or the terror and mystery of the process of childbirth. In some of the stories, such as Richard Sherman's "Barrow Street" and Kristin Hunter's "Debut," social pressures and profound fears account for the particular female perspective of the character. Finally, "male looks at female" describes the informing vision in John Updike's "Wife-wooing" and George P. Elliott's "Sandra," two tales in which male narrators record varied attitudes toward a woman.

In Ernest Hemingway's "Hills Like White Elephants" (1927), the pregnant Jig does not wish to have the abortion which her lover believes will solve all of their problems. She appears pathetically weak and dependent as she asks him, " 'And if I do it you'll be happy and things will be like they were and you'll love me?' " Asserting that she no longer cares what happens to her, Jig, like Catherine Barkley of *A Farewell to Arms*, is willing to abandon all sense of a separate self and live through pleasing another. Yet in an important respect, Hemingway considers Jig superior to the man she would serve and portrays her as a kind of female hero. Unlike her lover, who insists on disguising the situation with empty words, she refuses to lie to herself. In spite of all of his naive assurances, she faces the fact that after this crisis, their world can never be the same and neither can they. He vainly attempts to deny reality; she exhibits "grace under pressure" as she reassures him that she feels fine.

William Carlos Williams' "A Night in June" (1932), recounts the delivery of a poor Italian woman's eighth child as observed by the physician attending her. During the long evening of the labor, the physician is able to sleep intermittently since the pregnant woman never cries out during the hours of labor pains, nor during the subsequent delivery. She does not want to awaken the small child who sleeps next to her throughout the night. Certainly, the physician admires her courage and is impressed by the ex-

nt to which she has collaborated with him during the
elivery. He recalls: "The flesh of my arm lay against the
esh of her knee gratefully. It was I who was being com-
orted and soothed." Yet in spite of his fondness and
espect for Angelina, she is distinctly "the other," a crea-
ure he tenderly observes but one with whom he
an never identify. Earlier he had described her comments in
alian to her husband as "some high pitched animalistic
ound." Now the most expansive compliment he can
estow on her is to think of her as a clean beast: "This
oman in her present condition would have seemed re-
ulsive to me ten years ago—now, poor soul, I see her to
e as clean as a cow that calves." The gulf between the
oman's experience and the physician's is such that he
urns to an image of animal reproduction to ennoble her
xperience. And never does he raise the question which
ould be natural to many women: "In her condition could
have acted with similar control and fortitude?"

In a story which takes place in a very different milieu,
Richard Sherman's "Barrow Street" (1948), the encounter
etween the woman and man occurs in an expensive and
astefully furnished apartment. This attractive home and the
oung child asleep in his crib are the tangible badges of
uccess which Dorothy flaunts before George Hargrave, who
ad been her lover only a few years earlier. When George in-
uires about the changes which have taken place in Dorothy,
he indicates that her husband has "brought out" these traits
n her character.

The story's surprising conclusion raises several issues. Is
ur principal response admiration for the way in which
Dorothy has contrived this visit and revenged herself on the
man who ended their relationship with a flimsy pretext? Or
do we, instead, feel pity for a woman with such an inade-
quate self-image that she must usurp another woman's identity in order to triumph over George? And finally, do we,
with the sensibilities of the 1970s, think that the story's prem-
ise is pernicious? After all, Dorothy proclaims that the
right husband can confer a new and dignified identity on
his wife. Her new identity is that of serene caretaker of the
sleeping child and comfortable rooms. Doesn't Dorothy's
need for a beautiful home, handsome husband, and well-
loved child reflect society's narrowest vision of success for
a woman? It is intriguing to toy with the idea of a different
version of "Barrow Street," one with a reversal or roles.

How would a rejected young man go about impressing an
taunting his former mistress and proving that his fine
traits had lain dormant because she failed to inspire th
best within him?

An entirely dehumanized encounter between a female an
several males is the subject of Kristin Hunter's "Debut
(1973). Judy Simmons is at first an invisible eavesdroppe
listening to the exchange between three ghetto boys and th
streetwise Lucy Mae, a tough neighborhood teenager. A wal
divides Judy's middle-class world of aspirations urged upo
her by her social-climbing mother from the crude dram
played out below. "She had heard them at their dirty tal
in the alley before and had always been successful in ig
noring it; it had nothing to do with her, the wall protecte
her from their kind."

In a few hours Judy is to attend the Debutantes' Bal
marking her official entrance into the marriage market as sh
seeks a suitable husband. But her real initiation comes in he
own darkened room where she has been discovered by th
boys below. Intimidated by their taunts and threats, Jud
transforms herself into a creature who will triumph ove
the enemy. She abandons the peace and warmth of huma
relationships to enlist as a soldier in the war of social an
economic competition her mother has always been fighting.

In John Updike's "Wife-wooing" (1960), a somewhat so
phisticated and literary husband has made an effort to ar
range an evening in which his wife will be responsive to th
sexual excitation he feels. His attitude, as he watches hi
wife and their three children sitting before the fireplace, i
playful and imaginative. Exploring the sound that for hin
describes his wife, he contrives a number of alliterativ
statements:

> What soul took thought and knew that adding "wo" to mai
> would make a woman? The difference exactly. The wide w, th
> receptive o. Womb. In our crescent the children for all thei
> size seem to come out of you toward me, wet fingers and eye
> tinted bronze. Three children, five persons, seven years. Seve
> years since I wed wide warm woman, white-thighed. Wooe
> and wed. Wife. A knife of a word that for all its final bite di
> not end the wooing. To my wonderment.

Is this, perhaps, a description which is distinctly "mas
culine," a means of self-definition which would neve
occur to a woman? The husband expresses the tension o

eing married yet separate, the frustration of sexual
vertures which have come to nothing, and then candidly
eveals the meanness and spite with which he examines his
vife's appearance the following morning. Although the nar-
ator's central insight revolves about the value of the un-
xpected as opposed to the expected gift, the story conveys
nuch about the essential isolation of the individual in mar-
iage and the egotism and futility of expecting another to
narch to precisely the same inner rhythm by which we
nove.

In George Elliott's "Sandra" (1968), the male narrator,
Dell Oakes, has purchased a domestic slave, an eighteen-
year-old female named "Sandra." In this satire on power and
ole-playing in marriage, Elliott recounts Oakes's experiences
with his slave, first as the completely satisfied master, then as
the benevolent employer who has granted freedom to the
creature who pleased him, and later as the disgruntled husband of a self-centered wife. Although Elliott satirizes the behavior and expectations of the male narrator, the most telling
criticism is of Sandra's behavior after she has become Mrs.
Oakes. Her husband explains:

> First of all, as a wife, she was much frailer than she had
> been as a slave. I had to buy all sorts of things for her, auto-
> matic machines to wash the clothes and the dishes, a cooking
> stove with nine dials and two clocks, an electric ironer that
> could iron a shirt in two minutes, a vacuum cleaner, one
> machine to grind the garbage up and another to mix pancake
> batter, a thermostatic furnace, an electric floor waxer, and a
> town coupe for her to drive about to do her errands in. She had
> to get other people to wash her hair now, and shave her legs
> and armpits, and polish her toenails and fingernails for her. She
> took out subscriptions to five ladies' magazines, which printed
> among them half a million words a month for her to read, and
> she had her very bathrobe designed in Paris.

Only somewhat exaggerated, this criticism closely parallels
classic denunciations of husbands against their wives, women
who have lived out the roles of their husbands' housekeepers
and sex objects. Evaluating what their wives do while they
are away at work, men are often deluded about the joys of
the home and the pleasures of the female pursuit of continuing youth and beauty. Only in the last decade with the appearance of such works as Betty Friedan's *The Feminine
Mystique* (1963) have women begun to supply realistic

descriptions of the insecurity, frustration, and anger of those
wives who have supposedly been given everything they could
possibly desire.

Women Among Women

The one subject in this collection rendered only through
stories written by women is that of women's relationship
with one another. As Virginia Woolf first pointed out, significant relationships between women are rarely the central subject in the fiction of male writers. Generally, in their work
women are characterized as wives, mothers, lovers, daughters,
or sisters who are in conflict with or give assistance to an important male character. Strikingly absent from American
literature about women are the depictions of camaraderie
which are so easily discovered in fiction about men at
school, men at work, and men at war. Yet as Carroll
Smith-Rosenberg has demonstrated, in nineteenth-century
America relationships of lifelong love and friendship between women were among the strongest bonds recognized
by society.[5]

Five stories in this anthology depict women in an environment in which men either play a minimal role or are entirely absent: "The Guests of Mrs. Timms," "The Pocketbook Game," "The Condemned Librarian," "Gloss on a
Decision of the Council of Nicaea," and "Raymond's
Run." Perhaps it is meaningful that in the most recent of
these, "Raymond's Run," Toni Cade Bambara's heroine is
well on the way to enjoying the healthy sense of competition, cooperation, and camaraderie which heretofore have
been strictly masculine territory.

The earliest of these stories, Sarah Orne Jewett's "The
Guests of Mrs. Timms" (1895), typically expresses Jewett's
feminine perspective. As Edward Garnett observed, in her
stories

> woman herself it is that decides, arranges and criticises her
> own life, and the life of her friends, enemies, relations, and of
> the whole parish—and the reader has a sense in her pages that
> should the curtain be dropped on the feminine understanding,
> the most interesting side of life would become a mere darkened
> chaos to the isolated masculine understanding.[6]

A series of visits, welcome and unwelcome, provides the framework for the delineation of the traits of several New England women. The pompous Mrs. Persis Flagg and her timid acquaintance Miss Cynthia Pickett set out by stage-coach to visit the socially superior Mrs. Timms. Her casual invitation, extended to them the previous week, was obviously nothing more than an empty phrase. The arrival of the two visitors from Woodville is an unexpected inconvenience to Mrs. Timms who has a genius for simultaneously observing social forms and making her guests squirm with discomfort and shame. Mrs. Flagg and Miss Pickett are able to salvage their dignity and self-image, after all, through their successful visit to the less prestigious Nancy Fell who provides gracious hospitality for her unexpected callers. Jewett exercises gentle irony as she probes the illusions, rationalizations, and defensive reactions of the two self-conscious travelers. In addition, the story is virtually a miniature treatise on the social hierarchy of small New England towns and on such matters as housekeeping, fashion, and religious activities.

The relationship between Mildred, the black domestic worker, and her white employer Mrs. E, is captured with barbed irony in Alice Childress's sketch "The Pocketbook Game" (1956). As Mildred recounts her experience, she communicates her own straightforward and spontaneous attitudes toward people, attitudes which must make Mrs. E's behavior particularly offensive to her. Mildred, who has been personally insulted, becomes an acute social critic as she responds to her employer's lame explanation. Her honest and simple retort says it all.

In Jessamyn West's "The Condemned Librarian" (1955), Louise McKay is the extraordinary librarian who has fulfilled her dream of becoming a physician. She is the symbol of achievement that obsesses Miss McCullars, the frightened, insecure narrator of the story. This twenty-six-year-old teacher develops an intense desire to defeat Dr. McKay, to rob her of the admiration she inspires in other women, and to make her suffer. Although Miss McCullars has resigned her teaching position in a one-room schoolhouse in order to pursue her own dream of becoming an artist, she lacks the courage to carry out her plan. Instead, at the last minute she enrolls at a university to study for a secondary teaching credential which means nothing to her. This is one of the rare stories concerned with the significance of work in a woman's life. In it, West has explored the devastation caused when a woman is too fearful and has too impoverished a self-image to attempt to live up to her potential.

A very different sort of librarian, Miss Myra of the small southern town of Tugwell, is the central character of Joanne Greenberg's "Gloss on a Decision of the Council of Nicaea" (1966). She is the only white among eight women, all jailed for protesting against the racist practices of the town's public library. Ironically, the major conflict of this story is not between Myra and the brutal sheriff. He will treat her according to a familiar southern code for white women: they are all ladies. Her real adversary is Delphine, the educated young black woman who is the leader of this group of protesters. The two of them, as Myra comes to realize, are much alike. The librarian has made herself a storehouse of knowledge about the world's heroic leaders and victims of injustice. Delphine, on the other hand, is a storehouse of practical advice on the tactics of demonstrating and surviving police brutality. She regards the librarian not as an ally, but as an intruder, and does all she can to alienate the others from this white woman. Yet, through Myra's struggle with this fearless, arrogant, hate-filled adversary, Myra gains a glimpse into the sources of the very human emotions which motivated the historical figures who have always inspired her.

Toni Cade Bambara's "Raymond's Run" (1971) is a two-day chronicle of the life of a young female track star in Harlem. Squeaky, as the narrator is nicknamed, is a heroine of character and ability. Capable of protecting her retarded brother Raymond, she is strong, assertive, determined, and beautifully honest. She knows who she is and likes what she is. In contrast to her phony classmate Cynthia Procter, who pretends disdain for hard work or serious competition, Squeaky enjoys getting herself in shape for the May Day races. A perceptive critic of the dishonesty of females, she notices the way that Gretchen, her only serious competitor in the race, smiles at her. Squeaky thinks that "girls never really smile at each other because they don't know how to and don't want to know how and there's probably no one to teach us how, cause grown-up girls don't know either." As we can see from Squeaky's reactions while the judges decide who has won the fifty-yard dash, whatever the cards life deals to Squeaky, she will always be able to arrange them into a winning hand.

Insights and Identities

In a society in which women are so often described in terms of other people—"*his* wife" or "*her* mother"—women develop an intense awareness of the need to achieve a sense of self which grows from within. They need to learn to value their own beings apart from any services they render to others. In each of the stories in this group, women achieve an insight which enables them to better define themselves and their relationships to the outer world. Thus, in most of these stories experiences involving insight also involve identity.

Lydia Tillotson in Edith Wharton's "Souls Belated" (1899) gains an unexpected insight upon receipt of the official notification that her husband has divorced her. The story dramatizes the process by which this woman in search of freedom learns of the inexorable forces, both within and without, which are moving her toward a new identity—that of Ralph Gannett's wife. When Lydia fled her husband's stifling New York household, with its round of deadening social obligations, she believed that she and Ralph were beyond conventional moral dictates and that the bond of personal commitment should always be all that was necessary to keep them together. Lydia, who has a consciousness which might easily belong to a feminist heroine of the 1970s, is horrified by the thought that Ralph may feel obligated to marry her in order to "rehabilitate" her socially. And as she describes to Ralph her behavior with acquaintances at the small European hotel where they have been staying, she is filled with self-derision:

> "These people—the very prototypes of the bores you took me away from, with the same fenced-in view of life, the same keep-off-the-grass morality, the same little cautious virtues and the same little frightened vices—well, I've clung to them, I've delighted in them, I've done my best to please them. I've toadied Lady Susan, I've gossiped with Miss Pinsent, I've pretended to be shocked with Mrs. Ainger. Respectability! It was the one thing in life that I was sure I didn't care about, and it's grown so precious to me that I've stolen it because I couldn't get it in any other way."

Although Lydia deeply loves Gannett and attempts to live by an honest personal moral code, it is not these but other irresistible forces which are steadily shaping the identity that awaits her.

In another nineteenth-century story which exemplifies its author's modern view of human nature, Kate Chopin's "A Respectable Woman" (1894), the author depicts a woman involved in a predicament much more often associated with husbands than with wives in literature: namely a happily married person is sexually attracted to a stranger. Mrs. Baroda is at first merely disconcerted by the apparently irreproachable behavior of her husband's old college classmate and guest Gouvernail. Later, they sit together on a pleasant spring evening, she is bewildered by the emotion stirring within her:

> She wanted to reach out her hand in the darkness and touch him with the sensitive tips of her fingers upon the face or the lips. She wanted to draw close to him and whisper against his cheek—she did not care what—as she might have done if she had not been a respectable woman.

Her escape to an aunt's house on the pretext of needing to have alterations on some clothes puts an end to her present temptation and gives her time to examine her feelings. Although the revelation of an inexplicable passion is central to the story, Chopin withholds any description of Mrs. Baroda's insight nor does she explain the wife's final remarks to her husband, thus creating an intriguing open-ended tale.

The woman writer in Katherine Anne Porter's "Theft" (1930) discovers the damage she has been doing to herself. The final theft of her purse is the culmination of a number of spiritual robberies which have taken place during the preceding evening. In all of these, she unconsciously was a co-conspirator with the "thief." Her companion at a party, Camilo, has evolved, "a fairly complete set of smaller courtesies, ignoring the larger and more troublesome ones." Thus, he can accompany her to the New York subway station, pay her fare, yet not trouble himself to ride home with her. Her lack of belief in her own self-worth is quickly made apparent. After he deposits her near the station, "she stood watching him, for he was a very graceful young man, thinking that tomorrow morning he would gaze soberly at his spoiled hat and soggy shoes and possibly associate her with his misery." Here is a woman who feels guilty for a bad turn a the weather. Busy analyzing Camilo's possible reactions, he fails to have any emotions of her own about the trip home.

When she arrives at her apartment house, sopping wet, as her neighbor, Bill, notes, she demonstrates once again her willingness to be used by others. Bill, who can afford a ninety-five-dollar rug as well as payments on a piano and a Victrola, claims that he cannot afford to pay the fifty dollars he owes her for the portion of his play she had written for him. His response is to tell her: "'Have another drink and forget about it,'" and although she had resolved to be firm, she is unable to stand up for her rights. She will not be unpleasant, not make demands, not protect herself, since she obviously lacks self-respect. And although the theft of her purse acts as a catalyst to make this woman understand what she has been doing, we may wonder whether this insight will lead to a new attitude toward herself.

In John Steinbeck's "The Chrysanthemums" (1933), Elisa Allen's moment of insight comes as she spies the place on the road where her new chrysanthemum sprouts have been dumped. She learns that she has been manipulated by the itinerant workman who managed to earn fifty cents by his pretended interest in the flowers. The incident forces on Elisa a painful recognition of an emptiness in her life. A popular interpretation of the story is that Elisa is lacking in some feminine type of fulfillment. At thirty-five she is childless and has superabundant energy for both housework and gardening. But an alternate—and perhaps more realistic—interpretation would be that Elisa is not an example of suppressed femininity, a potential mother with no children, but an example of suppressed "masculinity," a human being who has been relegated to performing activities which require only a fraction of her ability. Her husband, it is clear, is solely responsible for the real business of selling cattle and raising crops.

When the workman describes the way he freely travels across the country, sleeping in his wagon, Elisa enviously responds: "'It must be very nice. I wish women could do such things.'" The workman asserts that his is not "the right kind of a life for a woman." Elisa seems very sure that he is wrong: "'How do you know? How can you tell?'" A few moments later, as she pays for his labor, she seems determined to convince him of his error: "'You might be surprised to have a rival some time. I can sharpen scissors, too.

And I can beat the dents out of little pots. I would show you what a woman might do.' " In the careless destruction of the sprouts, Elisa experiences an emotional jolt, possibly because the flowers are surrogate children. But the destruction of the plants may well reveal to Elisa how completely she has been deluded in her sense of accomplishment and what a meager outlet she has for the energy and talent she possesses.

In Dorothy Canfield's "Sex Education" (1947), a single incident provides three quite different insights. True self-knowledge is achieved only in the last of these. The narrator first hears about the incident in the form of an anecdote told by her Aunt Minnie as a conventional warning to a group of young girls who want to sleep out-of-doors. Aunt Minnie, then in her thirties, relates the terrifying experience of her own girlhood, complete with a breathless escape from the animal sensuality of Malcolm, the ordinarily mild minister in whose household she was a guest. The story is typical of those used to make young females aware of their particular vulnerability and to make them self-conscious and cautious.

But after many years of experience with human nature, Aunt Minnie has a much different interpretation of the experience. In the second recounting of the incident, she perceives the feelings and reactions of the minister with genuine concern and understanding. Her final insight comes almost fifty years after her first description of Malcolm's embrace in the cornfield. Well into her eighties, Minnie finally has the self-knowledge and freedom from conventional attitudes to evaluate honestly her own behavior. She no longer visualizes herself and Malcolm as stereotypes in the melodrama created when, as a young girl, she was warned that there were plenty of men around who would like nothing better than to catch an unsuspecting and helpless girl out in a cornfield. Minnie is finally able to assess the damage done to young women who are taught to lead timid lives of fear and loathing and whose training teaches them to see male demons lurking behind every bush. Many feminists, in fact, argue that the process by which female children are educated to avoid situations which might lead to rape is in itself a kind of rape of the mind—a damaging process which male children need never experience.

Women and Madness

Once again, the strain inherent in the roles assigned to women is crucial in all three stories which deal with mental abnormality. In Jean Stafford's "Beatrice Trueblood's Story," the aberration is relatively mild and temporary. Beatrice's deafness is an obvious defense mechanism produced by an unbearable situation. Discovering herself engaged to precisely the sort of man who is most destructive to her and not wishing to hear another venomous word from Marten ten Brink, she awakens one morning to find that her "wish" has been granted with a vengeance.

Haunted by the discordant relationship of her parents, Beatrice is horrified by any "altercation between a man and a woman whose conjunction had had as its origin tenderness and a concord of desire." Thus deluded by an impossible romantic vision, "she was certain that sweetness could put an end to strife; she believed that her tolerance was limitless, and she vowed that when she married there would be no quarrels." Both in her avoidance of a direct confrontation with Marten and in her unrealistic goal, which would require superhuman powers of adaptablity, Beatrice exhibits traits which are characteristic of the female role. Entirely willing as she is to become a submissive, malleable wife, she can avoid neither normal human friction nor her husband's bad temper. Interestingly, in American literature, although there are numerous examples of the stereotype of the argumentative or strong-willed wife—a comic figure—to whom terms such as "shrew," "scold," "termagant," and more recently "bitch," have been applied, there is no corresponding stereotypical male figure. The four men in Beatrice's life, her father, her first husband, Marten ten Brink, and Arthur Talbot, may be unpleasant, quarrelsome, and difficult, but they act within the socially acceptable perimeters of the masculine role; they simply take advantage of or distort it. In literature as well as in life, the husband who is the deplorable failure is commonly pictured as one who is not powerful enough, a "milquetoast" or a "henpecked husband."

In William Faulkner's "A Rose for Emily" (1930), the narrator insists that we understand Emily Grierson as southern woman, almost as southern institution. For the townspeople, she is far more a type than a human being. Thus, the same mayor, Colonel Sartoris, who decreed "that no Negro woman should appear on the streets without an apron" remitted the town's taxes on Emily's house after her father's death. Just as the aprons would symbolize the status of the black woman, this remission would testify to the inviolate aristocracy of this impoverished southern white woman. After the narrator describes the farfetched tale about the tax money the Colonel told Emily, he makes an interesting judgment: "Only a man of Colonel Sartoris' generation and thought could have invented it, and only a woman could have believed it." The town's attitudes toward Emily and subsequent treatment of her are predicated entirely on an antebellum ideal of southern gentility.

Faulkner's tale fits into an identifiable pattern of American fiction about the older single woman. In the work of male writers on this subject, the woman is generally described by an outsider, seems to act out of incomprehensible or foreign motives, and ends by revealing that she, the "old maid," is indeed the grotesque creature whose inability to find a husband—or worse still, whose preference for existing without one—has always made her suspect. The crazed, rejected Emily, like Miss Burden in *Light in August*, is one of Faulkner's "sexually insatiable daughters of the aristocracy" analyzed by Leslie Fiedler not as women, but as nightmarish "myths of masculine protest."[7] For sympathetic portraits of normal, healthy, single old women we must look to the writing of an earlier period, to the work of such authors as Sarah Orne Jewett and Mary Wilkins Freeman.

The third story to deal with madness portrays the narrator of Charlotte Perkins Gilman's "The Yellow Wallpaper" (1899). She is the wife of a physician who has taken over caring for her as both husband and doctor. His diagnosis, and that of another male authority, her brother who is also a physician, is that she is suffering from a "temporary nervous depression" and "a slight hysterical tendency." I think we may interpret the words "temporary" and "slight" as the products of wishful thinking.

All of the methods by which John hopes to cure his wife involve transferring the control of her life into his hands. He has chosen the room they will use—one that suits him and disturbs her. He has refused to repaper the room because they will occupy the house for only three months and he does

ot wish his wife to indulge her fancies. He prohibits stimu-
ating company for his wife such as her Cousin Henry and
ulia. He absolutely refuses to leave the house three weeks
efore the expiration of his lease merely because his wife
leads that they do so. And throughout their stay, he
aises such serious objections to his wife's doing any
writing that she must do it secretly. Her writing provides
er only opportunity for honest emotion and freedom of
xpression. For example, early in the story she asserts:
'John is a physician, and *perhaps*—(I would not say it to
living soul, of course, but this is dead paper and a great
elief to my mind)—*perhaps* that is one reason I do not
get well faster."

In "The Yellow Wallpaper," Gilman contributes a valuable
personal and historical document for which she drew upon
both the private agony of her own mental breakdown and her
understanding of the physical and mental distress experienced
by many nineteenth-century women and the sexist treatments
to which they were subjected. In *Complaints and Disorders:
The Sexual Politics of Sickness* (1973), Barbara Ehrenreich
and Deidre English provide a startling feminist study of the
theories and practices of the medical profession in dealing
with women patients during that period.[8] As the authors make
clear, much feminine hysteria and depression were obviously
related to the restrictiveness and emptiness of the lives of
middle-class American women. What was often interpreted as
illness was simply generalized rebelliousness. Gilman's character believes that she is sometimes "unreasonably angry"
with her husband, but given a society in which acceptable
wifely behavior is roughly equivalent to that expected of a
dutiful eight-year-old daughter, she lacks the experience and
a social context by which to judge her individual dissatisfaction and her yearning for personal autonomy.

Courtships

Only three of these stories are essentially concerned with
the most commonly explored crisis in literature about
women: whom will she marry, or will she marry at all? The

earliest of these, "The Old Woman and the New" (1914) by Anne Warner, offers a surprisingly modern view of marriage as an economic institution, and of wifehood as an exacting career of unpaid labor.

The "old woman" of the title is Mrs. Reed, who is thrilled when the only remaining bachelor in town proposes to her thirty-year-old daughter Emily. She unquestionably believes in the desirability of a woman marrying—no matter the cost. Thus, Mrs. Reed glories in her vision of Emily's engagement which she will shortly be enabled to proclaim throughout their small New England town. Although Mrs. Reed has vague romantic ideas about the relationship between Emily and her fiancé James Dwight, the proprietor and headmaster of a local private school, we realize that his proposal of marriage is precipitated by the forthcoming departure of his sister Hildegarde, who has served him both at home and at school. Mrs. Reed, who seems oblivious to Dwight's motivation, wants to rearrange the furniture before his next visit because she believes " 'It's so nice to sit on a sofa and be in love.' " Dwight has very little need for such accommodations as he outlines his plans for the future to his bride-to-be. He will no need to hire a housekeeper:

> "For I'll soon have you," he remarked not tenderly, but with quiet assertion. "Neither shall I need a teacher for the younges classes; you're absolutely qualified to teach them." A few minutes later he imparted to her that she "could easily do the drawing and music, too."

> "I've been thinking," he continued, "that I could rent some rooms in the next house and double the boarders. They pay and every extra one is money in my pocket. You could look ou for them. Yes, you could."

To Mrs. Reed, nothing that Dwight may desire from Emily seems too high a price to pay for the exalted role of a married woman. A husband's selfish demands are simply part of the unalterable scheme of the universe. She attempts to enlighten her daughter:

> "But all women have to work all day and till midnight, Emily I always sewed till midnight. A woman can't possibly get every thing brought up before midnight. Your father always had his evenings and went to bed at eleven, but I was always on the jump."

This story dramatizes the intense pressure on women to marry, as well as the emergence of the image of "a new woman" at the turn of the century in America. Emily will weigh the advantages of the kind of marriage she has been offered against a sense of self, which is quite different from her mother's.

Shirley, in Theodore Dreiser's "The Second Choice" (1918), is a typical example of the young woman who feels she must soon marry. Yet the man with whom she has fallen in love, Arthur, has grown tired of her and has moved to a distant city to pursue a new career. He is the stereotyped fun-loving bachelor whose romantic dreams and hazy plans have never really included Shirley. The very traits which make Arthur seem so exciting make it unlikely that he will ever marry her.

Trapped by her own sense of inadequacy, Shirley feels doomed to a future of uninspiring middle-class domesticity from which she believes only Arthur could have rescued her. In Shirley, Dreiser dramatizes the generally accepted view that a woman's identity is formed essentially as a result of the mate whom she has chosen or, more important, who has chosen her. Because Shirley has had an affair with Arthur, she feels contempt for both herself and for Barton, her long-time boyfriend, who still loves her and wishes to marry her. She thinks of herself as Arthur's leavings, and is disgusted to find Barton so grateful for her first gesture of reconciliation. Although Shirley thinks of Arthur as a kind of fairytale prince who could take her away from the petty routines of daily existence, Dreiser makes certain that we have a far more realistic view of him. For Shirley, who seems to have few inner resources, disillusionment with Arthur must have come sooner or later. But why, we ask from our contemporary perspective, must she scurry to reestablish a relationship with Barton? Does a woman without a suitor feel so vulnerable, so fearful of becoming "an old maid," that she must marry, whatever the circumstances?

The third story, Rona Jaffe's "Rima the Bird Girl" (1960), deals with a series of one-sided courtships since Rima loves and wishes to marry each of the men with whom she becomes involved. Thus, she dedicates herself to convincing each man that she would make a far more suitable mate than the woman to whom he is presently married. In spite of her intelligence and attractiveness, Rima is continually redesigning her lifestyle, treating herself as a piece of merchandise which can be made quite salable with a few new touches here and there. She is the girl to whom the myriad articles on self-improvement in women's magazines might well have been addressed. These articles—which have no counterpart in masculine culture—suggest ways in which any female may make herself more attractive by means of considerable changes which range from new hairdos and makeup through new hobbies and interests to the cultivation of new personality traits. They presuppose a female who is entirely raw material, ready and eager to be molded into a revised version of herself, one which men will find pleasing and desirable but, most important, which will be highly valued in the marriage market.

Lacking any inner goals or ambition but marriage, Rima comes alive only in the presence of another, a man. The pattern of her behavior is suggested in the narrator's early description of Rima at college.

> I remember her always hiding in her room, the shades down studying, or reading the poetry she loved, and then the sound of the phone bell . . . and ten minutes later she emerged—a swirl of orange skirt, a cloud of Arpege drifting after her, as if she had suddenly been told she existed.

The narrator of Rima's story is a classmate and later a roommate who begins with much the same lack of identity as her friend. Although she has succeeded in securing a husband, she describes the result of having abandoned all her own personal plans after graduation from college:

> My husband's work took him to New York where we lived in a three-room apartment that I cleaned carefully every day. I went to the grocery store, read his magazines, his books, played his records, and waited for him to come home to eat the dinners I cooked.

The narrator finally achieves an understanding of her need for a separate identity. This insight never comes to Rima, whose impressive creativity and intelligence are devoted to endlessly refurbishing herself in the service of another.

Married Women

Among the following stories four depict the problems of oppressed wives. Although the personality traits of each husband contribute substantially to each woman's suffering, the stories demonstrate the general disadvantages and burdens of the woman in marriage as well as her individual problem. Significantly, in a society which is permeated by the romantic myth that her husband and her home are a woman's refuge from a threatening world, American writers continually dramatize the disparity between the ideal and the reality of that most revered institution: marriage. Literature has long reflected what sociologists and psychologists have only recently come to understand—i.e., that every marriage is really two marriages, his and hers, and that the two may be very unlike. We have only just begun to be sensitive to the unique demands made upon women and the strain which they experience in the role of wife.

In two of the stories, Shirley Schoonover's "The Star Blanket" (1961) and J. F. Powers's "Blue Island" (1955), the married couples live in vastly different circumstances. Yet in spite of the gulf between the lives of nomadic California sheepherders and nouveau riche Minnesota suburbanites, there is a remarkable parallel in the roles of the wives and the oppressive behavior of their mates.

Although Schoonover's strangely primitive story takes place in twentieth-century America, with a few minor changes it might easily have been a tale of biblical times. Throughout the narrative, wife and husband are referred to as "the woman" (although she is merely fifteen years old) and "the man." The absence of names suggests a timeless, archetypal relationship between the two. The woman is her husband's property, having been traded to him by her father for three pregnant ewes when she was thirteen. Thus the sheepherder takes the girl to live with him, to cook and sew, to help with the lambs, and to satisfy his sexual needs. Her role is explained by her mother as she prepares to leave home:

"I never had time to tell you what to expect from a man. I can't tell you now except to be good to him. When he comes to you at night, take him." The girl had looked at her mother with mute eyes. "There's no way to find out about men and their ways except by doing. In ten years you'll not remember what it was like not to know a man. It seems to have been going on forever, and it will go on that way until he's too old." The mother held her daughter for the last time. "If you can take joy from his man's ways, that's good. If you can't, try to give him what you can, there's some joy in that too." She kissed her daughter's round forehead. "Now go to him, he seems to be kind, and you'd have to marry someone someday."

Following her husband and his flock up and down the mountains, she is totally dependent upon him. Her powerlessness is exemplified in her inability to control the dogs who herd the sheep. When they nip the heels of the windbroken horse her husband has acquired, she tries unsuccessfully to stop them. But only the whistled command of the master has any effect on the dogs. After a cowboy mistakenly thinks his wife must be his daughter, and speaks to her in a friendly way, the husband ceases to take her along on his infrequent trips to town. His possessiveness grows, as does his resentment of his wife's dreamy moods and simple pleasures. Isolated from the outside world as his restrictions become increasingly harsh and destructive, she obeys his wishes as a submissive wife.

In "Blue Island" Powers explores the basis of power in the relationship of a newly-wed couple, Ethel and Ralph Davicci. In many respects, Ethel is just as dependent, powerless, and subservient as the woman in "The Star Blanket." Once a waitress in Ralph's club, The Mohawk Inn, Ethel has taken on an even more exacting job, that of his wife. She is deeply aware that her husband need not have married her when she became pregnant. Ralph, vulgar and tasteless, makes all of the decisions. Ethel lives in a house he has chosen (she had never even seen it before they moved in), shops at the store he singles out, and returns to the store the pictures he scorns to hang in his house. Fearful of displeasing him, she lies about where she purchased the offending pictures. Initiated into a new existence of defensive living, of subterfuge and anxiety, Ethel is a vulnerable ornament in an expensive house in the suburbs.

Two other stories deal with intelligent and talented women who have had important goals outside of marriage. In Tillie Olsen's "Tell Me a Riddle" (1960), Eva and David are grandparents who have been married for forty-seven years.

They are engaged in a bitter dispute in which no compromise is possible. David wants to sell their house and to buy a place for them at "The Haven," a condominium for senior citizens which is run by his lodge. There, with the money from the house and a small pension, they can be free of all economic concerns. Eva vehemently opposes the plan, protesting that now that the children are grown, she can enjoy her home with a minimum of cleaning. It is no trouble to prepare a simple meal for two people. But behind all these practical objections lies the overwhelming principle which Eva will never relinquish and which her husband cannot comprehend. She knows that "*Never again*" will she "*be forced to move to the rhythms of others*." A lifetime of serving others, of caring for children and husband, of adapting her behavior, changing her goals, sacrificing her needs, has left her angry and determined.

The conflict of their old age is the result of the price paid by Eva in her marriage. Although both husband and wife have known hardships and poverty in raising their family, hers was the more painful and restrictive experience. She recalls the desperate remaking of old clothes to see what could be salvaged, pleading for credit, and cooking "soups of meat bones begged 'for-the-dog' one winter. . . ." In an attempt to make the proposed move attractive to Eva, her husband describes a reading circle which meets there, reminding her how much she used to enjoy such writers as Chekhov. Eva's bitterness overflows. "Now, when it pleases you, you find a reading circle for me. And forty years ago when the children were morsels and there was a Circle, did you stay home with them once so I could go? Even once? You trained me well. I do not need others to enjoy. Others!" There is nothing in the present which can recompense Eva for what she had given up in the past. Once a rebellious young woman who defied her father to seek an education, once a political prisoner in Siberia, still an idealist with deeply humanistic values, she exemplifies the tragedy of wasted potential and unfulfilled ideals—unheeded in a world in which women are only wives and mothers.

Another woman who is primarily defined by her role as a wife and mother is Barbara Scott Arber in "Accomplished Desires" (1965) by Joyce Carol Oates. Although she is a successful poet who has won a Pulitzer Prize for a volume of sonnets, Barbara is preoccupied with family relationships. She continues to write with facility at a battered desk in the attic, but feels a sense of inadequacy in dealing with her three sons.

> She did not always know what she had given birth to: they were so remote, even in their struggles and assaults, they were so fictional, as if she had imagined them herself. It had been she who'd imagined them not Mark. Their father had no time. He was always in a hurry, he had three aged typewriters in his study and paper in each one . . . and he had no time for the children except to nod grimly at them or tell them to be quiet.

In contrast, Mark, who is defined as a novelist and English professor, is experiencing a crisis as he attempts to live up to the promise of his early novels. Unlike Barbara, he has a good deal of freedom, to write, to travel, to be with people. When Dorie, an attractive student of his, abruptly informs Mark that she is in love with him, he immediately arranges family matters to his satisfaction. He brings the girl, now his mistress, home and announces that she will be living with them as housekeeper or babysitter. Thus, Mark flaunts his relationship with Dorie before Barbara, and soon the slender, well-dressed girl begins to accompany him wherever he can present her as his "secretary." Barbara is trapped. She is convinced that everyone is talking about her and gloating over her situation: "high-school baton twirlers were better off than Barbara Scott who had no dignity." When she offers Mark a divorce so that he can marry the girl, he is dismayed by the idea because he hates any disruptions in his life.

Dorie does become Mrs. Mark Arber after Barbara's suicide, but her life is very different from the one she had imagined. Interestingly, her despair is only partially caused by Mark's selfish actions. It is also the result of the qualities inherent in the role of wife and mother—a role she had intensely coveted when it was Barbara's. As Dorie sits at the attic desk she realizes that

> It did no good to read Barbara Scott's poetry because she did not understand it. Her understanding had dropped to tending the baby and the boys, fixing meals, cleaning up and shopping, and taking the station wagon to the garage perpetually . . . and she had no time to go with others to the tennis courts, or to accompany Mark to New York . . . and around her were human beings whose lives consisted of language, the grace of language, and she could no longer understand them. She felt strangely cheated, a part of her murdered. . . .

The dream marriage Dorie struggled so ruthlessly to achieve is now her private nightmare.

Women with Children

The pervasive American image of a mother is that of a tireless, selfless figure who happily serves her husband and children, and who achieves most of her satisfaction from the joys and successes of her offspring. In other words, the female parent is expected to live a vicarious existence, as compared to that of a father who may be proud of his children's achievements but never substitutes them for his own. Thus, the roles conventionally assigned to mothers and fathers are thoroughly dissimilar.

Three of the stories in this volume, "The Revolt of Mother," "A Day's Pleasure," and "Mother," explore the emotions of women who have lived painfully restricted lives imposed by marriage and motherhood. Conversely, Wright Morris's "The Ram in the Thicket" is a dramatization of the destructive wife and mother, a woman whose behavior is a travesty of society's image of motherhood.

Sarah Penn, an industrious farm wife with two grown children, is the heroine of Mary Wilkins Freeman's "The Revolt of Mother" (1890). She discovers that her husband, Adoniram, is building still another barn while his family is expected to continue living in the small, shabby dwelling he had promised to replace forty years before. Her anger and frustration are entirely justified. Adoniram, a distinctly patriarchal figure, refuses to answer her arguments or to change his plans. In spite of this serious dispute with her husband, Sarah continues to bake his favorite pies, to sew new shirts for him, and to process the milk of their six cows. Of course, the new barn will accommodate more cows and mean more work for her.

In this nineteenth-century story, family solidarity is sacred and Sarah's actions are not a threat to it. When Nancy, their daughter, criticizes her father's building of the barn, even though these thoughts reflect Sarah's own bitter ones, she attempts to defend her husband, asserting that his perceptions differ from those of a woman. Sarah suggests that there is some consolation in the fact that Father has kept their own roof well shingled and that it has never leaked—but once. Sarah's ultimate victory restores harmony and peace to the family, but the essential relationships have remained constant and loyal throughout the strife. In Freeman's story, members of the family can learn about one another's feelings, and when they do, they alter their behavior in keeping with their new understanding.

Hamlin Garland's "A Day's Pleasure" (1891), set on a far less successful farm than that of the Penns, depicts the endless toil and hardship of a poor farm wife on the prairie. Delia Markham has not been away from her own house for six months. When Sam Markham announces that he is going to town to sell some sacks of wheat, his wife is determined to go along. Since that means that she won't have the time to help with the sacks in the morning, she and her husband work together late into the night to fill and load the sacks. The next day, by the time she has gotten the older children off to school and finished her work in the kitchen, Delia feels weak and discouraged.

> She lay down on the bed a moment to ease that dull pain in her back. She had a moment's distaste for going out at all. The thought of sleep was more alluring. Then the thought of the long, long day, and the sickening sameness of her life, swept over her again, and she rose and prepared the baby for the journey.

While her husband socializes with some of the other men in town and pursues farm business, Delia finds that she has exhausted the few activities open to her. The day of escape from drudgery turns into a day of misery and discomfort as she aimlessly walks the hot, dusty street trying to quiet the restless baby in her arms. Through the intervention of some kind townspeople Delia's day is saved, but the most powerful images of the story are those of the impoverished woman, awkward and self-conscious in stores lined with items she cannot afford.

In Sherwood Anderson's "Mother" (1919), Elizabeth Willard is a shabby and defeated woman. Whatever future she has will be lived vicariously, and depends upon the escape of her son, George, from the environment in which she is imprisoned. Anderson characterizes her as an unfulfilled woman whose vague childhood longings have come to nothing.

For years she had been what is called "stage-struck" and had paraded through the streets with traveling men guests at her father's hotel, wearing loud clothes and urging them to tell her of life in the cities out of which they had come. Once she startled the town by putting on men's clothes and riding a bicycle down Main Street.

Anderson depicts her as triumphing over the husband she despises in that their only son is much the way she was in her youth and is resentful of his father. George announces that he must leave home, an action Elizabeth joyously understands as a repudiation of the life she would have left had she found the opportunity so many years before. Anderson ignores the ultimate price Elizabeth will pay for her "victory." George will leave behind not only his father, but his isolated and inarticulate mother.

Worlds apart from these self-sacrificing mothers is Violet Ormsby, the anti-heroine of Wright Morris's "The Ram in the Thicket" (1948). Both the stereotyped "great American bitch" and wicked witch of fairy tales, she has emasculated her husband and driven their only son away from home. Though vividly portrayed, Mrs. Ormsby, or Mother as she is called, is nevertheless a female stereotype, a literary sister of such American bitches as Margot Macomber of Hemingway's "The Short Happy Life of Francis Macomber" and of Mrs. Stoner in J. F. Powers's "The Valiant Woman." Mother's power, like that of the other two women, is gained entirely through a continuous struggle with the male character who would ordinarily—and naturally, in the male author's view— dominate the relationship. She acquires her strength through the diminution of her husband's confidence and power. As Dolores Barracano Schmidt has noted, this stereotyped "man-eating female in American literature . . . is always wife and quite often, mother; she does not work outside the home, except, perhaps, as a volunteer . . . she is educated, but not intellectual; well-informed, but not cultivated; her house is usually clean, orderly, well-run, though she is not a house-wife in the sense of one devoted to domesticity."[9] Thus, as the critic has indicated, this type of woman lacks a meaningful identity of her own and though apparently a powerful force in the home, "she is rarely viewed in her true powerlessness far removed from any source of significant decision-making."

Mother, of course, neither cooks nor shops because of her extensive work with the League for Wild Life Conservation and the League of Women Voters. Morris skillfully displays the horrors of this unnatural creature who is incapable of providing affection or warmth. Violet Ormsby's house is a parody of a home with its newspaper-covered furniture and jars of moldy leftovers in the refrigerator.

To a feminist critic, "The Ram in the Thicket," suggests several haunting insights about the conventional roles of wives and husbands. Morris certainly intends for us to feel pity and outrage for Ormsby when after cooking four eggs and dropping two of them on the floor, he serves Mother both of the remaining eggs. But to what extent would a reader feel pity and outrage on behalf of a wife who automatically regarded the ruined eggs as hers and who, therefore, served the edible two to her husband? Morris's story, in dramatizing the horrible results of role reversal, reveals some pernicious principles of traditional marital roles. Like other bitches of American fiction, Mother may well represent a male fantasy, a nightmare vision of the vicious enemy a man may unsuspectingly bring into his home when he weds the girl of his dreams.

BARBARA H. SOLOMON
Iona College
New Rochelle, New York

NOTES

1. "A Mirror for Men: Stereotypes of Women in Literature,"
   Woman: An Issue eds. Lee R. Edwards, Mary Heath, and
   Lisa Baskin (Boston: Little, Brown and Company, 1972),
   pp. 205-218. This volume duplicates the material of Volume
   XIII, Numbers 1 and 2, of *The Massachusetts Review*.

2. Published by the University of Washington Press in Seattle.

3. Published by Harcourt, Brace, and World, Inc. in New York.

4. "What Can a Heroine Do? or Why Women Can't Write,"
   Images of Women in Fiction: Feminist Perspectives, ed.
   Susan Koppelman Cornillon (Bowling Green: Bowling
   Green University Popular Press, 1972), p. 3.

5. "The Female World of Love and Ritual: Relations between
   Women in Nineteenth-Century America," *Signs: Journal of
   Women in Culture and Society* 1 (Autumn 1975), 1-29.

6. "Miss Sarah Orne Jewett's Tales," reprinted from *Academy and
   Literature* LXV (July 11, 1903), in *Appreciation of Sarah
   Orne Jewett*, ed. Richard Cary (Waterville, Maine: Colby
   College Press, 1973), p. 23.

7. *Love and Death in the American Novel* (New York: Dell Publishing Co., 1960), p. 321.

8. Published by The Feminist Press in Old Westbury, N.Y.

9. "The Great American Bitch," *College English*, 32 (May 1971),
   901, 904.

The Revolt of "Mother"

Mary Wilkins Freeman

"Father!"

"What is it?"

"What are them men diggin' over there in the field for?"

There was a sudden dropping and enlarging of the lower part of the old man's face, as if some heavy weight had settled therein; he shut his mouth tight, and went on harnessing the great bay mare. He hustled the collar on to her neck with a jerk.

"Father!"

The old man slapped the saddle upon the mare's back.

"Look here, father, I want to know what them men are diggin' over in the field for, an' I'm goin' to know."

"I wish you'd go into the house, mother, an' tend to your own affairs," the old man said then. He ran his words together, and his speech was almost as inarticulate as a growl.

But the woman understood; it was her most native tongue. "I ain't goin' into the house till you tell me what them men are doin' over there in the field," said she.

Then she stood waiting. She was a small woman, short and straight-waisted like a child in her brown cotton gown. Her forehead was mild and benevolent between the smooth curves of gray hair; there were meek downward lines about her nose and mouth; but her eyes, fixed upon the old man, looked as if the meekness had been the result of her own will, never of the will of another.

They were in the barn, standing before the wide open doors. The spring air, full of the smell of growing grass and unseen blossoms, came in their faces. The deep yard in front was littered with farm wagons and piles of wood; on the edges, close to the fence and the house, the grass was a vivid green, and there were some dandelions.

The old man glanced doggedly at his wife as he tightened the last buckles on the harness. She looked as immovable to him as one of the rocks in his pasture-land, bound to the

31

earth with generations of blackberry vines. He slapped the reins over the horse, and started forth from the barn.

"*Father!*" said she.

The old man pulled up. "What is it?"

"I want to know what them men are diggin' over there in that field for."

"They're diggin' a cellar, I s'pose, if you've got to know."

"A cellar for what?"

"A barn."

"A barn? You ain't goin' to build a barn over there where we was goin' to have a house, father?"

The old man said not another word. He hurried the horse into the farm wagon, and clattered out of the yard, jouncing as sturdily on his seat as a boy.

The woman stood a moment looking after him, then she went out of the barn across a corner of the yard to the house. The house, standing at right angles with the great barn and a long reach of sheds and out-buildings, was infinitesimal compared with them. It was scarcely as commodious for people as the little boxes under the barn eaves were for doves.

A pretty girl's face, pink and delicate as a flower, was looking out of one of the house windows. She was watching three men who were digging over in the field which bounded the yard near the road line. She turned quietly when the woman entered.

"What are they digging for, mother?" said she. "Did he tell you?"

"They're diggin' for—a cellar for a new barn."

"Oh, mother, he ain't going to build another barn?"

"That's what he says."

A boy stood before the kitchen glass combing his hair. He combed slowly and painstakingly, arranging his brown hair in a smooth hillock over his forehead. He did not seem to pay any attention to the conversation.

"Sammy, did you know father was going to build a new barn?" asked the girl.

The boy combed assiduously.

"Sammy!"

He turned, and showed a face like his father's under his smooth crest of hair. "Yes, I s'pose I did," he said, reluctantly.

"How long have you known it?" asked his mother.

"'Bout three months, I guess."

"Why didn't you tell of it?"

"Didn't think 'twould do no good."

"I don't see what father wants another barn for," said the girl, in her sweet, slow voice. She turned again to the window, and stared out at the digging men in the field. Her tender, sweet face was full of gentle distress. Her forehead was as bald and innocent as a baby's with the light hair strained back from it in a row of curl-papers. She was quite large, but her soft curves did not look as if they covered muscles.

Her mother looked sternly at the boy. "Is he goin' to buy more cows?"

The boy did not reply; he was tying his shoes.

"Sammy, I want you to tell me if he's goin' to buy more cows."

"I s'pose he is."

"How many?"

"Four, I guess."

His mother said nothing more. She went into the pantry, and there was a clatter of dishes. The boy got his cap from a nail behind the door, took an old arithmetic from the shelf, and started for school. He was lightly built, but clumsy. He went out of the yard with a curious spring in the hips, that made his loose home-made jacket tilt up in the rear.

The girl went to the sink, and began to wash the dishes that were piled there. Her mother came promptly out of the pantry, and shoved her aside. "You wipe 'em," said she, "I'll wash. There's a good many this mornin'."

The mother plunged her hands vigorously into the water, the girl wiped the plates slowly and dreamily. "Mother," said she, "don't you think it's too bad father's going to build that new barn, much as we need a decent house to live in?"

Her mother scrubbed a dish fiercely. "You ain't found out yet we're women-folks, Nanny Penn," said she. "You ain't seen enough of men-folks yet to. One of these days you'll find it out, an' then you'll know that we know only what men-folks think we do, so far as any use of it goes, an' how we'd ought to reckon men-folks in with Providence, an' not complain of what they do any more than we do of the weather."

"I don't care; I don't believe George is anything like that, anyhow," said Nanny. Her delicate face flushed pink, her lips pouted softly, as if she were going to cry.

"You wait an' see. I guess George Eastman ain't no better than other men. You hadn't ought to judge father though. He can't help it, 'cause he don't look at things jest the way we do. An' we've been pretty comfortable here, after all. The roof don't leak—ain't never but once—that's one thing. Father's kept it shingled right up."

"I do wish we had a parlor."

"I guess it won't hurt George Eastman any to come to see you in a nice clean kitchen. I guess a good many girls don't have as good a place as this. Nobody's ever heard me complain."

"I ain't complaining either, mother."

"Well, I don't think you'd better, a good father an' a good home as you've got. S'pose your father made you go out an' work for your livin'? Lots of girls have to that ain't no stronger an' better able to than you be."

Sarah Penn washed the frying-pan with a conclusive air. She scrubbed the outside of it as faithfully as the inside. She was a masterly keeper of her box of a house. Her one living-room never seemed to have in it any of the dust which the friction of life with inanimate matter produces. She swept, and there seemed to be no dirt to go before the broom; she cleaned, and one could see no difference. She was like an artist so perfect that he has apparently no art. To-day she got out a mixing bowl and a board, and rolled some pies, and there was no more flour upon her than upon her daughter who was doing finer work. Nanny was to be married in the fall, and she was sewing on some white cambric and embroidery. She sewed industriously while her mother cooked; her soft milk-white hands and wrists showed whiter than her delicate work.

"We must have the stove moved out in the shed before long," said Mrs. Penn. "Talk about not havin' things, it's been a real blessin' to be able to put a stove up in that shed in hot weather. Father did one good thing when he fixed that stove-pipe out there."

Sarah Penn's face as she rolled her pies had that expression of meek vigor which might have characterized one of the New Testament saints. She was making mince-pies. Her husband, Adoniram Penn, liked them better than any other kind. She baked twice a week. Adoniram often liked a piece of pie between meals. She hurried this morning. It had been later than usual when she began, and she wanted to have a pie baked for dinner. However deep a resentment she might be forced to hold against her husband, she would never fail in sedulous attention to his wants.

Nobility of character manifests itself at loop-holes when it is not provided with large doors. Sarah Penn's showed itself to-day in flaky dishes of pastry. So she made the pies faithfully, while across the table she could see, when she glanced up from her work, the sight that rankled in her patient and steadfast soul—the digging of the cellar of the new barn in the place where Adoniram forty years ago had promised her their new house should stand.

The pies were done for dinner. Adoniram and Sammy were home a few minutes after twelve o'clock. The dinner was eaten with serious haste. There was never much conversation at the table in the Penn family. Adoniram asked a blessing, and they ate promptly, then rose up and went about their work.

Sammy went back to school, taking soft sly lopes out of the yard like a rabbit. He wanted a game of marbles before school, and feared his father would give him some chores to do. Adoniram hastened to the door and called after him, but he was out of sight.

"I don't see what you let him go for, mother," said he. "I wanted him to help me unload that wood."

Adoniram went to work out in the yard unloading wood from the wagon. Sarah put away the dinner dishes, while Nanny took down her curl papers and changed her dress. She was going down to the store to buy some more embroidery and thread.

When Nanny was gone, Mrs. Penn went to the door. "Father!" she called.

"Well, what is it?"

"I want to see you jest a minute, father."

"I can't leave this wood nohow. I've got to git it unloaded an' go for a load of gravel afore two o'clock. Sammy had ought to helped me. You hadn't ought to let him go to school so early."

"I want to see you jest a minute."

"I tell ye I can't, nohow, mother."

"Father, you come here." Sarah Penn stood in the door like a queen; she held her head as if it bore a crown; there was that patience which makes authority royal in her voice. Adoniram went.

Mrs. Penn led the way into the kitchen and pointed to a chair. "Sit down, father," she said; "I've got somethin' I want to say to you."

He sat down heavily; his face was quite stolid, but he looked at her with restive eyes. "Well, what is it, mother?"

"I want to know what you're buildin' that new barn for, father?"

"I ain't got nothin' to say about it."

"It can't be you think you need another barn?"

"I tell ye I ain't got nothin' to say about it, mother; an' I ain't going to say nothin."

"Be you goin' to buy more cows?"

Adoniram did not reply; he shut his mouth tight.

"I know you be, as well as I want to. Now, father, look here"—Sarah Penn had not sat down; she stood before her husband in the humble fashion of a Scripture woman—"I'm goin' to talk real plain to you; I never have sence I married you, but I'm goin' to now. I ain't never complained, an' I ain't goin' to complain now, but I'm goin' to talk plain. You see this room here, father; you look at it well. You see there ain't no carpet on the floor, an' you see the paper is all dirty, an' droppin' off the wall. We ain't had no new paper on it for ten year, an' then I put it on myself, an' it didn't cost but ninepence a roll. You see this room, father; it's all the one I've had to work in an' eat in an' sit in sence we was married. There ain't another woman in the whole town whose husband ain't got half the means you have but what's got better. It's all the room Nanny's got to have her company in; an' there ain't one of her mates but what's got better, an' their fathers not so able as hers is. It's all the room she'll have to be married in. What would you have thought, father, if we had had our weddin' in a room no better than this? I was married in my mother's parlor, with a carpet on the floor, an' stuffed furniture, an' a mahogany cardtable. An' this is all the room my daughter will have to be married in. Look here, father!"

Sarah Penn went across the room as though it were a tragic stage. She flung open a door and disclosed a tiny bedroom, only large enough for a bed and bureau, with a path between. "There, father," said she—"there's all the room I've had to sleep in forty year. All my children were born there—the two that died, an' the two that's livin'. I was sick with a fever there."

She stepped to another door and opened it. It led into the small, ill-lighted pantry. "Here," said she, "is all the buttery I've got—every place I've got for my dishes, to set away my victuals in, an' to keep my milk-pans in. Father, I've been takin' care of the milk of six cows in this place, an' now you're goin' to build a new barn, an' keep more cows, an' give me more to do in it."

She threw open another door. A narrow crooked flight of stairs wound upward from it. "There, father," said she. "I want you to look at the stairs that go up to them two unfinished chambers that are all the places our son an' daughter have had to sleep in all their lives. There ain't a prettier girl in town nor a more ladylike one than Nanny, an' that's the place she has to sleep in. It ain't so good as your horse's stall, it ain't so warm an' tight."

Sarah Penn went back and stood before her husband. "Now, father," said she, "I want to know if you think you're doin' right an' accordin' to what you profess. Here, when we was married, forty year ago, you promised me faithful that we should have a new house built in that lot over in the field before the year was out. You said you had money enough, an' you wouldn't ask me to live in no such place as this. It is forty year now, an' you've been makin' more money, an' I've been savin' of it for you ever since, an' you ain't built no house yet. You've built sheds an' cow-houses an' one new barn, an' now you're going to build another. Father, I want to know if you think it's right. You're lodgin' your dumb beasts better than you are your own flesh an' blood. I want to know if you think it's right."

"I ain't got nothin' to say."

"You can't say nothin' without ownin' it ain't right, father. An' there's another thing—I ain't complained; I've got along forty year, an' I s'pose I should forty more, if it wasn't for that—if we don't have another house. Nanny she can't live with us after she's married. She'll have to go somewhere else to live away from us, an' it don't seem as if I could have it so, noways, father. She wasn't ever strong. She's got considerable color, but there wasn't never any backbone to her. I've always took the heft of everything off her, an' she ain't fit to keep house an' do everything herself. She'll be all worn out inside of a year. Think of her doin' all the washin' an' ironin' an' bakin' with them soft white hands an' arms, an' sweepin'! I can't have it so, noways, father."

Mrs. Penn's face was burning; her mild eyes gleamed. She had pleaded her little cause like a Webster; she had ranged from severity to pathos; but her opponent employed that obstinate silence which makes eloquence futile with mocking echoes. Adoniram arose clumsily.

"Father, ain't you got nothin' to say?" said Mrs. Penn.

"I've got to go off after that load of gravel. I can't stan' here talkin' all day."

"Father, won't you think it over, an' have a house built there instead of a barn?"

"I ain't got nothin' to say."

Adoniram shuffled out. Mrs. Penn went into her bedroom. When she came out, her eyes were red. She had a roll of unbleached cotton cloth. She spread it out on the kitchen table, and began cutting out some shirts for her husband. The men over in the field had a team to help them this afternoon; she could hear their halloos. She had a scanty pattern for the shirts; she had to plan and piece the sleeves.

Nanny came home with her embroidery, and sat down with her needlework. She had taken down her curl-papers, and there was a soft roll of fair hair like an aureole over her forehead; her face was as delicately fine and clear as porcelain. Suddenly she looked up, and the tender red flamed all over her face and neck. "Mother," said she.

"What say?"

"I've been thinking—I don't see how we're goin' to have any—wedding in this room. I'd be ashamed to have his folks come if we didn't have anybody else."

"Mebbe we can have some new paper before then; I can put it on. I guess you won't have no call to be ashamed of your belongin's."

"We might have the wedding in the new barn," said Nanny, with gentle pettishness. "Why, mother, what makes you look so?"

Mrs. Penn had started, and was staring at her with a curious expression. She turned again to her work, and spread out a pattern carefully on the cloth. "Nothin'," said she.

Presently Adoniram clattered out of the yard in his two-wheeled dump cart, standing as proudly upright as a Roman charioteer. Mrs. Penn opened the door and stood there a minute looking out; the halloos of the men sounded louder.

It seemed to her all through the spring months that she heard nothing but the halloos and the noises of saws and hammers. The new barn grew fast. It was a fine edifice for this little village. Men came on pleasant Sundays, in their meeting suits and clean shirt bosoms, and stood around it admiringly. Mrs. Penn did not speak of it, and Adoniram did not mention it to her, although sometimes, upon a return from inspecting it, he bore himself with injured dignity.

"It's a strange thing how your mother feels about the new barn," he said, confidentially, to Sammy one day.

Sammy only grunted after an odd fashion for a boy; he had learned it from his father.

The barn was all completed ready for use by the third week in July. Adoniram had planned to move his stock in on Wednesday; on Tuesday he received a letter which changed his plans. He came in with it early in the morning. "Sammy's been to the post-office," said he, "an' I've got a letter from Hiram." Hiram was Mrs. Penn's brother, who lived in Vermont.

"Well," said Mrs. Penn, "what does he say about the folks?"

"I guess they're all right. He says he thinks if I come up country right off there's a chance to buy jest the kind of a horse I want." He stared reflectively out of the window at the new barn.

Mrs. Penn was making pies. She went on clapping the rolling-pin into the crust, although she was very pale, and her heart beat loudly.

"I dun' know but what I'd better go," said Adoniram. "I hate to go off jest now, right in the midst of hayin', but the ten-acre lot's cut, an' I guess Rufus an' the others can git along without me three or four days. I can't get a horse around here to suit me, nohow, an' I've got to have another for all that wood-haulin' in the fall. I told Hiram to watch out, an' if he got wind of a good horse to let me know. I guess I'd better go."

"I'll get out your clean shirt an' collar," said Mrs. Penn calmly.

She laid out Adoniram's Sunday suit and his clean clothes on the bed in the little bedroom. She got his shaving-water and razor ready. At last she buttoned on his collar and fastened his black cravat.

Adoniram never wore his collar and cravat except on extra occasions. He held his head high, with a rasped dignity. When he was all ready, with his coat and hat brushed, and a lunch of pie and cheese in a paper bag, he hesitated on the threshold of the door. He looked at his wife, and his manner was definitely apologetic. "*If* them cows come to-day, Sammy can drive 'em into the new barn," said he; "an' when they bring the hay up, they can pitch it in there."

"Well," replied Mrs. Penn.

Adoniram set his shaven face ahead and started. When he had cleared the door-step, he turned and looked back with a kind of nervous solemnity. "I shall be back by Saturday if nothin' happens," said he.

"Do be careful, father," returned his wife.

She stood in the door with Nanny at her elbow and watched him out of sight. Her eyes had a strange, doubtful expression in them; her peaceful forehead was contracted. She went in, and about her baking again. Nanny sat sewing. Her wedding-day was drawing nearer, and she was getting pale and thin with her steady sewing. Her mother kept glancing at her.

"Have you got that pain in your side this mornin'?" she asked.

"A little."

Mrs. Penn's face, as she worked, changed, her perplexed forehead smoothed, her eyes were steady, her lips firmly set. She formed a maxim for herself, although incoherently with her unlettered thoughts. "Unsolicited opportunities are the guide-posts of the Lord to the new roads of life," she repeated in effect, and she made up her mind to her course of action.

"S'posin' I *had* wrote to Hiram," she muttered once, when she was in the pantry—"s'posin' I had wrote, an' asked him if he knew of any horse? But I didn't an' father's goin' wa'n't none of my doing'. It looks like a providence." Her voice rang out quite loud at the last.

"What you talkin' about, mother?" called Nanny.

"Nothin'."

Mrs. Penn hurried her baking; at eleven o'clock it was all done. The load of hay from the west field came slowly down the cart track, and drew up at the new barn. Mrs. Penn ran out. "Stop!" she screamed, "stop!"

The men stopped and looked; Sammy upreared from the top of the load, and stared at his mother.

"Stop!" she cried out again. "Don't put the hay in that barn; put it in the old one."

"Why, he said to put it in here," returned one of the haymakers, wonderingly. He was a young man, a neighbor's son, whom Adoniram hired by the year to help on the farm.

"Don't you put the hay in the new barn; there's room enough in the old one, ain't there?" said Mrs. Penn.

"Room enough," returned the hired man, in his thick, rustic tones. "Didn't need the new barn, nohow, far as room's concerned. Well, I s'pose he changed his mind." He took hold of the horses' bridles.

Mrs. Penn went back to the house. Soon the kitchen windows were darkened, and a fragrance like warm honey came into the room.

Nanny laid down her work. "I thought father wanted them to put the hay into the new barn?" she said, wonderingly.

"It's all right," replied her mother.

Sammy slid down from the load of hay, and came in to see if dinner was ready.

"I ain't going to get a regular dinner to-day, as long as father's gone," said his mother. "I've let the fire go out. You can have some bread an' milk an' pie. I thought we could get along." She set out some bowls of milk, some bread, and a pie on the kitchen table. "You'd better eat your dinner now," said she. "You might jest as well get through with it. I want you to help me afterwards."

Nanny and Sammy stared at each other. There was something strange in their mother's manner. Mrs. Penn did not eat anything herself. She went into the pantry, and they heard her moving dishes while they ate. Presently she came out with a pile of plates. She got the clothes-basket out of the shed, and packed them in it. Nanny and Sammy watched. She brought out cups and saucers, and put them in with the plates.

"What you goin' to do, mother?" inquired Nanny, in a timid voice. A sense of something unusual made her tremble, as if it were a ghost. Sammy rolled his eyes over his pie.

"You'll see what I'm goin' to do," replied Mrs. Penn. "If you're through Nanny, I want you to go upstairs an' pack up your things; an' I want you, Sammy, to help me take down the bed in the bedroom."

"Oh, mother, what for?" gasped Nanny.

"You'll see."

During the next few hours a feat was performed by this simple, pious New England mother which was equal in its way to Wolfe's storming of the Heights of Abraham. It took no more genius and audacity or bravery for Wolfe to cheer his wondering soldiers up those steep precipices, under the sleeping eyes of the enemy, than for Sarah Penn, at the head of her children, to move all their little household goods into the new barn while her husband was away.

Nanny and Sammy followed their mother's instructions without a murmur; indeed, they were overawed. There is a certain uncanny and superhuman quality about all such purely original undertakings as their mother's was to them.

Nanny went back and forth with her light load, and Sammy tugged with sober energy.

At five o'clock in the afternoon the little house in which the Penns had lived for forty years had emptied itself into the new barn.

Every builder builds somewhat for unknown purposes, and is in a measure a prophet. The architect of Adoniram Penn's barn, while he designed it for the comfort of four-footed animals, had planned better than he knew for the comfort of humans. Sarah Penn saw at a glance its possibilities. Those great box-stalls, with quilts hung before them, would make better bedrooms than the one she had occupied for forty years, and there was a tight carriage-room. The harness-room, with its chimney and shelves, would make a kitchen of her dreams. The great middle space would make a parlor, by-and-by, fit for a palace. Up-stairs there was as much room as down. With partitions and windows, what a house would there be! Sarah looked at the row of stanchions before the allotted space for cows, and reflected that she would have her front entry there.

At six o'clock the stove was up in the harness room, the kettle was boiling, and the table was set for tea. It looked almost as home-like as the abandoned house across the yard had ever done. The young hired man milked, and Sarah directed him calmly to bring the milk to the new barn. He came gaping, dropping little blots of foam from the brimming pails on the grass. Before the next morning he had spread the story of Adoniram Penn's wife moving into the new barn all over the little village. Men assembled in the store and talked it over, women with shawls over their heads scuttled into each other's houses before their work was done. Any deviation from the ordinary course of life in this quiet town was enough to stop all progress in it. Everybody paused to look at the staid, independent figure on the side track. There was a difference of opinion with regard to her. Some held her to be insane; some, of a lawless and rebellious spirit.

Friday the minister went to see her. It was in the forenoon, and she was at the barn door shelling peas for dinner. She looked up and returned his salutation with dignity, then she went on with her work. She did not invite him in. The saintly expression on her face remained fixed, but there was an angry flush over it.

The minister stood awkwardly before her, and talked. She handled the peas as if they were bullets. At last she looked up, and her eyes showed the spirit that her meek front had covered for a lifetime.

"There ain't no use talkin', Mr. Hersey," said she. "I've thought it all over an' over, an' I believe I'm doin' what's right. I've made it the subject of prayer, an' it's betwixt me an' the Lord an' Adoniram. There ain't no call for nobody else to worry about it."

"Well, of course, if you have brought it to the Lord in prayer, and feel satisfied that you are doing right, Mrs. Penn," said the minister, helplessly. His thin gray-bearded face was pathetic. He was a sickly man; his youthful confidence had cooled; he had to scourge himself up to some of his pastoral duties as relentlessly as a Catholic ascetic, and then he was prostrated by the smart.

"I think it's right jest as much as I think it was right for our forefathers to come over here from the old country 'cause they didn't have what belonged to 'em." said Mrs. Penn. She arose. The barn threshold might have been Plymouth Rock from her bearing. "I don't doubt you mean well, Mr. Hersey," said she, "but there are things people hadn't ought to interfere with. I've been a member of the church for over forty years. I've got my own mind an' my own feet, an' I'm goin' to think my own thoughts an' go my own way, an' nobody but the Lord is goin' to dictate to me unless I've a mind to have him. Won't you come in an' set down? How is Mis' Hersey?"

"She is well, I thank you," replied the minister. He added some more perplexed apologetic remarks; then he retreated.

He could expound the intricacies of every character study in the Scriptures, he was competent to grasp the Pilgrim Fathers and all historical innovators, but Sarah Penn was beyond him. He could deal with primal cases, but parallel ones worsted him. But, after all, although it was aside from his province, he wondered more how Adoniram Penn would deal with his wife than how the Lord would. Everybody shared the wonder. When Adoniram's four new cows arrived, Sarah ordered three to be put in the old barn, the other in the house shed where the cooking-stove had stood. That added to the excitement. It was whispered that all four cows were domiciled in the house.

Towards sunset on Saturday, when Adoniram was expected home, there was a knot of men in the road near the new barn. The hired man had milked, but he still hung around the premises. Sarah Penn had supper all ready. There were brown-bread and baked beans and a custard pie; it was the supper that Adoniram loved on a Saturday night. She had on a clean calico, and she bore herself imperturbably. Nanny and Sammy kept close at her heels. Their eyes were large, and Nanny was full of nervous tremors. Still there was to them more pleasant excitement than anything else. An inborn confidence in their mother over their father asserted itself.

Sammy looked out of the harness-room window. "There he is," he announced, in an awed whisper. He and Nanny peeped around the casing. Mrs. Penn kept on about her work. The children watched Adoniram leave the new horse standing in the drive while he went to the house door. It was fastened. Then he went around to the shed. That door was seldom locked, even when the family was away. The thought how her father would be confronted by the cow flashed upon Nanny. There was a hysterical sob in her throat. Adoniram emerged from the shed and stood looking about in a dazed fashion. His lips moved, he was saying something, but they could not hear what it was. The hired man was peeping around the corner of the old barn, but nobody saw him.

Adoniram took the new horse by the bridle and led him across the yard to the new barn. Nanny and Sammy slunk close to their mother. The barn doors rolled back, and there stood Adoniram, with the long mild face of the great Canadian farm horse looking over his shoulder.

Nanny kept behind her mother, but Sammy stepped suddenly forward, and stood in front of her.

Adoniram stared at the group. "What on airth you all down here for?" said he. "What's the matter over to the house?"

"We've come here to live, father," said Sammy. His shrill voice quavered out bravely.

"What"—Adoniram sniffed—"what is it smells like cookin'?" said he. He stepped forward and looked in the open door of the harness-room. Then he turned to his wife. His old bristling face was pale and frightened. "What on airth does this mean, mother?" he gasped.

"You come in here, father," said Sarah. She led the way into the harness-room and shut the door. "Now, father," said she, "you needn't be scared. I ain't crazy. There ain't nothin' to be upset over. But we've come here to live, an' we're goin' to live here. We've got jest as good a right here as new horses an' cows. The house wasn't fit for us to live in any longer, an' I made up my mind I wa'n't goin' to stay there. I've done my duty by you forty year, an' I'm goin' to do it now; but I'm goin' to live here. You've got to put in some windows and partitions; an' you'll have to buy some furniture."

"Why, mother!" the old man gasped.

"You'd better take your coat off an' get washed—there's the wash basin—an' then we'll have supper."

"Why, mother!"

Sammy went past the window, leading the new horse to the old barn. The old man saw him, and shook his head speechlessly. He tried to take off his coat, but his arms seemed to lack the power. His wife helped him. She poured some water into the tin basin, and put in a piece of soap. She got the comb and brush, and smoothed his thin gray hair after he had washed. Then she put the beans, hot bread, and tea on the table. Sammy came in, and the family drew up. Adoniram sat looking dazedly at his plate, and they waited.

"Ain't you goin' to ask a blessin', father?" said Sarah.

And the old man bent his head and mumbled.

All through the meal he stopped eating at intervals, and stared furtively at his wife; but he ate well. The home food tasted good to him, and his old frame was too sturdily healthy to be affected by his mind. But after supper he went out, and sat down on the step of the smaller door at the right of the barn, through which he had meant his Jerseys to pass in stately file, but which Sarah designed for her front house door, and he leaned his head on his hands.

After the supper dishes were cleared away and the milkpans washed, Sarah went out to him. The twilight was deepening. There was a clear green glow in the sky. Before them stretched the smooth level of field; in the distance was a cluster of hay-stacks like the huts of a village; the air was very cool and calm and sweet. The landscape might have been an ideal one of peace.

Sarah bent over and touched her husband on one of his thin, sinewy shoulders. "Father!"

The old man's shoulders heaved: he was weeping.

"Why, don't do so, father," said Sarah.

"I'll—put up the—partitions, an'—everything you—want, mother."

Sarah put her apron up to her face; she was overcome by her own triumph.

Adoniram was like a fortress whose walls had no active resistance, and went down the instant the right besieging tools were used. "Why, mother," he said, hoarsely, "I hadn't no idee you was so set on't as all this comes to."

The Yellow Wallpaper

Charlotte Perkins Gilman

It is very seldom that mere ordinary people like John and myself secure ancestral halls for the summer.

A colonial mansion, a hereditary estate, I would say a haunted house, and reach the height of romantic felicity—but that would be asking too much of fate!

Still I will proudly declare that there is something queer about it.

Else, why should it be let so cheaply? And why have stood so long untenanted?

John laughs at me, of course, but one expects that in marriage.

John is practical in the extreme. He has no patience with faith, an intense horror of superstition, and he scoffs openly at any talk of things not to be felt and seen and put down in figures.

John is a physician, and *perhaps*—(I would not say it to a living soul, of course, but this is dead paper and a great relief to my mind)—*perhaps* that is one reason I do not get well faster.

You see he does not believe I am sick!

And what can one do?

If a physician of high standing, and one's own husband, assures friends and relatives that there is really nothing the matter with one but temporary nervous depression—a slight hysterical tendency—what is one to do?

My brother is also a physician, and also of high standing, and he says the same thing.

So I take phosphates or phospites—whichever it is, and tonics, and journeys, and air, and exercise, and am absolutely forbidden to "work" until I am well again.

Personally, I disagree with their ideas.

Personally, I believe that congenial work, with excitement and change, would do me good.

But what is one to do?

I did write for a while in spite of them; but it *does* exhaust me a good deal—having to be so sly about it, or else meet with heavy opposition.

I sometimes fancy that in my condition if I had less opposition and more society and stimulus—but John says the very worst thing I can do is to think about my condition, and I confess it always makes me feel bad.

So I will let it alone and talk about the house.

The most beautiful place! It is quite alone, standing well back from the road, quite three miles from the village. It makes me think of English places that you read about, for there are hedges and walls and gates that lock, and lots of separate little houses for the gardeners and people.

There is a *delicious* garden! I never saw such a garden—large and shady, full of box-bordered paths, and lined with long grape-covered arbors with seats under them.

There were greenhouses, too, but they are all broken now.

There was some legal trouble, I believe, something about the heirs and coheirs; anyhow, the place has been empty for years.

That spoils my ghostliness, I am afraid, but I don't care—there is something strange about the house—I can feel it.

I even said so to John one moonlight evening, but he said what I felt was a *draught*, and shut the window.

I get unreasonably angry with John sometimes. I'm sure I never used to be so sensitive. I think it is due to this nervous condition.

But John says if I feel so, I shall neglect proper self-control; so I take pains to control myself—before him, at least, and that makes me very tired.

I don't like our room a bit. I wanted one downstairs that opened on the piazza and had roses all over the window, and such pretty old-fashioned chintz hangings! but John would not hear of it.

He said there was only one window and not room for two beds, and no near room for him if he took another.

He is very careful and loving, and hardly lets me stir without special direction.

I have a schedule prescription for each hour in the day; he takes all care from me, and so I feel basely ungrateful not to value it more.

He said we came here solely on my account, that I was to have perfect rest and all the air I could get. "Your exercise depends on your strength, my dear," said he, "and your food somewhat on your appetite; but air you can absorb all the time." So we took the nursery at the top of the house.

It is a big, airy room, the whole floor nearly, with windows that look all ways, and air and sunshine galore. It was nursery first and then playroom and gymnasium, I should judge; for the windows are barred for little children, and there are rings and things in the walls.

The paint and paper look as if a boys' school had used it. It is stripped off—the paper—in great patches all around the head of my bed, about as far as I can reach, and in a great place on the other side of the room low down. I never saw a worse paper in my life.

One of those sprawling flamboyant patterns committing every artistic sin.

It is dull enough to confuse the eye in following, pronounced enough to constantly irritate and provoke study, and when you follow the lame uncertain curves for a little distance they suddenly commit suicide—plunge off at outrageous angles, destroy themselves in unheard of contradictions.

The color is repellent, almost revolting; a smouldering unclean yellow, strangely faded by the slow-turning sunlight.

It is a dull yet lurid orange in some places, a sickly sulphur tint in others.

No wonder the children hated it! I should hate it myself if I had to live in this room long.

There comes John, and I must put this away,—he hates to have me write a word.

We have been here two weeks, and I haven't felt like writing before, since that first day.

I am sitting by the window now, up in this atrocious nursery, and there is nothing to hinder my writing as much as I please, save lack of strength.

John is away all day, and even some nights when his cases are serious.

I am glad my case is not serious!

But these nervous troubles are dreadfully depressing.

John does not know how much I really suffer. He knows there is no *reason* to suffer, and that satisfies him.

Of course it is only nervousness. It does weigh on me so not to do my duty in any way!

I meant to be such a help to John, such a real rest and comfort, and here I am a comparative burden already!

Nobody would believe what an effort it is to do what little I am able—to dress and entertain, and order things.

It is fortunate Mary is so good with the baby. Such a dear baby!

And yet I *cannot* be with him, it makes me so nervous.

I suppose John never was nervous in his life. He laughs at me so about this wallpaper!

At first he meant to repaper the room, but afterwards he said that I was letting it get the better of me, and that nothing was worse for a nervous patient than to give way to such fancies.

He said that after the wallpaper was changed it would be the heavy bedstead, and then the barred windows, and then that gate at the head of the stairs, and so on.

"You know the place is doing you good," he said, "and really, dear, I don't care to renovate the house just for a three months' rental."

"Then do let us go downstairs," I said, "there are such pretty rooms there."

Then he took me in his arms and called me a blessed little goose, and said he would go down to the cellar, if I wished, and have it whitewashed into the bargain.

But he is right enough about the beds and windows and things.

It is an airy and comfortable room as any one need wish, and, of course, I would not be so silly as to make him uncomfortable just for a whim.

I'm really getting quite fond of the big room, all but that horrid paper.

Out of one window I can see the garden, those mysterious deepshaded arbors, the riotous old-fashioned flowers, and bushes and gnarly trees.

Out of another I get a lovely view of the bay and a little private wharf belonging to the estate. There is a beautiful shaded lane that runs down there from the house. I always fancy I see people walking in these numerous paths and arbors, but John has cautioned me not to give way to fancy in the least. He says that with my imaginative power and habit of story-making, a nervous weakness like mine is sure to lead to all manner of excited fancies, and that I ought to use my will and good sense to check the tendency. So I try.

I think sometimes that if I were only well enough to write a little it would relieve the press of ideas and rest me.

But I find I get pretty tired when I try.

It is so discouraging not to have any advice and companionship about my work. When I get really well, John says we will ask Cousin Henry and Julia down for a long visit; but he says he would as soon put fireworks in my pillowcase as to let me have those stimulating people about now.

I wish I could get well faster.

But I must not think about that. This paper looks to me as if it *knew* what a vicious influence it had!

There is a recurrent spot where the pattern lolls like a broken neck and two bulbous eyes stare at you upside down.

I get positively angry with the impertinence of it and the everlastingness. Up and down and sideways they crawl, and those absurb, unblinking eyes are everywhere. There is one place where two breadths didn't match, and the eyes go all up and down the line, one a little higher than the other.

I never saw so much expression in an inanimate thing before, and we all know how much expression they have! I used to lie awake as a child and get more entertainment and terror out of blank walls and plain furniture than most children could find in a toy-store.

I remember what a kindly wink the knobs of our big, old bureau used to have, and there was one chair that always seemed like a strong friend.

I used to feel that if any of the other things looked too fierce I could always hop into that chair and be safe.

The furniture in this room is no worse than inharmonious, however, for we had to bring it all from downstairs. I suppose when this was used as a playroom they had to take the nursery things out, and no wonder! I never saw such ravages as the children have made here.

The wallpaper, as I said before, is torn off in spots, and it sticketh closer than a brother—they must have had perseverance as well as hatred.

Then the floor is scratched and gouged and splintered, the plaster itself is dug out here and there, and this great heavy bed which is all we found in the room, looks as if it had been through the wars.

But I don't mind it a bit—only the paper.

There comes John's sister. Such a dear girl as she is, and so careful of me! I must not let her find me writing.

She is a perfect and enthusiastic housekeeper, and hopes for no better profession. I verily believe she thinks it is the writing which made me sick!

But I can write when she is out, and see her a long way off from these windows.

There is one that commands the road, a lovely shaded winding road, and one that just looks off over the country. A lovely country, too, full of great elms and velvet meadows.

This wallpaper has a kind of sub-pattern in a different shade, a particularly irritating one, for you can only see it in certain lights, and not clearly then.

But in the places where it isn't faded and where the sun is just so—I can see a strange, provoking, formless sort of figure, that seems to skulk about behind that silly and conspicuous front design.

There's sister on the stairs!

Well, the Fourth of July is over! The people are all gone and I am tired out. John thought it might do me good to see a little company, so we just had mother and Nellie and the children down for a week.

Of course I didn't do a thing. Jennie sees to everything now.

But it tired me all the same.

John says if I don't pick up faster he shall send me to Weir Mitchell in the fall.

But I don't want to go there at all. I had a friend who was in his hands once, and she says he is just like John and my brother, only more so!

Besides, it is such an undertaking to go so far.

I don't feel as if it was worth while to turn my hand over for anything, and I'm getting dreadfully fretful and querulous.

I cry at nothing,. and cry most of the time.

Of course I don't when John is here, or anybody else, but when I am alone.

And I am alone a good deal just now. John is kept in town very often by serious cases, and Jennie is good and lets me alone when I want her to.

So I walk a little in the garden or down that lovely lane, sit on the porch under the roses, and lie down up here a good deal.

I'm getting really fond of the room in spite of the wallpaper. Perhaps *because* of the wallpaper.

It dwells in my mind so!

I lie here on this great immovable bed—it is nailed down, I believe—and follow that pattern about by the hour. It is as good as gymnastics, I assure you. I start, we'll say, at the bottom, down in the corner over there where it has not been touched, and I determine for the thousandth time that I *will* follow that pointless pattern to some sort of a conclusion.

I know a little of the principle of design, and I know this thing was not arranged on any laws of radiation, or alternation, or repetition, or symmetry, or anything else that I ever heard of.

It is repeated, of course, by the breadths, but not otherwise.

Looked at in one way each breadth stands alone, the bloated curves and flourishes—a kind of "debased Romanesque" with *delirium tremens*—go waddling up and down in isolated columns of fatuity.

But, on the other hand, they connect diagonally, and the sprawling outlines run off in great slanting waves of optic horror, like a lot of wallowing seaweeds in full chase.

The whole thing goes horizontally, too, at least it seems so, and I exhaust myself in trying to distinguish the order of its going in that direction.

They have used a horizontal breadth for a frieze, and that adds wonderfully to the confusion.

There is one end of the room where it is almost intact, and there, when the crosslights fade and the low sun shines directly upon it, I can almost fancy radiation after all—the interminable grotesques seem to form around a common centre and rush off in headlong plunges of equal distraction.

It makes me tired to follow it. I will take a nap I guess.

I don't know why I should write this.

I don't want to.

I don't feel able.

And I know John would think it absurd. But I *must* say what I feel and think in some way—it is such a relief!

But the effort is getting to be greater than the relief.

Half the time now I am awfully lazy, and lie down ever so much.

John says I mustn't lose my strength, and has me take cod liver oil and lots of tonics and things, to say nothing of ale and wine and rare meat.

Dear John! He loves me very dearly, and hates to have me sick. I tried to have a real earnest reasonable talk with him the other day, and tell him how I wish he would let me go and make a visit to Cousin Henry and Julia.

But he said I wasn't able to go, nor able to stand it after I got there; and I did not make out a very good case for myself, for I was crying before I had finished.

It is getting to be a great effort for me to think straight. Just this nervous weakness I suppose.

And dear John gathered me up in his arms, and just carried me upstairs and laid me on the bed, and sat by me and read to me till it tired my head.

He said I was his darling and his comfort and all he had, and that I must take care of myself for his sake, and keep well.

He says no one but myself can help me out of it, that I must use my will and self-control and not let any silly fancies run away with me.

There's one comfort, the baby is well and happy, and does not have to occupy this nursery with the horrid wallpaper.

If we had not used it, that blessed child would have! What a fortunate escape! Why, I wouldn't have a child of mine, an impressionable little thing, live in such a room for worlds.

I never thought of it before, but it is lucky that John kept me here after all, I can stand it so much easier than a baby, you see.

Of course I never mention it to them any more—I am too wise—but I keep watch of it all the same.

There are things in that paper that nobody knows but me, or ever will.

Behind that outside pattern the dim shapes get clearer every day.

It is always the same shape, only very numerous.

And it is like a woman stooping down and creeping about behind that pattern. I don't like it a bit. I wonder—I begin to think—I wish John would take me away from here!

It is so hard to talk with John about my case, because he is so wise, and because he loves me so.

But I tried it last night.

It was moonlight. The moon shines in all around just as the sun does.

I hate to see it sometimes, it creeps so slowly, and always comes in by one window or another.

John was asleep and I hated to waken him, so I kept still and watched the moonlight on that undulating wallpaper till I felt creepy.

The faint figure behind seemed to shake the pattern, just as if she wanted to get out.

I got up softly and went to feel and see if the paper *did* move, and when I came back John was awake.

"What is it, little girl?" he said. "Don't go walking about like that—you'll get cold."

I thought it was a good time to talk, so I told him that I really was not gaining here, and that I wished he would take me away.

"Why darling!" said he, "our lease will be up in three weeks, and I can't see how to leave before.

"The repairs are not done at home, and I cannot possibly leave town just now. Of course if you were in any danger, I could and would, but you really are better, dear, whether you can see it or not. I am a doctor, dear, and I know. You are gaining flesh and color, your appetite is better, I feel really much easier about you."

"I don't weigh a bit more," said I, "nor as much; and my appetite may be better in the evening when you are here, but it is worse in the morning when you are away!"

"Bless her little heart!" said he with a big hug, "she shall be as sick as she pleases! But now let's improve the shining hours by going to sleep, and talk about it in the morning!"

"And you won't go away?" I asked gloomily.

"Why, how can I, dear? It is only three weeks more and then we will take a nice little trip of a few days while Jennie is getting the house ready. Really, dear, you are better!"

"Better in body perhaps—" I began, and stopped short, for he sat up straight and looked at me with such a stern, reproachful look that I could not say another word.

"My darling," said he, "I beg of you, for my sake and for our child's sake, as well as for your own, that you will never for one instant let that idea enter your mind! There is nothing so dangerous, so fascinating, to a temperament like yours. It is a false and foolish fancy. Can you not trust me as a physician when I tell you so?"

So of course I said no more on that score, and we went to sleep before long. He thought I was asleep first, but I wasn't, and lay there for hours trying to decide whether that front pattern and the back pattern really did move together or separately.

On a pattern like this, by daylight, there is a lack of sequence, a defiance of law, that is a constant irritant to a normal mind.

The color is hideous enough, and unreliable enough, and infuriating enough, but the pattern is torturing.

You think you have mastered it, but just as you get well underway in following, it turns a back-somersault and there you are. It slaps you in the face, knocks you down, and tramples upon you. It is like a bad dream.

The outside pattern is a florid arabesque, reminding one of a fungus. If you can imagine a toadstool in joints, an interminable string of toadstools, budding and sprouting in endless convolutions—why, that is something like it.

That is, sometimes!

There is one marked peculiarity about this paper, a thing nobody seems to notice but myself, and that is that it changes as the light changes.

When the sun shoots in through the east window—I always watch for that first long, straight ray—it changes so quickly that I never can quite believe it.

That is why I watch it always.

By moonlight—the moon shines in all night when there is a moon—I wouldn't know it was the same paper.

At night in any kind of light, in twilight, candle light, lamplight, and worst of all by moonlight, it becomes bars! The outside pattern I mean, and the woman behind it is as plain as can be.

I didn't realize for a long time what the thing was that showed behind, that dim sub-pattern, but now I am quite sure it is a woman.

By daylight she is subdued, quiet. I fancy it is the pattern that keeps her so still. It is so puzzling. It keeps me quiet by the hour.

I lie down ever so much now. John says it is good for me, and to sleep all I can.

Indeed he started the habit by making me lie down for an hour after each meal.

It is a very bad habit I am convinced, for you see I don't sleep.

And that cultivates deceit, for I don't tell them I'm awake—O no!

The fact is I am getting a little afraid of John.

He seems very queer sometimes, and even Jennie has an inexplicable look.

It strikes me occasionally, just as a scientific hypothesis,—that perhaps it is the paper!

I have watched John when he did not know I was looking,

and come into the room suddenly on the most innocent excuses, and I've caught him several times *looking at the paper!* And Jennie too. I caught Jennie with her hand on it once.

She didn't know I was in the room, and when I asked her in a quiet, a very quiet voice, with the most restrained manner possible, what she was doing with the paper—she turned around as if she had been caught stealing, and looked quite angry—asked me why I should frighten her so!

Then she said that the paper stained everything it touched, and that she had found yellow smooches on all my clothes and John's, and she wished we would be more careful!

Did not that sound innocent? But I know she was studying that pattern, and I am determined that nobody shall find it out but myself!

Life is very much more exciting now than it used to be. You see I have something more to expect, to look forward to, to watch. I really do eat better, and am more quiet than I was.

John is so pleased to see me improve! He laughed a little the other day, and said I seemed to be flourishing in spite of my wallpaper.

I turned it off with a laugh. I had no intention of telling him it was *because* of the wallpaper—he would make fun of me. He might even want to take me away.

I don't want to leave now until I have found it out. There is a week more, and I think that will be enough.

I'm feeling ever so much better! I don't sleep much at night, for it is so interesting to watch developments; but I sleep a good deal in the daytime.

In the daytime it is tiresome and perplexing.

There are always new shoots on the fungus, and new shades of yellow all over it. I cannot keep count of them, though I have tried conscientiously.

It is the strangest yellow, that wallpaper! It makes me think of all the yellow things I ever saw—not beautiful ones like buttercups, but old foul, bad yellow things.

But there is something else about that paper—the smell! I noticed it the moment we came into the room, but with so much air and sun it was not bad. Now we have had a week of fog and rain, and whether the windows are open or not, the smell is here.

It creeps all over the house.

I find it hovering in the dining-room, skulking in the parlor, hiding in the hall, lying in wait for me on the stairs.

It gets into my hair.

Even when I go to ride, if I turn my head suddenly and surprise it—there is that smell!

Such a peculiar odor, too! I have spent hours in trying to analyze it, to find what it smelled like.

It is not bad—at first, and very gentle, but quite the subtlest, most enduring odor I ever met.

In this damp weather it is awful, I wake up in the night and find it hanging over me.

It used to disturb me at first. I thought seriously of burning the house—to reach the smell.

But now I am used to it. The only thing I can think of that it is like is the *color* of the paper! A yellow smell.

There is a very funny mark on this wall, low down, near the mopboard. A streak that runs round the room. It goes behind every piece of furniture, except the bed, a long, straight, even *smooch*, as if it had been rubbed over and over.

I wonder how it was done and who did it, and what they did it for. Round and round and round—round and round and round—it makes me dizzy!

I really have discovered something at last.

Through watching so much at night, when it changes so, I have finally found out.

The front pattern *does* move—and no wonder! The woman behind shakes it!

Sometimes I think there are a great many women behind, and sometimes only one, and she crawls around fast, and her crawling shakes it all over.

Then in the very bright spots she keeps still, and in the very shady spots she just takes hold of the bars and shakes them hard.

And she is all the time trying to climb through. But nobody could climb through that pattern—it strangles so: I think that is why it has so many heads.

They get through, and then the pattern strangles them off and turns them upside down, and makes their eyes white!

If those heads were covered or taken off it would not be half so bad.

I think that woman gets out in the daytime!

And I'll tell you why—privately—I've seen her!

I can see her out of every one of my windows!

It is the same woman, I know, for she is always creeping, and most women do not creep by daylight.

I see her on that long road under the trees, creeping along, and when a carriage comes she hides under the blackberry vines.

I don't blame her a bit. It must be very humiliating to be caught creeping by daylight.

I always lock the door when I creep by daylight. I can't do it at night, for I know John would suspect something at once.

And John is so queer now, that I don't want to irritate him. I wish he would take another room! Besides, I don't want anybody to get that woman out at night but myself.

I often wonder if I could see her out of all the windows at once.

But, turn as fast as I can, I can only see out of one at one time.

And though I always see her, she *may* be able to creep faster than I can turn!

I have watched her sometimes away off in the open country, creeping as fast as a cloud shadow in a high wind.

If only that top pattern could be gotten off from the under one! I mean to try it, little by little.

I have found out another funny thing, but I shan't tell it this time! It does not do to trust people too much.

There are only two more days to get this paper off, and I believe John is beginning to notice. I don't like the look in his eyes.

And I heard him ask Jennie a lot of professional questions about me. She had a very good report to give.

She said I slept a good deal in the daytime.

John knows I don't sleep very well at night, for all I'm so quiet!

He asked me all sorts of questions, too, and pretended to be very loving and kind.

As if I couldn't see through him!

Still, I don't wonder he acts so, sleeping under this paper for three months.

It only interests me, but I feel sure John and Jennie are secretly affected by it.

Hurrah! This is the last day, but it is enough. John to stay in town over night, and won't be out until this evening.

Jennie wanted to sleep with me—the sly thing! but I told her I should undoubtedly rest better for a night all alone.

That was clever, for really I wasn't alone a bit! As soon as it was moonlight and that poor thing began to crawl and shake the pattern, I got up and ran to help her.

I pulled and she shook, I shook and she pulled, and before morning we had peeled off yards of that paper.

A strip about as high as my head and half around the room.

And then when the sun came and that awful pattern began to laugh at me, I declared I would finish it to-day!

We go away to-morrow, and they are moving all my furniture down again to leave things as they were before.

Jennie looked at the wall in amazement, but I told her merrily that I did it out of pure spite at the vicious thing.

She laughed and said she wouldn't mind doing it herself, but I must not get tired.

How she betrayed herself that time!

But I am here, and no person touches this paper but me—not *alive!*

She tried to get me out of the room—it was too patent! But I said it was so quiet and empty and clean now that I believed I would lie down again and sleep all I could; and not to wake me even for dinner—I would call when I woke.

So now she is gone, and the servants are gone, and the things are gone, and there is nothing left but that great bedstead nailed down, with the canvas mattress we found on it.

We shall sleep downstairs to-night, and take the boat home to-morrow.

I quite enjoy the room, now it is bare again.

How those children did tear about here!

This bedstead is fairly gnawed!

But I must get to work.

I have locked the door and thrown the key down into the front path.

I don't want to go out, and I don't want to have anybody come in, till John comes.

I want to astonish him.

I've got a rope up here that even Jennie did not find. If that woman does get out, and tries to get away, I can tie her.

But I forgot I could not reach far without anything to stand on!

This bed will *not* move!

I tried to lift and push it until I was lame, and then I got so angry I bit off a little piece at one corner—but it hurt my teeth.

Then I peeled off all the paper I could reach standing on the floor. It sticks horribly and the pattern just enjoys it! All those strangled heads and bulbous eyes and waddling fungus growths just shriek with derision!

I am getting angry enough to do something desperate. To jump out of the window would be admirable exercise, but the bars are too strong even to try.

Besides I wouldn't do it. Of course not. I know well enough that a step like that is improper and might be misconstrued.

I don't like to *look* out of the windows even—there are so many of those creeping women, and they creep so fast.

I wonder if they all come out of that wallpaper as I did?

But I am securely fastened now by my well-hidden rope— you don't get *me* out in the road there!

I suppose I shall have to get back behind the pattern when it comes night, and that is hard!

It is so pleasant to be out in this great room and creep around as I please!

I don't want to go outside. I won't, even if Jennie asks me to.

For outside you have to creep on the ground, and everything is green instead of yellow.

But here I can creep smoothly on the floor, and my shoulder just fits in that long smooch around the wall, so I cannot lose my way.

Why there's John at the door!

It is no use, young man, you can't open it!

How he does call and pound!

Now he's crying for an axe.

It would be a shame to break down that beautiful door!

"John dear!" said I in the gentlest voice, "the key is down by the front steps, under a plantain leaf!"

That silenced him for a few moments.

Then he said—very quietly indeed, "Open the door, my darling!"

"I can't," said I. "The key is down by the front door under a plantain leaf!"

And then I said it again, several times, very gently and slowly, and said it so often that he had to go and see, and he got it of course, and came in. He stopped short by the door.

"What is the matter?" he cried. "For God's sake, what are you doing?"

I kept on creeping just the same, but I looked at him over my shoulder.

"I've got out at last," said I, "in spite of you and Jane. And I've pulled off most of the paper, so you can't put me back!"

Now why should that man have fainted? But he did, and right across my path by the wall, so that I had to creep over him every time!

A Respectable Woman

Kate Chopin

Mrs. Baroda was a little provoked to learn that her husband expected his friend, Gouvernail, up to spend a week or
two on the plantation.

They had entertained a good deal during the winter; much
of the time had also been passed in New Orleans in various
forms of mild dissipation. She was looking forward to a
period of unbroken rest, now, and undisturbed tête-à-tête
with her husband, when he informed her that Gouvernail was
coming up to stay a week or two.

This was a man she had heard much of but never seen.
He had been her husband's college friend; was now a journal-
ist, and in no sense a society man or "a man about town,"
which were, perhaps, some of the reasons she had never met
him. But she had unconsciously formed an image of him in
her mind. She pictured him tall, slim, cynical; with eye-glasses, and his hands in his pockets; and she did not like him.
Gouvernail was slim enough, but he wasn't very tall nor very
cynical; neither did he wear eye-glasses nor carry his hands in
his pockets. And she rather liked him when he first presented
himself.

But why she liked him she could not explain satisfactorily
to herself when she partly attempted to do so. She could discover in him none of those brilliant and promising traits
which Gaston, her husband, had often assured her that he
possessed. On the contrary, he sat rather mute and receptive
before her chatty eagerness to make him feel at home and in
face of Gaston's frank and wordy hospitality. His manner
was as courteous toward her as the most exacting woman
could require; but he made no direct appeal to her approval
or even esteem.

Once settled at the plantation he seemed to like to sit upon
the wide portico in the shade of one of the big Corinthian
pillars, smoking his cigar lazily and listening attentively to
Gaston's experience as a sugar planter.

"This is what I call living," he would utter with deep satisfaction, as the air that swept across the sugar field caressed him with its warm and scented velvety touch. It pleased him also to get on familiar terms with the big dogs that came about him, rubbing themselves sociably against his legs. He did not care to fish, and displayed no eagerness to go out and kill grosbecs when Gaston proposed doing so.

Gouvernail's personality puzzled Mrs. Baroda, but she liked him. Indeed, he was a lovable, inoffensive fellow. After a few days, when she could understand him no better than at first, she gave over being puzzled and remained piqued. In this mood she left her husband and her guest, for the most part, alone together. Then finding that Gouvernail took no manner of exception to her action, she imposed her society upon him, accompanying him in his idle strolls to the mill and walks along the batture. She persistently sought to penetrate the reserve in which he had unconsciously enveloped himself.

"When is he going—your friend?" she one day asked her husband. "For my part, he tires me frightfully."

"Not for a week yet, dear. I can't understand; he gives you no trouble."

"No. I should like him better if he did; if he were more like others, and I had to plan somewhat for his comfort and enjoyment."

Gaston took his wife's pretty face between his hands and looked tenderly and laughingly into her troubled eyes. They were making a bit of toilet sociably together in Mrs. Baroda's dressing-room.

"You are full of surprises, ma belle," he said to her. "Even I can never count upon how you are going to act under given conditions." He kissed her and turned to fasten his cravat before the mirror.

"Here you are," he went on, "taking poor Gouvernail seriously and making a commotion over him, the last thing he would desire or expect."

"Commotion!" she hotly resented. "Nonsense! How can you say such a thing? Commotion, indeed! But, you know, you said he was clever."

"So he is. But the poor fellow is run down by overwork now. That's why I asked him here to take a rest."

"You used to say he was a man of ideas," she retorted, unconciliated. "I expected him to be interesting, at least. I'm going to the city in the morning to have my spring gowns fitted. Let me know when Mr. Gouvernail is gone; I shall be at my Aunt Octavie's."

That night she went and sat alone upon a bench that stood beneath a live oak tree at the edge of the gravel walk.

She had never known her thoughts or her intentions to be so confused. She could gather nothing from them but the feeling of a distinct necessity to quit her home in the morning.

Mrs. Baroda heard footsteps crunching the gravel; but could discern in the darkness only the approaching red point of a lighted cigar. She knew it was Gouvernail, for her husband did not smoke. She hoped to remain unnoticed, but her white gown revealed her to him. He threw away his cigar and seated himself upon the bench beside her; without a suspicion that she might object to his presence.

"Your husband told me to bring this to you, Mrs. Baroda," he said, handing her a filmy, white scarf with which she sometimes enveloped her head and shoulders. She accepted the scarf from him with a murmur of thanks, and let it lie in her lap.

He made some commonplace observation upon the baneful effect of the night air at that season. Then as his gaze reached out into the darkness, he murmured, half to himself:

" 'Night of south winds—night of the large few stars!
    Still nodding night—' "

She made no reply to this apostrophe to the night, which indeed, was not addressed to her.

Gouvernail was in no sense a diffident man, for he was not a self-conscious one. His periods of reserve were not constitutional, but the result of moods. Sitting there beside Mrs. Baroda, his silence melted for the time.

He talked freely and intimately in a low, hesitating drawl that was not unpleasant to hear. He talked of the old college days when he and Gaston had been a good deal to each other; of the days of keen and blind ambitions and large intentions. Now there was left with him, at least, a philosophic acquiescence to the existing order—only a desire to be permitted to exist, with now and then a little whiff of genuine life, such as he was breathing now.

Her mind only vaguely grasped what he was saying. Her physical being was for the moment predominant. She was not thinking of his words, only drinking in the tones of his voice.

She wanted to reach out her hand in the darkness and touch him with the sensitive tips of her fingers upon the face or the lips. She wanted to draw close to him and whisper against his cheek—she did not care what—as she might have done if she had not been a respectable woman.

The stronger the impulse grew to bring herself near him, the further, in fact, did she draw away from him. As soon as she could do so without an appearance of too great rudeness, she rose and left him there alone.

Before she reached the house, Gouvernail had lighted a fresh cigar and ended his apostrophe to the night.

Mrs. Baroda was greatly tempted that night to tell her husband—who was also her friend—of this folly that had seized her. But she did not yield to the temptation. Beside being a respectable woman she was a very sensible one; and she knew there are some battles in life which a human being must fight alone.

When Gaston arose in the morning, his wife had already departed. She had taken an early morning train to the city. She did not return till Gouvernail was gone from under her roof.

There was some talk of having him back during the summer that followed. That is, Gaston greatly desired it; but this desire yielded to his wife's strenuous opposition.

However, before the year ended, she proposed, wholly from herself, to have Gouvernail visit them again. Her husband was surprised and delighted with the suggestion coming from her.

"I am glad, chère amie, to know that you have finally overcome your dislike for him; truly he did not deserve it."

"Oh," she told him, laughingly, after pressing a long, tender kiss upon his lips, "I have overcome everything! you will see. This time I shall be very nice to him."

The Guests of
Mrs. Timms

Sarah Orne Jewett

1   Mrs. Persis Flagg stood in her front doorway taking leave
of Miss Cynthia Pickett, who had been making a long call.
They were not intimate friends. Miss Pickett always came
formally to the front door and rang when she paid her visits,
but, the week before, they had met at the county conference, and happened to be sent to the same house for entertainment, and so had deepened and renewed the pleasures of
acquaintance.

It was an afternoon in early June; the syringa-bushes were
tall and green on each side of the stone doorsteps, and were
covered with their lovely white and golden flowers. Miss
Pickett broke off the nearest twig, and held it before her prim
face as she talked. She had a pretty childlike smile that came
and went suddenly, but her face was not one that bore the
marks of many pleasures. Mrs. Flagg was a tall, commanding
sort of person, with an air of satisfaction and authority.

"Oh, yes, gather all you want," she said stiffly, as Miss
Pickett took the syringa without having asked beforehand;
but she had an amiable expression, and just now her large
countenance was lighted up by pleasant anticipation.

"We can tell early what sort of a day it's goin' to be," she
said eagerly. "There ain't a cloud in the sky now. I'll stop for
you as I come along, or if there should be anything unforeseen to detain me, I'll send you word. I don't expect you'd
want to go if it wa'n't so that I could?"

"Oh my sakes, no!" answered Miss Pickett discreetly, with
a timid flush. "You feel certain that Mis' Timms won't be put
out? I shouldn't feel free to go unless I went 'long o' you."

"Why, nothin' could be plainer than her words," said Mrs.
Flagg in a tone of reproval. "You saw how she urged me, an'
had over all that talk about how we used to see each other

66

often when we both lived to Longport, and told how she'd been thinkin' of writin', and askin' if it wa'n't so I should be able to come over and stop three or four days as soon as settled weather come, because she couldn't make no fire in her best chamber on account of the chimbley smokin' if the wind wa'n't just right. You see how she felt toward me, kissin' of me comin' and goin'? Why, she even asked me who I employed to do over my bonnet, Miss Pickett, just as interested as if she was a sister; an' she remarked she should look for us any pleasant day after we all got home, an' were settled after the conference."

Miss Pickett smiled, but did not speak, as if she expected more arguments still.

"An' she seemed just about as much gratified to meet with you again. She seemed to desire to meet you again very particular," continued Mrs. Flagg. "She really urged us to come together an' have a real good day talkin' over old times— there, don't le' 's go all over it again! I've always heard she'd made that old house of her aunt Bascoms' where she lives look real handsome. I once heard her best parlor carpet described as being an elegant carpet, different from any there was round here. Why, nobody couldn't be more cordial, Miss Pickett; you ain't goin' to give out just at the last?"

"Oh, no!" answered the visitor hastily; "no, 'm! I want to go full as much as you do, Mis' Flagg, but you see I never was so well acquainted with Mis' Cap'n Timms, an' I always seem to dread putting myself for'ard. She certain was very urgent, an' she said plain enough to come any day next week, an' here 't is Wednesday, though of course she wouldn't look for us either Monday or Tuesday. 'T will be a real pleasant occasion, an' now we've been to the conference it don't seem near so much effort to start."

"Why, I don't think nothin' of it," said Mrs. Flagg proudly. "We shall have a grand good time, goin' together an' all, I feel sure."

Miss Pickett still played with her syringa flower, tapping her thin cheek, and twirling the stem with her fingers. She looked as if she were going to say something more, but after a moment's hesitation she turned away.

"Good-afternoon, Mis' Flagg," she said formally, looking up with a quick little smile; "I enjoyed my call; I hope I ain't kep' you too late; I don't know but what it's 'most tea-time. Well, I shall look for you in the mornin'."

"Good-afternoon, Miss Pickett; I'm glad I was in when you

came. Call again, won't you?" said Mrs. Flagg. "Yes; you may expect me in good season," and so they parted. Miss Pickett went out at the neat clicking gate in the white fence, and Mrs. Flagg a moment later looked out of her sitting-room window to see if the gate were latched, and felt the least bit disappointed to find that it was. She sometimes went out after the departure of a guest, and fastened the gate herself with a loud, rebuking sound. Both of these Woodville women lived alone, and were very precise in their way of doing things.

2   The next morning dawned clear and bright, and Miss Pickett rose even earlier than usual. She found it most difficult to decide which of her dresses would be best to wear. Summer was still so young that the day had all the freshness of spring, but when the two friends walked away together along the shady street, with a chorus of golden robins singing high overhead in the elms, Miss Pickett decided that she had made a wise choice of her second-best black silk gown, which she had just turned again and freshened. It was neither too warm for the season nor too cool, nor did it look overdressed. She wore her large cameo pin, and this, with a long watch-chain, gave an air of proper mural decoration. She was a straight, flat little person, as if, when not in use, she kept herself, silk dress and all, between the leaves of a book. She carried a noticeable parasol with a fringe, and a small shawl, with a pretty border, neatly folded over her left arm. Mrs. Flagg always dressed in black cashmere, and looked, to hasty observers, much the same one day as another; but her companion recognized the fact that this was the best black cashmere of all, and for a moment quailed at the thought that Mrs. Flagg was paying such extreme deference to their prospective hostess. The visit turned for a moment into an unexpectedly solemn formality, and pleasure seemed to wane before Cynthia Pickett's eyes, yet with great courage she never slackened a single step. Miss Flagg carried a somewhat worn black leather handbag, which Miss Pickett regretted; it did not give the visit that casual and unpremeditated air which she felt to be more elegant.

"Sha'n't I carry your bag for you?" she asked timidly. Mrs. Flagg was the older and more important person.

"Oh, dear me, no," answered Mrs. Flagg. "My pocket's so remote, in case I should desire to sneeze or anything, that I

thought 't would be convenient for carrying my handkerchief
and pocket-book; an' then I just tucked in a couple o' glasses
o' my crab-apple jelly for Mis' Timms. She used to be a great
hand for preserves of every sort, an' I thought 't would be a
kind of an attention, an' give rise to conversation. I know she
used to make excellent drop-cakes when we was both
residin' to Longport; folks used to say she never would give
the right receipt, but if I get a real good chance, I mean to
ask her. Or why can't you, if I start talkin' about receipts—
why can't you say, sort of innocent, that I have always spoken frequently of her drop-cakes, an' ask for the rule? She
would be very sensible to the compliment, and could pass it
off if she didn't feel to indulge us. There, I do so wish you
would!"

"Yes, 'm," said Miss Pickett doubtfully; "I'll try to make
the opportunity. I'm very partial to drop-cakes. Was they
flour or rye, Mis' Flagg?"

"They was flour, dear," replied Mrs. Flagg approvingly;
"crisp an' light as any you ever see."

"I wish I had thought to carry somethin' to make it
pleasant," said Miss Pickett, after they had walked a little
farther; "but there, I don't know's 't would look just right,
this first visit, to offer anything to such a person as Mis'
Timms. In case I ever go over to Baxter again I won't forget
to make her some little present, as nice as I've got. 'T was certain very polite of her to urge me to come with you. I did feel
very doubtful at first. I didn't know but she thought it be-
hooved her, because I was in your company at the conference, and she wanted to save my feelin's, and yet expected I
would decline. I never was well acquainted with her; our
folks wasn't well off when I first knew her; 't was before uncle
Cap'n Dyer passed away an' remembered mother an' me in
his will. We couldn't make no han'some companies in them
days, so we didn't go to none, an' kep' to ourselves; but in
my grandmother's time, mother always said, the families was
very friendly. I shouldn't feel like goin' over to pass the day
with Mis' Timms if I didn't mean to ask her to return the
visit. Some don't think o' these things, but mother was very
set about not bein' done for when she couldn't make no return."

" 'When it rains porridge hold up your dish,' " said Mrs.
Flagg; but Miss Pickett made no response beyond a feeble
"Yes, 'm," which somehow got caught in her pale-green bon-
net-strings.

"There, 't ain't no use to fuss too much over all them things," proclaimed Mrs. Flagg, walking alone at a good pace with a fine sway of her skirts, and carrying her head high. "Folks walks right by an' forgits all about you; folks can't always be going through with just so much. You'd had a good deal better time, you an' your ma, if you'd been freer in your ways; now don't you s'pose you would? 'T ain't what you give folks to eat so much as 't is makin' 'em feel welcome. Now, there's Mis' Timms; when we was to Longport she was dreadful methodical. She wouldn't let Cap'n Timms fetch nobody home to dinner without lettin' of her know, same's other cap'ns' wives had to submit to. I was thinkin', when she was so cordial over to Danby, how she'd softened with time. Years do learn folks somethin'! She did seem very pleasant an' desirous. There, I am so glad we got started; if she'd gone an' got up a real good dinner to-day, an' then not had us come till to-morrow, 't would have been real too bad. Where anybody lives alone such a thing is very tryin'."

"Oh, so 't is!" said Miss Pickett. "There, I'd like to tell you what I went through with year before last. They come an' asked me one Saturday night to entertain the minister, that time we was having candidates"—

"I guess we'd better step along faster," said Mrs. Flagg suddenly. "Why, Miss Pickett, there's the stage comin' now! It's dreadful prompt, seems to me. Quick! there's folks awaitin', an' I sha'n't get to Baxter in no state to visit Mis' Cap'n Timms if I have to ride all the way there backward!"

3   The stage was not full inside. The group before the store proved to be made up of spectators, except one man, who climbed at once to a vacant seat by the driver. Inside there was only one person, after two passengers got out, and she preferred to sit with her back to the horses, so that Mrs. Flagg and Miss Pickett settled themselves comfortably in the coveted corners of the back seat. At first they took no notice of their companion, and spoke to each other in low tones, but presently something attracted the attention of all three and engaged them in conversation.

"I never was over this road before," said the stranger. "I s'pose you ladies are well acquainted all along."

"We have often traveled it in past years. We was over this part of it last week goin' and comin' from the county conference," said Mrs. Flagg in a dignified manner.

"What persuasion?" inquired the fellow-traveler, with interest.

"Orthodox," said Miss Pickett quickly, before Mrs. Flagg could speak. "It was a very interestin' occasion; this other lady an' me stayed through all the meetin's."

"I ain't Orthodox," announced the stranger, waiving any interest in personalities. "I was brought up amongst the Freewill Baptists."

"We're well acquainted with several of that denomination in our place," said Mrs. Flagg, not without an air of patronage. "They've never built 'em no church; there ain't but a scattered few."

"They prevail where I come from," said the traveler. "I'm goin' now to visit with a Freewill lady. We was to a conference together once, same's you an' your friend, but 't was a state conference. She asked me to come some time an' make her a good visit, and I'm on my way now. I didn't seem to have nothin' to keep me to home."

"We're all goin' visitin' to-day, ain't we?" said Mrs. Flagg sociably; but no one carried on the conversation.

The day was growing very warm, there was dust in the sandy road, but the fields of grass and young growing crops looked fresh and fair. There was a light haze over the hills, and birds were thick in the air. When the stage-horses stopped to walk, you could hear the crows caw, and the bobolinks singing, in the meadows. All the farmers were busy in their fields.

"It don't seem but little ways to Baxter, does it?" said Miss Pickett, after a while. "I felt we should pass a good deal o' time on the road, but we must be pretty near half-way there a'ready."

"Why, more'n half!" exclaimed Mrs. Flagg. "Yes; there's Beckett's Corner right ahead, an' the old Beckett house. I haven't been on this part of the road for so long that I feel kind of strange. I used to visit over here when I was a girl. There's a nephew's widow owns the place now. Old Miss Susan Beckett willed it to him, an' he died; but she resides there an' carries on the farm, an unusual smart woman, everybody says. Ain't it pleasant here, right out among the farms!"

"Mis' Beckett's place, did you observe?" said the stranger, leaning forward to listen to what her companions said. "I expect that's where I'm goin'—Mis' Ezra Beckett's?"

"That's the one," said Miss Pickett and Mrs. Flagg together, and they both looked out eagerly as the coach drew up to the front door of a large old yellow house that stood close upon the green turf of the roadside.

The passenger looked pleased and eager, and made haste to leave the stage with her many bundles and bags. While she stood impatiently tapping at the brass knocker, the stage-driver landed a large trunk, and dragged it toward the door across the grass. Just then a busy-looking middle-aged woman made her appearance, with floury hands and a look as if she were prepared to be somewhat on the defensive.

"Why, how do you do, Mis' Beckett?" exclaimed the guest. "Well, here I be at last. I didn't know's you thought I was ever comin'. Why, I do declare, I believe you don't recognize me, Mis' Beckett."

"I believe I don't," said the self-possessed hostess. "Ain't you made some mistake, ma'am?"

"Why, don't you recollect we was together that time to the state conference, an' you said you should be pleased to have me come an' make you a visit some time, an' I said I would certain. There, I expect I look more natural to you now."

Mrs. Beckett appeared to be making the best possible effort, and gave a bewildered glance, first at her unexpected visitor, and then at the trunk. The stage-driver, who watched this encounter with evident delight, turned away with reluctance. "I can't wait all day to see how they settle it," he said, and mounted briskly to the box, and the stage rolled on.

"He might have waited just a minute to see," said Miss Pickett indignantly, but Mrs. Flagg's head and shoulders were already far out of the stage window—the house was on her side. "She ain't got in yet," she told Miss Pickett triumphantly. "I could see 'em quite a spell. With that trunk, too! I do declare, how inconsiderate some folks is!"

"'T was pushin' an acquaintance most too far, wa'n't it?" agreed Miss Pickett. "There, 't will be somethin' laughable to tell Mis' Timms. I never see anything more divertin'. I shall kind of pity that woman if we have to stop an' git her as we go back this afternoon."

"Oh, don't let's forgit to watch for her," exclaimed Mrs. Flagg, beginning to brush off the dust of travel. "There, I feel an excellent appetite, don't you? And we ain't got more'n three or four miles to go, if we have that. I wonder what Mis' Timms is likely to give us for dinner; she spoke of makin' a good many chicken-pies, an' I happened to remark how partial I was to 'em. She felt above most of the things we had provided for us over to the conference. I know she was always counted the best o' cooks when I knew her so well to Longport. Now, don't you forget, if there's a suitable opportunity, to inquire about the drop-cakes," and Miss Pickett, a little less doubtful than before, renewed her promise.

4   "My gracious, won't Mis' Timms be pleased to see us! It's just exactly the day to have company. And ain't Baxter a sweet pretty place?" said Mrs. Flagg, as they walked up the main street. "Cynthia Pickett, now ain't you proper glad you come? I felt sort o' calm about it part o' the time yesterday, but I ain't felt so like a girl for a good while. I do believe I'm goin' to have a splendid time."

Miss Pickett glowed with equal pleasure as she paced along. She was less expansive and enthusiastic than her companion, but now that they were fairly in Baxter, she lent herself generously to the occasion. The social distinction of going away to spend a day in company with Mrs. Flagg was by no means small. She arranged the folds of her shawl more carefully over her arm so as to show the pretty palm-leaf border, and then looked up with great approval to the row of great maples that shaded the broad sidewalk. "I wonder if we can't contrive to make time to go an' see old Miss Nancy Fell?" she ventured to ask Mrs. Flagg. "There ain't a great deal o' time before the stage goes at four o'clock; 't will pass quickly, but I should hate to have her feel hurt. If she was one we had visited often at home, I shouldn't care so much, but such folks feel any little slight. She was a member of our church; I think a good deal of that."

"Well, I hardly know what to say," faltered Mrs. Flagg coldly. "We might just look in a minute; I shouldn't want her to feel hurt."

"She was one that always did her part, too," said Miss Pickett, more boldly. "Mr. Cronin used to say that she was more generous with her little than many was with their much. If she hadn't lived in a poor part of the town, and so been occupied with a different kind of people from us, 't would have made a difference. They say she's got a comfortable little home over here, an' keeps house for a nephew. You know she was to our meeting one Sunday last winter, and 'peared dreadful glad to get back; folks seemed glad to see her, too. I don't know as you were out."

"She always wore a friendly look," said Mrs. Flagg indulgently. "There now, there's Mis' Timms's residence: it's handsome, ain't it, with them big spruce-trees? I expect she may be at the window now, an' see us as we come along. Is my bonnet on straight, an' everything? The blinds looks open in the room this way; I guess she's to home fast enough."

The friends quickened their steps, and with shining eyes and beating hearts hastened forward. The slightest mists of uncertainty were now cleared away; they gazed at the house with deepest pleasure; the visit was about to begin.

They opened the front gate and went up the short walk, noticing the pretty herringbone pattern of the bricks, and as they stood on the high steps Cynthia Pickett wondered whether she ought not to have worn her best dress, even though there was lace at the neck and sleeves, and she usually kept it for the most formal of tea-parties and exceptional parish festivals. In her heart she commended Mrs. Flagg for that familiarity with the ways of a wider social world which had led her to wear the very best among her black cashmeres.

"She's a good while coming to the door," whispered Mrs. Flagg presently. "Either she didn't see us, or else she's slipped upstairs to make some change, an' is just goin' to let us ring again. I've done it myself sometimes. I'm glad we come right over after her urgin' us so; it seems more cordial than to keep her expectin' us. I expect she'll urge us terribly to remain with her over-night."

"Oh, I ain't prepared," began Miss Pickett, but she looked pleased. At that moment there was a slow withdrawal of the bolt inside, and a key was turned, the front door opened, and Mrs. Timms stood before them with a smile. Nobody stopped to think at that moment what kind of smile it was.

"Why, if it ain't Mis' Flagg," she exclaimed politely, "an' Miss Pickett too! I am surprised!"

The front entry behind her looked well furnished, but not exactly hospitable; the stairs with their brass rods looked so clean and bright that it did not seem as if anybody had ever gone up or come down. A cat came purring out, but Mrs. Timms pushed her back with a determined foot, and hastily closed the sitting-room door. Then Miss Pickett let Mrs. Flagg precede her, as was becoming, and they went into a darkened parlor, and found their way to some chairs, and seated themselves solemnly.

"'T is a beautiful day, ain't it?" said Mrs. Flagg, speaking first. "I don't know's I ever enjoyed the ride more. We've been having a good deal of rain since we saw you at the conference, and the country looks beautiful."

"Did you leave Woodville this morning? I thought I hadn't heard you was in town," replied Mrs. Timms formally. She was seated just a little too far away to make things seem exactly pleasant. The darkness of the best room seemed to retreat somewhat, and Miss Pickett looked over by the door, where there was a pale gleam from the sidelights in the hall, to try to see the pattern of the carpet; but her effort failed.

"Yes, 'm," replied Mrs. Flagg to the question. "We left Woodville about half past eight, but it is quite a ways from where we live to where you take the stage. The stage does come slow, but you don't seem to mind it such a beautiful day."

"Why, you must have come right to see me first!" said Mrs. Timms, warming a little as the visit went on. "I hope you're going to make some stop in town. I'm sure it was very polite of you to come right an' see me; well, it's very pleasant, I declare. I wish you'd been in Baxter last Sabbath; our minister did give us an elegant sermon on faith an' works. He spoke of the conference, and gave his views on some o' the questions that came up, at Friday evenin' meetin'; but I felt tired after getting home an' so I wasn't out. We feel very much favored to have such a man amon'st us. He's building up the parish very considerable. I understand the pew-rents come to thirty-six dollars more this quarter than they did last."

"We also feel grateful in Woodville for our pastor's efforts," said Miss Pickett; but Mrs. Timms turned her head away sharply, as if the speech had been untimely, and trembling Miss Pickett had interrupted.

"They're thinking here of raisin' Mr. Barlow's salary another year," the hostess added; "a good many of the old parishioners have died off, but every one feels to do what they can. Is there much interest among the young people in Woodville, Mis' Flagg?"

"Considerable at this time, ma'am," answered Mrs. Flagg, without enthusiasm, and she listened with unusual silence to the subsequent fluent remarks of Mrs. Timms.

The parlor seemed to be undergoing the slow processes of a winter dawn. After a while the three women could begin to see one another's faces, which aided them somewhat in carrying on a serious and impersonal conversation. There were a good many subjects to be touched upon, and Mrs.

Timms said everything that she should have said, except to invite her visitors to walk upstairs and take off their bonnets. Mrs. Flagg sat her parlor-chair as if it were a throne, and carried her banner of self-possession as high as she knew how, but toward the end of the call even she began to feel hurried.

"Won't you ladies take a glass of wine an' a piece of cake after your ride?" inquired Mrs. Timms, with an air of hospitality that almost concealed the fact that neither cake nor wine was anywhere to be seen; but the ladies bowed and declined with particular elegance. Altogether it was a visit of extreme propriety on both sides, and Mrs. Timms was very pressing in her invitation that her guests should stay longer.

"Thank you, but we ought to be going," answered Mrs. Flagg, with a little show of ostentation, and looking over her shoulder to be sure that Miss Pickett had risen too. "We've got some little ways to go," she added with dignity. "We should be pleased to have you call an' see us in case you have occasion to come to Woodville," and Miss Pickett faintly seconded the invitation. It was in her heart to add, "Come any day next week," but her courage did not rise so high as to make the words audible. She looked as if she were ready to cry; her usual smile had burnt itself out into gray ashes; there was a white, appealing look about her mouth. As they emerged from the dim parlor and stood at the open front door, the bright June day, the golden-green trees, almost blinded their eyes. Mrs. Timms was more smiling and cordial than ever.

"There, I ought to have thought to offer you fans; I am afraid you was warm after walking," she exclaimed, as if to leave no stone of courtesy unturned. "I have so enjoyed meeting you again, I wish it was so you could stop longer. Why, Mis' Flagg, we haven't said one word about old times when we lived to Longport. I've had news from there, too, since I saw you; my brother's daughter-in-law was here to pass the Sabbath after I returned."

Mrs. Flagg did not turn back to ask any questions as she stepped stiffly away down the brick walk. Miss Pickett followed her, raising the fringed parasol; they both made ceremonious little bows as they shut the high white gate behind them. "Good-by," said Mrs. Timms finally, as she stood in the door with her set smile, and as they departed she came out and began to fasten up a rosebush that climbed a narrow white ladder by the steps.

"Oh, my goodness alive!" exclaimed Mrs. Flagg, after they had gone some distance in aggrieved silence, "if I haven't gone and forgotten my bag! I ain't goin' back, whatever happens. I expect she'll trip over it in that dark room and break her neck!"

"I brought it; I noticed you'd forgotten it," said Miss Pickett timidly, as if she hated to deprive her companion of even that slight consolation.

"There, I'll tell you what we'd better do," said Mrs. Flagg gallantly; "we'll go right over an' see poor old Miss Nancy Fell; 't will please her about to death. We can say we felt like goin' somewhere to-day an' 't was a good many years since either one of us had seen Baxter, so we come just for the ride, an' to make a few calls. She'll like to hear all about the conference; Miss Fell was always one that took a real interest in religious matters."

Miss Pickett brightened, and they quickened their step. It was nearly twelve o'clock, they had breakfasted early, and now felt as if they had eaten nothing since they were grown up. An awful feeling of tiredness and uncertainty settled down upon their once buoyant spirits.

"I can forgive a person," said Mrs. Flagg, once, as if she were speaking to herself; "I can forgive a person, but when I'm done with 'em, I'm done."

5 "I do declare, 't was like a scene in Scriptur' to see that poor good-hearted Nancy Fell run down her walk to open the gate for us!" said Mrs. Persis Flagg later that afternoon, when she and Miss Pickett were going home in the stage. Miss Pickett nodded her head approvingly.

"I had a good sight better time with her than I should have had at the other place," she said with fearless honesty. "If I'd been Mis' Cap'n Timms, I'd made some apology or just passed us the compliment. If it wa'n't convenient, why couldn't she just tell us so after all her urgin' an' sayin' how she should expect us?"

"I thought then she'd altered from what she used to be," said Mrs. Flagg. "She seemed real sincere an' open away from home. If she wa'n't prepared to-day, 't was easy enough to say so; we was reasonable folks, an' should have gone away with none but friendly feelin's. We did have a grand good time with Nancy. She was as happy to see us as if we'd been queens."

"'T was a real nice little dinner," said Miss Pickett grate
fully. "I thought I was goin' to faint away just before we go
to the house, and I didn't know how I should hold out if she
undertook to do anything extra, and keep us awaitin'; bu
there, she just made us welcome, simple-hearted; to what she
had. I never tasted such dandelion greens; an' that nice littl
piece o' pork and new biscuit, why, they was just splendid
She must have an excellent good cellar, if 't is such a smal
house. Her potatoes was truly remarkable for this time o
year. I myself don't deem it necessary to cook potatoes when
I'm goin' to have dandelion greens. Now, didn't it put you i
mind of that verse in the Bible that says, 'Better is a dinne
of herbs where love is'? An' how desirous she'd been to see
somebody that could tell her some particulars about the con
ference!"

"She'll enjoy tellin' folks about our comin' over to see her.
Yes, I'm glad we went; 't will be of advantage every way, an
our bein' of the same church an' all, to Woodville. If Mis'
Timms hears of our bein' there, she'll see we had reason, an
knew of a place to go. Well, I needn't have brought this old
bag!"

Miss Pickett gave her companion a quick resentful glance
which was followed by one of triumph directed at the dus
that was collecting on the shoulders of the best black cashmere; then she looked at the bag on the front seat, and suddenly felt illuminated with the suspicion that Mrs. Flagg had
secretly made preparations to pass the night in Baxter. The
bag looked plump, as if it held much more than the pocketbook and the jelly.

Mrs. Flagg looked up with unusual humility. "I did think
about that jelly," she said, as if Miss Pickett had openly
reproached her. "I was afraid it might look as if I was tryin'
to pay Nancy for her kindness."

"Well, I don't know," said Cynthia; "I guess she'd been
pleased. She'd thought you just brought her over a little
present; but I do' know as 't would been any good to her after all, she'd thought so much of it, comin' from you, that
she'd kep' it till 't was all candied." But Mrs. Flagg didn't
look exactly pleased by this unexpected compliment, and her
fellow-traveler colored with confusion and a sudden feeling
that she had shown undue forwardness.

Presently they remembered the Beckett house, to their
great relief, and, as they approached, Mrs. Flagg reached over
and moved her hand-bag from the front seat to make room

for another passenger. But nobody came out to stop the stage, and they saw the unexpected guest sitting by one of the front windows comfortably swaying a palm-leaf fan, and rocking to and fro in calm content. They shrank back into their corners, and tried not to be seen. Mrs. Flagg's face grew very red.

"She got in, didn't she?" said Miss Pickett, snipping her words angrily, as if her lips were scissors. Then she heard a call, and bent forward to see Mrs. Beckett herself appear in the front doorway, very smiling and eager to stop the stage.

The driver was only too ready to stop his horses. "Got a passenger for me to carry back, ain't ye?" said he facetiously. "Them's the kind I like; carry both ways, make somethin' on a double trip," and he gave Mrs. Flagg and Miss Pickett a friendly wink as he stepped down over the wheel. Then he hurried toward the house, evidently in a hurry to put the baggage on; but the expected passenger still sat rocking and fanning at the window.

"No, sir; I ain't got any passengers," exclaimed Mrs. Beckett, advancing a step or two to meet him, and speaking very loud in her pleasant excitement. "This lady that come this morning wants her large trunk with her summer things that she left to the depot in Woodville. She's very desirous to git into it, so don't you go an' forgit; ain't you got a book or somethin', Mr. Ma'sh? Don't you forgit to make a note of it; here's her check, an' we've kep' the number in case you should mislay it or anything. There's things in the trunk she needs; you know how you overlooked stoppin' to the milliner's for my bunnit last week."

"Other folks disremembers things as well's me," grumbled Mr. Marsh. He turned to give the passengers another wink more familiar than the first, but they wore an offended air, and were looking the other way. The horses had backed a few steps, and the guest at the front window had ceased the steady motion of her fan to make them a handsome bow, and been puzzled at the lofty manner of their acknowledgment.

"Go 'long with your foolish jokes, John Ma'sh!" Mrs. Beckett said cheerfully, as she turned away. She was a comfortable, hearty person, whose appearance adjusted the beauties of hospitality. The driver climbed to his seat, chuckling, and drove away with the dust flying after the wheels.

"Now, she's a friendly sort of a woman, that Mis' Beckett," said Mrs. Flagg unexpectedly, after a few moments of silence, when she and her friend had been unable to look at each other. "I really ought to call over an' see her some o' these days, knowing her husband's folks as well as I used to, an' visitin' of 'em when I was a girl." But Miss Pickett made no answer.

"I expect it was all for the best, that woman's comin'," suggested Mrs. Flagg again hopefully. "She looked like a willing person who would take right hold. I guess Mis' Beckett knows what she's about, and must have had her reasons. Perhaps she thought she'd chance it for a couple o' weeks anyway, after the lady'd come so fur, an' bein' one o' her own denomination. Hayin'-time'll be here before we know it. I think myself, gen'rally speakin', 't is just as well to let anybody know you're comin'."

"Them seemed to be Mis' Cap'n Timms's views," said Miss Pickett in a low tone; but the stage rattled a good deal, and Mrs. Flagg looked up inquiringly, as if she had not heard.

A Day's Pleasure

Hamlin Garland

"Mainly it is long and wearyful, and has a home of toil at one end and a dull little town at the other"

When Markham came in from shovelling his last wagon-load of corn into the crib he found that his wife had put the children to bed, and was kneading a batch of dough with the dogged action of a tired and sullen woman.

He slipped his soggy boots off his feet, and having laid a piece of wood on top of the stove, put his heels on it comfortably. His chair squeaked as he leaned back on its hinder legs, but he paid no attention; he was used to it, exactly as he was used to his wife's lameness and ceaseless toil.

"That closes up my corn," he said after a silence. "I guess I'll go to town to-morrow to git my horses shod."

"I guess I'll git ready and go along," said his wife, in a sorry attempt to be firm and confident of tone.

"What do you want to go to town fer?" he grumbled.

"What does anybody want to go to town fer?" she burst out, facing him. "I ain't been out o' this house fer six months, while you go an' go!"

"Oh, it ain't six months. You went down that day I got the mower."

"When was that? The tenth of July, and you know it."

"Well, mebbe 'twas. I didn't think it was so long ago. I ain't no objection to your goin', only I'm goin' to take a load of wheat."

"Well, jest leave off a sack, an' that'll balance me an' the baby," she said spiritedly.

"All right," he replied good-naturedly, seeing she was roused. "Only that wheat ought to be put up to-night if you're goin'. You won't have any time to hold sacks for me in the morning with them young ones to get off to school."

"Well, let's go do it then," she said, sullenly resolute.

"I hate to go out agin; but I s'pose we'd better."

81

He yawned dismally and began pulling his boots on again, stamping his swollen feet into them with grunts of pain. She put on his coat and one of the boy's caps, and they went out to the granary. The night was cold and clear.

"Don't look so much like snow as it did last night," said Sam. "It may turn warm."

Laying out the sacks in the light of the lantern, they sorted out those which were whole, and Sam climbed into the bin with a tin pail in his hand, and the work began.

He was a sturdy fellow, and he worked desperately fast; the shining tin pail dived deep into the cold wheat and dragged heavily on the woman's tired hands as it came to the mouth of the sack, and she trembled with fatigue, but held on and dragged the sacks away when filled, and brought others, till at last Sam climbed out, puffing and wheezing, to tie them up.

"I guess I'll load 'em in the morning," he said. "You needn't wait for me. I'll tie 'em up alone."

"Oh, I don't mind," she replied, feeling a little touched by his unexpectedly easy acquiescence to her request. When they went back to the house the moon had risen.

It had scarcely set when they were wakened by the crowing roosters. The man rolled stiffly out of bed and began rattling the stove in the dark, cold kitchen.

His wife arose lamer and stiffer than usual, and began twisting her thin hair into a knot.

Sam did not stop to wash, but went out to the barn. The woman, however, hastily soused her face into the hard limestone water at the sink, and put the kettle on. Then she called the children. She knew it was early, and they would need several callings. She pushed breakfast forward, running over in her mind the things she must have: two spools of thread, six yards of cotton flannel, a can of coffee, and mittens for Kitty. These she must have—there were oceans of things she needed.

The children soon came scudding down out of the darkness of the upstairs to dress tumultuously at the kitchen stove. They humped and shivered, holding up their bare feet from the cold floor, like chickens in new fallen snow. They were irritable, and snarled and snapped and struck like cats and dogs. Mrs. Markham stood it for a while with mere commands to "hush up," but at last her patience gave out, and she charged down on the struggling mob and cuffed them right and left.

They ate their breakfast by lamplight, and when Sam went back to his work around the barnyard it was scarcely dawn. The children, left alone with their mother, began to tease her to let them go to town also.

"No sir—nobody goes but baby. Your father's goin' to take a load of wheat."

She was weak with the worry of it all when she had sent the older children away to school and the kitchen work was finished. She went into the cold bedroom off the little sitting room and put on her best dress. It had never been a good fit, and now she was getting so thin it hung in wrinkled folds everywhere about the shoulders and waist. She lay down on the bed a moment to ease that dull pain in her back. She had a moment's distaste for going out at all. The thought of sleep was more alluring. Then the thought of the long, long day, and the sickening sameness of her life, swept over her again, and she rose and prepared the baby for the journey.

It was but little after sunrise when Sam drove out into the road and started for Belleplain. His wife sat perched upon the wheat-sacks behind him, holding the baby in her lap, a cotton quilt under her, and a cotton horse-blanket over her knees.

Sam was disposed to be very good-natured, and he talked back at her occasionally, though she could only understand him when he turned his face toward her. The baby stared out at the passing fence-posts, and wiggled his hands out of his mittens at every opportunity. He was merry at least.

It grew warmer as they went on, and a strong south wind arose. The dust settled upon the woman's shawl and hat. Her hair loosened and blew unkemptly about her face. The road which led across the high, level prairie was quite smooth and dry, but still it jolted her, and the pain in her back increased. She had nothing to lean against, and the weight of the child grew greater, till she was forced to place him on the sacks beside her, though she could not loose her hold for a moment.

The town drew in sight—a cluster of small frame houses and stores on the dry prairie beside a railway station. There were no trees yet which could be called shade trees. The pitilessly severe light of the sun flooded everything. A few teams were hitched about, and in the lee of the stores a few men could be seen seated comfortably, their broad hat-rims flopping up and down, their faces brown as leather.

Markham put his wife out at one of the grocery-stores, and drove off down toward the elevators to sell his wheat.

The grocer greeted Mrs. Markham in a perfunctorily kind manner, and offered her a chair, which she took gratefully. She sat for a quarter of an hour almost without moving, leaning against the back of the high chair. At last the child began to get restless and troublesome, and she spent half an hour helping him amuse himself around the nail-kegs.

At length she rose and went out on the walk, carrying the baby. She went into the dry-goods store and took a seat on one of the little revolving stools. A woman was buying some woollen goods for a dress. It was worth twenty-seven cents a yard, the clerk said, but he would knock off two cents if she took ten yards. It looked warm, and Mrs. Markham wished she could afford it for Mary.

A pretty young girl came in and laughed and chatted with the clerk, and bought a pair of gloves. She was the daughter of the grocer. Her happiness made the wife and mother sad. When Sam came back she asked him for some money.

"What do you want to do with it?" he asked.

"I want to spend it," she said.

She was not to be trifled with, so he gave her a dollar.

"I need a dollar more."

"Well, I've got to go take up that note at the bank."

"Well, the children's got to have some new underclo'es," she said.

He handed her a two-dollar bill and then went out to pay his note.

She bought her cotton flannel and mittens and thread, and then sat leaning against the counter. It was noon, and she was hungry. She went out to the wagon, got the lunch she had brought, and took it into the grocery to eat it—where she could get a drink of water.

The grocer gave the baby a stick of candy and handed the mother an apple.

"It'll kind o' go down with your doughnuts," he said.

After eating her lunch she got up and went out. She felt ashamed to sit there any longer. She entered another dry-goods store, but when the clerk came toward her saying, "Anything to-day, Mrs.——?" she answered, "No, I guess not," and turned away with foolish face.

She walked up and down the street, desolately homeless. She did not know what to do with herself. She knew no one except the grocer. She grew bitter as she saw a couple of ladies pass, holding their demi-trains in the latest city fashion. Another woman went by pushing a baby carriage, in which sat a child just about as big as her own. It was bouncing itself up and down on the long slender springs, and laughing and shouting. Its clean round face glowed from its pretty fringed hood. She looked down at the dusty clothes and grimy face of her own little one, and walked on savagely.

She went into the drug store where the soda fountain was, but it made her thirsty to sit there and she went out on the street again. She heard Sam laugh, and saw him in a group of men over by the blacksmith shop. He was having a good time and had forgotten her.

Her back ached so intolerably that she concluded to go in and rest once more in the grocer's chair. The baby was growing cross and fretful. She bought five cents' worth of candy to take home to the children, and gave baby a little piece to keep him quiet. She wished Sam would come. It must be getting late. The grocer said it was not much after one. Time seemed terribly long. She felt that she ought to do something while she was in town. She ran over her purchases—yes, that was all she had planned to buy. She fell to figuring on the things she needed. It was terrible. It ran away up into twenty or thirty dollars at the least. Sam, as well as she, needed underwear for the cold winter, but they would have to wear the old ones, even if they were thin and ragged. She would not need a dress, she thought bitterly, because she never went anywhere. She rose and went out on the street once more, and wandered up and down, looking at everything in the hope of enjoying something.

A man from Boon Creek backed a load of apples up to the sidewalk, and as he stood waiting for the grocer he noticed Mrs. Markham and the baby, and gave the baby an apple. This was a pleasure. He had such a hearty way about him. He on his part saw an ordinary farmer's wife with dusty dress, unkempt hair, and tired face. He did not know exactly why she appealed to him, but he tried to cheer her up.

The grocer was familiar with these bedraggled and weary wives. He was accustomed to see them sit for hours in his big wooden chair, and nurse tired and fretful children. Their forlorn, aimless, pathetic wandering up and down the street was a daily occurrence, and had never possessed any special meaning to him.

II

In a cottage around the corner from the grocery store two men and a woman were finishing a dainty luncheon. The woman was dressed in cool, white garments, and she seemed to make the day one of perfect comfort.

The home of the Honorable Mr. Hall was by no means the costliest in the town, but his wife made it the most attractive. He was one of the leading lawyers of the county, and a man of culture and progressive views. He was entertaining a friend who had lectured the night before in the Congregational church.

They were by no means in serious discussion. The talk was rather frivolous. Hall had the ability to caricature men with a few gestures and attitudes, and was giving to his Eastern friend some descriptions of the old-fashioned Western lawyers he had met in his practice. He was very amusing, and his guest laughed heartily for a time.

But suddenly Hall became aware that Otis was not listening. Then he perceived that he was peering out of the window at some one, and that on his face a look of bitter sadness was falling.

Hall stopped, "What do you see, Otis?"

Otis replied, "I see a forlorn, weary woman."

Mrs. Hall rose and went to the window. Mrs. Markham was walking by the house, her baby in her arms. Savage anger and weeping were in her eyes and on her lips, and there was hopeless tragedy in her shambling walk and weak back.

In the silence Otis went on: "I saw the poor, dejected creature twice this morning. I couldn't forget her."

"Who is she?" asked Mrs. Hall, very softly.

"Her name is Markham; she's Sam Markham's wife," said Hall.

The young wife led the way into the sitting room, and the men took seats and lit their cigars. Hall was meditating a diversion when Otis resumed suddenly:

"That woman came to town to-day to get a change, to have a little play-spell, and she's wandering around like a starved and weary cat. I wonder if there is a woman in this town with sympathy enough and courage enough to go out and help that woman? The saloon-keepers, the politicians, and the grocers make it pleasant for the man—so pleasant that he forgets his wife. But the wife is left without a word."

Mrs. Hall's work dropped, and on her pretty face was a look of pain. The man's harsh words had wounded her—and wakened her. She took up her hat and hurried out on the walk. The men looked at each other, and then the husband said:

"It's going to be a little sultry for the men around these diggings. Suppose we go out for a walk."

Delia felt a hand on her arm as she stood at the corner.

"You look tired, Mrs. Markham; won't you come in a little while? I'm Mrs. Hall."

Mrs. Markham turned with a scowl on her face and a biting word on her tongue, but something in the sweet, round little face of the other woman silenced her, and her brow smoothed out.

"Thank you kindly, but it's most time to go home. I'm looking fer Mr. Markham now."

"Oh, come in a little while, the baby is cross and tired out; please do."

Mrs. Markham yielded to the friendly voice, and together the two women reached the gate just as two men hurriedly turned the other corner.

"Let me relieve you," said Mrs. Hall.

The mother hesitated. "He's so dusty."

"Oh, that won't matter. Oh, what a big fellow he is! I haven't any of my own," said Mrs. Hall, and a look passed like an electric spark between the two women, and Delia was her willing guest from that moment.

They went into the little sitting room, so dainty and lovely to the farmer's wife, and as she sank into an easy-chair she was faint and drowsy with the pleasure of it. She submitted to being brushed. She gave the baby into the hands of the Swedish girl, who washed its face and hands and sang it to sleep, while its mother sipped some tea. Through it all she lay back in her easy-chair, not speaking a word, while the ache passed out of her back, and her hot, swollen head ceased to throb.

But she saw everything—the piano, the pictures, the curtains, the wall-paper, the little tea-stand. They were almost as grateful to her as the food and fragrant tea. Such housekeeping as this she had never seen. Her mother had worn her kitchen floor as thin as brown paper in keeping a speckless

house, and she had been in houses that were larger and cost-
lier, but something of the charm of her hostess was in the arrangement of vases, chairs, or pictures. It was tasteful.

Mrs. Hall did not ask about her affairs. She talked to her
about the sturdy little baby, and about the things upon which
Delia's eyes dwelt. If she seemed interested in a vase she was
told what it was and where it was made. She was shown all
the pictures and books. Mrs. Hall seemed to read her visitor's
mind. She kept as far from the farm and her guest's affairs as
possible, and at last she opened the piano and sang to her—
not slow-moving hymns, but catchy love-songs full of senti-
ment, and then played some simple melodies, knowing that
Mrs. Markham's eyes were studying her hands, her rings, and
the flash of her fingers on the keys—seeing more than she
heard—and through it all Mrs. Hall conveyed the impression
that she, too, was having a good time.

The rattle of the wagon outside roused them both. Sam
was at the gate for her. Mrs. Markham rose hastily. "Oh, it's
almost sundown!" she gasped in astonishment as she looked
out of the window.

"Oh, that won't kill anybody," replied her hostess. "Don't
hurry. Carrie, take the baby out to the wagon for Mrs. Markham while I help her with her things."

"Oh, I've had such a good time," Mrs. Markham said as
they went down the little walk.

"So have I," replied Mrs. Hall. She took the baby a moment as her guest climbed in. "Oh, you big, fat fellow!" she
cried as she gave him a squeeze. "You must bring your wife
in oftener, Mr. Markham," she said, as she handed the baby
up.

Sam was staring with amazement.

"Thank you, I will," he finally managed to say.

"Good-night," said Mrs. Markham.

"Good-night, dear," called Mrs. Hall, and the wagon began
to rattle off.

The tenderness and sympathy in her voice brought the
tears to Delia's eyes—not hot nor bitter tears, but tears that
cooled her eyes and cleared her mind.

The wind had gone down, and the red sunlight fell mistily
over the world of corn and stubble. The crickets were still
chirping and the feeding cattle were drifting toward the farm-
yards. The day had been made beautiful by human sympathy.

Souls Belated

Edith Wharton

I

Their railway-carriage had been full when the train left Bologna; but at the first station beyond Milan their only remaining companion—a courtly person who ate garlic out of a carpet-bag—had left his crumb-strewn seat with a bow.

Lydia's eyes regretfully followed the shiny broadcloth of his retreating back till it lost itself in the cloud of touts and cabdrivers hanging about the station; then she glanced across at Gannett and caught the same regret in his look. They were both sorry to be alone.

"Par-ten-za!" shouted the guard. The train vibrated to a sudden slamming of doors; a waiter ran along the platform with a tray of fossilized sandwiches; a belated porter flung a bundle of shawls and band-boxes into a third-class carriage; the guard snapped out a brief *Partenza!* which indicated the purely ornamental nature of his first shout; and the train swung out of the station.

The direction of the road had changed, and a shaft of sunlight struck across the dusty red velvet seats into Lydia's corner. Gannett did not notice it. He had returned to his *Revue de Paris*, and she had to rise and lower the shade of the farther window. Against the vast horizon of their leisure such incidents stood out sharply.

Having lowered the shade, Lydia sat down, leaving the length of the carriage between herself and Gannett. At length he missed her and looked up.

"I moved out of the sun," she hastily explained.

He looked at her curiously; the sun was beating on her through the shade.

"Very well," he said pleasantly; adding, "You don't mind?" as he drew a cigarette-case from his pocket.

It was a refreshing touch, relieving the tension of her spirit with the suggestion that, after all, if he could *smoke*—! The relief was only momentary. Her experience of smokers was limited (her husband had disapproved of the use of tobacco) but she knew from hearsay that men sometimes smoked to get away from things; that a cigar might be a masculine equivalent of darkened windows and a headache. Gannett, after a puff or two, returned to his review.

It was just as she had foreseen; he feared to speak as much as she did. It was one of the misfortunes of their situation that they were never busy enough to necessitate, or even to justify, the postponement of unpleasant discussions. If they avoided a question it was obviously, unconcealably because the question was disagreeable. They had unlimited leisure and an accumulation of mental energy to devote to any subject that presented itself; new topics were in fact at a premium. Lydia sometimes had premonitions of a famine-stricken period when there would be nothing left to talk about, and she had already caught herself doling out piecemeal what, in the first prodigality of their confidences, she would have flung to him in a breath. Their silence therefore might simply mean that they had nothing to say; but it was another disadvantage of their position that it allowed infinite opportunity for the classification of minute differences. Lydia had learned to distinguish between real and factitious silences; and under Gannett's she now detected a hum of speech to which her own thoughts made breathless answer.

How could it be otherwise, with that thing between them? She glanced up at the rack overhead. The *thing* was there, in her dressing-bag, symbolically suspended over her head and his. He was thinking of it now, just as she was; they had been thinking of it in unison ever since they had entered the train. While the carriage had held other travellers they had screened her from his thoughts; but now that he and she were alone she knew exactly what was passing through his mind; she could almost hear him asking himself what he should say to her. . . .

The thing had come that morning, brought up to her in an innocent-looking envelope with the rest of their letters, as they were leaving the hotel in Bologna. As she tore it open, she and Gannett were laughing over some ineptitude of the local guidebook—they had been driven, of late, to make the most of such incidental humors of travel. Even when she had unfolded the document she took it for some unimportant business paper sent abroad for her signature, and her eye travelled inattentively over the curly *Whereases* of the preamble until a word arrested her:—Divorce. There it stood, an impassable barrier, between her husband's name and hers.

She had been prepared for it, of course, as healthy people are said to be prepared for death, in the sense of knowing it must come without in the least expecting that it will. She had known from the first that Tillotson meant to divorce her—but what did it matter? Nothing mattered, in those first days of supreme deliverance, but the fact that she was free; and not so much (she had begun to be aware) that freedom had released her from Tillotson as that it had given her to Gannett. This discovery had not been agreeable to her self-esteem. She had preferred to think that Tillotson had himself embodied all her reasons for leaving him; and those he represented had seemed cogent enough to stand in no need of reinforcement. Yet she had not left him till she met Gannett. It was her love for Gannett that had made life with Tillotson so poor and incomplete a business. If she had never, from the first, regarded her marriage as a full cancelling of her claims upon life, she had at least, for a number of years, accepted it as a provisional compensation—she had made it "do." Existence in the commodious Tillotson mansion in Fifth Avenue—with Mrs. Tillotson senior commanding the approaches from the second-story front windows—had been reduced to a series of purely automatic acts. The moral atmosphere of the Tillotson interior was as carefully screened and curtained as the house itself: Mrs. Tillotson senior dreaded ideas as much as a draught in her back. Prudent people liked an even temperature; and to do anything unexpected was as foolish as going out in the rain. One of the chief advantages of being rich was that one need not be exposed to unforeseen contingencies: by the use of ordinary firmness and common sense one could make sure of doing exactly the same thing every day at the same hour. These doctrines, reverentially imbibed with his mother's milk, Tillotson (a model son who had never given his parents an hour's anxiety) complacently expounded to his wife, testifying to his sense of their importance by the regularity with which he wore goloshes on damp days, his punctuality at meals, and his elaborate precautions against burglars and contagious diseases. Lydia, coming from a smaller town, and entering New York life through the portals of the Tillotson mansion, had mechanically accepted this point of view as inseparable from having a front pew in church and a parterre box at the opera. All the people who came to the house revolved in the same circle of prejudices. It was the kind of society in which, after dinner, the ladies compared the exorbitant charges of their children's teachers, and agreed that, even with the new duties on French clothes, it was cheaper in the end to get everything from Worth; while the husbands, over their cigars, lamented municipal corruption, and decided that the men to start a reform were those who had no private interests at stake.

To Lydia, this view of life had become a matter of course, just as lumbering about in her mother-in-law's landau had come to seem the only possible means of locomotion, and listening every Sunday to a fashionable Presbyterian divine the inevitable atonement for having thought oneself bored on the other six days of the week. Before she met Gannett her life had seemed merely dull: his coming made it appear like one of those dismal Cruikshank prints in which the people are all ugly and all engaged in occupations that are either vulgar or stupid.

It was natural that Tillotson should be the chief sufferer from this readjustment of focus. Gannett's nearness had made her husband ridiculous, and a part of the ridicule had been reflected on herself. Her tolerance laid her open to a suspicion of obtuseness from which she must, at all costs, clear herself in Gannett's eyes.

She did not understand this until afterwards. At the time she fancied that she had merely reached the limits of endurance. In so large a charter of liberties as the mere act of leaving Tillotson seemed to confer, the small question of divorce or no divorce did not count. It was when she saw that she had left her husband only to be with Gannett that she perceived the significance of anything affecting their relations. Her husband, in casting her off, had virtually flung her at Gannett: it was thus that the world viewed it. The measure of alacrity with which Gannett would receive her would be the subject of curious speculation over afternoon-tea tables and in club corners. She knew what would be said—she had heard it so often of others! The recollection bathed her in misery. The men would probably back Gannett to "do the decent thing"; but the ladies' eye-brows would emphasize the worthlessness of such enforced fidelity; and after all, they would be right. She had put herself in a position where Gannett "owed" her something; where, as a gentleman, he was bound to "stand the damage." The idea of accepting such compensation had never crossed her mind; the so-called rehabilitation of such a marriage had always seemed to her the only real disgrace. What she dreaded was the necessity of having to explain herself; of having to combat his arguments; of calculating, in spite of herself, the exact measure of insistence with which he pressed them. She knew not whether she most shrank from his insisting too much or too little. In such a case the nicest sense of proportion might be at fault; and how easy to fall into the error of taking her resistance for a test of his sincerity! Whichever way she turned, an ironical implication confronted her: she had the exasperated sense of having walked into the trap of some stupid practical joke.

Beneath all these preoccupations lurked the dread of what he was thinking. Sooner or later, of course, he would have to speak; but that, in the meantime, he should think, even for a moment, that there was any use in speaking, seemed to her simply unendurable. Her sensitiveness on this point was aggravated by another fear, as yet barely on the level of consciousness; the fear of unwillingly involving Gannett in the trammels of her dependence. To look upon him as the instrument of her liberation; to resist in herself the least tendency to a wifely taking possession of his future; had seemed to Lydia the one way of maintaining the dignity of their relation. Her view had not changed, but she was aware of a growing inability to keep her thoughts fixed on the essential point—the point of parting with Gannett. It was easy to face as long as he kept it sufficiently far off: but what was this act of mental postponement but a gradual encroachment on his future? What was needful was the courage to recognize the moment when, by some word or look, their voluntary fellowship should be transformed into a bondage the more wearing that it was based on none of those common obligations which make the most imperfect marriage in some sort a centre of gravity.

When the porter, at the next station, threw the door open, Lydia drew back, making way for the hoped-for intruder; but none came, and the train took up its leisurely progress through the spring wheat-fields and budding copses. She now began to hope that Gannett would speak before the next station. She watched him furtively, half disposed to return to the seat opposite his, but there was an artificiality about his absorption that restrained her. She had never before seen him read with so conspicuous an air of warding off interruption.

What could he be thinking of? Why should he be afraid to speak? Or was it her answer that he dreaded?

The train paused for the passing of an express, and he put down his book and leaned out of the window. Presently he turned to her with a smile.

"There's a jolly old villa out here," he said.

His easy tone relieved her, and she smiled back at him as she crossed over to his corner.

Beyond the embankment, through the opening in a mossy wall, she caught sight of the villa, with its broken balustrades, its stagnant fountains, and the stone satyr closing the perspective of a dusky grass-walk.

"How should you like to live there?" he asked as the train moved on.

"There?"

"In some such place, I mean. One might do worse, don't you think so? There must be at least two centuries of solitude under those yew-trees. Shouldn't you like it?"

"I—I don't know," she faltered. She knew now that he meant to speak.

He lit another cigarette. "We shall have to live somewhere, you know," he said as he bent over the match.

Lydia tried to speak carelessly. *"Je n'en vois pas la nécessité!* Why not live everywhere, as we have been doing?"

"But we can't travel forever, can we?"

"Oh, forever's a long word," she objected, picking up the review he had thrown aside.

"For the rest of our lives then," he said, moving nearer.

She made a slight gesture which caused his hand to slip from hers.

"Why should we make plans? I thought you agreed with me that it's pleasanter to drift."

He looked at her hesitatingly. "It's been pleasant, certainly; but I suppose I shall have to get at my work again some day. You know I haven't written a line since—all this time," he hastily emended.

She flamed with sympathy and self-reproach. "Oh, if you mean *that*— if you want to write—of course we must settle down. How stupid of me not to have thought of that sooner! Where shall we go? Where do you think you could work best? We oughtn't to lose any more time."

He hesitated again. "I had thought of a villa in these parts. It's quiet; we shouldn't be bothered. Should you like it?"

"Of course I should like it." She paused and looked away.

"But I thought—I remember your telling me once that your best work had been done in a crowd—in big cities. Why should you shut yourself up in a desert?"

Gannett, for a moment, made no reply. At length he said, avoiding her eye as carefully as she avoided his: "It might be different now; I can't tell, of course, till I try. A writer ought not to be dependent on his *milieu;* it's a mistake to humor oneself in that way; and I thought that just at first you might prefer to be—"

She faced him. "To be what?"

"Well—quiet. I mean—"

"What do you mean by 'at first'?" she interrupted.

He paused again. "I mean after we are married."

She thrust up her chin and turned toward the window. "Thank you!" she tossed back at him.

"Lydia!" he exclaimed blankly; and she felt in every fibre of her averted person that he had made the inconceivable, the unpardonable mistake of anticipating her acquiescence.

The train rattled on and he groped for a third cigarette. Lydia remained silent.

"I haven't offended you?" he ventured at length, in the tone of a man who feels his way.

She shook her head with a sigh. "I thought you understood," she moaned. Their eyes met and she moved back to his side.

"Do you want to know how not to offend me? By taking it for granted, once for all, that you've said your say on this odious question and that I've said mine, and that we stand just where we did this morning before that—that hateful paper came to spoil everything between us!"

"To spoil everything between us? What on earth do you mean? Aren't you glad to be free?"

"I was free before."

"Not to marry me," he suggested.

"But I don't *want* to marry you!" she cried.

She saw that he turned pale. "I'm obtuse, I suppose," he said slowly. "I confess I don't see what you're driving at. Are you tired of the whole business? Or was I simply a—an excuse for getting away? Perhaps you didn't care to travel alone? Was that it? And now you want to chuck me?" His voice had grown harsh. "You owe me a straight answer, you know; don't be tenderhearted!"

Her eyes swam as she leaned to him. "Don't you see it's because I care—because I care so much? Oh, Ralph! Can't you see how it would humiliate me? Try to feel it as a woman would! Don't you see the misery of being made your wife in this way? If I'd known you as a girl—that would have been a real marriage! But now—this vulgar fraud upon society—and upon a society we despised and laughed at—this sneaking back into a position that we've voluntarily forfeited: don't you see what a cheap compromise it is? We neither of us believe in the abstract 'sacredness' of marriage; we both know that no ceremony is needed to consecrate our love for each other; what object can we have in marrying, except the secret fear of each that the other may escape, or the secret longing to work our way back gradually—oh, very gradually—into the esteem of the people whose conventional morality we have always ridiculed and hated? And the very fact that, after a decent interval, the same people would come and dine with us—the women who talk about the indissolubility of marriage, and who would let me die in a gutter to-day because I am 'leading a life of sin'—doesn't that disgust you more than their turning their backs on us now? I can stand being cut by them, but I couldn't stand their coming to call and asking what I meant to do about visiting that unfortunate Mrs. So-and-So!"

She paused and Gannett maintained a perplexed silence.

"You judge things too theoretically," he said at length, slowly. "Life is made up of compromises."

"The life we ran away from—yes! If we had been willing to accept them"—she flushed—"we might have gone on meeting each other at Mrs. Tillotson's dinners."

He smiled slightly. "I didn't know that we ran away to found a new system of ethics. I supposed it was because we loved each other."

"Life is complex, of course; isn't it the very recognition of that fact that separates us from the people who see it *tout d'une pièce*? If *they* are right—if marriage is sacred in itself and the individual must always be sacrificed to the family—then there can be no real marriage between us, since our—our being together is a protest against the sacrifice of the individual to the family." She interrupted herself with a laugh. "You'll say now that I'm giving you a lecture on sociology! Of course one acts as one can—as one must, perhaps—pulled by all sorts of invisible threads; but at least one needn't pretend, for social advantages, to subscribe to a creed that ignores the complexity of human motives—that classifies people by arbitrary signs, and puts it in everybody's reach to be on Mrs. Tillotson's visiting-list. It may be necessary that the world should be ruled by conventions—but if we believed in them, why did we break through them? And if we don't believe in them, is it honest to take advantage of the protection they afford?"

Gannett hestiated. "One may believe in them or not; but as long as they do rule the world it is only by taking advantage of their protection that one can find a *modus vivendi*."

"Do outlaws need a *modus vivendi*?"

He looked at her hopelessly. Nothing is more perplexing to man than the mental process of a woman who reasons her emotions.

She thought she had scored a point and followed it up passionately. "You do understand, don't you? You see how the very thought of the thing humiliates me! We are together to-day because we choose to be—don't let us look any farther than that!" She caught his hands. "*Promise* me you'll never speak of it again; promise me you'll never *think* of it even," she implored, with a tearful prodigality of italics.

Through what followed—his protests, his arguments, his final unconvinced submission to her wishes—she had a sense of his but half-discerning all that, for her, had made the moment so tumultuous. They had reached the memorable point in every heart-history when, for the first time, the man seems obtuse and the woman irrational. It was the abundance of his intentions that consoled her, on reflection, for what they lacked in quality. After all, it would have been worse, incalculably worse, to have detected any overreadiness to understand her.

II

When the train at night-fall brought them to their journey's end at the edge of one of the lakes, Lydia was glad that they were not, as usual, to pass from one solitude to another. Their wanderings during the year had indeed been like the flight of outlaws: through Sicily, Dalmatia, Transylvania and Southern Italy they had persisted in their tacit avoidance of their kind. Isolation, at first, had deepened the flavor of their happiness, as night intensifies the scent of certain flowers; but in the new phase on which they were entering, Lydia's chief wish was that they should be less abnormally exposed to the action of each other's thoughts.

She shrank, nevertheless, as the brightly-looming bulk of the fashionable Anglo-American hotel on the water's brink began to radiate toward their advancing boat its vivid suggestion of social order, visitors' lists, Church services, and the bland inquisition of the *table-d'hôte*. The mere fact that in a moment or two she must take her place on the hotel register as Mrs. Gannett seemed to weaken the springs of her resistance.

They had meant to stay for a night only, on their way to a lofty village among the glaciers of Monte Rosa; but after the first plunge into publicity, when they entered the dining-room, Lydia felt the relief of being lost in a crowd, of ceasing for a moment to be the centre of Gannett's scrutiny; and in his face she caught the reflection of her feeling. After dinner, when she went upstairs, he strolled into the smoking-room, and an hour or two later, sitting in the darkness of her window, she heard his voice below and saw him walking up and down the terrace with a companion cigar at his side. When he came up he told her he had been talking to the hotel chaplain—a very good sort of fellow.

"Queer little microcosms, these hotels! Most of these people live here all summer and then migrate to Italy or the Riviera. The English are the only people who can lead that kind of life with dignity—those soft-voiced old ladies in Shetland shawls somehow carry the British Empire under their caps. *Civis Romanus sum.* It's a curious study—there might be some good things to work up here."

He stood before her with the vivid preoccupied stare of the novelist on the trail of a "subject." With a relief that was half painful she noticed that, for the first time since they had been together, he was hardly aware of her presence.

"Do you think you could write here?"

"Here? I don't know." His stare dropped. "After being out of things so long one's first impressions are bound to be tremendously vivid, you know. I see a dozen threads already that one might follow——"

He broke off with a touch of embarrassment.

"Then follow them. We'll stay," she said with sudden decision.

"Stay here?" He glanced at her in surprise, and then, walking to the window, looked out upon the dusky slumber of the garden.

"Why not?" she said at length, in a tone of veiled irritation.

"The place is full of old cats in caps who gossip with the chaplain. Shall you like—I mean, it would be different if—"

She flamed up.

"Do you suppose I care? It's none of their business."

"Of course not; but you won't get them to think so."

"They may think what they please."

He looked at her doubtfully.

"It's for you to decide."

"We'll stay," she repeated.

Gannett, before they met, had made himself known as a successful writer of short stories and of a novel which had achieved the distinction of being widely discussed. The reviewers called him "promising," and Lydia now accused herself of having too long interfered with the fulfilment of his promise. There was a special irony in the fact, since his passionate assurances that only the stimulus of her companionship could bring out his latent faculty had almost given the dignity of a "vocation" to her course: there had been moments when she had felt unable to assume, before posterity, the responsibility of thwarting his career. And, after all, he had not written a line since they had been together: his first desire to write had come from renewed contact with the world! Was it all a mistake then? Must the most intelligent choice work more disastrously than the blundering combinations of chance? Or was there a still more humiliating answer to her perplexities? His sudden impulse of activity so exactly coincided with her own wish to withdraw, for a time, from the range of his observation, that she wondered if he too were not seeking sanctuary fron intolerable problems.

"You must begin to-morrow!" she cried, hiding a tremor under the laugh with which she added, "I wonder if there's any ink in the inkstand?"

Whatever else they had at the Hotel Bellosguardo, they had, as Miss Pinsent said, "a certain tone." It was to Lady Susan Condit that they owed this inestimable benefit; an advantage ranking in Miss Pinsent's opinion above even the lawn tennis courts and the resident chaplain. It was the fact of Lady Susan's annual visit that made the hotel what it was. Miss Pinsent was certainly the last to underrate such a privilege:—"It's so important, my dear, forming as we do a little family, that there should be some one to give *the tone;* and no one could do it better than Lady Susan—an earl's daughter and a person of such determination. Dear Mrs. Ainger now—who really *ought,* you know, when Lady Susan's away—absolutely refuses to assert herself." Miss Pinsent sniffed derisively. "A bishop's niece!—my dear, I saw her once actually give in to some South Americans—and before us all. She gave up her seat at table to oblige them—such a lack of dignity! Lady Susan spoke to her very plainly about it afterwards."

Miss Pinsent glanced across the lake and adjusted her auburn front.

"But of course I don't deny that the stand Lady Susan takes is not always easy to live up to—for the rest of us, I mean. Monsieur Grossart, our good proprietor, finds it trying at times, I know—he has said as much, privately, to Mrs. Ainger and me. After all, the poor man is not to blame for wanting to fill his hotel, is he? And Lady Susan is so difficult—so very difficult—about new people. One might almost say that she disapproves of them beforehand, on principle. And yet she's had warnings—she very nearly made a dreadful mistake once with the Duchess of Levens, who dyed her hair and—well, swore and smoked. One would have thought that might have been a lesson to Lady Susan." Miss Pinsent resumed her knitting with a sigh. "There are exceptions, of course. She took at once to you and Mr. Gannett—it was quite remarkable, really. Oh, I don't mean that either—of course not! It was perfectly natural—we *all* thought you so charming and interesting from the first day—we knew at once that Mr. Gannett was intellectual, by the magazines you took in; but you know what I mean. Lady Susan is so very—well, I won't say prejudiced, as Mrs. Ainger does—but so prepared *not* to like new people, that her taking to you in that way was a surprise to us all, I confess."

Miss Pinsent sent a significant glance down the long laurustinus alley from the other end of which two people—a lady and gentleman—were strolling toward them through the smiling neglect of the garden.

"In this case, of course, it's very different; that I'm willing to admit. Their looks are against them; but, as Mrs. Ainger says, one can't exactly tell them so."

"She's very handsome," Lydia ventured, with her eyes on the lady, who showed, under the dome of a vivid sunshade, the hourglass figure and superlative coloring of a Christmas chromo.

"That's the worst of it. She's too handsome."

"Well, after all, she can't help that."

"Other people manage, to," said Miss Pinsent skeptically.

"But isn't it rather unfair of Lady Susan—considering that nothing is known about them?"

"But, my dear, that's the very thing that's against them. It's infinitely worse than any actual knowledge."

Lydia mentally agreed that, in the case of Mrs. Linton, it possibly might be.

"I wonder why they came here?" she mused.

"That's against them too. It's always a bad sign when loud people come to a quiet place. And they've brought van-loads of boxes—her maid told Mrs. Ainger's that they meant to stop indefinitely."

"And Lady Susan actually turned her back on her in the *salon?*"

"My dear, she said it was for our sakes: that makes it so unanswerable! But poor Grossart *is* in a way! The Lintons have taken his most expensive *suite*, you know—the yellow damask drawing-room above the portico—and they have champagne with every meal!"

They were silent as Mr. and Mrs. Linton sauntered by; the lady with tempestuous brows and challenging chin; the gentleman, a blond stripling, trailing after her, head downward, like a reluctant child dragged by his nurse.

"What does your husband think of them, my dear?" Miss Pinsent whispered as they passed out of earshot.

Lydia stooped to pick a violet in the border.

"He hasn't told me."

"Of your speaking to them, I mean. Would he approve of that? I know how very particular nice Americans are. I think your action might make a difference; it would certainly carry weight with Lady Susan."

"Dear Miss Pinsent, you flatter me!"

Lydia rose and gathered up her book and sunshade.

"Well, if you're asked for an opinion—if Lady Susan asks you for one—I think you ought to be prepared," Miss Pinsent admonished her as she moved away.

III

Lady Susan held her own. She ignored the Lintons, and her little family, as Miss Pinsent phrased it, followed suit. Even Mrs. Ainger agreed that it was obligatory. If Lady Susan owed it to the others not to speak to the Lintons, the others clearly owed it to Lady Susan to back her up. It was generally found expedient, at the Hotel Bellosguardo, to adopt this form of reasoning.

Whatever effect this combined action may have had upon the Lintons, it did not at least have that of driving them away. Monsieur Grossart, after a few days of suspense, had the satisfaction of seeing them settle down in his yellow damask *premier* with what looked like a permanent installation of palm-trees and silk sofa-cushions, and a gratifying continuance in the consumption of champagne. Mrs. Linton trailed her Doucet draperies up and down the garden with the same challenging air, while her husband, smoking innumerable cigarettes, dragged himself dejectedly in her wake; but neither of them, after the first encounter with Lady Susan, made any attempt to extend their acquaintance. They simply ignored their ignorers. As Miss Pinsent resentfully observed, they behaved exactly as though the hotel were empty.

It was therefore a matter of surprise, as well as of displeasure, to Lydia, to find, on glancing up one day from her seat in the garden, that the shadow which had fallen across her book was that of the enigmatic Mrs. Linton.

"I want to speak to you," that lady said, in a rich hard voice that seemed the audible expression of her gown and her complexion.

Lydia started. She certainly did not want to speak to Mrs. Linton.

"Shall I sit down here?" the latter continued, fixing her intensely-shaded eyes on Lydia's face, "or are you afraid of being seen with me?"

"Afraid?" Lydia colored. "Sit down, please. What is it that you wish to say?"

Mrs. Linton, with a smile, drew up a garden-chair and crossed one open-work ankle above the other.

"I want you to tell me what my husband said to your husband last night."

Lydia turned pale.

"My husband—to yours?" she faltered, staring at the other.

"Didn't you know they were closeted together for hours in the smoking-room after you went upstairs? My man didn't get to bed until nearly two o'clock and when he did I couldn't get a word out of him. When he wants to be aggravating I'll back him against anybody living!" Her teeth and eyes flashed persuasively upon Lydia. "But you'll tell me what they were talking about, won't you? I know I can trust you—you look so awfully kind. And it's for his own good. He's such a precious donkey, and I'm so afraid he's got into some beastly scrape or other. If he'd only trust his own old woman! But they're always writing to him and setting him against me. And I've got nobody to turn to." She laid her hand on Lydia's with a rattle of bracelets. "You'll help me, won't you?"

Lydia drew back from the smiling fierceness of her brows.

"I'm sorry—but I don't think I understand. My husband has said nothing to me of—of yours."

The great black crescents above Mrs. Linton's eyes met angrily.

"I say—is that true?" she demanded.

Lydia rose from her seat.

"Oh, look here, I didn't mean that, you know—you mustn't take one up so! Can't you see how rattled I am?"

Lydia saw that, in fact, her beautiful mouth was quivering beneath softened eyes.

"I'm beside myself!" the splendid creature wailed, dropping into her seat.

"I'm so sorry," Lydia repeated, forcing herself to speak kindly; "but how can I help you?"

Mrs. Linton raised her head sharply.

"By finding out—there's a darling!"

"Finding what out?"

"What Trevenna told him."

"Trevenna—?" Lydia echoed in bewilderment.

Mrs. Linton clapped her hand to her mouth.

"Oh Lord—there, it's out! What a fool I am! But I supposed of course you knew; I supposed everybody knew." She dried her eyes and bridled. "Didn't you know that he's Lord Trevenna? I'm Mrs. Cope."

Lydia recognized the names. They had figured in a flamboyant elopement which had thrilled fashionable London some six months earlier.

"Now you see how it is—you understand, don't you?" Mrs. Cope continued on a note of appeal. "I knew you would—that's the reason I came to you. I suppose *he* felt the same thing about your husband; he's not spoken to another soul in this place." Her face grew anxious again. "He's awfully sensitive, generally—he feels our position, he says—as if it wasn't *my* place to feel that! But when he does get talking there's no knowing what he'll say. I know he's been brooding over something lately, and I *must* find out what it is—it's to his interest that I should. I always tell him that I think only of his interest; if he'd only trust me! But he's been so odd lately—I can't think what he's plotting. You will help me, dear?"

Lydia, who had remained standing, looked away uncomfortably.

"If you mean by finding out what Lord Trevenna has told my husband, I'm afraid it's impossible."

"Why impossible?"

"Because I infer that it was told in confidence."

Mrs. Cope stared incredulously.

"Well, what of that? Your husband looks such a dear—any one can see he's awfully gone on you. What's to prevent your getting it out of him?"

Lydia flushed.

"I'm not a spy!" she exclaimed.

"A spy—a spy? How dare you?" Mrs. Cope flamed out. "Oh, I don't mean that either! Don't be angry with me—I'm so miserable." She essayed a softer note. "Do you call that spying—for one woman to help out another? I do need help so dreadfully! I'm at my wits' end with Trevenna, I am indeed. He's such a boy—a mere baby, you know; he's only two-and-twenty." She dropped her orbed lids. "He's younger than me—only fancy! a few months younger. I tell him he ought to listen to me as if I was his mother; oughtn't he now? But he won't, he won't! All his people are at him, you see—oh, I know *their* little game! Trying to get him away from me before I can get my divorce—that's what they're up to. At first he wouldn't listen to them; he used to toss their letters over to me to read; but now he reads them himself, and answers 'em too, I fancy; he's always shut up in his room, writing. If I only knew what his plan is I could stop him fast enough—he's such a simpleton. But he's dreadfully deep too—at times I can't make him out. But I know he's told your husband everything—I knew that last night the minute I laid eyes on him. And I *must* find out—you must help me—I've got no one else to turn to!"

She caught Lydia's fingers in a stormy pressure.

"Say you'll help me—you and your husband."

Lydia tried to free herself.

"What you ask is impossible; you must see that it is. No one could interfere in—in the way you ask."

Mrs. Cope's clutch tightened.

"You won't, then? You won't?"

"Certainly not. Let me go, please."

Mrs. Cope released her with a laugh.

"Oh, go by all means—pray don't let me detain you! Shall you go and tell Lady Susan Condit that there's a pair of us—or shall I save you the trouble of enlightening her?"

Lydia stood still in the middle of the path, seeing her antagonist through a mist of terror. Mrs. Cope was still laughing.

"Oh, I'm not spiteful by nature, my dear; but you're a little more than flesh and blood can stand! It's impossible, is it? Let you go, indeed! You're too good to be mixed up in my affairs, are you? Why, you little fool, the first day I laid eyes on you I saw that you and I were both in the same box—that's the reason I spoke to you."

She stepped nearer, her smile dilating on Lydia like a lamp through a fog.

"You can take your choice, you know; I always play fair. If you'll tell I'll promise not to. Now then, which is it to be?"

Lydia, involuntarily, had begun to move away from the pelting storm of words; but at this she turned and sat down again.

"You may go," she said simply. "I shall stay here."

IV

She stayed there for a long time, in the hypnotized contemplation, not of Mrs. Cope's present, but of her own past. Gannett, early that morning, had gone off on a long walk—he had fallen into the habit of taking these mountain-tramps with various fellow-lodgers; but even had he been within reach she could not have gone to him just then. She had to deal with herself first. She was surprised to find how, in the last months, she had lost the habit of introspection. Since their coming to the Hotel Bellosguardo she and Gannett had tacitly avoided themselves and each other.

She was aroused by the whistle of the three o'clock steam-boat as it neared the landing just beyond the hotel gates. Three o'clock! Then Gannett would soon be back—he had told her to expect him before four. She rose hurriedly, her face averted from the inquisitorial façade of the hotel. She could not see him just yet; she could not go indoors. She slipped through one of the overgrown garden-alleys and climbed a steep path to the hills.

It was dark when she opened their sitting-room door. Gannett was sitting on the window-ledge smoking a cigarette. Cigarettes were now his chief resource: he had not written a line during the two months they had spent at the Hotel Bellosguardo. In that respect, it had turned out not to be the right *milieu* after all.

He started up at Lydia's entrance.

"Where have you been? I was getting anxious."

She sat down in a chair near the door.

"Up the mountain," she said wearily.

"Alone?"

"Yes."

Gannett threw away his cigarette; the sound of her voice made him want to see her face.

"Shall we have a little light?" he suggested.

She made no answer and he lifted the globe from the lamp and put a match to the wick. Then he looked at her.

"Anything wrong? You look done up."

She sat glancing vaguely about the little sitting-room, dimly lit by the pallid-globed lamp, which left in twilight the out-lines of the furniture, of his writing-table heaped with books and papers, of the tea-roses and jasmine drooping on the mantel-piece. How like home it had all grown—how like home!

"Lydia, what is wrong?" he repeated.

She moved away from him, feeling for her hatpins and turning to lay her hat and sunshade on the table.

Suddenly she said: "That woman has been talking to me."

Gannett stared.

"That woman? What woman?"

"Mrs. Linton—Mrs. Cope."

He gave a start of annoyance, still, as she perceived, not grasping the full import of her words.

"The deuce! She told you—?"

"She told me everything."

Gannett looked at her anxiously.

"What impudence! I'm so sorry that you should have been exposed to this, dear."

"Exposed!" Lydia laughed.

Gannett's brow clouded and they looked away from each other.

"Do you know *why* she told me? She had the best of reasons. The first time she laid eyes on me she saw that we were both in the same box."

"Lydia!"

"So it was natural, of course, that she should turn to me in a difficulty."

"What difficulty?"

"It seems she has reason to think that Lord Trevenna's people are trying to get him away from her before she gets her divorce—"

"Well?"

"And she fancied he had been consulting with you last night as to—as to the best way of escaping from her."

Gannett stood up with an angry forehead.

"Well—what concern of yours was all this dirty business? Why should she go to you?"

"Don't you see? It's so simple. I was to wheedle his secret out of you."

"To oblige that woman?"

"Yes; or, if I was unwilling to oblige her, then to protect myself."

"To protect yourself? Against whom?"

"Against her telling every one in the hotel that she and I are in the same box."

"She threatened that?"

"She left me the choice of telling it myself or of doing it for me."

"The beast!"

There was a long silence. Lydia had seated herself on the sofa, beyond the radius of the lamp, and he leaned against the window. His next question surprised her.

"When did this happen? At what time, I mean?"

She looked at him vaguely.

"I don't know—after luncheon, I think. Yes, I remember; it must have been at about three o'clock."

He stepped into the middle of the room and as he approached the light she saw that his brow had cleared.

"Why do you ask?" she said.

"Because when I came in, at about half-past three, the mail was just being distributed, and Mrs. Cope was waiting as usual to pounce on her letters; you know she was always watching for the postman. She was standing so close to me that I couldn't help seeing a big official-looking envelope that was handed to her. She tore it open, gave one look at the inside, and rushed off upstairs like a whirlwind, with the director shouting after her that she had left all her other letters behind. I don't believe she ever thought of you again after that paper was put into her hand."

"Why?"

"Because she was too busy. I was sitting in the window, watching for you, when the five o'clock boat left, and who should go on board, bag and baggage, valet and maid, dressing-bags and poodle, but Mrs. Cope and Trevenna. Just an hour and a half to pack up in! And you should have seen her when they started. She was radiant—shaking hands with everybody—waving her handkerchief from the deck—distributing bows and smiles like an empress. If ever a woman got what she wanted just in the nick of time that woman did. She'll be Lady Trevenna within a week, I'll wager."

"You think she has her divorce?"

"I'm sure of it. And she must have got it just after her talk with you."

Lydia was silent.

At length she said, with a kind of reluctance, "She was horribly angry when she left me. It wouldn't have taken long to tell Lady Susan Condit."

"Lady Susan Condit has not been told."

"How do you know?"

"Because when I went downstairs half an hour ago I met Lady Susan on the way—"

He stopped, half smiling.

"Well?"

"And she stopped to ask if I thought you would act as patroness to a charity concert she is getting up."

In spite of themselves they both broke into a laugh. Lydia's ended in sobs and she sank down with her face hidden. Gannett bent over her, seeking her hands.

"That vile woman—I ought to have warned you to keep away from her; I can't forgive myself! But he spoke to me in confidence; and I never dreamed—well, it's all over now."

Lydia lifted her head.

"Not for me. It's only just beginning."

"What do you mean?"

She put him gently aside and moved in her turn to the window. Then she went on, with her face turned toward the shimmering blackness of the lake, "You see of course that it might happen again at any moment."

"What?"

"This—this risk of being found out. And we could hardly count again on such a lucky combination of chances, could we?"

He sat down with a groan.

Still keeping her face toward the darkness, she said, "I want you to go and tell Lady Susan—and the others."

Gannett, who had moved towards her, paused a few feet off.

"Why do you wish me to do this?" he said at length, with less surprise in his voice than she had been prepared for.

"Because I've behaved basely, abominably, since we came here: letting these people believe we were married—lying with every breath I drew—"

"Yes, I've felt that too," Gannett exclaimed with sudden energy.

The words shook her like a tempest: all her thoughts seemed to fall about her in ruins.

"You—you've felt so?"

"Of course I have." He spoke with low-voiced vehemence. "Do you suppose I like playing the sneak any better than you do? It's damnable."

He had dropped on the arm of a chair, and they stared at each other like blind people who suddenly see.

"But you have liked it here," she faltered.

"Oh, I've liked it—I've liked it." He moved impatiently. "Haven't you?"

"Yes," she burst out; "that's the worst of it—that's what I can't bear. I fancied it was for your sake that I insisted on staying—because you thought you could write here; and perhaps just at first that really was the reason. But afterwards I wanted to stay myself—I loved it." She broke into a laugh. "Oh, do you see the full derision of it? These people—the very prototypes of the bores you took me away from, with

the same fenced-in view of life, the same keep-off-the-grass
morality, the same little cautious virtues and the same little
frightened voices—well, I've clung to them. I've delighted in
them. I've done my best to please them. I've toadied Lady
Susan, I've gossipped with Miss Pinsent, I've pretended to be
shocked with Mrs. Ainger. Respectability! It was the one
thing in life that I was sure I didn't care about, and it's grown
so precious to me that I've stolen it because I couldn't get it
in any other way."

She moved across the room and returned to his side with
another laugh.

"I who used to fancy myself unconventional! I must have
been born with a card-case in my hand. You should have
seen me with that poor woman in the garden. She came to
me for help, poor creature, because she fancied that, having
'sinned,' as they call it, I might feel some pity for others who
had been tempted in the same way. Not I! She didn't know
me. Lady Susan would have been kinder, because Lady Susan
wouldn't have been afraid. I hated the woman—my one
thought was not to be seen with her—I could have killed her
for guessing my secret. The one thing that mattered to me at
that moment was my standing with Lady Susan!"

Gannett did not speak.

"And you—you've felt it too!" she broke out accusingly.
"You've enjoyed being with these people as much as I have;
you've let the chaplain talk to you by the hour about 'The
Reign of Law' and Professor Drummond. When they asked
you to hand the plate in church I was watching you—*you
wanted to accept.*"

She stepped close, laying her hand on his arms.

"Do you know, I begin to see what marriage is for. It's to
keep people away from each other. Sometimes I think that
two people who love each other can be saved from madness
only by the things that come between them—children, duties,
visits, bores, relations—the things that protect married people
from each other. We've been too close together—that has
been our sin. We've seen the nakedness of each other's souls."

She sank again on the sofa, hiding her face in her hands.

Gannett stood above her perplexedly: he felt as though she
were being swept away by some implacable current while he
stood helpless on its bank.

At length he said, "Lydia, don't think me a brute—but
don't you see yourself that it won't do?"

"Yes, I see it won't do," she said without raising her head.

His face cleared.

"Then we'll go to-morrow."

"Go—where?"

"To Paris; to be married."

For a long time she made no answer; then she asked slowly, "Would they have us here if we were married?"

"Have us here?"

"I mean Lady Susan—and the others."

"Have us here? Of course they would."

"Not if they knew—at least, not unless they could pretend not to know."

He made an impatient gesture.

"We shouldn't come back here, of course; and other people needn't know—no one need know."

She sighed. "Then it's only another form of deception and a meaner one. Don't you see that?"

"I see that we're not accountable to any Lady Susans on earth!"

"Then why are you ashamed of what we are doing here?"

"Because I'm sick of pretending that you're my wife when you're not—when you won't be."

She looked at him sadly.

"If I were your wife you'd have to go on pretending. You'd have to pretend that I'd never been—anything else. And our friends would have to pretend that they believed what you pretended."

Gannett pulled off the sofa-tassel and flung it away.

"You're impossible," he groaned.

"It's not I—it's our being together that's impossible. I only want you to see that marriage won't help it."

"What will help it then?"

She raised her head.

"My leaving you."

"Your leaving me?" He sat motionless, staring at the tassel which lay at the other end of the room. At length some impulse of retaliation for the pain she was inflicting made him say deliberately:

"And where would you go if you left me?"

"Oh!" she cried, wincing.

He was at her side in an instant.

"Lydia—Lydia—you know I didn't mean it; I couldn't mean it! But you've driven me out of my senses; I don't know what I'm saying. Can't you get out of this labyrinth of self-torture? It's destroying us both."

"That's why I must leave you."

"How easily you say it!" He drew her hands down and made her face him. "You're very scrupulous about yourself—and others. But have you thought of me? You have no right to leave me unless you've ceased to care—"

"It's because I care—"

"Then I have a right to be heard. If you love me you can't leave me."

Her eyes defied him.

"Why not?"

He dropped her hands and rose from her side.

"Can you?" he said sadly.

The hour was late and the lamp flickered and sank. She stood up with a shiver and turned toward the door of her room.

V

At daylight a sound in Lydia's room woke Gannett from a troubled sleep. He sat up and listened. She was moving about softly, as though fearful of disturbing him. He heard her push back one of the creaking shutters; then there was a moment's silence, which seemed to indicate that she was waiting to see if the noise had roused him.

Presently she began to move again. She had spent a sleepless night, probably, and was dressing to go down to the garden for a breath of air. Gannett rose also; but some undefinable instinct made his movements as cautious as hers. He stole to his window and looked out through the slats of the shutter.

It had rained in the night and the dawn was gray and lifeless. The cloud-muffled hills across the lake were reflected in its surface as in a tarnished mirror. In the garden, the birds were beginning to shake the drops from the motionless laurustinus-boughs.

An immense pity for Lydia filled Gannett's soul. Her seeming intellectual independence had blinded him for a time to the feminine cast of her mind. He had never thought of her as a woman who wept and clung: there was a lucidity in her intuitions that made them appear to be the result of reasoning. Now he saw the cruelty he had committed in detaching her from the normal conditions of life; he felt, too, the insight with which she had hit upon the real cause of their suffering. Their life was "impossible," as she had said—and its worst penalty was that it had made any other life impossible for them. Even had his love lessened, he was bound to her now by a hundred ties of pity and self-reproach; and she, poor child! must turn back as Latude returned to his cell . . .

A new sound startled him: it was the stealthy closing of Lydia's door. He crept to his own and heard her footsteps passing down the corridor. Then he went back to the window and looked out.

A minute or two later he saw her go down the steps of the porch and enter the garden. From his post of observation her face was invisible, but something about her appearance struck him. She wore a long travelling cloak and under its folds he detected the outline of a bag or bundle. He drew a deep breath and stood watching her.

She walked quickly down the laurustinus alley toward the gate; there she paused a moment, glancing about the little shady square. The stone benches under the trees were empty, and she seemed to gather resolution from the solitude about her, for she crossed the square to the steam-boat landing, and he saw her pause before the ticket-office at the head of the wharf. Now she was buying her ticket. Gannett turned his head a moment to look at the clock: the boat was due in five minutes. He had time to jump into his clothes and overtake her—

He made no attempt to move; an obscure reluctance restrained him. If any thought emerged from the tumult of his sensations, it was that he must let her go if she wished it. He had spoken last night of his rights: what were they? At the last issue, he and she were two separate beings, not made one by the miracle of common forebearances, duties, abnegations, but bound together in a *noyade* of passion that left them resisting yet clinging as they went down.

After buying her ticket, Lydia had stood for a moment looking out across the lake; then he saw her seat herself on one of the benches near the landing. He and she, at that moment, were both listening for the same sound: the whistle of the boat as it rounded the nearest promontory. Gannett turned again to glance at the clock; the boat was due now.

Where would she go? What would her life be when she had left him? She had no near relations and few friends. There was money enough . . . but she asked so much of life, in ways so complex and immaterial. He thought of her as walking barefooted through a stony waste. No one would understand her—no one would pity her—and he, who did both, was powerless to come to her aid . . .

He saw that she had risen from the bench and walked toward the edge of the lake. She stood looking in the direction from which the steamboat was to come; then she turned to the ticket office, doubtless to ask the cause of the delay. After that she went back to the bench and sat down with bent head. What was she thinking of?

The whistle sounded; she started up, and Gannett involuntarily made a movement toward the door. But he turned back and continued to watch her. She stood motionless, her eyes on the trail of smoke that preceded the appearance of the boat. Then the little craft rounded the point, a dead-white object on the leaden water: a minute later it was puffing and backing at the wharf.

The few passengers who were waiting—two or three peasants and a snuffy priest—were clustered near the ticket-office. Lydia stood apart under the trees.

The boat lay alongside now; the gang-plank was run out and the peasants went on board with their baskets of vegetables, followed by the priest. Still Lydia did not move. A bell began to ring querulously; there was a shriek of steam, and some one must have called to her that she would be late, for she started forward, as though in answer to a summons. She moved waveringly, and at the edge of the wharf she paused. Gannett saw a sailor beckon to her; the bell rang again and she stepped upon the gang-plank.

Half-way down the short incline to the deck she stopped again; then she turned and ran back to the land. The gang-plank was drawn in, the bell ceased to ring, and the boat backed out into the lake. Lydia, with slow steps, was walking toward the garden . . .

As she approached the hotel she looked up furtively and Gannett drew back into the room. He sat down beside a table; a Bradshaw lay at his elbow, and mechanically, without knowing what he did, he began looking out the trains to Paris . . .

The New Woman and the Old

Anne Warner

It was a quiet, pleasant room of a certain well-known variety. Inexpensive wall-paper, curtains, and carpet, with one small Turkish rug spread carefully cornerwise on the largest vacant floor-space; a couch, with hand-embroidered pillows in the far corner; a bookcase filled with well-worn old authors and bright, new editions of the kind given away with "a year's subscription"; three easy-chairs and four that were frankly uneasy; a center-table, with an excellent lamp, three good magazines, "The Simple Life," a well-known novel, a work-box, and a vase of flowers—that was all. And that was enough. It was the vase of flowers that gave the key-note of the whole, for it was a special vase of flowers and betrayed the fact at a glance. The every-day vase of flowers stands about as carelessly as a clubman in his favorite club; the special vase of flowers acts like a country stranger who has never seen the inside of a club before. This special vase had been tried on both the mantelpiece and the bookcase, also on the little table in the corner; but in the end it seemed as if the center-table was really the only place. "I think it looks best there," Mrs. Reed had said, half in assertion and half in question; and so Emily had left it there.

Mrs. Reed herself sat just to the left of the vase, and Emily sat just to its right. Mrs. Reed wore her dark-blue dress, with a lace collar that her cousin Ann Hamilton had sent her from Brussels. Emily wore a red merino house frock shaped at the waist with smocking. She was a large, well-built young woman of about thirty, with fine eyes and hair. In her hair she wore a little silver comb which her mother's cousin Ann Hamilton had sent her from Venice.

Mrs. Reed was sewing. Her sewing was non-committal, and of a kind which any one could have out anywhere: it looked like a large bag, but it might have been a small pillow-case.

Every time she adjusted its intricacies, she glanced at the clock, and its intricacies certainly required a deal of adjusting. Emily was reading, and scorned to look at the clock at all, but her cheeks grew more and more flushed each minute. Finally the clock struck the half-hour.

"It's half-past six," Mrs. Reed then said, taking off her thimble and putting it on again at once—"half-past, Emily."

"Yes, I heard it," said Emily, turning a page—Emily was bound that she would be absolutely indifferent, if it killed her,—"but supper isn't till seven."

"I wonder if Julia has left the table just as I laid it."

"She wouldn't change anything, Mother."

"Hadn't I better just go and look?"

"She wouldn't change anything."

"I guess I'll just look at it, anyway."

Mrs. Reed left the room for five minutes, then returned and took up her work, "It's twenty minutes to seven now, Emily."

"He wasn't asked till seven."

"I know; I wasn't thinking of him. I only said it was twenty minutes to seven."

Emily said nothing.

"Really, Emily, I wasn't thinking of him at all."

Just here the bell pealed violently.

"Oh, there he is!" exclaimed Mrs. Reed. "Shall I go to the door, or will you?"

"Julia will go."

"Did you tell her?"

"Yes, I told her."

"Did you remind her about tying on a fresh apron before she went?"

"Yes, I laid it out so she couldn't forget."

"But she isn't going, Emily. He's standing out there all this time. Let me go."

"No, Mother. She'll go. She was down cellar; I heard her running up the steps."

"Oh, Emily, she's sure to forget the clean apron!"

"No, she won't, Mother."

"And what is he thinking of? Invited to supper, and then left out on the step all this time!" Mrs. Reed's distress was pitiable.

"There's Julia going to the door now, Mother." From where she sat Emily commanded a view not visible to her mother's anxious eyes.

"Has she the apron?"

"She's tying it on."

Mrs. Reed mastered her emotion by a desperate effort of will, and took up her work. Emily turned another page. Her face was crimson, but still impassive.

They could hear the front door opened and closed, then some one was busy by the hat-rack in the hall.

"Don't you think you ought to go out there, Emily?" Mrs. Reed whispered.

Emily shook her head.

A man's step sounded in the front parlor, and the next second Dwight was before them, rubbing his big, cold hands together. He was tall and bald. Both ladies rose and welcomed him warmly, to the casual observer even more warmly than he appeared to merit, for he was neither an interesting nor a prepossessing man.

"Sit down by the fire," said Mrs. Reed, pushing up one big chair, while Emily pushed up another; "you must be frozen."

"No, oh, no," said Dwight; "oh, no, I'm not frozen. Oh, no it isn't cold enough for that. No—no."

"I think it's very cold to-day," said Mrs. Reed. "I've thought it was cold all day. You know I remarked it to you, Emily. But I feel the cold. My cousin Ann Hamilton and I feel the cold just alike."

Dwight sat down in the easier of the two easy-chairs. "How is Mrs. Hamilton?" he inquired.

"Oh, she's so well!" said Mrs. Reed, "I had a letter from her last week. Not a long letter, just the half of a postal-card—that half that's left to write on, you know. She's motoring up the Nile cataracts this month. Emily and I keep right along with her in the cyclopedia. Ann Hamilton *does* enjoy life."

"Yes," Dwight said—"yes, I thought so: yes. And what have you been doing to-day?" he asked Emily.

Emily blushed. "My usual routine," she said. "Life will never hold anything different for me."

"Oh Emily," protested her mother, "how can you say that? Something nice may happen any minute to change all your future."

Emily, helplessly purple, looked at her mother in desperate pleading for a discretion that didn't exist.

"Very true," said Dwight, solemnly; "*very* true."

There was a slight pause; both mother and daughter were one in a subconscious desire to be alone together, to the end that they might carefully discuss that remark of their caller's and weigh well whether it did or did not mean anything.

Dwight ended the silence by saying abruptly: "And so Mrs. Hamilton is in Egypt. Well, I *am* glad to hear that. Yes—yes."

Just here Julia, still clean-aproned, opened the dining-room door and jangled the tea-bell vigorously.

"Oh, I guess supper's ready," said Mrs. Reed, smiling and rising. "You must be hungry from your walk, Mr. Dwight?"

"Oh, I don't know," said Dwight, dubiously. "Well, maybe. Yes, I think I am. Yes, I think I am. Yes—yes."

They went out to the table, which was decorated with another vase of flowers, and cheered by a platter of cold sliced ham, a dish of Saratoga chips, two plates of hot bread, and two kinds of preserves.

"You see, we don't put on any style for you," said Mrs. Reed—"just a plain home supper." She and Emily sat opposite each other, and Dwight sat at the end, right in front of one plate of hot bread.

The supper was very successful, the guest eating all in sight. He was one of those cavernous-looking men, and cavernous-looking men are often cavernous in many directions at once. The conversation that accompanied the food was highly edifying. Dwight and Emily had been reading "The Master of Ballantrae," and a pleasant discussion as to the possibility of being buried alive arose. Mrs. Reed declared them both too young to have to begin to think of that for years to come, but Dwight, plunging in among the Saratoga chips for the sixth time, said you never could tell. Emily asked him if he had ever known any one well who had "been through it." This reminded him of some one he had known who had "come through" drowning. Mrs. Reed remembered then how just before she was married a neighbor had taken rat poison.

"What an experience for you!" said Dwight, with his mouth full.

"Yes; but I went on and got married just the same," said Mrs. Reed. "And I've never regretted it," she added, with emphasis.

Dwight helped himself to more ham.

"Put the platter right by him, Emily," said Mrs. Reed. "It just does me good to see you eat, Mr. Dwight."

"I didn't know I was so hungry," said Dwight; "I didn't really. No, really I didn't; no."

After supper they went back into the sitting-room and sat

down. In a few minutes Mrs. Reed got up, said she had a bad headache, and went away. Dwight and Emily were left alone with only the vase of flowers to look out for them.

"I suppose your sister is very busy these days?" Emily said, keenly aware that some one must say something.

"Yes, she is," said Dwight, nervously; "yes—yes."

"Let me see—why, the wedding's only three weeks from to-day."

"It's the twenty-fourth."

"That's not long."

"No," said the man. "No, I really don't know what to do. Hildegarde's been a great help to me with the school."

"You'll have to get a—a housekeeper, won't you?"

Dwight wrung his big hands together, but no words came.

"If you can find the right one," said Emily.

"Yes, that's it," he said.

There were a few more acute interchanges and then he did get the proposal out—and Emily Reed became engaged.

After Dwight went—and he didn't stay late—the daughter locked the door, put out the lights, and went up-stairs.

"I'm awake," Mrs. Reed cried softly from her room. "Come in here, Emily. Oh, Emily, I didn't really have a headache. I just said that to get out of the way."

Emily groped her way to the bed and sat down on its side.

"*Did* he say anything?" Mrs. Reed asked, and Emily could feel the bed shake with her nervousness.

"Yes, Mother; he asked me to marry him."

"*Emily!* Oh, Emily! Then it's really settled?"

"Yes, Mother."

"Oh, can I tell Julia the first thing in the morning?"

"Oh, no, Mother."

"And you'll really be married! *Emily!* Me with a married daughter! *Can't* you tell me what he said—just a little, you know?"

"I hardly know what he said, Mother."

"I know—I know just what you mean. It isn't so much what's said—it's the whole thing together. Oh, to think I can write Ann Hamilton that you're going to be married! She'll be sure to make you a handsome present." Mrs. Reed put forth her hand in the darkness and got hold of her daughter's. "I almost thought you never would marry," she said, with a quiver in her voice.

Emily stroked her mother's hand gently.

"Did you plan anything about when?" Mrs. Reed asked.

"No; we didn't say a word about that."

"But—but, Emily—he kissed you, didn't he?"

There was a second or so of silence. "Yes," Emily said then, "he kissed me."

"Wasn't it splendid?—Wasn't it different from all the rest of your life before? You know that old black hair-ribbon I've got in my work-basket? I had it on the first time I was ever kissed."

"Didn't it please father your treasuring it so?" Emily's tone was lacking in interest; her mind seemed far way.

"Oh, it wasn't him; it was my first beau. I had so many, Emily! You don't know anything about life, my poor child. When I think of the kind of men I wouldn't have, and then of the kind you've got to have! Why, Emily, I wouldn't have looked at a man that age when I was your age, and now only see how glad we both are to get him! I don't know where all the young men have gone to these days, I'm sure."

Emily leaned forward and kissed her mother. "You must go to sleep now, and so must I," she said.

"Yes; and I want to say a prayer of gratitude too. I'm *so* grateful, you can't think."

It was long before Mrs. Reed slept, but longer yet before her daughter even undressed. Emily Reed was not an ordinary young woman; she was endowed much beyond the ordinary, and her betrothal held almost no satisfaction for her. Like all girls, she had had dreams; and this was their end in her eyes. She never for one second had looked upon marriage with Dwight as their beginning. The big waves of progress take their rise in the centers of active life, where there is plenty of force for them to keep to their purpose; only their spent remains, their faltering outer edge, their more insignificant wreckage and dead debris, find their end along that by-path of civilization, the smaller town. There was one preëminently interesting wave washing the world at this time; Emily Reed had felt its influence, but had not been drawn fully into the current: she had lost all her illusions; she had not yet received much in their place. It was three years since she had begun to call herself, to herself, a "new woman"—three years of thorns and briars, for her mother had no sympathy with any such notions. Her mother wished her to marry. Her mother was forever putting it to Emily that she, Mrs. Reed, and her cousin Ann Hamilton had both married. Emily, in bed at last, reflected over it all. Well, now she was going to marry. She was going to marry James Dwight. She was going to go the way of the majority of her sex. She sighed, and then later, much later, she slept.

It was a strange awakening. At first she could not recall what had happened. The first spring rain was coming down on the tin roof outside her window. It had been fiercely cold the night before, and now here was spring come all of a sudden. She sighed, and just as she sighed her mother came in, her hair still in curl-papers and her face all smiles.

"Emily," I'm so happy I don't know what to say. I could hardly sleep at all. I cried twice just because I was so happy. I suppose you'll have to live at the school, but you'll take dinner here every Sunday. When I think of you coming walking up the street with your own husband! He's so fine-looking, too. My gracious, Emily! but you're a lucky girl! I never dared really hope he'd really ask you."

Emily looked at her mother and smiled. It made her happier now that she saw how happy it made her mother.

"I wonder if he's woke up yet?" pursued Mrs. Reed. "I suppose you've been wondering that, too. You see, I don't forget what love is. Oh, my goodness! think of the wedding! I do wonder if it can be this summer."

There was a certain pathos in the daughter's face, a touch of wistful envy of her mother's joy. "We never spoke of it," she said.

"I'm not curious, Emily, but how did he begin? Did he take your hand, or did he put his arm around you? I've always wondered about proposals; I didn't have a real one myself, I just stepped on a snake when I was out walking with your father."

The easy red went coursing over Emily's face. "He was very quiet, Mother," she said. "I—I don't really remember just what did begin—just what was said."

"I wonder how soon we can tell every one. I'd like to tell Julia first of any one. I couldn't help just hinting to her last night that there was a reason for her not going around on the porch to shut the outside blinds, and I should like to tell her what it was to-day."

"I shouldn't tell her yet, Mother."

"Well, I won't, if you don't want me to. But she's so discreet, Emily; I tell her so many things. She's just like one of us, you know."

"I don't think we ought to say anything yet."

"Well, just as you say, Emily; but there's this about it; it does hold a man a good deal firmer. In cities they always tell right off. It makes it a settled thing."

Again the red in Emily's cheeks. "I shouldn't want to hold him if he wanted to go, Mother."

"Oh, Emily, you're *so* queer with your notions! Why, he's asked you, and he ought to want to be held now. He ought to want every one to know. He ought to be proud over getting you. Of course he isn't proud, because he could marry any woman in town, because he's the only man in town for anybody to marry; but if you'd had any choice, he might well be proud." Mrs. Reed sounded aggrieved.

Emily began to get up.

"After breakfast we'll look over all my linen," said Mrs. Reed, turning to go; "we'll want to begin hemming your napkins right off."

Emily tried to smile.

Her mother got as far as the door, stopped there, and looked back. Emily was squeezing the tube of tooth-paste over her brush. "Emily, I know who I can tell."

"Who, Mother?"

"Ann Hamilton; I may write to her." Emily poured out a glass of water.

"I may write to her, mayn't I, Emily?"

"Yes, Mother." Emily began to brush her teeth.

Mrs. Reed went away. They breakfasted half an hour later. The breakfast-table conversation ebbed and flowed between a second and yet more serious discussion as to the telling of Julia and another equally serious, as to writing to the city for linen samples.

"I want you to have *some* nice linen," Mrs. Reed declared; "but, oh, dear! I do want to consult Julia! She'd be *so* interested. She's got a beau, too, you know. And I'm sure she'd *never* tell."

But Emily was firm, and Mrs. Reed did not tell Julia.

It rained all day, and no one came to the house, and no one left it. The mother continued blissfully happy and full of plans for the future.

"You may make a great big school out of it," she said hopefully, "like Harvard College and Mount Holyoke. They began small, too, and now look at them. And Mr. Dwight is so clever, Emily, I shouldn't be surprised over anything he did. He's a remarkable man. Will he come to-night?"

"Yes," said Emily. "He has a book that he wishes me to read, and he said he'd bring it to-night."

"Oh, Emily, that just shows that you don't know anything about love. He doesn't want you to read that book one bit; he just wants an excuse to see you soon again. My goodness! I should think you'd have seen right straight through that."

"It's a book on modern education," said Emily; "he's going to read the preface aloud to me."

"I don't believe that preface will get read much," said Mrs. Reed, with a preternaturally wise air. "Oh, Emily, do you think it would look too much as if you asked me to do it if we brought the sofa out of the corner and put it along in front of the fire? It's so nice to sit on a sofa and be in love. You don't know about it now, but if we bring the sofa out, you'll see."

Emily objected to the moving of the sofa, and Mrs. Reed was soon diverted into the channel of writing her cousin Ann Hamilton. "I guess I won't come in at all to-night. You can say I've still got my headache, and I can write Ann. That'll be best."

Poor Mrs. Reed's ideas of Dwight were far removed from the truth, for the first thing he did after his arrival that evening was to sit down and read the whole twenty-six pages of the preface aloud. Emily sat on the opposite side of the table, her eyelids drooping over her eyes, and listened. It was quarter after nine before he finished, and the conversation that followed was edifying in the extreme. Dwight opened his heart to his future wife and outlined her life to come for her benefit. When his sister married, he should get no housekeeper. "For I'll soon have you," he remarked not tenderly, but with quiet assertion. "Neither shall I need a teacher for the youngest classes; you're absolutely qualified to teach them." A few minutes later he imparted to her that she "could easily do the drawing and music, too."

"I've been thinking," he continued, "that I could rent some rooms in the next house and double the boarders. They pay, and every extra one is money in my pocket. You could look out for them. Yes, you could."

Emily sat on her own side of the table in silence.

"And I believe that I could lay out a course for you that would bring you up to where you could take some of my classes," Dwight went on, "it would relieve me so much just to know that there was some one who *could* take my place if I was tired or wanted to go away for a few days."

Emily remained silent under the appalling avalanche of marital plans; but within her soul she was not passive; on the contrary, she was mentally very active, listening, wondering, pondering.

"Marriage, as I understand it, is a partnership," Dwight went on. "I know you have some money, and of course you'll take it in now and invest it in the school. We'll work together. I want to go to Germany next summer and investigate the newer methods, and we'll be married before I go or after I return, just as you prefer. If we're married before I go, you can have your mother with you while I'm gone. You'll have to superintend the cleaning of the school during my vacation, you know."

Emily opened her mother's work-box at that and looked idly inside. She was taking breath for mighty speech.

"I must be going now," said Dwight, rising abruptly. "I'm sorry your mother couldn't see me; I hope she'll be better tomorrow."

Emily turned her head and looked at him. "Don't go for a minute," she said a little huskily; "I've something to say to you."

"What is it?" said Dwight, still standing.

"Sit down," she bade him.

He sat down then and looked at her. She had turned toward him and crossed her hands on the table; her eyes were leveled straight upon him.

"Well, what is it?" he asked.

She flushed crimson. There was resolution and purpose gathering in her face, but a latent regret over the blow so soon to fall upon her mother softened her eyes and lips so that she was almost lovely for the moment.

"Well?" Dwight repeated.

"I wish to give it up," Emily said then very steadily, but with finality.

"Give it up!"

"Yes."

The man stared at her. "Give it up!" he repeated.

"Yes," she said again.

He seemed not to understand. "Give *what* up?" he asked.

"Our engagement," said Emily. There was a short, rather awful silence. Then she spoke further; "I'm not equal to what you want of me. I couldn't possibly do all that work."

He was looking straight at her. She went on: "And I don't want to try to do it. I'd rather not marry you. I've been considering all the while that you were talking, and I no longer desire to marry you."

This was rather a bald way of putting it, but Emily was such an extremely new woman that she was more than crude; she was absolutely raw.

Dwight now understood clearly and was angry.

"Oh, very well," he said, starting to his feet. "I'm sure, if you feel that way, I don't wish to marry you. By no means. No—no."

She looked after him as he went out of the room, but with no faintest shadow of regret. After she had heard the front door bang she went into the entry and locked it; then she put out the lights and went up-stairs.

Mrs. Reed was awake and called softly from her room. Emily went in.

"Do you know *now* when you'll be married?" the mother asked.

"No." Emily was deliberating whether to tell her at once or wait until the morning.

"I've been lying here all the evening so happy, so awful happy. I've been thinking about when every one will know. Kate Black would have gone out of her senses for joy if he wanted Kitty, and you know how all the Motts have run after him. Oh, Emily, I don't know what I've ever done to be so happy as to see you married! I've always thought you never would be. Not that it was your fault, but with only one man to marry, how could I dare to hope he'd marry you. I haven't dared hope. I've prayed a lot, but I never had a mite of real hope."

Poor Emily! She sat down on the side of the bed and took her mother's hand. There was a striking contrast in the repetition of so much of the night before—her seat on the bed, and the secret to tell—all, all. Mrs. Reed clung affectionately to her child in the dark.

"I wrote to Ann Hamilton, Emily. The letter's over there on my table. I left it unsealed so I could put in the marriage date, if you knew it. And, oh, Emily, how I have regretted not moving the sofa! We must do that to-morrow. It won't look pointed now; it'll just look as if the room had been swept. Did he kiss you much?"

"No." said Emily, painfully.

"There, I knew you'd miss the sofa. But he kissed you good-by, didn't he?"

"No. Mother."

"He didn't kiss you good-by!"

"No."

Mrs. Reed gave a start, then agitation again shook the bed.

"Emily, I do hope and trust you haven't had any trouble."

Emily drew a long breath. "He wanted more than I could learn to do, Mother; so we've given it up."

Mrs. Reed sprang to a sitting posture like a Jack-in-the-box. "Not the engagement? Oh, Emily, you haven't given up your engagement?"

"Yes, Mother; I had to. I hadn't any choice. He told me all that he expected of his wife, and no mortal woman could undertake to do all that; so I gave the engagement up. Oh, don't cry, Mother dear." For Mrs. Reed had burst into tears.

"I—I—I can't help it. Oh, Emily! Oh, Emily!"

"Mother, it's much better as it is. I'm so glad that I found out his views at once."

But Mrs. Reed was not to be thus easily comforted. "If I'd only told people, then you couldn't have g-g-given it up. Oh, oh!"

"But, Mother, it's so much better as—"

"You'll never be married now, Emily; you'll never have another chance. There isn't any other man to give you a chance. I was too happy! I was too happy!"

"But, Mother dear, I—"

"Suppose he did want you to do a great deal of work, Emily; all women have to do ever so much more work than they ever expect to. It's just he was so noble to try and save you that surprise. And instead of being grateful and taking it in the right spirit, you—oh, oh!"

"But, Mother, he wanted me to work hard all day and then study till midnight every night."

"But all women have to work all day and till midnight, Emily. I *always* sewed till midnight. A woman can't possibly get everything brought up before midnight. Your father always had his evenings and went to bed at eleven, but I was always on the jump. And you thought it was something uncommon, and so you've broken your engagement with the only man in town. Get me a handkerchief out of my top drawer, please—one of the big ones."

Emily sought the handkerchief. "He was so selfish, Mother," she said, coming back to the bed; "that was another thing that frightened me."

Mrs. Reed seized the handkerchief. "But all men are selfish," she wailed from its folds; "even in a cityful of men

you won't find any one that isn't selfish. Your father ate all
the giblets up to the day he died. If you think there's such a
thing as an unselfish man, you'll be an old maid sure. Oh, my
goodness me! to think you've sent Mr. Dwight away for a
little thing like that! Oh, oh!"

"I don't want to marry just to be a slave," protested Emily.
"I—"

"But you can't be married without being a slave." Mrs.
Reed's voice was faint with emotion for a little while, and
then it swelled suddenly strong: "That isn't any kind of reason for giving a man up. What difference does being a slave
make, anyhow, if only you're married? The thing is to be
married, Emily; and you've let the only man in town go. And
for such silly reasons—just because he told you beforehand
what most men leave the girl to find out afterward. He'll
marry one of the Motts now—I just know it,—and instead of
me telling Mrs. Mott, it'll be Mrs. Mott telling me!" Mrs.
Reed's voice rose again, this time most dramatically until it
succeeded in perching the last word on a hitherto unattained
altitude of woe. Then she began to cry again.

"Mother," said Emily, gently, but in a tone of penetrating
force, "would you choose to have me a mere drudge for the
rest of my life just for the sake of being married? Do you
really feel that way?"

"You'd have soon gotten used to it," sobbed Mrs. Reed.
"Women always do. I wasn't married more than six months
before I was used to it."

"I don't wish to get used to it," the daughter declared. "I
don't wish to marry in that way."

"Well, you won't be married in that way. You won't be
married at all now," her mother said. "I can just see Mrs.
Mott's face when she comes to tell me! She'd go down on her
knees and scrub floors for James Dwight. I would, too. I
know what getting married means. Oh, Emily, to think that
you've had such a chance and lost it! To think of it!"

Emily leaned forward and kissed her mother on the forehead. "It's no use our talking longer," she said; "if I leave
you, you'll think it over quietly and see that I am right—"

"No, I sha'n't," interposed Mrs. Reed.

"And in the morning we'll try and take a brighter view of
it. I'm well content, absolutely content."

"Get me another handkerchief before you go," said Mrs.
Reed. "I know I'm going to need it. Oh, Emily, you've broken my heart! Yes, you have. You were so difficult to raise

with your notions, and now just see the end you've made! Oh, oh!"

Emily brought the handkerchief. She was sorry for her mother, but she could not possibly regret James Dwight. "Good night, dear," she said gently. "Try to bear it bravely. I know it's very hard for you, but think if I had married him, how hard all my future would have been!"

"But you'd have been married!" wailed the poor mother, "and now you never will be. Oh, oh!"

Emily turned and walked quietly out of the room. Neither her lips nor her resolution trembled; she had meant all that she had said—all that she had said to Dwight, and also all that she had said to her mother. She went to bed, and on this night she slept soundly.

And later, much later, Mrs. Reed slept, too.

The Second Choice

Theodore Dreiser

SHIRLEY DEAR:

You don't want the letters. There are only six of them, anyhow, and think, they're all I have of you to cheer me on my travels. What good would they be to you—little bits of notes telling me you're sure to meet me—but me—think of me! If I send them to you, you'll tear them up, whereas if you leave them with me I can dab them with musk and ambergis and keep them in a little silver box, always beside me.

Ah, Shirley dear, you really don't know how sweet I think you are, how dear! There isn't a thing we have ever done together that isn't as clear in my mind as this great big skyscraper over the way here in Pittsburgh, and far more pleasing. In fact, my thoughts of you are the most precious and delicious things I have, Shirley.

But I'm too young to marry now. You know that, Shirley, don't you? I haven't placed myself in any way yet, and I'm so restless that I don't know whether I ever will, really. Only yesterday, old Roxbaum—that's my new employer here—came to me and wanted to know if I would like an assistant overseership on one of his coffee plantations in Java, said there would not be much money in it for a year or two, a bare living, but later there would be more—and I jumped at it. Just the thought of Java and going there did that, although I knew I could make more staying right here. Can't you see how it is with me, Shirl? I'm too restless and too young. I couldn't take care of you right, and you wouldn't like me after a while if I didn't.

But ah, Shirley sweet, I think the dearest things of you! There isn't an hour, it seems, but some little bit of you comes back—a dear, sweet, bit—the night we sat on the grass in Tregore Park and counted the stars through the trees; that first evening at Sparrows Point when we missed the last train and had to walk to Langley. Remember the tree-toads, Shirl? And then that warm April Sunday in Atholby woods! Ah, Shirl, you don't want the six notes! Let me keep them. But think of me, will you, sweet, wherever you go and whatever you do? I'll always think of you, and wish that you had met a better, saner man than me, and that I really could have married you and been all you wanted me to be. By-by, sweet. I may start for

129

Java within the month. If so, and you would want them, I'll
send you some cards from there if they have any.

Your worthless
ARTHUR

She sat and turned the letter in her hand, dumb with
despair. It was the very last letter she would ever get from
him. Of that she was certain. He was gone now, once and for
all. She had written him only once, not making an open plea
but asking him to return her letters, and then there had come
this tender but evasive reply, saying nothing of a possible return but desiring to keep her letters for old times' sake—the
happy hours they had spent together.

The happy hours! Oh, yes, yes, yes—the happy hours!

In her memory now, as she sat here in her home after the
day's work, meditating on all that had been in the few short
months since he had come and gone, was a world of color
and light—a color and light so transfiguring as to seem celestial, but now, alas, wholly dissipated. It had contained so
much of all she had desired—love, romance, amusement,
laughter. He had been so gay and thoughtless, or headstrong,
so youthfully romantic, and with such a love of play and
change and to be saying and doing anything and everything.
Arthur could dance in a gay way, whistle, sing after a fashion, play. He could play cards and do tricks, and he had such
a superior air, so genial and brisk, with a kind of innate
courtesy in it and yet an intolerance for slowness and stodg-
iness or anything dull or dingy, such as characterized—but
here her thoughts fled from him. She refused to think of any
one but Arthur.

Sitting in her little bedroom now, off the parlor on the
ground floor in her home in Bethune Street, and looking out
over the Kessels' yard, and beyond that—there being no
fences in Bethune Street—over the "yards" or lawns of the
Pollards, Bakers, Cryders, and others, she thought of how
dull it must all have seemed to him, with his fine imaginative
mind and experiences, his love of change and gaiety, his atmosphere of something better than she had ever known. How
little she had been fitted, perhaps, by beauty or temperament
to overcome this—the something—dullness in her work or
her home, which possibly had driven him away. For, although many had admired her to date, and she was young
and pretty in her simple way and constantly receiving sugges-

tions that her beauty was disturbing to some, still, he had not cared for her—he had gone.

And now, as she meditated, it seemed that this scene, and all that it stood for—her parents, her work, her daily shuttling to and fro between the drug company for which she worked and this street and house—was typical of her life and what she was destined to endure always. Some girls were so much more fortunate. They had fine clothes, fine homes, a world of pleasure and opportunity in which to move. They did not have to scrimp and save and work to pay their own way. And yet she had always been compelled to do it, but had never complained until now—or until he came, and after. Bethune Street, with its commonplace front yards and houses nearly all alike, and this house, so like the others, room for room and porch for porch, and her parents, too, really like all the others, had seemed good enough, quite satisfactory, indeed, until then. But now, now!

Here, in their kitchen, was her mother, a thin, pale, but kindly woman, peeling potatoes and washing lettuce, and putting a bit of steak or a chop or a piece of liver in a frying pan day after day, morning and evening, month after month, year after year. And next door was Mrs. Kessel doing the same thing. And next door Mrs. Cryder. And next door Mrs. Pollard. But, until now, she had not thought it so bad. But now—now—oh! And on all the porches or lawns all along this street were the husbands and fathers, mostly middle-aged or old men like her father, reading their papers or cutting the grass before dinner, or smoking and meditating afterward. Her father was out in front now, a stooped, forebearing, meditative soul, who had rarely anything to say—leaving it all to his wife, her mother, but who was fond of her in his dull, quiet way. He was a pattern-maker by trade, and had come into possession of this small, ordinary home via years of toil and saving, her mother helping him. They had no particular religion, as he often said, thinking reasonably human conduct a sufficient passport to heaven, but they had gone occasionally to the Methodist Church over in Nicholas Street, and she had once joined it. But of late she had not gone, weaned away by the other commonplace pleasures of her world.

And then in the midst of it, the dull drift of things, as she now saw them to be, he had come—Arthur Bristow—young, energetic, good-looking, ambitious, dreamful, and instanter, and with her never knowing quite how, the whole thing had been changed. He had appeared so swiftly—out of nothing, as it were.

Previous to him had been Barton Williams, stout, phlegmatic, good-natured, well-meaning, who was, or had been before Arthur came, asking her to marry him, and whom she allowed to half assume that she would. She had liked him in a feeble, albeit, as she thought, tender way, thinking him the kind, according to the logic of her neighborhood, who would make her a good husband, and, until Arthur appeared on the scene, had really intended to marry him. It was not really a love-match, as she saw now, but she thought it was, which was much the same thing, perhaps. But, as she now recalled, when Arthur came, how the scales fell from her eyes! In a trice, as it were, nearly, there was a new heaven and a new earth. Arthur had arrived, and with him a sense of something different.

Mabel Gove had asked her to come over to her house in Westleigh, the adjoining suburb, for Thanksgiving eve and day, and without a thought of anything, and because Barton was busy handling a part of the work in the despatcher's office of the Great Eastern and could not see her, she had gone. And then, to her surprise and strange, almost ineffable delight, the moment she had seen him, he was there—Arthur, with his slim, straight figure and dark hair and eyes and clean-cut features, as clean and attractive as those of a coin. And as he had looked at her and smiled and narrated humorous bits of things that had happened to him, something had come over her—a spell—and after dinner they had all gone round to Edith Barringer's to dance, and there as she had danced with him, somehow, without any seeming boldness on his part, he had taken possession of her, as it were, drawn her close, and told her she had beautiful eyes and hair and such a delicately rounded chin, and that he thought she danced gracefully and was sweet. She had nearly fainted with delight.

"Do you like me?" he had asked in one place in the dance, and, in spite of herself, she had looked up into his eyes, and from that moment she was almost mad over him, could think of nothing else but his hair and eyes and his smile and graceful figure.

Mabel Gove had seen it all, in spite of her determination that no one should, and on their going to bed later, back at Mabel's home, she had whispered:

"Ah, Shirley, I saw. You like Arthur, don't you?"

"I think he's very nice," Shirley recalled replying, for Mabel knew of her affair with Barton and liked him, "but I'm not crazy over him." And for this bit of treason she had sighed in her dreams nearly all night.

And the next day, true to a request and a promise made by him, Arthur had called again at Mabel's to take her and Mabel to a "movie" which was not so far away, and from there they had gone to an ice-cream parlor, and during it all, when Mabel was not looking, he had squeezed her arm and hand and kissed her neck, and she had held her breath, and her heart had seemed to stop.

"And now you're going to let me come out to your place to see you, aren't you?" he had whispered.

And she had replied, "Wednesday evening," and then written the address on a little piece of paper and given it to him.

But now it was all gone, gone!

This house, which now looked so dreary—how romantic it had seemed that first night *he* called—the front room with its commonplace furniture, and later in the spring, the veranda, with its vines just sprouting, and the moon in May. Oh, the moon in May, and June and July, when he was here! How she had lied to Barton to make evenings for Arthur, and occasionally to Arthur to keep him from contact with Barton. She had not even mentioned Barton to Arthur because—because—well, because Arthur was so much better, and somehow (she admitted it to herself now) she had not been sure that Arthur would care for her long, if at all, and then—well, and then, to be quite frank, Barton might be good enough. She did not exactly hate him because she had found Arthur—not at all. She still liked him in a way—he was so kind and faithful, so very dull and straightforward and thoughtful of her, which Arthur was certainly not. Before Arthur had appeared, as she well remembered, Barton had seemed to be plenty good enough—in fact, all that she desired in a pleasant, companionable way, calling for her, taking her places, bringing her flowers and candy, which Arthur rarely did, and for that, if nothing more, she could not help continuing to like him and to feel sorry for him, and besides, as she had admitted to herself before, if Arthur left her— . . . Weren't his parents better off than hers—and hadn't he a good position for such a man as he—one hundred and fifty dollars a month and the certainty of more later on? A little while before meeting Arthur, she had thought this very good, enough for two to live on at least, and she had thought some of trying it at some time or other—but now—now—

And that first night he had called—how well she remembered it—how it had transfigured the parlor next this in which she was now, filling it with something it had never had before, and the porch outside, too, for that matter, with its gaunt, leafless vine, and this street, too, even—dull, commonplace Bethune Street. There had been a flurry of snow during the afternoon while she was working at the store, and the ground was white with it. All the neighboring homes seemed to look sweeter and happier and more inviting than ever they had as she came past them, with their lights peeping from under curtains and drawn shades. She had hurried into hers and lighted the big red-shaded parlor lamp, her one artistic treasure, as she thought, and put it near the piano, between it and the window, and arranged the chairs, and then bustled to the task of making herself as pleasing as she might. For him she had gotten out her one best filmy house dress and done up her hair in the fashion she thought most becoming—and that he had not seen before—and powdered her cheeks and nose and darkened her eyelashes, as some of the girls at the store did, and put on her new gray satin slippers, and then, being so arrayed, waited nervously, unable to eat anything or to think of anything but him.

And at last, just when she had begun to think he might not be coming, he had appeared with that arch smile and a "Hello! It's here you live, is it? I was wondering. George, but you're twice as sweet as I thought you were, aren't you?" And then, in the little entryway, behind the closed door, he had held her and kissed her on the mouth a dozen times while she pretended to push against his coat and struggle and say that her parents might hear.

And, oh, the room afterward, with him in it in the red glow of the lamp, and with his pale handsome face made handsomer thereby, as she thought! He had made her sit near him and had held her hands and told her about his work and his dreams—all that he expected to do in the future—and then she had found herself wishing intensely to share just such a life—his life—anything that he might wish to do; only, she kept wondering, with a slight pain, whether he would want her to—he was so young, dreamful, ambitious, much younger and more dreamful than herself, although, in reality, he was several years older.

And then followed that glorious period from December to this late September, in which everything which was worth happening in love had happened. Oh, those wondrous days the following spring, when, with the first burst of buds and leaves, he had taken her one Sunday to Atholby, where all the great woods were, and they had hunted spring beauties in the grass, and sat on a slope and looked at the river below and watched some boys fixing up a sailboat and setting forth in it quite as she wished she and Arthur might be doing—going somewhere together—far, far away from all commonplace things and life! And then he had slipped his arm about her and kissed her cheek and neck, and tweaked her ear and smoothed her hair—and oh, there on the grass, with the spring flowers about her and a canopy of small green leaves above, the perfection of love had come—love so wonderful that the mere thought of it made her eyes brim now! And then had been days, Saturday afternoons and Sundays, at Atholby and Sparrows Point, where the great beach was, and in lovely Tregore Park, a mile or two from her home, where they could go of an evening and sit in or near the pavilion and have ice-cream and dance or watch the dancers. Oh, the stars, the winds, the summer breath of those days! Ah, me! Ah, me!

Naturally, her parents had wondered from the first about her and Arthur, and her and Barton, since Barton had already assumed a proprietary interest in her and she had seemed to like him. But then she was an only child and a pet, and used to presuming on that, and they could not think of saying anything to her. After all, she was young and pretty and was entitled to change her mind; only, only—she had had to indulge in a career of lying and subterfuge in connection with Barton, since Arthur was headstrong and wanted every evening that he chose—to call for her at the store and keep her downtown to dinner and a show.

Arthur had never been like Barton, shy, phlegmatic, obedient, waiting long and patiently for each little favor, but, instead, masterful and eager, rifling her of kisses and caresses and every delight of love, and teasing and playing with her as a cat would a mouse. She could never resist him. He demanded of her her time and her affection without let or hindrance. He was not exactly selfish or cruel, as some might have been, but gay and unthinking at times, unconsciously so, and yet loving and tender at others—nearly always so. But always he would talk of things in the future as if they really did not include her—and this troubled her greatly—of places he might go, things he might do, which, somehow, he seemed to think or assume that she could not or would not do with him. He was always going to Australia sometime, he thought, in a business way, or to South Africa, or possibly to India. He never seemed to have any fixed clear future for himself in mind.

A dreadful sense of helplessness and of impending disaster came over her at these times, of being involved in some predicament over which she had no control, and which would lead her on to some sad end. Arthur, although plainly in love, as she thought, and apparently delighted with her, might not always love her. She began, timidly at first (and always, for that matter), to ask him pretty, seeking questions about himself and her, whether their future was certain to be together, whether he really wanted her—loved her—whether he might not want to marry some one else or just her, and whether she wouldn't look nice in a pearl satin wedding-dress with a long creamy veil and satin slippers and a bouquet of bridalwreath. She had been so slowly but surely saving to that end, even before he came, in connection with Barton; only, after *he* came, all thought of the import of it had been transferred to him. But now, also, she was beginning to ask herself sadly, "Would it ever be?" He was so airy, so inconsequential, so ready to say: "Yes, yes," and "Sure, sure! that's right! Yes, indeedy; you bet! Say, kiddie, but you'll look sweet!" but, somehow, it had always seemed as if this whole thing were a glorious interlude and that it could not last. Arthur was too gay and ethereal and too little settled in his own mind. His ideas of travel and living in different cities, finally winding up in New York or San Francisco, but never with her exactly until she asked him, were too ominous, although he always reassured her gaily: "Of course! Of course!" But somehow she could never believe it really, and it made her intensely sad at times, horribly gloomy. So often she wanted to cry, and she could scarcely tell why.

And then, because of her affection for him, she had finally quarreled with Barton, or nearly that, if one could say that one ever really quarreled with him. It had been because of a certain Thursday evening a few weeks before about which she had disappointed him. In a fit of generosity, knowing that Arthur was coming Wednesday, and because Barton had stopped in at the store to see her, she had told him that he might come, having regretted it afterwards, so enamored was she of Arthur. And then when Wednesday came, Arthur had changed his mind, telling her he would come Friday instead, but on Thursday evening he had stopped in at the store and

THE SECOND CHOICE 137

asked her to go to Sparrows Point, with the result that she had no time to notify Barton. He had gone to the house and sat with her parents until ten-thirty, and then, a few days later, although she had written him offering an excuse, had called at the store to complain slightly.

"Do you think you did just right, Shirley? You might have sent word, mightn't you? Who was it—the new fellow you won't tell me about?"

Shirley flared on the instant.

"Supposing it was? What's it to you? I don't belong to you yet, do I? I told you there wasn't any one, and I wish you'd let me alone about that. I couldn't help it last Thursday— that's all—and I don't want you to be fussing with me—that's all. If you don't want to, you needn't come any more, any-how."

"Don't say that, Shirley," pleaded Barton. "You don't mean that. I won't bother you, though, if you don't want me any more."

And because Shirley sulked, not knowing what else to do, he had gone and she had not seen him since.

And then sometime later when she had thus broken with Barton, avoiding the railway station where he worked, Arthur had failed to come at his appointed time, sending no word until the next day, when a note came to the store saying that he had been out of town for his firm over Sunday and had not been able to notify her, but that he would call Tuesday. It was an awful blow. At the time, Shirley had a vision of what was to follow. It seemed for the moment as if the whole world had suddenly been reduced to ashes, that there was nothing but black charred cinders anywhere—she felt that about all life. Yet, it all came to her clearly then that this was but the beginning of just such days and just such excuses, and that soon, soon, he would come no more. He was begin-ning to be tired of her and soon he would not even make ex-cuses. She felt it, and it froze and terrified her.

And then, soon after, the indifference which she feared did follow—almost created by her own thoughts, as it were. First, it was a meeting he had to attend somewhere one Wednesday night when he was to have come for her. Then he was going out of town again, over Sunday. Then he was going away for a whole week—it was absolutely unavoidable, he said, his commercial duties were increasing—and once he had casually remarked that nothing could stand in the way where she was concerned—never! She did not think of reproaching him with this; she was too proud. If he was going, he must go. She would not be willing to say to herself that she had ever attempted to hold any man. But, just the same, she was agonized by the thought. When he was with her, he seemed tender enough; only, at times, his eyes wandered and he seemed slightly bored. Other girls, particularly pretty ones, seemed to interest him as much as she did.

And the agony of the long days when he did not come any more for a week or two at a time! The waiting, the brooding, the wondering, at the store and here in her home—in the former place making mistakes at times because she could not get her mind off him and being reminded of them, and here at her own home at nights, being so absent-minded that her parents remarked on it. She felt sure that her parents must be noticing that Arthur was not coming any more, or as much as he had—for she pretended to be going out with him, going to Mabel Gove's instead—and that Barton had deserted her too, he having been driven off by her indifference, never to come any more, perhaps, unless she sought him out.

And then it was that the thought of saving her own face by taking up with Barton once more occurred to her, of using him and his affections and faithfulness and dullness, if you will, to cover up her own dilemma. Only, this ruse was not to be tried until she had written Arthur this one letter—a pretext merely to see if there was a single ray of hope, a letter to be written in a gentle-enough way and asking for the return of the few notes she had written him. She had not seen him now in nearly a month, and the last time she had, he had said he might soon be compelled to leave her awhile—to go to Pittsburgh to work. And it was his reply to this that she now held in her hand—from Pittsburgh! It was frightful! The future without him!

But Barton would never know really what had transpired, if she went back to him. In spite of all her delicious hours with Arthur, she could call him back, she felt sure. She had never really entirely dropped him, and he knew it. He had bored her dreadfully on occasion, arriving on off days when Arthur was not about, with flowers or candy, or both, and sitting on the porch steps and talking of the railroad business and of the whereabouts and doings of some of their old friends. It was shameful, she had thought at times, to see a man so patient, so hopeful, so good-natured as Barton, deceived in this way, and by her, who was so miserable over another. Her parents must see and know, she had thought at these times, but still, what else was she to do?

"I'm a bad girl," she kept telling herself. "I'm all wrong. What right have I to offer Barton what is left?" But still, somehow, she realized that Barton, if she chose to favor him, would only be too grateful for even the leavings of others where she was concerned, and that even yet, if she but deigned to crook a finger, she could have him. He was so simple, so good-natured, so stolid and matter of fact, so different to Arthur whom (she could not help smiling at the thought of it) she was loving now about as Barton loved her—slavishly, hopelessly.

And then, as the days passed and Arthur did not write any more—just this one brief note—she at first grieved horribly, and then in a fit of numb despair attempted, bravely enough from one point of view, to adjust herself to the new situation. Why should she despair? Why die of agony where there were plenty who would still sigh for her—Barton among others? She was young, pretty, very—many told her so. She could, if she chose, achieve a vivacity which she did not feel. Why should she brook this unkindness without a thought of retaliation? Why shouldn't she enter upon a gay and heartless career, indulging in a dozen flirtations at once—dancing and killing all thoughts of Arthur in a round of frivolities? There were many who beckoned to her. She stood at her counter in the drug store on many a day and brooded over this, but at the thought of which one to begin with, she faltered. After her late love, all were so tame, for the present anyhow.

And then—and then—always there was Barton, the humble or faithful, to whom she had been so unkind and whom she had used and whom she still really liked. So often self-reproaching thoughts in connection with him crept over her. He must have known, must have seen how badly she was using him all this while, and yet he had not failed to come and come, until she had actually quarreled with him, and any one would have seen that it was literally hopeless. She could not help remembering, especially now in her pain, that he adored her. He was not calling on her now at all—by her indifference she had finally driven him away—but a word, a word—she waited for days, weeks, hoping against hope, and then—

The office of Barton's superior in the Great Eastern terminal had always made him an easy object for her blandishments, coming and going, as she frequently did, via this very station. He was in the office of the assistant train-despatcher on the ground floor, where passing to and from the local, which, at times, was quicker than a street-car, she could easily see him by peering in; only, she had carefully avoided him for nearly a year. If she chose now, and would call for a message blank at the adjacent telegraph-window which was a part of his room, and raised her voice as she often had in the past, he could scarcely fail to hear, if he did not see her. And if he did, he would rise and come over—of that she was sure, for he never could resist her. It had been a wile of hers in the old days to do this or to make her presence felt by idling outside. After a month of brooding, she felt that she must act—her position as a deserted girl was too much. She could not stand it any longer really—the eyes of her mother, for one.

It was six-fifteen one evening when, coming out of the store in which she worked, she turned her step disconsolately homeward. Her heart was heavy, her face rather pale and drawn. She had stopped in the store's retiring-room before coming out to add to her charms as much as possible by a little powder and rouge and to smooth her hair. It would not take much to reallure her former sweetheart, she felt sure— and yet it might not be so easy after all. Suppose he had found another? But she could not believe that. It had scarcely been long enough since he had last attempted to see her, and he was really so very, very fond of her and so faithful. He was too slow and certain in his choosing—he had been so with her. Still, who knows? With this thought, she went forward in the evening, feeling for the first time the shame and pain that comes of deception, the agony of having to relinquish an ideal and the feeling of despair that comes to those who find themselves in the position of suppliants, stooping to something which in better days and better fortune they would not know. Arthur was the cause of this.

When she reached the station, the crowd that usually filled it at this hour was swarming. There were so many pairs like Arthur and herself laughing and hurrying away or so she felt. First glancing in the small mirror of a weighing scale to see if she were still of her former charm, she stopped thoughtfully at a little flower stand which stood outside, and for a few pennies purchased a tiny bunch of violets. She then went inside and stood near the window, peering first furtively to see if he were present. He was. Bent over his work, a green shade over his eyes, she could see his solid genial figure at a table. Stepping back a moment to ponder, she finally went forward and, in a clear voice asked.

"May I have a blank, please?"

The infatuation of the discarded Barton was such that it brought him instantly to his feet. In his stodgy, stocky way he rose, his eyes glowing with a friendly hope, his mouth wreathed in smiles, and came over. At the sight of her, pale, but pretty—paler and prettier, really, than he had ever seen her—he thrilled dumbly.

"How are you, Shirley?" he asked sweetly, as he drew near, his eyes searching her face hopefully. He had not seen her for so long that he was intensely hungry, and her paler beauty appealed to him more than ever. Why wouldn't she have him? he was asking himself. Why wouldn't his persistent love yet win her? Perhaps it might. "I haven't seen you in a month of Sundays, it seems. How are the folks?"

"They're all right, Bart," she smiled archly, "and so am I. How have you been? It has been a long time since I've seen you. I've been wondering how you were. Have you been all right? I was just going to send a message."

As he had approached, Shirley had pretended at first not to see him, a moment later to affect surprise, although she was really suppressing a heavy sigh. The sight of him, after Arthur, was not reassuring. Could she really interest herself in him any more? Could she?

"Sure, sure," he replied genially; "I'm always all right. You couldn't kill me, you know. Not going away, are you, Shirl?" he queried interestedly.

"No; I'm just telegraphing to Mabel. She promised to meet me to-morrow, and I want to be sure she will."

"You don't come past here as often as you did, Shirley," he complained tenderly. "At least, I don't seem to see you so often," he added with a smile. "It isn't anything I have done, is it?" he queried, and then, when she protested quickly, added: "What's the trouble, Shirl? Haven't been sick, have you?"

She affected all her old gaiety and ease, feeling as though she would like to cry.

"Oh, no," she returned; "I've been all right. I've been going through the other door, I suppose, or coming in and going out on the Langdon Avenue car." (This was true, because she had been wanting to avoid him.) "I've been in such a hurry, most nights, and I haven't had time to stop, Bart. You know how late the store keeps us at times."

He remembered, too, that in the old days she had made time to stop or meet him occasionally.

"Yes, I know," he said tactfully. "But you haven't been to any of our old card-parties either of late, have you? At least, I haven't seen you. I've gone to two or three, thinking you might be there."

That was another thing Arthur had done—broken up her interest in these old store and neighborhood parties and a banjo-and-mandolin club to which she had once belonged. They had all seemed so pleasing and amusing in the old days, but now. . . . In those days Bart had been her usual companion when his work permitted.

"No," she replied evasively, but with a forced air of pleasant remembrance; "I have often thought of how much fun we had at those, though. It was a shame to drop them. You haven't seen Harry Stull or Trina Trask recently, have you?" she inquired, more to be saying something than for any interest she felt.

He shook his head negatively, then added:

"Yes, I did, too; here in the waiting-room a few nights ago. They were coming down-town to a theater, I suppose."

His face fell slightly as he recalled how it had been their custom to do this, and what their one quarrel had been about. Shirley noticed it. She felt the least bit sorry for him, but much more for herself, coming back so disconsolately to all this.

"Well, you're looking as pretty as ever, Shirley," he continued, noting that she had not written the telegram and that there was something wistful in her glance. "Prettier, I think," and she smiled sadly. Every word that she tolerated from him was as so much gold to him, so much of dead ashes to her. "You wouldn't like to come down some evening this week and see 'The Mouse-Trap,' would you? We haven't been to a threater together in I don't know when." His eyes sought hers in a hopeful, doglike way.

So—she could have him again—that was the pity of it! To have what she really did not want, did not care for! At the least nod now he would come, and this very devotion made it all but worthless, and so sad. She ought to marry him now for certain, if she began in this way, and could in a month's time if she chose, but oh, oh—could she? For the moment she decided that she could not, would not. If he had only re-

pulsed her—told her to go—ignored her—but no; it was her
fate to be loved by him in this moving, pleading way, and
hers not to love him as she wished to love—to be loved.
Plainly, he needed some one like her, whereas, she, she—She
turned a little sick, a sense of the sacrilege of gaiety at this
time creeping into her voice, and exclaimed:

"No, no!" Then seeing his face change, a heavy sadness
come over it, "Not this week, anyhow, I mean" ("Not so
soon," she had almost said). "I have several engagements this
week and I'm not feeling well. But"—seeing his face change,
and the thought of her own state returning—"you might
come out to the house some evening instead, and then we can
go some other time."

His face brightened intensely. It was wonderful how he
longed to be with her, how the least favor from her comforted and lifted him up. She could see also now, however, how
little it meant to her, how little it could ever mean, even if to
him it was heaven. The old relationship would have to be
resumed in toto, once and for all, but did she want it that
way now that she was feeling so miserable about this other
affair? As she meditated, these various moods racing to and
fro in her mind, Barton seemed to notice, and now it occurred to him that perhaps he had not pursued her enough—
was too easily put off. She probably did like him yet. This
evening, her present visit, seemed to prove it.

"Sure, sure!" he agreed. "I'd like that. I'll come out Sunday, if you say. We can go any time to the play. I'm sorry,
Shirley, if you're not feeling well. I've thought of you a lot
these days. I'll come out Wednesday, if you don't mind."

She smiled a wan smile. It was all so much easier than
she had expected—her triumph—and so ashenlike in conse-
quence, a flavor of dead-sea fruit and defeat about it all, that
it was pathetic. How could she, after Arthur? How could he,
really?

"Make it Sunday," she pleaded, naming the farthest day
off, and then hurried out.

Her faithful lover gazed after her, while she suffered an intense nausea. To think—to think—it should all be coming to
this! She had not used her telegraph-blank, and now had forgotten all about it. It was not the simple trickery that discouraged her, but her own future which could find no better
outlet than this, could not rise above it apparently, or that she
had no heart to make it rise above it. Why couldn't she interest herself in some one different to Barton? Why did she have

to return to him? Why not wait and meet some other—ignore him as before? But no, no; nothing mattered now—no one—it might as well be Barton as any one, and she would at least make him happy and at the same time solve her own problem. She went out into the train-shed and climbed into her train. Slowly, after the usual pushing and jostling of a crowd, it drew out toward Latonia, that suburban region in which her home lay. As she rode, she thought.

"What have I just done? What am I doing?" she kept asking herself as the clacking wheels on the rails fell into a rhythmic dance and the houses of the brown, dry, endless city fled past in a maze. "Severing myself decisively from the past—the happy past—for supposing, once I am married, Arthur should return and want me again—suppose! Suppose!"

Below at one place, under a shed, were some market-gardeners disposing of the last remnants of their day's wares—a sickly, dull life, she thought. Here was Rutgers Avenue, with its line of red street-cars, many wagons and tracks and counterstreams of automobiles—how often had she passed it morning and evening in a shuttle-like way, and how often would, unless she got married! And here, now, was the river flowing smoothly between its banks lined with coal-pockets and wharves—away, away to the huge deep sea which she and Arthur had enjoyed so much. Oh, to be in a small boat and drift out, out into the endless, restless, pathless deep! Somehow the sight of this water, to-night and every night, brought back those evenings in the open with Arthur at Sparrows Point, the long line of dancers in Eckert's Pavilion, the woods at Atholby, the park, with the dancers in the pavilion—she choked back a sob. Once Arthur had come this way with her on just such an evening as this, pressing her hand and saying how wonderful she was. Oh, Arthur! Arthur! And now Barton was to take his old place again—forever, no doubt. She could not trifle with her life longer in this foolish way, or his. What was the use? But think of it!

Yes, it must be—forever now, she told herself. She must marry. Time would be slipping by and she would become too old. It was her only future—marriage. It was the only future she had ever contemplated really, a home, children, the love of some man whom she could love as she loved Arthur. Ah, what a happy home that would have been for her! But now, now—

But there must be no turning back now, either. There was no other way. If Arthur ever came back—but fear not, he wouldn't! She had risked so much and lost—lost him. Her little venture into true love had been such a failure. Before Arthur had come all had been well enough. Barton, stout and simple and frank and direct, had in some way—how, she could scarcely realize now—offered sufficient of a future. But now, now! He had enough money, she knew, to build a cottage for the two of them. He had told her so. He would do his best always to make her happy, she was sure of that. They could live in about the state her parents were living in—or a little better, not much—and would never want. No doubt there would be children, because he craved them—several of them—and that would take up her time, long years of it—the sad, gray years! But then Arthur, whose children she would have thrilled to bear, would be no more, a mere memory—think of that!—and Barton, the dull, the commonplace, would have achieved his finest dream—and why?

Because love was a failure for her—that was why—and in her life there would be no more true love. She would never love any one again as she had Arthur. It could not be, she was sure of it. He was too fascinating, too wonderful. Always, always, wherever she might be, whoever she might marry, he would be coming back, intruding between her and any possible love, receiving any possible kiss. It would be Arthur she would be loving or kissing. She dabbed at her eyes with a tiny handkerchief, turned her face close to the window and stared out, and then as the environs of Latonia came into view, wondered (so deep is romance): What if Arthur should come back at some time—or now! Supposing he should be here at the station now, accidentally or on purpose, to welcome her, to soothe her weary heart. He had met her here before. How she would fly to him, lay her head on his shoulder, forget forever that Barton ever was, that they had ever separated for an hour. Oh, Arthur! Arthur!

But no, no; here was Latonia—here the viaduct over her train, the long business street and the cars marked "Center" and "Langdon Avenue" running back into the great city. A few blocks away in treeshaded Bethune Street, duller and plainer than ever, was her parents' cottage and the routine of that old life which was now, she felt, more fully fastened upon her than ever before—the lawn-mowers, the lawns, the front porches all alike. Now would come the going to and fro of Barton to business as her father and she now went to business, her keeping house, cooking, washing, ironing, sewing for Barton as her mother now did these things for her father and herself. And she would not be in love really, as she wanted to be. Oh, dreadful! She could never escape it really, now that she could endure it less, scarcely for another hour. And yet she must, must, for the sake of—for the sake of— she closed her eyes and dreamed.

She walked up the street under the trees, past the houses and lawns all alike to her own, and found her father on their veranda reading the evening paper. She sighed at the sight.

"Back, daughter?" he called pleasantly.

"Yes."

"Your mother is wondering if you would like steak or liver for dinner. Better tell her."

"Oh, it doesn't matter."

She hurried into her bedroom, threw down her hat and gloves, and herself on the bed to rest silently, and groaned in her soul. To think that it had all come to this!—Never to see him any more!—To see only Barton, and marry him and live in such a street, have four or five children, forget all her youthful companionships—and all to save her face before her parents, and her future. Why must it be? Should it be, really? She choked and stifled. After a little time her mother, hearing her come in, came to the door—thin, practical, affectionate, conventional.

"What's wrong, honey? Aren't you feeling well tonight? Have you a headache? Let me feel."

Her thin cool fingers crept over her temples and hair. She suggested something to eat or a headache powder right away.

"I'm all right, mother. I'm just not feeling well now. Don't bother. I'll get up soon. Please don't."

"Would you rather have liver or steak to-night, dear?"

"Oh, anything—nothing—please don't bother—steak will do—anything"—if only she could get rid of her and be at rest.

Her mother looked at her and shook her head sympathetically, then retreated quietly, saying no more. Lying so, she thought and thought—grinding, destroying thoughts about the beauty of the past, the darkness of the future—until able to endure them no longer she got up and, looking distractedly out of the window into the yard and the house next door, stared at her future fixedly. What should she do? What should she really do? There was Mrs. Kessel in her kitchen getting her dinner as usual, just as her own mother was now, and Mr. Kessel out on the front porch in his shirt-sleeves reading the evening paper. Beyond was Mr. Pollard in his yard, cutting the grass. All along Bethune Street were such houses and such people—simple, commonplace souls all— clerks, managers, fairly successful craftsmen, like her father and Barton, excellent in their way but not like Arthur the beloved, the lost—and here was she, perforce, or by decision of necessity, soon to be one of them, in some such street as this no doubt, forever and—. For the moment it choked and stifled her.

She decided that she would not. No, no, no! There must be some other way—many ways. She did not have to do this unless she really wished to—would not—only—. Then going to the mirror she looked at her face and smoothed her hair.

"But what's the use?" she asked herself wearily and resignedly after a time. "Why should I cry? Why shouldn't I marry Barton? I don't amount to anything, anyhow. Arthur wouldn't have me. I wanted him, and I am compelled to take some one else—or no one—what difference does it really make who? My dreams are too high, that's all. I wanted Arthur, and he wouldn't have me. I don't want Barton, and he crawls at my feet. I'm a failure, that's what's the matter with me."

And then, turning up her sleeves and removing a fichu which stood out too prominently from her breast, she went into the kitchen and looking about for an apron, observed:

"Can't I help? Where's the tablecloth?" and finding it among napkins and silverware in a drawer in the adjoining room, proceeded to set the table.

Mother

Sherwood Anderson

Elizabeth Willard, the mother of George Willard, was tall and gaunt and her face was marked with smallpox scars. Although she was but forty-five, some obscure disease had taken the fire out of her figure. Listlessly she went about the disorderly old hotel looking at the faded wall-paper and the ragged carpets and, when she was able to be about, doing the work of a chambermaid among beds soiled by the slumbers of fat traveling men. Her husband, Tom Willard, a slender, graceful man with square shoulders, a quick military step, and a black mustache trained to turn sharply up at the ends, tried to put the wife out of his mind. The presence of the tall ghostly figure, moving slowly through the halls, he took as a reproach to himself. When he thought of her he grew angry and swore. The hotel was unprofitable and forever on the edge of failure and he wished himself out of it. He thought of the old house and the woman who lived there with him as things defeated and done for. The hotel in which he had begun life so hopefully was now a mere ghost of what a hotel should be. As he went spruce and business-like through the streets of Winesburg, he sometimes stopped and turned quickly about as though fearing that the spirit of the hotel and of the woman would follow him even into the streets. "Damn such a life, damn it!" he sputtered aimlessly.

Tom Willard had a passion for village politics and for years had been the leading Democrat in a strongly Republican community. Some day, he told himself, the tide of things political will turn in my favor and the years of ineffectual service count big in a bestowal of rewards. He dreamed of going to Congress and even of becoming governor. Once when a younger member of the party arose at a political conference and began to boast of his faithful service, Tom Willard grew white with fury. "Shut up, you," he roared, glaring about. "What do you know of service? What are you but a boy? Look at what I've done here! I was a Democrat here in

148

Winesburg when it was a crime to be a Democrat. In the old days they fairly hunted us with guns."

Between Elizabeth and her one son George there was a deep unexpressed bond of sympathy, based on a girlhood dream that had long ago died. In the son's presence she was timid and reserved, but sometimes while he hurried about town intent upon his duties as a reporter, she went into his room and closing the door knelt by a little desk, made of a kitchen table, that sat near a window. In the room by the desk she went through a ceremony that was half a prayer, half a demand, addressed to the skies. In the boyish figure she yearned to see something half forgotten that had once been a part of herself re-created. The prayer concerned that. "Even though I die, I will in some way keep defeat from you," she cried, and so deep was her determination that her whole body shook. Her eyes glowed and she clenched her fists. "If I am dead and see him becoming a meaningless drab figure like myself, I will come back," she declared. "I ask God now to give me that privilege. I demand it. I will pay for it. God may beat me with his fists. I will take any blow that may befall if but this my boy be allowed to express something for us both." Pausing uncertainly, the woman stared about the boy's room. "And do not let him become smart and successful either," she added vaguely.

The communion between George Willard and his mother was outwardly a formal thing without meaning. When she was ill and sat by the window in her room he sometimes went in the evening to make her a visit. They sat by a window that looked over the roof of a small frame building into Main Street. By turning their heads they could see through another window, along an alleyway that ran behind the Main Street stores and into the back door of Abner Groff's bakery. Sometimes as they sat thus a picture of village life presented itself to them. At the back door of his shop appeared Abner Groff with a stick or an empty milk bottle in his hand. For a long time there was a feud between the baker and a grey cat that belonged to Sylvester West, the druggist. The boy and his mother saw the cat creep into the door of the bakery and presently emerge followed by the baker, who swore and waved his arms about. The baker's eyes were small and red and his black hair and beard were filled with flour dust. Sometimes he was so angry that, although the cat had disappeared, he hurled sticks, bits of broken glass, and even some of the tools of his trade about. Once he broke a window at the back of Sinning's Hardware Store. In the alley the grey cat crouched behind barrels filled with torn paper and broken bottles above which flew a black swarm of flies. Once when she was alone, and after watching a prolonged and ineffectual outburst on the part of the baker, Elizabeth Willard put her head down on her long white hands and wept. After that she did not look along the alleyways any more, but tried to forget the contest between the bearded man and the cat. It seemed like a rehearsal of her own life, terrible in its vividness.

In the evening when the son sat in the room with his mother, the silence made them both feel awkward. Darkness came on and the evening train came in at the station. In the street below feet tramped up and down upon a board side-walk. In the station yard, after the evening train had gone, there was a heavy silence. Perhaps Skinner Leason, the express agent, moved a truck the length of the station platform. Over on Main Street sounded a man's voice, laughing. The door of the express office banged. George Willard arose and crossing the room fumbled for the doorknob. Sometimes he knocked against a chair, making it scrape along the floor. By the window sat the sick woman, perfectly still, listless. Her long hands, white and bloodless, could be seen drooping over the ends of the arms of the chair. "I think you had better be out among the boys. You are too much indoors," she said, striving to relieve the embarrassment of the departure. "I thought I would take a walk," replied George Willard, who felt awkward and confused.

One evening in July, when the transient guests who made the New Willard House their temporary home had become scarce, and the hallways, lighted only by kerosene lamps turned low, were plunged in gloom, Elizabeth Willard had an adventure. She had been ill in bed for several days and her son had not come to visit her. She was alarmed. The feeble blaze of life that remained in her body was blown into a flame by her anxiety and she crept out of bed, dressed and hurried along the hallway toward her son's room, shaking with exaggerated fears. As she went along she steadied herself with her hand, slipped along the papered walls of the hall and breathed with difficulty. The air whistled through her teeth. As she hurried forward she thought how foolish she was. "He is concerned with boyish affairs," she told herself. "Perhaps he has now begun to walk about in the evening with girls."

Elizabeth Willard had a dread of being seen by guests in

the hotel that had once belonged to her father and the ownership of which still stood recorded in her name in the county
courthouse. The hotel was continually losing patronage because of its shabbiness and she thought of herself as also
shabby. Her own room was in an obscure corner and when
she felt able to work she voluntarily worked among the beds,
preferring the labor that could be done when the guests were
abroad seeking trade among the merchants of Winesburg.

By the door of her son's room the mother knelt upon the
floor and listened for some sound from within. When she
heard the boy moving about and talking in low tones a smile
came to her lips. George Willard had a habit of talking aloud
to himself and to hear him doing so had always given his
mother a peculiar pleasure. The habit in him, she felt,
strengthened the secret bond that existed between them. A
thousand times she had whispered to herself of the matter.
"He is groping about, trying to find himself," she thought.
"He is not a dull clod, all words and smartness. Within him
there is a secret something that is striving to grow. It is the
thing I let be killed in myself."

In the darkness in the hallway by the door the sick woman
arose and started again toward her own room. She was afraid
that the door would open and the boy come upon her. When
she had reached a safe distance and was about to turn a corner into a second hallway she stopped and bracing herself
with her hands waited, thinking to shake off a trembling fit of
weakness that had come upon her. The presence of the boy
in the room had made her happy. In her bed, during the long
hours alone, the little fears that had visited her had become
giants. Now they were all gone. "When I get back to my
room I shall sleep," she murmured gratefully.

But Elizabeth Willard was not to return to her bed and to
sleep. As she stood trembling in the darkness the door of her
son's room opened and the boy's father, Tom Willard,
stepped out. In the light that streamed out at the door he
stood with the knob in his hand and talked. What he said in-
furiated the woman.

Tom Willard was ambitious for his son. He had always
thought of himself as a successful man, although nothing he
had ever done had turned out successfully. However, when he
was out of sight of the New Willard House and had no fear
of coming upon his wife, he swaggered and began to
dramatize himself as one of the chief men of the town. He
wanted his son to succeed. He it was who had secured for the

boy the position on the *Winesburg Eagle*. Now, with a ring of earnestness in his voice, he was advising concerning some course of conduct. "I tell you what, George, you've got to wake up," he said sharply. "Will Henderson has spoken to me three times concerning the matter. He says you go along for hours not hearing when you are spoken to and acting like a gawky girl. What ails you?" Tom Willard laughed good-naturedly. "Well, I guess you'll get over it," he said. "I told Will that. You're not a fool and you're not a woman. You're Tom Willard's son and you'll wake up. I'm not afraid. What you say clears things up. If being a newspaper man had put the notion of becoming a writer into your mind that's all right. Only I guess you'll have to wake up to do that too, eh?"

Tom Willard went briskly along the hallway and down a flight of stairs to the office. The woman in the darkness could hear him laughing and talking with a guest who was striving to wear away a dull evening by dozing in a chair by the office door. She returned to the door of her son's room. The weakness had passed from her body as by a miracle and she stepped boldly along. A thousand ideas raced through her head. When she heard the scraping of a chair and the sound of a pen scratching upon paper, she again turned and went back along the hallway to her own room.

A definite determination had come into the mind of the defeated wife of the Winesburg hotel keeper. The determination was the result of long years of quiet and rather ineffectual thinking. "Now," she told herself, "I will act. There is something threatening my boy and I will ward it off." The fact that the conversation between Tom Willard and his son had been rather quiet and natural, as though an understanding existed between them, maddened her. Although for years she had hated her husband, her hatred had always before been a quite impersonal thing. He had been merely a part of something else that she hated. Now, and by the few words at the door, he had become the thing personified. In the darkness of her own room she clenched her fists and glared about. Going to a cloth bag that hung on a nail by the wall she took out a long pair of sewing scissors and held them in her hand like a dagger. "I will stab him," she said aloud. "He has chosen to be the voice of evil and I will kill him. When I have killed him something will snap within myself and I will die also. It will be a release for all of us."

In her girlhood and before her marriage with Tom Willard, Elizabeth had borne a somewhat shaky reputation in Winesburg. For years she had been what is called "stage-struck" and had paraded through the streets with traveling men guests at her father's hotel, wearing loud clothes and urging them to tell her of life in the cities out of which they had come. Once she startled the town by putting on men's clothes and riding a bicycle down Main Street.

In her own mind the tall dark girl had been in those days much confused. A great restlessness was in her and it expressed itself in two ways. First there was an uneasy desire for change, for some big definite movement to her life. It was this feeling that had turned her mind to the stage. She dreamed of joining some company and wandering over the world, seeing always new faces and giving something out of herself to all people. Sometimes at night she was quite beside herself with the thought, but when she tried to talk of the matter to the members of the theatrical companies that came to Winesburg and stopped at her father's hotel, she got nowhere. They did not seem to know what she meant, or if she did get something of her passion expressed, they only laughed. "It's not like that," they said. "It's as dull and uninteresting as this here. Nothing comes of it."

With the traveling men when she walked about with them, and later with Tom Willard, it was quite different. Always they seemed to understand and sympathize with her. On the side streets of the village, in the darkness under the trees, they took hold of her hand and she thought that something unexpressed in herself came forth and became a part of an unexpressed something in them.

And then there was the second expression of her restlessness. When that came she felt for a time released and happy. She did not blame the men who walked with her and later she did not blame Tom Willard. It was always the same, beginning with kisses and ending, after strange wild emotions, with peace and then sobbing repentance. When she sobbed she put her hand upon the face of the man and had always the same thought. Even though he were large and bearded she thought he had become suddenly a little boy. She wondered why he did not sob also.

In her room, tucked away in a corner of the old Willard House, Elizabeth Willard lighted a lamp and put it on a dressing table that stood by the door. A thought had come into her mind and she went to a closet and brought out a small square box and set it on the table. The box contained material for make-up and had been left with other things by a theatrical company that had once been stranded in Winesburg. Elizabeth Willard had decided that she would be beautiful. Her hair was still black and there was a great mass of it braided and coiled about her head. The scene that was to take place in the office began to grow in her mind. No ghostly worn-out figure should confront Tom Willard, but something quite unexpected and startling. Tall and with dusky cheeks and hair that fell in a mass from her shoulders, a figure should come striding down the stairway before the startled loungers in the hotel office. The figure would be silent—it would be swift and terrible. As a tigress whose cub had been threatened would she appear, coming out of the shadows, stealing noiselessly along and holding the long wicked scissors in her hand.

With a little broken sob in her throat, Elizabeth Willard blew out the light that stood upon the table and stood weak and trembling in the darkness. The strength that had been as a miracle in her body left and she half reeled across the floor, clutching at the back of the chair in which she had spent so many long days staring out over the tin roofs into the main street of Winesburg. In the hallway there was the sound of footsteps and George Willard came in at the door. Sitting in a chair beside his mother he began to talk. "I'm going to get out of here," he said. "I don't know where I shall go or what I shall do but I am going away."

The woman in the chair waited and trembled. An impulse came to her. "I suppose you had better wake up," she said. "You think that? You will go to the city and make money, eh? It will be better for you, you think, to be a business man, to be brisk and smart and alive?" She waited and trembled.

The son shook his head. "I suppose I can't make you understand, but oh, I wish I could," he said earnestly. "I can't even talk to father about it. I don't try. There isn't any use. I don't know what I shall do. I just want to go away and look at people and think."

Silence fell upon the room where the boy and woman sat together. Again, as on the other evenings, they were embarrassed. After a time the boy tried to talk. "I suppose it won't be for a year or two but I've been thinking about it," he said, rising and going toward the door. "Something father said makes it sure that I shall have to go away." He fumbled with the door knob. In the room the silence became unbearable to the woman. She wanted to cry out with joy because of the words that had come from the lips of her son, but the expression of joy had become impossible to her. "I think you had better go out among the boys. You are too much indoors," she said. "I thought I would go for a little walk," replied the son stepping awkwardly out of the room and closing the door.

Hills Like White Elephants

Ernest Hemingway

The hills across the valley of the Ebro were long and white. On this side there was no shade and no trees and the station was between two lines of rails in the sun. Close against the side of the station there was the warm shadow of the building and a curtain, made of strings of bamboo beads, hung across the open door into the bar, to keep out flies. The American and the girl with him sat at a table in the shade, outside the building. It was very hot and the express from Barcelona would come in forty minutes. It stopped at this junction for two minutes and went on to Madrid.

"What should we drink?" the girl asked. She had taken off her hat and put it on the table.

"It's pretty hot," the man said.

"Let's drink beer."

"Dos cervezas," the man said into the curtain.

"Big ones?" a woman asked from the doorway.

"Yes. Two big ones."

The woman brought two glasses of beer and two felt pads. She put the felt pads and the beer glasses on the table and looked at the man and the girl. The girl was looking off at the line of hills. They were white in the sun and the country was brown and dry.

"They look like white elephants," she said.

"I've never seen one," the man drank his beer.

"No, you wouldn't have."

"I might have," the man said. "Just because you say I wouldn't have doesn't prove anything."

The girl looked at the bead curtain. "They've painted something on it," she said. "What does it say?"

"Anis del Toro. It's a drink."

"Could we try it?"

The man called "Listen" through the curtain. The woman came out from the bar.

"Four reales."

"We want two Anis del Toro."

"With water?"

"Do you want it with water?"

"I don't know," the girl said. "Is it good with water?"

"It's all right."

"You want them with water?" asked the woman.

"Yes, with water."

"It tastes like licorice," the girl said and put the glass down.

"That's the way with everything."

"Yes," said the girl. "Everything tastes of licorice. Especially all the things you've waited so long for, like absinthe."

"Oh, cut it out."

"You started it," the girl said. "I was being amused. I was having a fine time."

"Well, let's try and have a fine time."

"All right. I was trying. I said the mountains looked like white elephants. Wasn't that bright?"

"That was bright."

"I wanted to try this new drink. That's all we do, isn't it—look at things and try new drinks?"

"I guess so."

The girl looked across the hills.

"They're lovely hills," she said. "They don't really look like white elephants. I just meant the coloring of their skin through the trees."

"Should we have another drink?"

"All right."

The warm wind blew the bead curtain against the table.

"The beer's nice and cool," the man said.

"It's lovely," the girl said.

"It's really an awfully simple operation, Jig," the man said. "It's not really an operation at all."

The girl looked at the ground the table legs rested on.

"I know you wouldn't mind it, Jig. It's really not anything. It's just to let the air in."

The girl did not say anything.

"I'll go with you and I'll stay with you all the time. They just let the air in and then it's all perfectly natural."

"Then what will we do afterward?"

"We'll be fine afterward. Just like we were before."

"What makes you think so?"

"That's the only thing that bothers us. It's the only thing that's made us unhappy."

The girl looked at the bead curtain, put her hand out and took hold of two of the strings of beads.

"And you think then we'll be all right and be happy."

"I know we will. You don't have to be afraid. I've known lots of people that have done it."

"So have I," said the girl. "And afterward they were all so happy."

"Well," the man said, "if you don't want to you don't have to. I wouldn't have you do it if you didn't want to. But I know it's perfectly simple."

"And you really want to?"

"I think it's the best thing to do. But I don't want you to do it if you don't really want to."

"And if I do it you'll be happy and things will be like they were and you'll love me?"

"I love you now. You know I love you."

"I know. But if I do it, then it will be nice again if I say things are like white elephants, and you'll like it?"

"I'll love it. I love it now but I just can't think about it. You know how I get when I worry."

"If I do it you won't ever worry?"

"I won't worry about that because it's perfectly simple."

"Then I'll do it. Because I don't care about me."

"What do you mean?"

"I don't care about me."

"Well, I care about you."

"Oh, yes. But I don't care about me. And I'll do it and then everything will be fine."

"I don't want you to do it if you feel that way."

The girl stood up and walked to the end of the station. Across, on the other side, were fields of grain and trees along the banks of the Ebro. Far away, beyond the river, were mountains. The shadow of a cloud moved across the field of grain and she saw the river through the trees.

"And we could have all this," she said. "And we could have everything and every day we make it more impossible."

"What did you say?"

"I said we could have everything."

"We can have everything."

"No, we can't."

"We can have the whole world."

"No, we can't."

"We can go everywhere."

"No, we can't. It isn't ours any more."

"It's ours."

"No, it isn't. And once they take it away, you never get it back."

"But they haven't taken it away."

"We'll wait and see."

"Come on back in the shade," he said. "You mustn't feel that way."

"I don't feel any way," the girl said. "I just know things."

"I don't want you to do anything that you don't want to do—"

"Nor that isn't good for me," she said. "I know. Could we have another beer?"

"All right. But you've got to realize—"

"I realize," the girl said. "Can't we maybe stop talking?"

They sat down at the table and the girl looked across at the hills on the dry side of the valley and the man looked at her and at the table.

"You've got to realize," he said, "that I don't want you to do it if you don't want to. I'm perfectly willing to go through with it if it means anything to you."

"Doesn't it mean anything to you? We could get along."

"Of course it does. But I don't want anybody but you. I don't want any one else. And I know it's perfectly simple."

"Yes, you know it's perfectly simple."

"It's all right for you to say that, but I do know it."

"Would you do something for me now?"

"I'd do anything for you."

"Would you please please please please please please please stop talking?"

He did not say anything but looked at the bags against the wall of the station. There were labels on them from all the hotels where they had spent nights.

"But I don't want you to," he said, "I don't care anything about it."

"I'll scream," the girl said.

The woman came out through the curtains with two glasses of beer and put them down on the damp felt pads. "The train comes in five minutes," she said.

"What did she say?" asked the girl.

"That the train is coming in five minutes."

The girl smiled brightly at the woman, to thank her.

"I'd better take the bags over to the other side of the station," the man said. She smiled at him.

"All right. Then come back and we'll finish the beer."

He picked up the two heavy bags and carried them around the station to the other tracks. He looked up the tracks but could not see the train. Coming back, he walked through the barroom, where people waiting for the train were drinking. He drank an Anis at the bar and looked at the people. They were all waiting reasonably for the train. He went out through the bead curtain. She was sitting at the table and smiled at him.

"Do you feel better?" he asked.

"I feel fine," she said. "There's nothing wrong with me. I feel fine."

A Rose for Emily

William Faulkner

I

When Miss Emily Grierson died, our whole town went to her funeral: the men through a sort of respectful affection for a fallen monument, the women mostly out of curiosity to see the inside of her house, which no one save an old manservant—a combined gardener and cook—had seen in at least ten years.

It was a big, squarish frame house that had once been white, decorated with cupolas and spires and scrolled balconies in the heavily lightsome style of the seventies, set on what had once been our most select street. But garages and cotton gins had encroached and obliterated even the august names of that neighborhood; only Miss Emily's house was left, lifting its stubborn and coquettish decay about the cotton wagons and the gasoline pumps—an eyesore among eyesores. And now Miss Emily had gone to join the representatives of those august names where they lay in the cedar-bemused cemetery among the ranked and anonymous graves of Union and Confederate soldiers who fell at the battle of Jefferson.

Alive, Miss Emily had been a tradition, a duty, and a care; a sort of hereditary obligation upon the town, dating from that day in 1894 when Colonel Sartoris, the mayor—he who fathered the edict that no Negro woman should appear on the streets without an apron—remitted her taxes, the dispensation dating from the death of her father on into perpetuity. Not that Miss Emily would have accepted charity. Colonel Sartoris invented an involved tale to the effect that Miss Emily's father had loaned money to the town, which the town, as a matter of business, preferred this way of repaying. Only a man of Colonel Sartoris' generation and thought could have invented it, and only a woman could have believed it.

When the next generation, with its more modern ideas, became mayors and aldermen, this arrangement created some little dissatisfaction. On the first of the year they mailed her a tax notice. February came, and there was no reply. They wrote her a formal letter, asking her to call at the sheriff's office at her convenience. A week later the mayor wrote her himself, offering to call or to send his car for her, and received in reply a note on paper of an archaic shape, in a thin, flowing calligraphy in faded ink, to the effect that she no longer went out at all. The tax notice was also enclosed, without comment.

They called a special meeting of the Board of Aldermen. A deputation waited upon her, knocked at the door through which no visitor had passed since she ceased giving china-painting lessons eight or ten years earlier. They were admitted by the old Negro into a dim hall from which a stairway mounted into still more shadow. It smelled of dust and disuse—a close, dank smell. The Negro led them into the parlor. It was furnished in heavy, leather-covered furniture. When the Negro opened the blinds of one window, they could see that the leather was cracked; and when they sat down, a faint dust rose sluggishly about their thighs, spinning with slow motes in the single sun-ray. On a tarnished gilt easel before the fireplace stood a crayon portrait of Miss Emily's father.

They rose when she entered—a small, fat woman in black, with a thin gold chain descending to her waist and vanishing into her belt, leaning on an ebony cane with a tarnished gold head. Her skeleton was small and spare; perhaps that was why what would have been merely plumpness in another was obesity in her. She looked bloated, like a body long submerged in motionless water, and of that pallid hue. Her eyes, lost in the fatty ridges of her face, looked like two small pieces of coal pressed into a lump of dough as they moved from one face to another while the visitors stated their errand.

She did not ask them to sit. She just stood in the door and listened quietly until the spokesman came to a stumbling halt. Then they could hear the invisible watch ticking at the end of the gold chain.

Her voice was dry and cold. "I have no taxes in Jefferson. Colonel Sartoris explained it to me. Perhaps one of you can gain access to the city records and satisfy yourselves."

"But we have. We are the city authorities, Miss Emily. Didn't you get a notice from the sheriff, signed by him?"

"I received a paper, yes," Miss Emily said. "Perhaps he considers himself the sheriff . . . I have no taxes in Jefferson."

"But there is nothing on the books to show that, you see. We must go by the—"

"See Colonel Sartoris. I have no taxes in Jefferson."

"But, Miss Emily—"

"See Colonel Sartoris." (Colonel Sartoris had been dead almost ten years.) "I have no taxes in Jefferson. Tobe!" The Negro appeared. "Show these gentlemen out."

II

She she vanquished them, horse and foot, just as she had vanquished their fathers thirty years before about the smell. That was two years after her father's death and a short time after her sweetheart—the one we believed would marry her—had deserted her. After her father's death she went out very little; after her sweetheart went away, people hardly saw her at all. A few of the ladies had the temerity to call, but were not received, and the only sign of life about the place was the Negro man—a young man then—going in and out with a market basket.

"Just as if a man—any man—could keep a kitchen properly," the ladies said; so they were not surprised when the smell developed. It was another link between the gross, teeming world and the high and mighty Griersons.

A neighbor, a woman, complained to the mayor, Judge Stevens, eighty years old.

"But what will you have me do about it, madam?" he said.

"Why, send her word to stop it," the woman said. "Isn't there a law?"

"I'm sure that won't be necessary," Judge Stevens said. "It's probably just a snake or a rat that nigger of hers killed in the yard. I'll speak to him about it."

The next day he received two more complaints, one from a man who came in diffident deprecation. "We really must do something about it, Judge. I'd be the last one in the world to bother Miss Emily, but we've got to do something." That night the Board of Aldermen met—three graybeards and one younger man, a member of the rising generation.

"It's simple enough," he said. "Send her word to have her place cleaned up. Give her a certain time to do it in, and if she don't . . ."

"Dammit, sir," Judge Stevens said, "will you accuse a lady to her face of smelling bad?"

So the next night, after midnight, four men crossed Miss Emily's lawn and slunk about the house like burglars, sniffing along the base of the brickwork and at the cellar openings while one of them performed a regular sowing motion with his hand out of a sack slung from his shoulder. They broke open the cellar door and sprinkled lime there, and in all the outbuildings. As they recrossed the lawn, a window that had been dark was lighted and Miss Emily sat in it, the light behind her, and her upright torso motionless as that of an idol. They crept quietly across the lawn and into the shadow of the locusts that lined the street. After a week or two the smell went away.

That was when people had began to feel really sorry for her. People in our town, remembering how old lady Wyatt, her great-aunt, had gone completely crazy at last, believed that the Griersons held themselves a little too high for what they really were. None of the young men were quite good enough for Miss Emily and such. We had long thought of them as a tableau, Miss Emily a slender figure in white in the background, her father a spraddled silhouette in the foreground, his back to her and clutching a horsewhip, the two of them framed by the back-flung front door. So when she got to be thirty and was still single, we were not pleased exactly, but vindicated; even with insanity in the family she wouldn't have turned down all of her chances if they had really materialized.

When her father died, it got about that the house was all that was left to her; and in a way, people were glad. At last they could pity Miss Emily. Being left alone, and a pauper, she had become humanized. Now she too would know the old thrill and the old despair of a penny more or less.

The day after his death all the ladies prepared to call at the house and offer condolence and aid, as is our custom. Miss Emily met them at the door, dressed as usual and with no trace of grief on her face. She told them that her father was not dead. She did that for three days, with the ministers calling on her, and the doctors, trying to persuade her to let them dispose of the body. Just as they were about to resort to law and force, she broke down, and they buried her father quickly.

We did not say she was crazy then. We believed she had to do that. We remembered all the young men her father had driven away, and we knew that with nothing left, she would have to cling to that which had robbed her, as people will.

III

She was sick for a long time. When we saw her again, her hair was cut short, making her look like a girl, with a vague resemblance to those angels in colored church windows—sort of tragic and serene.

The town had just let the contracts for paving and sidewalks, and in the summer after her father's death they began the work. The construction company came with niggers and mules and machinery, and a foreman named Homer Barron, a Yankee—a big, dark, ready man, with a big voice and eyes lighter than his face. The little boys would follow in groups to hear him cuss the niggers, and the niggers singing in time to the rise and fall of picks. Pretty soon he knew everybody in town. Whenever you heard a lot of laughing anywhere about the square, Homer Barron would be in the center of the group. Presently we began to see him and Miss Emily on Sunday afternoons driving in the yellow-wheeled buggy and the matched team of bays from the livery stable.

At first we were glad that Miss Emily would have an interest, because the ladies all said, "Of course a Grierson would not think seriously of a Northerner, a day laborer." But there were still others, older people, who said that even grief could not cause a real lady to forget *noblesse oblige*—without calling it *noblesse oblige*. They just said, "Poor Emily. Her kinsfolk should come to her." She had some kin in Alabama; but years ago her father had fallen out with them over the estate of old lady Wyatt, the crazy woman, and there was no communication between the two families. They had not even been represented at the funeral.

And as soon as the old people said, "Poor Emily," the whispering began. "Do you suppose it's really so?" they said to one another. "Of course it is. What else could . . ." This behind their hands; rustling of craned silk and satin behind jalousies closed upon the sun of Sunday afternoon as the thin, swift clop-clop-clop of the matched team passed: "Poor Emily."

She carried her head high enough—even when we believed that she was fallen. It was as if she demanded more than ever the recognition of her dignity as the last Grierson; as if it had wanted that touch of earthiness to reaffirm her imperviousness. Like when she bought the rat poison, the arsenic. That was over a year after they had begun to say "Poor Emily," and while the two female cousins were visiting her.

"I want some poison," she said to the druggist. She was over thirty then, still a slight woman, though thinner than usual, with cold, haughty black eyes in a face the flesh of which was strained across the temples and about the eyesockets as you imagine a lighthouse-keeper's face ought to look. "I want some poison," she said.

"Yes, Miss Emily. What kind? For rats and such? I'd recom—"

"I want the best you have. I don't care what kind."

The druggist named several. "They'll kill anything up to an elephant. But what you want is—"

"Arsenic," Miss Emily said. "Is that a good one?"

"Is . . . arsenic? Yes, ma'am. But what you want—"

"I want arsenic."

The druggist looked down at her. She looked back at him, erect, her face like a strained flag. "Why, of course," the druggist said. "If that's what you want. But the law requires you to tell what you are going to use it for."

Miss Emily just stared at him, her head tilted back in order to look him eye to eye, until he looked away and went and got the arsenic and wrapped it up. The Negro delivery boy brought her the package; the druggist didn't come back. When she opened the package at home there was written on the box, under the skull and bones: "For rats."

IV

So the next day we all said, "She will kill herself"; and we said it would be the best thing. When she had first begun to be seen with Homer Barron, we had said, "She will marry

him." Then we said, "She will persuade him yet," because
Homer himself had remarked—he liked men, and it was
known that he drank with the younger men in the Elks'
Club—that he was not a marrying man. Later we said, "Poor
Emily" behind the jalousies as they passed on Sunday afternoon in the glittering buggy. Miss Emily with her head high
and Homer Barron with his hat cocked and a cigar in his
teeth, reins and whip in a yellow glove.

Then some of the ladies began to say that it was a disgrace
to the town and a bad example to the young people. The men
did not want to interfere, but at last the ladies forced the
Baptist minister—Miss Emily's people were Episcopal—to
call upon her. He would never divulge what happened during
that interview, but he refused to go back again. The next
Sunday they again drove about the streets, and the following
day the minister's wife wrote to Miss Emily's relations in Alabama.

So she had blood-kin under her roof again and we sat back
to watch developments. At first nothing happened. Then we
were sure that they were to be married. We learned that Miss
Emily had been to the jeweler's and ordered a man's toilet set
in silver, with the letters H.B. on each piece. Two days later
we learned that she had bought a complete outfit of men's
clothing, including a nightshirt, and we said, "They are married." We were really glad. We were glad because the two female cousins were even more Grierson than Miss Emily had
ever been.

So we were not surprised when Homer Barron—the
streets had been finished some time since—was gone. We
were a little disappointed that there was not a public blow-
ing-off, but we believed that he had gone on to prepare for
Miss Emily's coming, or to give her a chance to get rid of the
cousins. (By that time it was a cabal, and we were all Miss
Emily's allies to help circumvent the cousins.) Sure enough,
after another week they departed. And, as we had expected
all along, within three days, Homer Barron was back in town.
A neighbor saw the Negro man admit him at the kitchen
door at dusk one evening.

And that was the last we saw of Homer Barron. And of
Miss Emily for some time. The Negro man went in and out
with the market basket, but the front door remained closed.
Now and then we would see her at a window for a moment,
as the men did that night when they sprinkled the lime, but
for almost six months she did not appear on the streets. Then

we knew that this was to be expected too; as if that quality of her father which had thwarted her woman's life so many times had been too virulent and too furious to die.

When we next saw Miss Emily, she had grown fat and her hair was turning gray. During the next few years it grew grayer and grayer until it attained an even pepper-and-salt iron-gray, when it ceased turning. Up to the day of her death at seventy-four it was still that vigorous iron-gray, like the hair of an active man.

From that time on her front door remained closed, save for a period of six or seven years, when she was about forty, during which she gave lessons in china-painting. She fitted up a studio in one of the downstairs rooms, where the daughters and granddaughters of Colonel Sartoris' contemporaries were sent to her with the same regularity and in the same spirit that they were sent to church on Sundays with a twenty-five-cent piece for the collection plate. Meanwhile her taxes had been remitted.

Then the newer generation became the backbone and the spirit of the town, and the painting pupils grew up and fell away and did not send their children to her with boxes of color and tedious brushes and pictures cut from the ladies' magazines. The front door closed upon the last one and remained closed for good. When the town got free postal delivery, Miss Emily alone refused to let them fasten the metal numbers above her door and attach a mailbox to it. She would not listen to them.

Daily, monthly, yearly we watched the Negro grow grayer and more stooped, going in and out with the market basket. Each December we sent her a tax notice, which would be returned by the post office a week later, unclaimed. Now and then we would see her in one of the downstairs windows—she had evidently shut up the top floor of the house—like the carven torso of an idol in a niche, looking or not looking at us, we could never tell which. Thus she passed from generation to generation—dear, inescapable, impervious, tranquil, and perverse.

And so she died. Fell ill in the house filled with dust and shadows, with only a doddering Negro man to wait on her. We did not even know she was sick; we had long since given up trying to get any information from the Negro. He talked to no one, probably not even to her, for his voice had grown harsh and rusty, as if from disuse.

She died in one of the downstairs rooms, in a heavy walnut bed with a curtain, her gray head propped on a pillow yellow and moldly with age and lack of sunlight.

V

The Negro met the first of the ladies at the front door and let them in, with their hushed, sibilant voices and their quick, curious glances, and then he disappeared. He walked right through the house and out the back and was not seen again.

The two female cousins came at once. They held the funeral on the second day, with the town coming to look at Miss Emily beneath a mass of bought flowers, with the crayon face of her father musing profoundly above the bier and the ladies sibilant and macabre; and the very old men—some in their brushed Confederate uniforms—on the porch and the lawn, talking of Miss Emily as if she had been a contemporary of theirs, believing that they had danced with her and courted her perhaps, confusing time with its mathematical progression, as the old do, to whom all the past is not a diminishing road but, instead, a huge meadow which no winter ever quite touches, divided from them now by the narrow bottle-neck of the most recent decade of years.

Already we knew that there was one room in that region above stairs which no one had seen in forty years, and which would have to be forced. They waited until Miss Emily was decently in the ground before they opened it.

The violence of breaking down the door seemed to fill this room with pervading dust. A thin, acrid pall as of the tomb seemed to lie everywhere upon this room decked and furnished as for a bridal: upon the valance curtains of faded rose color, upon the rose-shaded lights, upon the dressing table, upon the delicate array of crystal and the man's toilet things backed with tarnished silver, silver so tarnished that the monogram was obscured. Among them lay a collar and tie, as if they had just been removed, which, lifted, left upon the surface a pale crescent in the dust. Upon a chair hung the suit, carefully folded; beneath it the two mute shoes and the discarded socks.

The man himself lay in the bed.

For a long while we just stood there, looking down at the

profound and fleshless grin. The body had apparently once lain in the attitude of an embrace, but now the long sleep that outlasts love, that conquers even the grimace of love, had cuckolded him. What was left of him, rotted beneath what was left of the nightshirt, had become inextricable from the bed in which he lay; and upon him and upon the pillow beside him lay that even coating of the patient and biding dust.

Then we noticed that in the second pillow was the indentation of a head. One of us lifted something from it, and leaning forward, that faint and invisible dust dry and acrid in the nostrils, we saw a long strand of iron-gray hair.

Theft

Katherine Anne Porter

She had the purse in her hand when she came in. Standing in the middle of the floor, holding her bathrobe around her and trailing a damp towel in one hand, she surveyed the immediate past and remembered everything clearly. Yes, she had opened the flap and spread it out on the bench after she had dried the purse with her handkerchief.

She had intended to take the Elevated, and naturally she looked in her purse to make certain she had the fare, and was pleased to find forty cents in the coin envelope. She was going to pay her own fare, too, even if Camilo did have the habit of seeing her up the steps and dropping a nickel in the machine before he gave the turnstile a little push and sent her through it with a bow. Camilo by a series of compromises had managed to make effective a fairly complete set of smaller courtesies, ignoring the larger and more troublesome ones. She had walked with him to the station in a pouring rain, because she knew he was almost as poor as she was, and when he insisted on a taxi, she was firm and said, "You know it simply will not do." He was wearing a new hat of a pretty biscuit shade, for it never occurred to him to buy anything of a practical color; he had put it on for the first time and the rain was spoiling it. She kept thinking, "But this is dreadful, where will he get another?" She compared it with Eddie's hats that always seemed to be precisely seven years old and as if they had been quite purposely left out in the rain, and yet they sat with a careless and incidental rightness on Eddie. But Camilo was far different; if he wore a shabby hat it would be merely shabby on him, and he would lose his spirits over it. If she had not feared Camilo would take it badly, for he insisted on the practice of his little ceremonies up to the point he had fixed for them, she would have said to him as they left Thora's house, "Do go home. I can surely reach the station by myself."

"It is written that we must be rained upon tonight," said Camilo, "so let it be together."

At the foot of the platform stairway she staggered slightly—they were both nicely set up on Thora's cocktails—and said: "At least, Camilo, do me the favor not to climb these stairs in your present state, since for you it is only a matter of coming down again at once, and you'll certainly break your neck."

He made three quick bows, he was Spanish, and leaped off through the rainy darkness. She stood watching him, for he was a very graceful young man, thinking that tomorrow morning he would gaze soberly at his spoiled hat and soggy shoes and possibly associate her with his misery. As she watched, he stopped at the far corner and took off his hat and hid it under his overcoat. She felt she had betrayed him by seeing, because he would have been humiliated if he thought she even suspected him of trying to save his hat.

Roger's voice sounded over her shoulder above the clang of the rain falling on the stairway shed, wanting to know what she was doing out in the rain at this time of night, and did she take herself for a duck? His long, imperturbable face was streaming with water, and he tapped a bulging spot on the breast of his buttoned-up overcoat: "Hat," he said. "Come on, let's take a taxi."

She settled back against Roger's arm which he laid around her shoulders, and with the gesture they exchanged a glance full of long amiable associations, then she looked through the window at the rain changing the shapes of everything, and the colors. The taxi dodged in and out between the pillars of the Elevated, skidding slightly on every curve, and she said: "The more it skids the calmer I feel, so I really must be drunk."

"You must be," said Roger. "This bird is a homicidal maniac, and I could do with a cocktail myself this minute."

They waited on the traffic at Fortieth Street and Sixth Avenue, and three boys walked before the nose of the taxi. Under the globes of light they were cheerful scarecrows, all very thin and all wearing very seedy snappy-cut suits and gay neckties. They were not very sober either, and they stood for a moment wobbling in front of the car, and there was an argument going on among them. They leaned toward each other as if they were getting ready to sing, and the first one said: "When I get married if won't be jus' for getting married, I'm gonna marry for *love*, see?" and the second one

id, "Aw, gwan and tell that stuff to *her,* why n't yuh?" and
he third one gave a kind of hoot, said, "Hell, dis guy? Wot
he hell's he got?" and the first one said; "Aaah, shurrup yuh
hush, I got plenty." Then they all squealed and scrambled
cross the street beating the first one on the back and pushing
im around.

"Nuts," commented Roger, "pure nuts."

Two girls went skittering by in short transparent raincoats,
he green, one red, their heads tucked against the drive of the
ain. One of them was saying to the other, "Yes, I know all
bout *that.* But what about me? You're always so sorry for
im . . ." and they ran on with their little pelican legs flash-
ng back and forth.

The taxi backed up suddenly and leaped forward again,
nd after a while Roger said: "I had a letter from Stella to-
lay, and she'll be home on the twenty-sixth, so I suppose
he's made up her mind and it's all settled."

"I had a sort of letter today too," she said, "making up my
mind for me. I think it is time for you and Stella to do some-
hing definite."

When the taxi stopped on the corner of West Fifty-third
Street, Roger said, "I've just enough if you'll add ten cents,"
o she opened her purse and gave him a dime, and he said,
"That's beautiful, that purse."

"It's a birthday present," she told him, "and I like it.
How's your show coming?"

"Oh, still hanging on, I guess. I don't go near the place.
Nothing sold yet. I mean to keep right on the way I'm going
nd they can take it or leave it. I'm through with the argument."

"It's absolutely a matter of holding out, isn't it?"

"Holding out's the tough part."

"Good night, Roger."

"Good night, you should take aspirin and push yourself
into a tub of hot water, you look as though you're catching
cold."

"I will."

With the purse under her arm she went upstairs, and on
the first landing Bill heard her step and poked his head out
with his hair tumbled and his eyes red, and he said: "For
Christ's sake, come in and have a drink with me. I've had
some bad news."

"You're perfectly sopping," said Bill, looking at her
drenched feet. They had two drinks, while Bill told how the

director had thrown his play out after the cast had bee
picked over twice, and had gone through three rehearsals. '
said to him, 'I didn't say it was a masterpiece, I said it woul
make a good show.' And he said, 'It just doesn't *play*, do yo
see? It needs a doctor.' So I'm stuck, absolutely stuck," sai
Bill, on the edge of weeping again. "I've been crying," he tol
her, "in my cups." And he went on to ask her if she realize
his wife was ruining him with her extravagance. "I send he
ten dollars every week of my unhappy life, and I don't reall
have to. She threatens to jail me if I don't, but she can't d
it. God, let her try it after the way she treated me! She's n
right to alimony and she knows it. She keeps on saying she
got to have it for the baby and I keep on sending it because
can't bear to see anybody suffer. So I'm way behind on th
piano and the victrola, both—"

"Well, this is a pretty rug, anyhow," she said.

Bill stared at it and blew his nose. "I got it at Ricci's fo
ninety-five dollars," he said. "Ricci told me it once belonge
to Marie Dressler, and cost fifteen hundred dollars, bu
there's a burnt place on it, under the divan. Can you bea
that?"

"No," she said. She was thinking about her empty purs
and that she could not possibly expect a check for her lates
review for another three days, and her arrangement with th
basement restaurant could not last much longer if she did no
pay something on the account. "It's no time to speak of it,
she said, "but I've been hoping you would have by now tha
fifty dollars you promised for my scene in the third act. Eve
if it doesn't play. You were to pay me for the work anyhov
out of your advance."

"Weeping Jesus," said Bill, "you, too?" He gave a loud sob
or hiccough, in his moist handkerchief. "Your stuff was n
better than mine, after all. Think of that."

"But you got something for it," she said. "Seven hundre
dollars."

Bill said, "Do me a favor, will you? Have another drin
and forget about it. I can't, you know I can't, I would if
could, but you know the fix I'm in."

"Let it go, then," she found herself saying almost in spit
of herself. She had meant to be quite firm about it. The
drank again without speaking, and she went to her apartmen
on the floor above.

There, she now remembered distinctly, she had taken th
letter out of the purse before she spread the purse out to dry.

She had sat down and read the letter over again: but there were phrases that insisted on being read many times, they had a life of their own separate from the others, and when she tried to read past and around them, they moved with the movement of her eyes, and she could not escape them . . . "thinking about you more than I mean to . . . yes, I even talk about you . . . why were you so anxious to destroy . . . even if I could see you now I would not . . . not worth all this abominable . . . the end . . ."

Carefully she tore the letter into narrow strips and touched a lighted match to them in the coal grate.

Early the next morning she was in the bathtub when the janitress knocked and then came in, calling out that she wished to examine the radiators before she started the furnace going for the winter. After moving about the room for a few minutes, the janitress went out, closing the door very sharply.

She came out of the bathroom to get a cigarette from the package in the purse. The purse was gone. She dressed and made coffee, and sat by the window while she drank it. Certainly the janitress had taken the purse, and certainly it would be impossible to get it back without a great deal of ridiculous excitement. Then let it go. With this decision of her mind, there rose coincidentally in her blood a deep almost murderous anger. She sat the cup carefully in the center of the table, and walked steadily downstairs, three long flights and a short hall and a steep short flight into the basement, where the janitress, her face streaked with coal dust, was shaking up the furnace. "Will you please give me back my purse? There isn't any money in it. It was a present, and I don't want to lose it."

The janitress turned without straightening up and peered at her with hot flickering eyes, a red light from the furnace reflected in them. "What do you mean, your purse?"

"The gold cloth purse you took from the wooden bench in my room," she said. "I must have it back."

"Before God I never laid eyes on your purse, and that's the holy truth," said the janitress.

"Oh, well then, keep it," she said, but in a very bitter voice; "keep it if you want it so much." And she walked away.

She remembered how she had never locked a door in her life, on some principle of rejection in her that made her uncomfortable in the ownership of things, and her paradox-

ical boast before the warnings of her friends, that she had
never lost a penny by theft; and she had been pleased with
the bleak humility of this concrete example designed to illus-
trate and justify a certain fixed, otherwise baseless and general faith which ordered the movements of her life without
regard to her will in the matter.

In this moment she felt that she had been robbed of an
enormous number of valuable things, whether material or in-
tangible: things lost or broken by her own fault, things she
had forgotten and left in houses when she moved: books borrowed from her and not returned, journeys she had planned
and had not made, words she had waited to hear spoken to
her and had not heard, and the words she had meant to answer with; bitter alternatives and intolerable substitutes worse
than nothing, and yet inescapable: the long patient suffering
of dying friendships, and the dark inexplicable death of
love—all that she had had, and all that she had missed, were
lost together, and were twice lost in this landslide of remembered losses.

The janitress was following her upstairs with the purse in
her hand and the same deep red fire flickering in her eyes. The
janitress thrust the purse towards her while they were still a
half dozen steps apart, and said: "Don't never tell on me. I
musta been crazy. I get crazy in the head sometimes, I swear
I do. My son can tell you."

She took the purse after a moment, and the janitress went
on: "I got a niece who is going on seventeen, and she's a nice
girl and I thought I'd give it to her. She needs a pretty purse.
I musta been crazy; I thought maybe you wouldn't mind, you
leave things around and don't seem to notice much."

She said: "I missed this because it was a present to me
from someone . . ."

The janitress said: "He'd get you another if you lost this
one. My niece is young and needs pretty things, we oughta
give the young ones a chance. She's got young men after her
maybe will want to marry her. She oughta have nice things.
She needs them bad right now. You're a grown woman,
you've had your chance, you ought to know how it is!"

She held the purse out to the janitress saying: "You don't
know what you're talking about. Here, take it, I've changed
my mind. I really don't want it."

The janitress looked up at her with hatred and said: "I
don't want it either, now. My niece is young and pretty, she

don't need fixin' up to be pretty, she's young and pretty any-how! I guess you need it worse than she does!"

"It wasn't really yours in the first place," she said, turning away. "You mustn't talk as if I had stolen it from you."

"It's not from me, it's from her you're stealing it," said the janitress, and went back downstairs.

She laid the purse on the table and sat down with the cup of chilled coffee, and thought: I was right not to be afraid of any thief but myself, who will end by leaving me nothing.

The Chrysanthemums

John Steinbeck

The high grey-flannel fog of winter closed off the Salinas Valley from the sky and from all the rest of the world. On every side it sat like a lid on the mountains and made of the great valley a closed pot. On the broad, level land floor the gang plows bit deep and left the black earth shining like metal where the shares had cut. On the foothill ranches across the Salinas River, the yellow stubble fields seemed to be bathed in pale cold sunshine, but there was no sunshine in the valley now in December. The thick willow scrub along the river flamed with sharp and positive yellow leaves.

It was a time of quiet and of waiting. The air was cold and tender. A light wind blew up from the southwest so that the farmers were mildly hopeful of a good rain before long; but fog and rain do not go together.

Across the river, on Henry Allen's foothill ranch there was little work to be done, for the hay was cut and stored and the orchards were plowed up to receive the rain deeply when it should come. The cattle on the higher slopes were becoming shaggy and rough-coated.

Elisa Allen, working in her flower garden, looked down across the yard and saw Henry, her husband, talking to two men in business suits. The three of them stood by the tractor shed, each man with one foot on the side of the little Fordson. They smoked cigarettes and studied the machine as they talked.

Elisa watched them for a moment and then went back to her work. She was thirty-five. Her face was lean and strong and her eyes were as clear as water. Her figure looked blocked and heavy in her gardening costume, a man's black hat pulled low down over her eyes, clod-hopper shoes, a figured print dress almost completely covered by a big corduroy apron with four big pockets to hold the snips, the trowel and scratcher, the seeds and the knife she worked with. She wore heavy leather gloves to protect her hands while she worked.

She was cutting down the old year's chrysanthemum stalks with a pair of short and powerful scissors. She looked down toward the men by the tractor shed now and then. Her face was eager and mature and handsome; even her work with the scissors was over-eager, over-powerful. The chrysanthemum stems seemed too small and easy for her energy.

She brushed a cloud of hair out of her eyes with the back of her glove, and left a smudge of earth on her cheek in doing it. Behind her stood the neat white farm house with red geraniums close-banked around it as high as the windows. It was a hard-swept looking little house, with hard-polished windows, and a clean mud-mat on the front steps.

Elisa cast another glance toward the tractor shed. The strangers were getting into their Ford coupe. She took off a glove and put her strong fingers down into the forest of new green chrysanthemum sprouts that were growing around the old roots. She spread the leaves and looked down among the close-growing stems. No aphids were there, no sowbugs or snails or cutworms. Her terrier fingers destroyed such pests before they could get started.

Elisa started at the sound of her husband's voice. He had come near quietly, and he leaned over the wire fence that protected her flower garden from cattle and dogs and chickens.

"At it again," he said. "You've got a strong new crop coming."

Elisa straightened her back and pulled on the gardening glove again. "Yes. They'll be strong this coming year." In her tone and on her face there was a little smugness.

"You've got a gift with things," Henry observed. "Some of those yellow chrysanthemums you had this year were ten inches across. I wish you'd work out in the orchard and raise some apples that big."

Her eyes sharpened. "Maybe I could do it, too. I've a gift with things, all right. My mother had it. She could stick anything in the ground and make it grow. She said it was having planters' hands that knew how to do it."

"Well, it sure works with flowers," he said.

"Henry, who were those men you were talking to?"

"Why, sure, that's what I came to tell you. They were from the Western Meat Company. I sold those thirty head of three-year-old steers. Got nearly my own price, too."

"Good," she said. "Good for you."

"And I thought," he continued, "I thought how it's Saturday afternoon, and we might go into Salinas for dinner at a restaurant, and then to a picture show—to celebrate, you see."

"Good," she repeated. "Oh, yes. That will be good."

Henry put on his joking tone. "There's fights tonight. How'd you like to go to the fights?"

"Oh, no," she said breathlessly. "No, I wouldn't like fights."

"Just fooling, Elisa. We'll go to a movie. Let's see. It's two now. I'm going to take Scotty and bring down those steers from the hill. It'll take us maybe two hours. We'll go in town about five and have dinner at the Cominos Hotel. Like that?"

"Of course I'll like it. It's good to eat away from home."

"All right, then. I'll go get up a couple of horses."

She said, "I'll have plenty of time to transplant some of these sets, I guess."

She heard her husband calling Scotty down by the barn. And a little later she saw the two men ride up the pale yellow hillside in search of the steers.

There was a little square sandy bed kept for rooting the chrysanthemums. With her trowel she turned the soil over and over, and smoothed it and patted it firm. Then she dug ten parallel trenches to receive the sets. Back at the chrysanthemum bed she pulled out the little crisp shoots, trimmed off the leaves of each one with her scissors and laid it on a small orderly pile.

A squeak of wheels and plod of hoofs came from the road. Elisa looked up. The country road ran along the dense bank of willows and cottonwoods that bordered the river, and up this road came a curious vehicle, curiously drawn. It was an old spring-wagon, with a round canvas top on it like the cover of a praire schooner. It was drawn by an old bay horse and a little grey-and-white burro. A big stubble-bearded man sat between the cover flaps and drove the crawling team. Underneath the wagon, between the hind wheels, a lean and rangy mongrel dog walked sedately. Words were painted on the canvas, in clumsy, crooked letters. "Pots, pans, knives, sisors, lawn mores, Fixed." Two rows of articles, and the triumphantly definitive "Fixed" below. The black paint had run down in little sharp points beneath each letter.

Elisa, squatting on the ground, watched to see the crazy, loose-jointed wagon pass by. But it didn't pass. It turned into the farm road in front of her house, crooked old wheels skirling and squeaking. The rangy dog darted from between the wheels and ran ahead. Instantly the two ranch shepherds flew out at him. Then all three stopped, and with stiff and quivering tails, with taut straight legs, with ambassadorial dignity, they slowly circled, sniffing daintily. The caravan pulled up to Elisa's wire fence and stopped. Now the newcomer dog, feeling out-numbered, lowered his tail and retired under the wagon with raised hackles and bared teeth.

The man on the wagon seat called out, "That's a bad dog in a fight when he gets started."

Elisa laughed. "I see he is. How soon does he generally get started?"

The man caught up her laughter and echoed it heartily. "Sometimes not for weeks and weeks," he said. He climbed stiffly down, over the wheel. The horse and the donkey drooped like unwatered flowers.

Elisa saw that he was a very big man. Although his hair and beard were greying, he did not look old. His worn black suit was wrinkled and spotted with grease. The laughter had disappeared from his face and eyes the moment his laughing voice ceased. His eyes were dark, and they were full of the brooding that gets in the eyes of teamsters and of sailors. The calloused hands he rested on the wire fence were cracked, and every crack was a black line. He took off his battered hat.

"I'm off my general road, ma'am," he said. "Does this dirt road cut over across the river to the Los Angeles highway?"

Elisa stood up and shoved the thick scissors in her apron pocket. "Well, yes, it does, but it winds around and then fords the river. I don't think your team could pull through the sand."

He replied with some asperity, "It might surprise you what them beasts can pull through."

"When they get started?" she asked.

He smiled for a second. "Yes. When they get started."

"Well," said Elisa, "I think you'll save time if you go back to the Salinas road and pick up the highway there."

He drew a big finger down the chicken wire and made it sing. "I ain't in any hurry, ma'am. I go from Seattle to San Diego and back every year. Takes all my time. About six months each way. I aim to follow nice weather."

Elisa took off her gloves and stuffed them in the apron pocket with the scissors. She touched the under edge of her man's hat, searching for fugitive hairs. "That sounds like a nice kind of way to live," she said.

He leaned confidentially over the fence. "Maybe you noticed the writing on my wagon. I mend pots and sharpen knives and scissors. You got any of them things to do?"

"Oh, no," she said quickly. "Nothing like that." Her eyes hardened with resistance.

"Scissors is the worst thing," he explained. "Most people just ruin scissors trying to sharpen 'em, but I know how. I got a special tool. It's a little bobbit kind of thing, and patented. But it sure does the trick."

"No. My scissors are all sharp."

"All right, then. Take a pot," he continued earnestly, "a bent pot, or a pot with a hole. I can make it like new so you don't have to buy no new ones. That's a saving for you."

"No," she said shortly. "I tell you I have nothing like that for you to do."

His face fell to an exaggerated sadness. His voice took on a whining undertone. "I ain't had a thing to do today. Maybe I won't have no supper tonight. You see I'm off my regular road. I know folks on the highway clear from Seattle to San Diego. They have their things for me to sharpen up because they know I do it so good and save them money."

"I'm sorry," Elisa said irritably. "I haven't anything for you to do."

His eyes left her face and fell to searching the ground. They roamed about until they came to the chrysanthemum bed where she had been working. "What's them plants, ma'am?"

The irritation and resistance melted from Elisa's face. "Oh, those are chrysanthemums, giant whites and yellows. I raise them every year, bigger than anybody around here."

"Kind of a long-stemmed flower? Looks like a quick puff of colored smoke?" he asked.

"That's it. What a nice way to describe them."

"They smell kind of nasty till you get used to them," he said.

"It's a good bitter smell," she retorted, "not nasty at all."

He changed his tone quickly. "I like the smell myself."

"I had ten-inch blooms this year," she said.

The man leaned farther over the fence. "Look. I know a lady down the road a piece, has got the nicest garden you ever seen. Got nearly every kind of flower but no chrysanthemums. Last time I was mending a copper-bottom washtub for her (that's a hard job but I do it good), she said to me, 'If you ever run acrost some nice chrysanthemums I wish you'd try to get me a few seeds.' That's what she told me."

Elisa's eyes grew alert and eager. "She couldn't have known much about chrysanthemums. You *can* raise them from seed, but it's much easier to root the little sprouts you see there."

"Oh," he said. "I s'pose I can't take none to her, then."

"Why yes you can," Elisa cried. "I can put some in damp sand, and you can carry them right along with you. They'll take root in the pot if you keep them damp. And then she can transplant them."

"She'd sure like to have some, ma'am. You say they're nice ones?"

"Beautiful," she said. "Oh, beautiful." Her eyes shone. She tore off the battered hat and shook out her dark pretty hair. "I'll put them in a flower pot, and you can take them right with you. Come into the yard."

While the man came through the picket gate Elisa ran excitedly along the geranium-bordered path to the back of the house. And she returned carrying a big red flower pot. The gloves were forgotten now. She kneeled on the ground by the starting bed and dug up the sandy soil with her fingers and scooped it into the bright new flower pot. Then she picked up the little pile of shoots she had prepared. With her strong fingers she pressed them into the sand and tamped around them with her knuckles. The man stood over her. "I'll tell you what to do," she said. "You remember so you can tell the lady."

"Yes, I'll try to remember."

"Well, look. These will take root in about a month. Then she must set them out, about a foot apart in good rich earth like this, see?" She lifted a handful of dark soil for him to look at. "They'll grow fast and tall. Now remember this: In July tell her to cut them down, about eight inches from the ground."

"Before they bloom?" he asked.

"Yes, before they bloom." Her face was tight with eagerness. "They'll grow right up again. About the last of September the buds will start."

She stopped and seemed perplexed. "It's the budding that takes the most care," she said hesitantly. "I don't know how to tell you." She looked deep into his eyes, searchingly. Her mouth opened a little, and she seemed to be listening. "I'll try to tell you," she said. "Did you ever hear of planting hands?"

"Can't say I have, ma'am."

"Well, I can only tell you what it feels like. It's when you're picking off the buds you don't want. Everything goes right down into your fingertips. You watch your fingers work. They do it themselves. You can feel how it is. They pick and pick the buds. They never make a mistake. They're with the plant. Do you see? Your fingers and the plant. You can feel that, right up your arm. They know. They never make a mistake. You can feel it. When you're like that you can't do anything wrong. Do you see that? Can you understand that?"

She was kneeling on the ground looking up at him. Her breast swelled passionately.

The man's eyes narrowed. He looked away self-consciously. "Maybe I know," he said. "Sometimes in the night in the wagon there—"

Elisa's voice grew husky. She broke in on him, "I've never lived as you do, but I know what you mean. When the night is dark—why, the stars are sharp-pointed, and there's quiet. Why, you rise up and up! Every pointed star gets driven into your body. It's like that. Hot and sharp and—lovely."

Kneeling there, her hand went out toward his legs in the greasy black trousers. Her hesitant fingers almost touched the cloth. Then her hand dropped to the ground. She crouched low like a fawning dog.

He said, "It's nice, just like you say. Only when you don't have no dinner, it ain't."

She stood up then, very straight, and her face was ashamed. She held the flower pot out to him and placed it gently in his arms. "Here. Put it in your wagon, on the seat, where you can watch it. Maybe I can find something for you to do."

At the back of the house she dug in the can pile and found two old and battered aluminum saucepans. She carried them back and gave them to him. "Here, maybe you can fix these."

His manner changed. He became professional. "Good as new I can fix them." At the back of his wagon he set a little anvil, and out of an oily tool box dug a small machine hammer. Elisa came through the gate to watch him while he pounded out the dents in the kettles. His mouth grew sure and knowing. At a difficult part of the work he sucked his under-lip.

"You sleep right in the wagon?" Elisa asked.

"Right in the wagon, ma'am. Rain or shine I'm dry as a cow in there."

"It must be nice," she said. "It must be very nice. I wish women could do such things."

"It ain't the right kind of life for a woman."

Her upper lip raised a little, showing her teeth. "How do you know? How can you tell?" she said.

"I don't know, ma'am," he protested. "Of course I don't know. Now here's your kettles done. You don't have to buy no new ones."

"How much?"

"Oh, fifty cents'll do. I keep my prices down and my work good. That's why I have all them satisfied customers up and down the highway."

Elisa brought him a fifty-cent piece from the house and dropped it in his hand. "You might be surprised to have a rival some time. I can sharpen scissors, too. And I can beat the dents out of little pots. I could show you what a woman might do."

He put his hammer back in the oily box and shoved the little anvil out of sight. "It would be a lonely life for a woman, ma'am, and a scarey life, too, with animals creeping under the wagon all night." He climbed over the singletree, steadying himself with a hand on the burro's white rump. He settled himself in the seat, picked up the lines. "Thank you kindly, ma'am," he said. "I'll do like you told me; I'll go back and catch the Salinas road."

"Mind," she called, "if you're long in getting there, keep the sand damp."

"Sand, ma'am? . . . Sand? Oh, sure. You mean around the chrysanthemums. Sure I will." He clucked his tongue. The beasts leaned luxuriously into their collars. The mongrel dog took his place between the back wheels. The wagon turned and crawled out the entrance road and back the way it had come, along the river.

Elisa stood in front of her wire fence watching the slow progress of the caravan. Her shoulders were straight, her head thrown back, her eyes half-closed, so that the scene came vaguely into them. Her lips moved silently, forming the words "Good-bye—good-bye." Then she whispered, "That's a bright direction. There's a glowing there." The sound of her whisper startled her. She shook herself free and looked about to see whether anyone had been listening. Only the dogs had heard. They lifted their heads toward her from their sleeping in the dust, and then stretched out their chins and settled asleep again. Elisa turned and ran hurriedly into the house.

In the kitchen she reached behind the stove and felt the water tank. It was full of hot water from the noonday cooking. In the bathroom she tore off her soiled clothes and flung them into the corner. And then she scrubbed herself with a little block of pumice, legs and thighs, loins and chest and arms, until her skin was scratched and red. When she had dried herself she stood in front of a mirror in her bedroom and looked at her body. She tightened her stomach and threw out her chest. She turned and looked over her shoulder at her back.

After a while she began to dress, slowly. She put on her newest underclothing and her nicest stockings and the dress which was the symbol of her prettiness. She worked carefully on her hair, penciled her eyebrows and rouged her lips.

Before she was finished she heard the little thunder of hoofs and the shouts of Henry and his helper as they drove the red steers into the corral. She heard the gate bang shut and set herself for Henry's arrival.

His step sounded on the porch. He entered the house calling, "Elisa, where are you?"

"In my room, dressing. I'm not ready. There's hot water for your bath. Hurry up. It's getting late."

When she heard him splashing in the tub, Elisa laid his dark suit on the bed, and shirt and socks and tie beside it. She stood his polished shoes on the floor beside the bed. Then she went to the porch and sat primly and stiffly down. She looked toward the river road where the willow-line was still yellow with frosted leaves so that under the high grey fog they seemed a thin band of sunshine. This was the only color in the grey afternoon. She sat unmoving for a long time. Her eyes blinked rarely.

Henry came banging out of the door, shoving his tie inside his vest as he came. Elisa stiffened and her face grew tight. Henry stopped short and looked at her. "Why—why, Elisa. You look so nice!"

"Nice? You think I look nice? What do you mean by 'nice'?"

Henry blundered on. "I don't know. I mean you look different, strong and happy."

"I am strong? Yes, strong. What do you mean 'strong'?"

He looked bewildered. "You're playing some kind of a game," he said helplessly. "It's a kind of a play. You look strong enough to break a calf over your knee, happy enough to eat it like a watermelon."

For a second she lost her rigidity. "Henry! Don't talk like that. You didn't know what you said." She grew complete again. "I'm strong," she boasted. "I never knew before how strong."

Henry looked down toward the tractor shed, and when he brought his eyes back to her, they were his own again. "I'll get out the car. You can put on your coat while I'm starting."

Elisa went into the house. She heard him drive to the gate and idle down his motor, and then she took a long time to put on her hat. She pulled it here and pressed it there. When Henry turned the motor off she slipped into her coat and went out.

The little roadster bounced along on the dirt road by the river, raising the birds and driving the rabbits into the brush. Two cranes flapped heavily over the willow-line and dropped into the river-bed.

Far ahead on the road Elisa saw a dark speck. She knew.

She tried not to look as they passed it, but her eyes would not obey. She whispered to herself sadly, "He might have thrown them off the road. That wouldn't have been much trouble, not very much. But he kept the pot," she explained. "He had to keep the pot. That's why he couldn't get them off the road."

The roadster turned a bend and she saw the caravan ahead. She swung full around toward her husband so she could not see the little covered wagon and the mismatched team as the car passed them.

In a moment it was over. The thing was done. She did not look back.

She said loudly, to be heard above the motor, "It will be good, tonight, a good dinner."

"Now you're changed again," Henry complained. He took one hand from the wheel and patted her knee. "I ought to take you in to dinner oftener. It would be good for both of us. We get so heavy out on the ranch."

"Henry," she asked, "could we have wine at dinner?"

"Sure we could. Say! That will be fine."

She was silent for a while; then she said, "Henry, at those prize fights, do the men hurt each other very much?"

"Sometimes a little, not often. Why?"

"Well, I've read how they break noses, and blood runs

down their chests. I've read how the fighting gloves get heavy and soggy with blood."

He looked around at her. "What's the matter, Elisa? I didn't know you read things like that." He brought the car to a stop, then turned to the right over the Salinas River bridge.

"Do any women ever go to the fights?" she asked.

"Oh, sure, some. What's the matter, Elisa? Do you want to go? I don't think you'd like it, but I'll take you if you really want to go."

She relaxed limply in the seat. "Oh, no. No. I don't want to go. I'm sure I don't." Her face was turned away from him. "It will be enough if we can have wine. It will be plenty." She turned up her coat collar so he could not see that she was crying weakly—like an old woman.

A Night in June

William Carlos Williams

I was a young man then—full of information and tenderness. It was her first baby. She lived just around the corner from her present abode, one room over a small general store kept by an old man.

It was a difficult forceps delivery and I lost the child, to my disgust; though without nurse, anesthetist, or even enough hot water in the place, I shouldn't have been overmuch blamed. I must have been fairly able not to have done worse. But I won a friend and I found another—to admire, a sort of love for the woman.

She was slightly older than her husband, a heavy-looking Italian boy. Both were short. A peasant woman who could scarcely talk a word of English, being recently come from the other side, a woman of great simplicity of character—docility, patience, with a fine direct look in her grey eyes. And courageous. Devoted to her instincts and convictions and to me.

Sometimes she'd cry out at her husband, as I got to know her later, with some high pitched animalistic sound when he would say something to her in Italian that I couldn't understand and I knew that she was holding out for me.

Usually though, she said very little, looking me straight in the eye with a smile, her voice pleasant and candid though I could scarcely understand her few broken words. Her sentences were seldom more than three or four words long. She always acted as though I must naturally know what was in her mind and her smile with a shrug always won me.

Apart from the second child, born a year after the first, during the absence of the family from town for a short time, I had delivered Angelina of all her children. This one would make my eighth attendance on her, her ninth labor.

Three A.M., June the 10th, I noticed the calendar as I flashed on the light in my office to pick up my satchel, the same, by the way, my uncle had given me when I graduated

189

from Medical School. One gets not to deliver women at home nowadays. The hospital is the place for it. The equipment is far better.

Smiling, I picked up the relic from where I had tossed it two or three years before under a table in my small laboratory hoping never to have to use it again. In it I found a brand new hypodermic syringe with the manufacturer's name still shiny with black enamel on the barrel. Also a pair of curved scissors I had been looking for for the last three years, thinking someone had stolen them.

I dusted off the top of the Lysol bottle when I took it from the shelf and quickly checking on the rest of my necessities, I went off, without a coat or necktie, wearing the same shirt I had had on during the day preceding, soiled but—better so.

It was a beautiful June night. The lighted clock in the tower over the factory said 3:20. The clock in the facade of the Trust Company across the track said it also. Paralleling the railroad I recognized the squat figure of the husband returning home ahead of me—whistling as he walked. I put my hand out of the car in sign of recognition and kept on, rounding the final triangular block a little way ahead to bring my car in to the right in front of the woman's house for parking.

The husband came up as I was trying to decide which of the two steep cobbled entry-ways to take. Got you up early, he said.

Where ya been? his sister said to him when we had got into the house from the rear.

I went down to the police to telephone, he said, that's the surest way.

I told you to go next door you dope. What did you go away down there for? Leaving me here alone.

Aw, I didn't want to wake nobody up.

I got two calls, I broke in.

Yes, he went away and left me alone. I got scared so I waked him up anyway to call you.

The kitchen where we stood was lighted by a somewhat damaged Welsbach mantel gaslight. Everything was quiet. The husband took off his cap and sat along the wall. I put my satchel on the tubs and began to take things out.

There was just one sterile umbilical tie left, two, really, in the same envelope, as always, for possible twins, but that detail aside, everything was ample and in order. I complimented myself. Even the Argyrol was there, in tablet form, insuring the full potency of a fresh solution. Nothing so satisfying as a kit of any sort prepared and in order even when picked up in an emergency after an interval of years.

I selected out two artery clamps and two scissors. One thing, there'd be no need of sutures afterward in this case.

You want hot water?

Not yet, I said. Might as well take my shirt off, though. Which I did, throwing it on a kitchen chair and donning the usual light rubber apron.

I'm sorry we ain't got no light in there. The electricity is turned off. Do you think you can see with a candle?

Sure. Why not? But it was very dark in the room where the woman lay on a low double bed. A three-year-old boy was asleep on the sheet beside her. She wore an abbreviated nightgown, to her hips. Her short thick legs had, as I knew, bunches of large varicose veins about them like vines. Everything was clean and in order. The sister-in-law held the candle. Few words were spoken.

I made the examination and found the head high but the cervix fully dilated. Oh yeah. If often happens in women who have had many children; pendulous abdomen, lack of muscular power resulting in a slight misdirection of the forces of labor and the thing may go on for days.

When I finished, Angelina got up and sat on the edge of the bed. I went back to the kitchen, the candle following me, leaving the room dark again.

Do you need it any more? the sister-in-law said, I'll put it out.

Then the husband spoke up. Ain't you got but that one candle?

No, said the sister.

Why didn't you get some at the store when you woke him up; use your head.

The woman had the candle in a holder on the cold coal range. She leaned over to blow it out but misdirecting her aim, she had to blow three times to do it. Three of four times.

What's the matter? said her brother, getting weak? Old ages counts, eh Doc? he said and got up finally to go out.

We could hear an engineer signaling outside in the still night—with short quick blasts of his whistle—very staccato—not, I suppose, to make any greater disturbance than necessary with people sleeping all about.

Later on the freights began to roar past shaking the whole house.

She doesn't seem to be having many strong pains, I said to

my companion in the kitchen, for there wasn't a sound from the labor room and hadn't been for the past half hour.

She don't want to make no noise and wake the kids.

How old is the oldest now? I asked.

He's sixteen. The girl would have been eighteen this year. You know the first one you took from her.

Where are they all?

In there, with a nod of the head toward the other room of the apartment, such as it was, the first floor of an old two-story house, the whole thing perhaps twenty-five feet each way.

I sat in a straight chair by the kitchen table, my right arm, bare to the shoulder, resting on the worn oil cloth.

She says she wants an enema, said the woman. O.K. But I don't know how to give it to her. She ain't got a bed-pan or nothing. I don't want to get the bed all wet.

Has she had a movement today?

Yeah, but she thinks an enema will help her.

Well, have you got a bag?

Yeah, she says there's one here somewhere.

Get it. She's got a chamber pot here, hasn't she?

Sure.

So the woman got the equipment, a blue rubber douche bag, the rubber of it feeling rather stiff to the touch. She laid in on the stove in its open box and looked at it holding her hands out helplessly. I'm afraid, she said.

All right, you hold the candle. Mix up a little warm soapy water. We'll need some vaseline.

The woman called out to us where to find it, having over-heard our conversation.

Lift up, till I put these newspapers under you, said my assistant. I don't want to wet the bed.

That's nothing, Angelina answered smiling. But she raised her buttocks high so we could fix her.

Returning ten minutes later to my chair, I saw the woman taking the pot out through the kitchen and upstairs to empty it. I crossed my legs, crossed my bare arms in my lap also and let my head fall forward. I must have slept, for when I opened my eyes again, both my legs and my arms were some-what numb. I felt deliciously relaxed though somewhat bewildered. I must have snored, waking myself with a start. Everything was quiet as before. The peace of the room was unchanged. Delicious.

I heard the woman and her attendant making some slight sounds in the next room and went in to her.

Examining her, I found things unchanged. It was about half past four. What to do? Do you mind if I give you the needle? I asked her gently. We'd been through this many times before. She shrugged her shoulders as much as to say, It's up to you. So I gave her a few minims of pituitrin to intensify the strength of the pains. I was cautious since the practice is not without danger. It is possible to get a ruptured uterus where the muscle has been stretched by many pregnancies if one does not know what one is doing. Then I returned to the kitchen to wait once more.

This time I took out the obstetric gown I had brought with me, it was in a roll as it had come from the satchel, and covering it with my shirt to make a better surface and a little more bulk, I placed it at the edge of the table and leaning forward, laid my face sidewise upon it, my arms resting on the table before me, my nose and mouth at the table edge between my arms. I could breathe freely. It was a pleasant position and as I lay there content, I thought as I often do of what painting it was in which I had seen men sleeping that way.

Then I fell asleep and, in my half sleep began to argue with myself—or some imaginary power—of science and humanity. Our exaggerated ways will have to pull in their horns, I said. We've learned from one teacher and neglected another. Now that I'm older, I'm finding the older school.

The pituitary extract and other simple devices represent science. Science, I dreamed, has crowded the stage more than is necessary. The process of selection will simplify the application. It touches us too crudely now, all newness is overcomplex. I couldn't tell whether I was asleep or awake.

But without science, without pituitrin, I'd be here till noon or maybe—what? Some others wouldn't wait so long but rush her now. A carefully guarded shot of pituitrin—ought to save her at least much exhaustion—if not more. But I don't want to have anything happen to her.

Now when I lifted my head, there was beginning to be a little light outside. The woman was quiet. No progress. This time I increased the dose of pituitrin. She had stronger pains but without effect.

Maybe I'd better give you a still larger dose, I said. She made no demur. Well, let me see if I can help you first. I sat on the edge of the bed while the sister-in-law held the candle again glancing at the window where the daylight was growing. With my left hand steering the child's head, I used my ungloved right hand outside of her bare abdomen to press upon the fundus. The woman and I then got to work. Her two hands grabbed me at first a little timidly about the right wrist and forearm. Go ahead, I said. Pull hard. I welcomed the feel of her hands and the strong pull. It quieted me in the way the whole house had quieted me all night.

This woman in her present condition would have seemed repulsive to me ten years ago—now, poor soul, I see her to be as clean as a cow that calves. The flesh of my arm lay against the flesh of her knee gratefully. It was I who was being comforted and soothed.

Finally the head began to move. I wasn't sorry, thinking perhaps I'd have to do something radical before long. We kept at it till the head was born and I could leave her for a moment to put on my other glove. It was almost light now. What time is it? I asked the other woman. Six o'clock, she said.

Just after I had tied the cord, cut it and lifted the baby, a girl, to hand it to the woman, I saw the mother clutch herself suddenly between her thighs and give a cry. I was startled.

The other woman turned with a flash and shouted, Get out of here, you damned kids! I'll slap your damned face for you. And the door through which a head had peered was pulled closed. The three-year-old on the bed beside the mother stirred when the baby cried at first shrilly but had not wakened.

Oh yes, the drops in the baby's eyes. No need. She's as clean as a beast. How do I know? Medical discipline says every case must have drops in the eyes. No chance of gonorrhoea though here—but—Do it.

I heard her husband come into the kitchen now so we gave him the afterbirth in a newspaper to bury. Keep them damned kids out of here, his sister told him. Lock that door. Of course, there was no lock on it.

How do you feel now? I asked the mother after everything had been cleaned up. All right, she said with the peculiar turn of her head and smile by which I knew her.

How many is that? I asked the other woman. Five boys and three girls, she said. I've forgotten how to fix a baby, she went on. What shall I do? Put a little boric acid powder on the belly button to help dry it up?

Sex Education

Dorothy Canfield

It was three times—but at intervals of many years—that I heard my Aunt Minnie tell about an experience of her girlhood that had made a never-to-be-forgotten impression on her. The first time she was in her thirties, still young. But she had then been married for ten years, so that to my group of friends, all in the early teens, she seemed quite of another generation.

The day she told us the story, we had been idling on one end of her porch as we made casual plans for a picnic supper in the woods. Darning stockings at the other end, she paid no attention to us until one of the girls said, "Let's take blankets and sleep out there. It'd be fun."

"No," Aunt Minnie broke in sharply, "you mustn't do that."

"Oh, for goodness' sakes, why not!" said one of the younger girls, rebelliously, "the boys are always doing it. Why can't we, just once?"

Aunt Minnie laid down her sewing. "Come here, girls," she said, "I want you should hear something that happened to me when I was your age."

Her voice had a special quality which, perhaps, young people of today would not recognize. But we did. We knew from experience that it was the dark voice grownups used when they were going to say something about sex.

Yet at first what she had to say was like any dull family anecdote; she had been ill when she was fifteen; and afterwards she was run down, thin, with no appetite. Her folks thought a change of air would do her good, and sent her from Vermont out to Ohio—or was it Illinois? I don't remember. Anyway, one of those places where the corn grows high. Her mother's Cousin Ella lived there, keeping house for her son-in-law.

The son-in-law was the minister of the village church. His wife had died some years before, leaving him a young

195

widower with two little girls and a baby boy. He had been a normally personable man then, but the next summer, on the Fourth of July when he was trying to set off some fireworks to amuse his children, an imperfectly manufactured rocket had burst in his face. The explosion had left one side of his face badly scarred. Aunt Minnie made us see it, as she still saw it, in horrid detail: the stiffened, scarlet scar tissue distorting one cheek, the lower lip turned so far out at one corner that the moist red mucous-membrane lining always showed, one lower eyelid hanging loose, and watering.

After the accident, his face had been a long time healing. It was then that his wife's elderly mother had gone to keep house and take care of the children. When he was well enough to be about again, he found his position as pastor of the little church waiting for him. The farmers and village people in his congregation, moved by his misfortune, by his faithful service and by his unblemished character, said they would rather have Mr. Fairchild, even with his scarred face, than any other minister. He was a good preacher, Aunt Minnie told us, "and the way he prayed was kind of exciting. I'd never known a preacher, not to live in the same house with him, before. And when he was in the pulpit, with everybody looking up at him, I felt the way his children did, kind of proud to think we had just eaten breakfast at the same table. I liked to call him 'Cousin Malcolm' before folks. One side of his face was all right, anyhow. You could see from that that he *had* been a good-looking man. In fact, probably one of those ministers that all the women——" Aunt Minnie paused, drew her lips together, and looked at us uncertainly.

Then she went back to the story as it happened—as it happened that first time I heard her tell it. "I thought he was a saint. Everybody out there did. That was all *they* knew. Of course, it made a person sick to look at that awful scar—the drooling corner of his mouth was the worst. He tried to keep that side of his face turned away from folks. But you always knew it was there. That was what kept him from marrying again, so Cousin Ella said. I heard her say lots of times that he knew no woman would touch any man who looked the way he did, not with a ten-foot pole.

"Well, the change of air did do me good. I got my appetite back, and ate a lot and played outdoors a lot with my cousins. They were younger than I (I had my sixteenth birthday there) but I still liked to play games. I got taller and laid on some weight. Cousin Ella used to say I grew as fast as the corn did. Their house stood at the edge of the village. Beyond it was one of those big cornfields they have out West. At the time when I first got there, the stalks were only up to a person's knee. You could see over their tops. But it grew like lightning, and before long, it was the way thick woods are here, way over your head, the stalks growing so close together it was dark under them.

"Cousin Ella told us youngsters that it was lots worse for getting lost in than woods, because there weren't any landmarks in it. One spot in a cornfield looked just like any other. 'You children keep out of it,' she used to tell us almost every day, *especially you girls.* It's no place for a decent girl. You could easy get so far from the house nobody could hear you if you hollered. There are plenty of men in this town that wouldn't like anything better than——' she never said what.

"In spite of what she said, my little cousins and I had figured out that if we went across one corner of the field, it would be a short cut to the village, and sometimes, without letting on to Cousin Ella, we'd go that way. After the corn got really tall, the farmer stopped cultivating, and we soon beat down a path in the loose dirt. The minute you were inside the field it was dark. You felt as if you were miles from anywhere. It sort of scared you. But in no time the path turned and brought you out on the far end of Main Street. Your breath was coming fast, maybe, but that was what made you like to do it.

"One day I missed the turn. Maybe I didn't keep my mind on it. Maybe it had rained and blurred the tramped-down look of the path. I don't know what. All of a sudden, I knew I was lost. And the minute I knew that, I began to run, just as hard as I could run. I couldn't help it, any more than you can help snatching your hand off a hot stove. I didn't know what I was scared of, I didn't even know I *was* running, till my heart was pounding so hard I had to stop.

"The minute I stood still, I could hear Cousin Ella saying, 'There are plenty of men in this town that wouldn't like anything better than——' I didn't know, not really, what she meant. But I knew she meant something horrible. I opened my mouth to scream. But I put both hands over my mouth to keep the scream in. If I made any noise, one of those men would hear me. I thought I heard one just behind me, and whirled around. And then I thought another one had tiptoed up behind me, the other way, and I spun around so fast I almost fell over. I stuffed my hands hard up against my mouth. And then—I couldn't help it—I ran again—but my legs were shaking so I soon had to stop. There I stood, scared to move for fear of rustling the corn and letting the men know where I was. My hair had come down, all over my face. I kept pushing it back and looking around, quick, to make sure one of the men hadn't found out where I was. Then I thought I saw a man coming towards me, and I ran away from him— and fell down, and burst some of the buttons off my dress, and was sick to my stomach—and thought I heard a man close to me and got up and staggered around, knocking into the corn because I couldn't even see where I was going.

"And then, off to one side, I saw Cousin Malcolm. Not a man. The minister. He was standing still, one hand up to his face, thinking. He hadn't heard me.

"I was so *terrible* glad to see him, instead of one of those men, I ran as fast as I could and just flung myself on him, to make myself feel how safe I was."

Aunt Minnie had become strangely agitated. Her hands were shaking, her face was crimson. She frightened us. We could not look away from her. As we waited for her to go on, I felt little spasms twitch at the muscles inside my body. "And what do you think that *saint,* that holy minister of the Gospel, did to an innocent child who clung to him for safety? The most terrible look came into his eyes—you girls are too young to know what he looked like. But once you're married, you'll find out. He grabbed hold of me—that dreadful face of his was *right on mine*—and began clawing the clothes off my back."

She stopped for a moment, panting. We were too frightened to speak. She went on, "He had torn my dress right down to the waist before I—then I *did* scream—all I could—and pulled away from him so hard I almost fell down, and ran and all of a sudden I came out of the corn, right in the back yard of the Fairchild house. The children were staring at the corn, and Cousin Ella ran out of the kitchen door. They had heard me screaming. Cousin Ella shrieked out, 'What is it? What happened? Did a man scare you?' And I said, 'Yes, yes, yes, a man—I ran——!' And then I fainted away. I must have. The next thing I knew I was on the sofa in the living room and Cousin Ella was slapping my face with a wet towel."

'She had to wet her lips with her tongue before she could go on. Her face was gray now. "There! that's the kind of thing girls' folks ought to tell them about—so they'll know what men are like."

She finished her story as if she were dismissing us. We wanted to go away, but we were too horrified to stir. Finally one of the youngest girls asked in a low trembling voice, "Aunt Minnie, did you tell on him?"

"No, I was ashamed to," she said briefly. "They sent me home the next day anyhow. Nobody ever said a word to me about it. And I never did either. Till now."

By what gets printed in some of the modern child-psychology books, you would think that girls to whom such a story had been told would never develop normally. Yet, as far as I can remember what happened to the girls in that group, we all grew up about like anybody. Most of us married, some happily, some not so well. We kept house. We learned—more or less—how to live with our husbands, we had children and struggled to bring them up right—we went forward into life, just as if we had never been warned not to.

Perhaps, young as we were that day, we had already had enough experience of life so that we were not quite blank paper for Aunt Minnie's frightening story. Whether we thought of it then or not, we couldn't have failed to see that at this very time, Aunt Minnie had been married for ten years or more, comfortably and well married, too. Against what she tried by that story to brand into our minds stood the cheerful home life in that house, the good-natured, kind, hard-working husband, and the children—the three rough-and-tumble, nice little boys, so adored by their parents, and the sweet girl baby who died, of whom they could never speak without tears. It was such actual contact with adult life that probably kept generation after generation of girls from being scared by tales like Aunt Minnie's into a neurotic horror of living.

Of course, since Aunt Minnie was so much older than we, her boys grew up to be adolescents and young men, while our children were still little enough so that our worries over them were nothing more serious than whooping cough and trying to get them to make their own beds. Two of our aunt's three boys followed, without losing their footing, the narrow path which leads across adolescence into normal adult life. But the middle one, Jake, repeatedly fell off into the morass. "Girl trouble," as the succinct family phrase put it. He was one of those boys who have "charm," whatever we mean by that, and was always being snatched at by girls who would be "all wrong" for him to marry. And once, at nineteen, he ran away from home, whether with one of these girls or not we never heard, for through all her ups and downs with this son, Aunt Minnie tried fiercely to protect him from scandal that might cloud his later life.

Her husband had to stay on his job to earn the family living. She was the one who went to find Jake. When it was gossiped around that Jake was in "bad company" his mother drew some money from the family savings-bank account, and silent, white-cheeked, took the train to the city where rumor said he had gone.

Some weeks later he came back with her. With no girl. She had cleared him of that entanglement. As of others, which followed, later. Her troubles seemed over when, at a "suitable" age, he fell in love with a "suitable" girl, married her and took her to live in our shire town, sixteen miles away, where he had a good position. Jake was always bright enough.

Sometimes, idly, people speculated as to what Aunt Minnie had seen that time she went after her runaway son, wondering where her search for him had taken her—very queer places for Aunt Minnie to be in, we imagined. And how could such an ignorant, homekeeping woman ever have known what to say to an errant willful boy to set him straight?

Well, of course, we reflected, watching her later struggles with Jake's erratic ways, she certainly could not have remained ignorant, after seeing over and over what she probably had; after talking with Jake about the things which, a good many times, must have come up with desperate openness between them.

She kept her own counsel. We never knew anything definite about the facts of those experiences of hers. But one day she told a group of us—all then married women—something which gave us a notion about what she had learned from them.

We were hastily making a layette for a not-especially welcome baby in a poor family. In those days, our town had no such thing as a district-nursing service. Aunt Minnie, a vigorous woman of fifty-five, had come in to help. As we sewed, we talked, of course; and because our daughters were near or in their teens, we were comparing notes about the bewildering responsibility of bringing up girls.

After a while, Aunt Minnie remarked, "Well, I hope you teach your girls some *sense*. From what I read, I know you're great on telling them 'the facts,' facts we never heard of when we were girls. Like as not, some facts I don't know, now. But knowing the facts isn't going to do them any more good than *not* knowing the facts ever did, unless they have some sense taught them, too."

"What do you mean, Aunt Minnie?" one of us asked her uncertainly.

She reflected, threading a needle, "Well, I don't know but what the best way to tell you what I mean is to tell you about something that happened to me, forty years ago. I've never said anything about it before. But I've thought about it a good deal. Maybe——"

She had hardly begun when I recognized the story—her visit to her Cousin Ella's Midwestern home, the widower with his scarred face and saintly reputation and, very vividly, her getting lost in the great cornfield. I knew every word she was going to say—to the very end, I thought.

But no, I did not. Not at all.

She broke off, suddenly, to exclaim with impatience, "Wasn't I the big ninny? But not so big a ninny as that old cousin of mine. I could wring her neck for getting me in such a state. Only she didn't know any better, herself. That was the way they brought young people up in those days, scaring them out of their wits about the awfulness of getting lost, but not telling them a thing about how *not* to get lost. Or how to act, if they did.

"If I had had the sense I was born with, I'd have known that running my legs off in a zigzag was the worst thing I could do. I couldn't have been more than a few feet from the path when I noticed I wasn't on it. My tracks in the loose plow dirt must have been perfectly plain. If I'd h' stood still, and collected my wits, I could have looked down to see which way my footsteps went and just walked back over them to the path and gone on about my business.

"Now I ask you, if I'd been told how to do that, wouldn't it have been a lot better protection for me—if protection was what my aunt thought she wanted to give me—than to scare me so at the idea of being lost that I turned deaf-dumb-and-blind when I thought I was?

"And anyhow that patch of corn wasn't as big as she let on. And she knew it wasn't. It was no more than a big field in a farming country. I was a well-grown girl of sixteen, as tall as I am now. If I couldn't have found the path, I could have just walked along one line of cornstalks—*straight*—and I'd have come out somewhere in ten minutes. Fifteen at the most. Maybe not just where I wanted to go. But all right, safe, where decent folks were living."

She paused, as if she had finished. But at the inquiring blankness in our faces, she went on, "Well, now, why isn't teaching girls—and boys, too, for the Lord's sake don't forget they need it as much as the girls—about this man-and-woman business, something like that? If you give them the idea—no matter whether it's *as* you tell them the facts, or as you *don't* tell them the facts, that it is such a terribly scary thing that if they take a step into it, something's likely to happen to them so awful that you're ashamed to tell them what—well, they'll lose their heads and run around like crazy things, first time they take one step away from the path.

"For they'll be trying out the paths, all right. You can't keep them from it. And a good thing too. How else are they going to find out what it's like? Boys' and girls' going to-gether is a path across one corner of growing up. And when they go together, they're likely to get off the path some. Seems to me, it's up to their folks to bring them up so when they do, they don't start screaming and running in circles, but stand tall, right where they are, and get their breath and fig-ure out how to get back.

"And anyhow, you don't tell 'em the truth about sex" (I was astonished to hear her use the actual word, taboo to women of her generation) "if they get the idea from you that it's all there is to living. It's not. If you don't get to where you want to go in it, well, there's a lot of landscape all around it a person can have a good time in.

"D'you know, I believe one thing that gives girls and boys the wrong idea is the way folks *look!* My old cousin's face, I can see her now, it was as red as a rooster's comb when she was telling me about men in that cornfield. I believe now she kind of *liked* to talk about it."

(Oh, Aunt Minnie—and yours! I thought.)

Someone asked, "But how *did* you get out, Aunt Minnie?"

She shook her head, laid down her sewing. "More foolish-ness. That minister my mother's cousin was keeping house for—her son-in-law—I caught sight of him, down along one of the aisles of cornstalks, looking down at the ground, thinking, the way he often did. And I was so glad to see him I rushed right up to him, and flung my arms around his neck and hugged him. He hadn't heard me coming. He gave a great start, put one arm around me and turned his face full towards me—I suppose for just a second he had forgotten how awful one side of it was. His expression, his eyes—well, you're all married women, you know how he looked, the way any able-bodied man thirty-six or -seven, who'd been married and begotten children, would look—for a minute anyhow, if a full-blooded girl of sixteen, who ought to have known better, flung herself at him without any warning, her hair tumbling down, her dress half unbottoned, and hugged him with all her might.

"I was what they called innocent in those days. That is, I knew just as little about what men are like as my folks could manage I should. But I was old enough to know all right what that look meant. And it gave me a start. But of course the real thing of it was that dreadful scar of his, so close to my face—that wet corner of his mouth, his eye drawn down with the red inside of the lower eyelid showing——

"It turned me so sick, I pulled away with all my might, so fast that I ripped one sleeve nearly loose, and let out a screech like a wildcat. And ran. Did I run? And in a minute, I was through the corn and had come out in the back yard of the house. I hadn't been more than a few feet from it, probably, any of the time. And then I fainted away. Girls were always fainting away; it was the way our corset strings were pulled tight, I suppose, and then—oh, a lot of fuss.

"But anyhow," she finished, picking up her work and going on, setting neat, firm stitches with steady hands, "there's one thing, I never told anybody it was Cousin Malcolm I had met in the cornfield. I told my old cousin that 'a man had scared me.' And nobody said anything more about it to me, not ever. That was the way they did in those days. They thought if they didn't let on about something, maybe it wouldn't have happened. I was sent back to Vermont right away and Cousin Malcolm went on being minister of the church. I've always been," said Aunt Minnie moderately, "kind of proud that I didn't go and ruin a man's life for just one second's slip-up. If you could have called it that. For it *would* have ruined him. You know how hard as stone people are about other folks' let-downs. If I'd have told, not one person in that town would have had any charity. Not one would have tried to understand. One slip, *once*, and they'd have pushed him down in the mud. If I had told, I'd have felt pretty bad about it, later—when I came to have more sense. But I declare, I can't see how I came to have the decency, dumb as I was then, to know that it wouldn't be fair."

It was not long after this talk that Aunt Minnie's elderly husband died, mourned by her, by all of us. She lived alone then. It was peaceful October weather for her, in which she kept a firm roundness of face and figure, as quiet-living country-women often do, on into her late sixties.

But then Jake, the boy who had had girl trouble, had wife trouble. We heard he had taken to running after a young girl, or was it that she was running after him? It was something serious. For his nice wife left him and came back with the children to live with her mother in our town. Poor Aunt Minnie used to go to see her for long talks which made them both cry. And she went to keep house for Jake, for months at a time.

She grew old, during those years. When finally she (or something) managed to get the marriage mended so that Jake's wife relented and went back to live with him, there was no trace left of her pleasant brisk freshness. She was stooped, and slow-footed and shrunken. We, her kins-people, although we would have given our lives for any one of our own children, wondered whether Jake was worth what it had cost his mother to—well, steady him, or reform him. Or perhaps just understand him. Whatever it took.

She came of a long-lived family and was able to go on keeping house for herself well into her eighties. Of course we and the other neighbors stepped in often to make sure she was all right. Mostly, during those brief calls, the talk turned on nothing more vital than her geraniums. But one midwinter afternoon, sitting with her in front of her cozy stove, I chanced to speak in rather hasty blame of someone who had, I thought, acted badly. To my surprise this brought from her the story about the cornfield which she had evidently quite forgotten telling me, twice before.

This time she told it almost dreamily, swaying to and fro in her rocking chair, her eyes fixed on the long slope of snow outside her window. When she came to the encounter with the minister she said, looking away from the distance and back into my eyes, "I know now that I had been, all along, kind of *interested* in him, the way any girl as old as I was would be, in any youngish man living in the same house with her. And a minister, too. They have to have the gift of gab so much more than most men, women get to thinking they are more alive than men who can't talk so well. I *thought* the reason I threw my arms around him was because I had been so scared. And I certainly had been scared, by my old cousin's horrible talk about the cornfield being full of men waiting to grab girls. But that wasn't all the reason I flung myself at Malcolm Fairchild and hugged him. I know that now. Why in the world shouldn't I have been taught *some* notion of it then? 'Twould do girls good to know that they are just like everybody else—human nature *and* sex, all mixed up together. I didn't have to hug him. I wouldn't have, if he'd been dirty or fat or old, or chewed tobacco."

I stirred in my chair, ready to say, "But it's not so simple as all that to tell girls——" and she hastily answered my unspoken protest. "I know, I know, most of it can't be put into words. There just aren't any words to say something that's so both-ways-at-once all the time as this man-and-woman business. But look here, you know as well as I do that there are lots more ways than in words to teach young folks what you want 'em to know."

The old woman stopped her swaying rocker to peer far back into the past with honest eyes. "What was in my mind back there in the cornfield—partly anyhow—was what had been there all the time I was living in the same house with Cousin Malcolm—that he had long straight legs, and broad shoulders, and lots of curly brown hair, and was nice and flat in front, and that one side of his face was good-looking. But most of all, that he and I were really alone, for the first time, without anybody to see us.

"I suppose if it hadn't been for that dreadful scar, he'd have drawn me up, tight, and—most any man would—kissed me. I know how I must have looked, all red and hot and my hair down and my dress torn open. And, used as he was to big cornfields, he probably never dreamed that the reason I looked that way was because I was scared to be by myself in one. He may have thought—you know what he may have thought."

"Well—if his face had been like anybody's—when he looked at me the way he did, the way a man does look at a woman he wants to have, it would have scared me—some. But I'd have cried, maybe. And probably he'd have kissed me again. You know how such things go. I might have come out of the cornfield halfway engaged to marry him. Why not? I was old enough, as people thought then. That would have been nature. That was probably what he thought of, in that first instant.

"But what did I do? I had one look at his poor, horrible face, and started back as though I'd stepped on a snake. And screamed and ran."

"What do you suppose *he* felt, left there in the corn? He must have been sure that I would tell everybody he had attacked me. He probably thought that when he came out and went back to the village he'd already be in disgrace and put out of the pulpit.

"But the worst must have been to find out, so rough, so plain from the way I acted—as if somebody had hit him with an ax—the way he would look to any woman he might try to get close to. That must have been——" she drew a long breath, "well, pretty hard on him."

After a silence, she murmured pityingly, "Poor man!"

The Ram in the Thicket

Wright Morris

In this dream Mr. Ormsby stood in the yard—at the edge of the yard where the weeds began—and stared at a figure that appeared to be on a rise. This figure had the head of a bird with a crown of bright, exotic plumage—visible, somehow,. in spite of the helmet he wore. Wisps of it appeared at the side, or shot through the top of it like a pillow leaking long sharp spears of yellow straw. Beneath the helmet was the face of a bird, a long face indescribably solemn, with eyes so pale they were like openings on the sky. The figure was clothed in a uniform, a fatigue suit that was dry at the top but wet and dripping about the waist and knees. Slung over the left arm, very casually, was a gun. The right arm was extended and above it hovered a procession of birds, an endless coming and going of all the birds he had ever seen. The figure did not speak—nor did the pale eyes turn to look at him—although it was for this, this alone, that Mr. Ormsby was there. The only sounds he heard were those his lips made for the birds, a wooing call of irresistible charm. As he stared Mr. Ormsby realized that he was pinned to something, a specimen pinned to a wall that had quietly moved up behind. His hands were fastened over his head and from the weight he felt in his wrists he knew he must be suspended there. He knew he had been brought there to be judged, sentenced, or whatever—and this would happen when the figure looked at him. He waited, but the sky-blue eyes seemed only to focus on the birds, and his lips continued to speak to them wooingly. They came and went, thousands of them, and there were so many, and all so friendly, that Mr. Ormsby, also, extended his hand. He did this although he knew that up to that moment his hands were tied—but strange to relate, in that gesture, he seemed to be free. Without effort he broke the bonds and his hand was free. No birds came—but in his palm he felt the dull drip of the alarm clock and he held it tenderly, like a living thing, until it ran down.

In the morning light the photograph at the foot of his bed was a little startling—for the boy stood alone on a rise, and he held, very casually, a gun. The face beneath the helmet had no features, but Mr. Ormsby would have known it just by the—well, just by the stance. He would have known it just by the way the boy held the gun. He held the gun like some women held their arms when their hands were idle, like parts of their body that for the moment were not much use. Without the gun it was as if some part of the boy had been amputated; the way he stood, even the way he walked was not quite right. But with the gun—what seemed out, fell into place.

He had given the boy a gun because he had never had a gun himself and not because he wanted him to kill anything. The boy didn't want to kill anything either—he couldn't very well with his first gun because of the awful racket the beebees made in the barrel. He had given him a thousand-shot gun—but the rattle the bee-bees made in the barrel made it impossible for the boy to get close to anything. And *that* was what had made a hunter out of him. He had to stalk everything in order to get close enough to hit it, and after you stalk it you naturally want to hit something. When he got a gun that would really shoot, and only made a racket after he shot it, it was only natural that he shot it better than anyone else. He said shoot, because the boy never seemed to realize that when he shot and hit something the something was dead. He simply didn't realize this side of things at all. But when he brought a rabbit home and fried it—by himself, for Mother wouldn't let *him* touch it—he never kidded them about the meat they ate themselves. He never really knew whether the boy did that out of kindness for Mother, or simply because he never thought about such things. He never seemed to feel like talking much about anything. He would sit and listen to Mother—he had never once been disrespectful—nor had he ever once heeded anything she said. He would listen, respectfully, and that was all. It was a known fact that Mother knew more about birds and bird migration than anyone in the state of Pennsylvania—except the boy. It was clear to him that the boy knew more, but for years it had been Mother's business and it meant more to her—the business did—than to the boy. But it was only natural that a woman who founded the League for Wild Life Conservation would be upset by a boy who lived with a gun. It was only natural—he was upset himself by the *idea* of it—but the boy and his gun somehow never bothered him. He had never seen a boy and a dog, or a boy and anything any closer—and if the truth were known both the boy's dogs knew it, nearly died of it. Not that he wasn't friendly, or as nice to them as any boy, but they knew they simply didn't rate in a class with his gun. Without that gun the boy himself really looked funny, didn't know how to stand, and nearly fell over if you talked to him. It was only natural that he enlisted, and there was nothing he ever heard that surprised him less than their making a hero out of him. Nothing more natural than that they should name something after him. If the boy had had his choice it would have been a gun rather than a boat, a thousand-shot non-rattle bee-bee gun named Ormsby. But it would kill Mother if she knew— maybe it would kill nearly anybody—what he thought was the most natural thing of all. Let God strike him dead if he had known anything righter, anything more natural, than that the boy should be killed. That was something he could not explain, and would certainly never mention to Mother unless he slipped up some night and talked in his sleep.

He turned slowly on the bed, careful to keep the springs quiet, and as he lowered his feet he scooped his socks from the floor. As a precaution Mother had slept the first few months of their marriage in her corset—as a precaution and as an aid to self-control. In the fall they had ordered twin beds. Carrying his shoes—today, of all days, would be a trial for Mother—he tiptoed to the closet and picked up his shirt and pants. There was simply no reason, as he had explained to her twenty years ago, why she should get up when he could just as well get a bite for himself. He had made that suggestion when the boy was just a baby and she needed her strength. Even as it was she didn't come out of it any too well. The truth was, Mother was so thorough about every- thing she did that her breakfasts usually took an hour or more. When he did it himself he was out of the kitchen in ten, twelve minutes and without leaving any pile of dishes around. By himself he could quick-rinse them in a little hot water, but with Mother there was the dish pan and all of the suds. Mother had the idea that a meal simply wasn't a meal without setting the table and using half the dishes in the place. It was easier to do it himself, and except for Sunday, when they had brunch, he was out of the house an hour be- fore she got up. He had a bite of lunch at the store and at four o'clock he did the day's shopping since he was right downtown anyway. There was a time he called her up and inquired as to what she thought she wanted, but since he did all the buying he knew that better himself. As secretary for the League of Women Voters she had enough on her mind in times like these without cluttering it up with food. Now that he left the store an hour early he usually got home in the midst of her nap or while she was taking her bath. As he had nothing else to do he prepared the vegetables, and dressed the meat, as Mother had never shown much of a flare for meat. There had been a year—when the boy was small and before he had taken up that gun—when she had made several marvelous lemon meringue pies. But feeling as she did about the gun—and she told them both how she felt about it—she didn't see why she should slave in the kitchen for people like that. She always spoke to them as *they*—or as *you* plural—from the time he had given the boy the gun. Whether this was because they were both men, both culprits, or both something else, they were never entirely separate things again. When she called *they* would both answer, and though the boy had been gone two years he still felt him *there,* right beside him, when Mother said *you.*

For some reason he could not understand—although the rest of the house was neat as a pin, too neat—the room they *lived* in was always a mess. Mother refused to let the cleaning woman set her foot in it. Whenever she left the house she locked the door. Long, long ago he had said something, and she had said something, and she had said she had wanted one room in the house where she could relax and just let her hair down. That had sounded so wonderfully human, so unusual for Mother, that he had been completely taken with it. As a matter of fact he still didn't know what to say. It was the only room in the house—except for the screened-in porch in the summer—where he could take off his shoes and open his shirt on his underwear. If the room was *clean,* it would be clean like all of the others, and that would leave him nothing but the basement and the porch. The way the boy took to the out-of-doors—he stopped looking for his cuff links, began to look for pins—was partially because he couldn't find a place in the house to sit down. They had just redecorated the house—the boy at that time was just a little shaver—and Mother had spread newspapers over everything. There hadn't been a chair in the place—except the straight-backed ones at the table—that hadn't been, that *wasn't* covered with a piece of newspaper. Anyone who had ever scrunched around on a paper knew what that was like. It was at that time that he had got the idea of having his pipe in the basement, reading in the bedroom, and the boy had taken to the out-of-doors. Because he had always wanted a gun himself, and because the boy was alone, with no kids around to play with, he had brought him home that damn gun. A thousand-shot gun by the name of Daisy—funny that he should remember the name and five thousand bee-bees in a drawstring canvas bag.

That gun had been a mistake—he began to shave himself in tepid, lukewarm water rather than let it run hot, which would bang the pipes and wake Mother up. That gun had been a mistake—when the telegram came that the boy had been killed Mother hadn't said a word, but she made it clear whose fault it was. There was never any doubt, *any* doubt, as to just whose fault it was.

He stopped thinking while he shaved, attentive to the mole at the edge of his mustache, and leaned to the mirror to avoid dropping suds on the rug. There had been a time when he had wondered about an oriental throw rug in the bathroom, but over twenty years he had become accustomed to it. As a matter of fact he sort of missed it whenever they had guests with children and Mother remembered to take it up. Without the rug he always felt just a little uneasy, a little naked, in the bathroom, and this made him whistle or turn on the water and let it run. If it hadn't been for that he might not have noticed as soon as he did that Mother did the same thing whenever anybody was in the house. She turned on the water and let it run until she was through with the toilet, then she would flush it before she turned the water off. If you happen to have old-fashioned plumbing, and have lived with a person for twenty years, you can't help noticing little things like that. He had got to be a little like that himself: since the boy had gone he used the one in the basement or waited until he got down to the store. As a matter of fact it was more convenient, didn't wake Mother up, and he could have his pipe while he was sitting there.

With his pants on, but carrying his shirt—for he might get it soiled preparing breakfast—he left the bathroom and tiptoed down the stairs.

Although the boy had gone, was gone, that is, Mother still liked to preserve her slip covers and the kitchen linoleum. It was a good piece, well worth preserving, but unless there were guests in the house he never saw it—he nearly forgot that it was there. The truth was he had to look at it once a week, every time he put down the papers—but right now he couldn't tell you what color that linoleum was! He couldn't do it, and wondering what in the world color it was he bent over and peeked at it—blue. Blue and white, Mother's favorite colors of course.

Suddenly he felt the stirring of his bowels. Usually this occurred while he was rinsing the dishes after his second cup of coffee or after the first long draw on his pipe. He was not supposed to smoke in the morning, but it was more important to be regular that way than irregular with his pipe. Mother had been the first to realize this—not in so many words—but she would rather he did anything than not be able to do *that*.

He measured out a pint and a half of water, put it over a medium fire, and added just a pinch of salt. Then he walked to the top of the basement stairs, turned on the light, and at the bottom turned it off. He dipped his head to pass beneath a sagging line of wash, the sleeves dripping, and with his hands out, for the corner was dark, he entered the cell.

The basement toilet had been put in to accommodate the help, who had to use something, and Mother would not have them on her oriental rug. Until the day he dropped some money out of his pants and had to strike a match to look for it, he had never noticed what kind of a stool it was. Mother had picked it up secondhand—she had never told him where—because she couldn't see buying something new for a place always in the dark. It was very old, with a chain pull, and operated on a principle that invariably produced quite a splash. But in spite of that, he preferred it to the one at the store and very much more than the one upstairs. This was rather hard to explain since the seat was pretty cold in the winter and the water sometimes nearly froze. But it was private like no other room in the house. Considering that the house was as good as empty, that was a strange thing to say, but it was the only way to say how he felt. If he went off for a walk like the boy, Mother would miss him, somebody would see him, and he wouldn't feel right about it anyhow. All he wanted was a dark quiet place and the feeling that for five minutes, just five minutes, nobody would be looking for him. Who would ever believe five minutes like that were so hard to come by? The closest he had ever been to the boy— after he had given him the gun—was the morning he had found him here on the stool. It was then that the boy had said, *et tu, Brutus,* and they had both laughed so hard they had had to hold their sides. The boy had put his head in a basket of wash so Mother wouldn't hear. Like everything the boy said there were two or three ways to take it, and in the dark Mr. Ormsby could not see his face. When he stopped laughing the boy said, *Well Pop, I suppose one flush ought to do*, but Mr. Ormsby had not been able to say anything. To be called Pop made him so weak that he had to sit right down on the stool, just like he was, and support his head in his hands. Just as he had never had a name for the boy, the boy had never had a name for him—none, that is, that Mother would permit him to use. Of all the names Mother couldn't stand, Pop was the worst, and he agreed with her, it was vulgar, common, and used by strangers to intimidate old men. He agreed with her, completely—until he heard the word in the boy's mouth. It was only natural that the boy would use it if he ever had the chance—but he never dreamed that any word, especially *that* word, could mean what it did. It made him weak, he had to sit down and pretend he was going about his business, and what a blessing it was that the place was dark. Nothing more was said, ever, but it remained their most important conversation—so important they were afraid to try and improve on it. Days later he remembered the rest of the boy's sentence, and how shocking it was but without any *sense* of shock. A blow so sharp that he had no sense of pain, only a knowing, as he had under gas, that he had been worked on. For two, maybe three minutes, there in the dark they had been what Mother called them, they were *they*—and they were there in the basement because they were so much alike. When the telegram came, and when he knew what he would find, he had brought it there, had struck a match, and read what it said. The match filled the cell with light and he saw—he couldn't help seeing—piles of tin goods in the space beneath the stairs. Several dozen cans of tuna fish and salmon, and since *he* was the one that had the points, bought the groceries, there was only one place Mother could have got such things. It had been a greater shock than the telegram—that was the honest-to-God's truth and anyone who knew Mother as well as he did would have felt the same. It was unthinkable, but there it was—and there were more on top of the water closet, where he peered while precariously balanced on the stool. Cans of pineapple, crabmeat, and tins of Argentine beef. He had been stunned, the match had burned down and actually scorched his fingers, and he nearly killed himself when he forgot and stepped off the seat. Only later in the morning—after he had sent the flowers to ease the blow for Mother—

did he realize how such a thing *must* have occurred. Mother
knew so many influential people, and before the war they
gave her so much, that they had very likely given her all of
this stuff as well. Rather than turn it down and needlessly
alienate people, influential people, Mother had done the next
best thing. While the war was on she refused to serve it, or
profiteer in any way—and at the same time not alienate
people foolishly. It had been an odd thing, certainly, that he
should discover all of that by the same match that he read
the telegram. Naturally, he never breathed a word of it to
Mother, as something like that, even though she was not su-
perstitious, would really upset her. It was one of those things
that he and the boy would keep to themselves.

It would be like Mother to think of putting it in here, the
very last place that the cleaning woman would look for it.
The new cleaning woman would neither go upstairs nor
down, and did whatever she did somewhere else. Mr. Ormsby
lit a match to see if everything was all right—hastily blew it
out when he saw that the can pile had increased. He stood
up—then hurried up the stairs without buttoning his pants as
he could hear the water boiling. He added half a cup, then
measured three heaping tablespoons of coffee into the bottom
of the double boiler, buttoned his pants. Looking at his watch
he saw that it was seven-thirty-five. As it would be a hard
day—sponsoring a boat was a man-size job—he would give
Mother another ten minutes or so. He took two bowls from
the cupboard, sat them on blue pottery saucers, and with the
grapefruit knife in his hand walked to the icebox.

As he put his head in the icebox door—in order to see he
had to—Mr. Ormsby stopped breathing and closed his eyes.
What had been dying for some time was now dead. He
leaned back, inhaled, leaned in again. The floor of the icebox
was covered with a fine assortment of jars full of leftovers
Mother simply could not throw away. Some of the jars were
covered with little oilskin hoods, some with saucers, and some
with paper snapped on with a rubber band. It was impossible
to tell, from the outside, which one it was. Seating himself on
the floor he removed them one at a time, starting at the front
and working toward the back. As he had done this many
times before, he got well into the problem, near the middle,
before troubling to sniff anything. A jar which might have
been carrots—it was hard to tell without probing—was now a
furry marvel of green mold. It smelled only mildly, however,
and Mr. Ormsby remembered that this was penicillin, the

ife-giver. A spoonful of cabbage—it had been three months ince they had had cabbage—had a powerful stench but was till not the one he had in mind. There were two more jars of nold, the one screwed tight he left alone as it had a frosted ook and the top of the lid bulged. The culprit, however, was ot that at all, but in an open saucer on the next shelf—part f an egg—Mr. Ormsby had beaten the white himself. He olaced the saucer on the sink and returned all but two of the ars to the icebox; the cabbage and the explosive looking one. f it smelled he took it out, otherwise Mother had to see for erself as she refused to take *their* word for these things. When he was just a little shaver the boy had walked into the iving room full of Mother's guests and showed them some-hing in a jar. Mother had been horrified—but she naturally hought it a frog or something and not a bottle out of her own cebox. When one of the ladies asked the boy where in the vorld he had found it, he naturally said, *In the icebox*. Mother had never forgiven him. After that she forbade him to ook in the box without permission, and the boy had not so nuch as peeked in it since. He would eat only what he found on the table, or ready to eat in the kitchen—or what he found at the end of those walks he took everywhere.

With the jar of cabbage and furry mold Mr. Ormsby made a trip to the garage, picked up the garden spade, walked around behind. At one time he had emptied the jars and nerely buried the contents, but recently, since the war that is, ne had buried it all. Part of it was a question of time—he nad more work to do at the store—but the bigger part of it vas to put an end to the jars. Not that it worked out that vay—all Mother had to do was open a new one—but it gave nim a real satisfaction to bury them. Now that the boy and nis dogs were gone there was simply no one around the house to eat up all the food Mother saved.

There were worms in the fork of earth he had turned and ne stood looking at them—*they* both had loved worms—vhen he remembered the water boiling on the stove. He dropped everything and ran, ran right into Emil Ludlow, the nilkman, before he noticed him. Still on the run he went up he steps and through the screen door into the kitchen—he vas clear to the stove before he remembered the door would slam. He started back, but too late, and in the silence that followed the BANG he stood with his eyes tightly closed, his ists clenched. Usually he remained in this condition until a sign from Mother—a thump on the floor or her voice at the

top of the stairs. None came, however, only the sound of the
milk bottles that Emil Ludlow was leaving on the porch. Mr.
Ormsby gave him time to get away, waited until he heard the
horse walking, then he went out and brought the milk in. At
the icebox he remembered the water—why it was he had
come running in the first place—and he left the door open
and hurried to the stove. It was down to half a cup but not,
thank heavens, dry. He added a full pint, then returned and
put the milk in the icebox; took out the butter, four eggs, and
a Flori-gold grapefruit. Before he cut the grapefruit he
looked at his watch and seeing that it was ten minutes to
eight, an hour before train time, he opened the stairway door.

"Ohhh Mother!" he called, and then he returned to the
grapefruit.

Ad astra per aspera, she said, and rose from the bed. In
the darkness she felt about for her corset then let herself go
completely for the thirty-five seconds it required to get it on.
This done, she pulled the cord to the light that hung in the
attic, and as it snapped on, in a firm voice she said, *Fiat lux*.
Light having been made, Mother opened her eyes.

As the bulb hung in the attic, thirty feet away and out of
sight, the closet remained in an afterglow, a twilight zone. It
was not light, strictly speaking, but it was all Mother wanted
to see. Seated on the attic stairs she trimmed her toenails with
a pearl handled knife that Mr. Ormsby had been missing for
several years. The blade was not so good any longer and
using it too freely had resulted in ingrown nails on both of
her big toes. But Mother preferred it to scissors which were
proven, along with bathtubs, to be one of the most dangerous
things in the home. *Even more than the battlefield, the most
dangerous place in the world. Dry feet and hands before
turning on lights, dry between toes.*

Without stooping she slipped into her sabots and left the
closet, the light burning, and with her eyes dimmed, but not
closed, went down the hall. Locking the bathroom door she
stepped to the basin and turned on the cold water, then she
removed several feet of paper from the toilet paper roll.
This took time, as in order to keep the roller from squeaking,
it had to be removed from its socket in the wall, then returned. One piece she put in the pocket of her kimono, the
other she folded into a wad and used as a blotter to dab up
spots on the floor. Turning up the water she sat down on the

stool—then she got up to get a pencil and pad from the table near the window. On the first sheet she wrote—

Ars longa, vita brevis
Wildflower club, sun. 4 pm.

She tore this off and filed it, tip showing, right at the front of her corset. On the next page—

ROGER—
Ivory Snow
Sani Flush on thurs.

As she placed this on top of the toilet paper roll she heard him call "First for breakfast." She waited until he closed the stairway door, then she stood up and turned on the shower. As it rained into the tub and splashed behind her in the basin, she lowered the lid, flushed the toilet. Until the water closet had filled, stopped gurgling, she stood at the window watching a squirrel cross the yard from tree to tree. Then she turned the shower off and noisily dragged the shower curtain, on its metal rings, back to the wall. She dampened her shower cap in the basin and hung it on the towel rack to dry, dropping the towel that was there down the laundry chute. This done, she returned to the basin and held her hands under the running water, now cold, until she was awake. With her index finger she massaged her gums—*there is no pyorrhea among the Indians*—and then, with the tips of her fingers, she dampened her eyes.

She drew the blind, and in the half light the room seemed to be full of lukewarm water, greenish in color. With a piece of Kleenex, she dried her eyes, then turned it to gently blow her nose, first the left side, then with a little more blow on the right. There was nothing to speak of, nothing, so she folded the tissue, slipped it into her pocket. Raising the blind, she faced the morning with her eyes softly closed, letting the light come in as prescribed—gradually. Eyes wide, she then stared for a full minute at the yard full of grackles, covered with grackles, before she *discovered* them. Running to the door, her head in the hall, her arm in the bathroom wildly pointing, she tried to whisper, loud-whisper to him, but her voice cracked.

"Roger," she called, a little hoarsely. "The window—run!"

She heard him turn from the stove and skid on the newspapers, bump into the sink, curse, then get up and on again.

"Blackbirds?" he whispered.

"Grackles!" she said, for the thousandth time she said *Grackles*.

"They're pretty!" he said.

"Family—" she said, ignoring him, "family *icteridae* American."

"Well—" he said.

"Roger!" she said, "something's burning."

She heard him leave the window and on his way back to the stove, on the same turn, skid on the papers again. She left him there and went down the hall to the bedroom, closed the door, and passed between the mirrors once more to the closet. From five dresses—*any woman with more than five dresses, at this time, should have the vote taken away from her*—she selected the navy blue sheer with pink lace yoke and kerchief, short bolero. At the back of the closet—but in order to see she had to return to the bathroom, look for the flashlight in the drawer full of rags and old tins of shoe polish—were three shelves, each supporting ten to twelve pairs of shoes, and a large selection of slippers were piled on the floor. On the second shelf were the navy blue pumps—*we all have one weakness, but between men and shoes you can give me shoes*—navy blue pumps with a cuban heel and a small bow. She hung the dress from the neck of the floor lamp, placed the shoes on the bed. From beneath the bed she pulled a hat box—the hat was new. Navy straw with shasta daisies, pink geraniums and a navy blue veil with pink and white fuzzy dots. She held it out where it could be seen in the mirror, front and side without seeing herself—*it's not every day that one sponsors a boat*. Not every day, and she turned to the calendar on her night table, a bird calendar featuring the natural-color male goldfinch for the month of June. Under the date of June 23rd she printed the words, *family icteridae—yardful*, and beneath it—

Met Captain Sudcliffe and gave him U. S. S. *Ormsby*

When he heard Mother's feet on the stairs Mr. Ormsby cracked her soft boiled eggs and spooned them carefully into her heated cup. He had spilled his own on the floor when he had run to look at the black—or whatever color they were—birds. As they were very, very soft he had merely wiped them

up. As he buttered the toast—the four burned slices were on
the back porch airing—Mother entered the kitchen and said,
"Roger—*more* toast?"

"I was watching blackbirds," he said.

"Grack-les," she said, "Any bird is a *black*bird if the males
are largely or entirely black."

Talk about male and female birds really bothered Mr.
Ormsby. Although she was a girl of the old school Mother
never hesitated, *anywhere*, to speak right out about male and
female birds. A cow was a cow, a bull was a bull, but to Mr.
Ormsby a bird was a bird.

"Among the birdfolk," said Mother, "the menfolk, so to
speak, wear the feathers. The female has more serious work
to do."

"How does that fit the blackbirds?" said Mr. Ormsby.

"Every rule" said Mother, "has an exception."

There was no denying the fact that the older Mother got
the more distinguished she appeared. As for himself, what he
saw in the mirror looked very much like the Roger Ormsby
that had married Violet Ames twenty years ago. As the top
of his head got hard the bottom tended to get a little soft, but
otherwise there wasn't much change. But it was hard to believe that Mother was the pretty little pop-eyed girl—he had
thought it was her corset that popped them—whose nipples
had been like buttons on her dress. Any other girl would
have looked like a you-know—but there wasn't a man in
Media county, or anywhere else, who ever mentioned it. A
man could think what he would think, but he was the only
man who really knew what Mother was like. And how little
she was like *that*.

"Three-seven-four east one-one-six," said Mother.

That was the way her mind worked, all over the place in
one cup of coffee—birds one moment, Mrs. Dinardo the
next.

He got up from the table and went after Mrs. Dinardo's
letter—Mother seldom had time to read them unless he read
them to her. Returning, he divided the rest of the coffee between them, unequally: three quarters for Mother, a swallow
of grounds for himself. He waited a moment, wiping his
glasses, while Mother looked through the window at another
black bird. "Cowbird," she said, "*Molothrus ater*."

"Dear Mrs. Ormsby," Mr. Ormsby began. Then he stopped
to scan the page, as Mrs. Dinardo had a strange style and
was not much given to writing letters. "Dear Mrs. Ormsby,"

he repeated, "I received your letter and I Sure was glad to know that you are both well and I know you often think of me I often think of you too—" He paused to get his breath—Mrs. Dinardo's style was not much for pauses—and to look at Mother. But Mother was still with the cowbird. "Well, Mrs. Ormsby," he continued, "I haven't a thing in a room that I know of the people that will be away from the room will be only a week next month. But come to See me I may have Something if you don't get Something." Mrs. Dinardo, for some reason, always capitalized the letter S which along with everything else didn't make it easier to read. "We are both well and he is Still in the Navy Yard. My I do wish the war was over it is So long. We are So tired of it do come and See us when you give them your boat. Wouldn't a Street be better than a boat? If you are going to name Something why not a Street? Here in my hand is news of a boat Sunk what is wrong with Ormsby on a Street? Well 116 is about the Same we have the river and its nice. If you don't find Something See me I may have something.

Best Love
Mrs. Myrtle Dinardo."

It was quite a letter to get from a woman that Mother had known, known Mother, that is, for nearly eighteen years. Brought in to nurse the boy—he could never understand why a woman like Mother, with her figure—but anyhow, Mrs. Dinardo was brought in. Something in her milk, Dr. Paige said, when it was plain as the nose on your face it was nothing in the milk, but something in the boy. He just refused, plain refused, to nurse with Mother. The way the little rascal would look at her, but not a sound out of him but gurgling when Mrs. Dinardo would scoop him up and go upstairs to their room—the only woman—other woman, that is, that Mother ever let step inside of it. She had answered an ad that Mother had run, on Dr. Paige's suggestion, and they had been like *that* from the first time he saw them.

"I'll telephone," said Mother.

On the slightest provocation Mother would call Mrs. Dinardo by long distance—she had to come down four flights of stairs to answer—and tell her she was going to broadcast over the radio or something. Although Mrs. Dinardo hardly knew one kind of bird from another, Mother sent her printed

copies of every single one of her bird-lore lectures. She also
sent her hand-pressed flowers from the garden.

"I'll telephone," repeated Mother.

"My own opinion—" began Mr. Ormsby, but stopped
when Mother picked up her eggcup, made a pile of her
plates, and started toward the sink. "I'll take care of that," he
said. "Now you run along and telephone." But Mother
walked right by him and took her stand at the sink. With one
hand—with the other she held her kimono close about her—
she let the water run into a large dish pan. Mr. Ormsby had
hoped to avoid this; now he would have to first rinse, then
dry, every piece of silver and every dish they had used. As
Mother could only use one hand it would be even slower
than usual.

"We don't want to miss our local," he said. "You better
run along and let me do it."

"Cold water," she said, "for the eggs." He had long ago
learned not to argue with Mother about the fine points of
washing pots, pans, or dishes with bits of egg. He stood at the
sink with the towel while she went about trying to make suds
with a piece of stale soap in a little wire cage. As Mother refused to use a fresh piece of soap, nothing remotely like suds
ever appeared. For this purpose, he kept a box of Gold Dust
Twins concealed beneath the sink, and when Mother turned
her back he slipped some in.

"There now," Mother said, and placed the rest of the
dishes in the water, rinsed her fingers under the tap, paused
to sniff at them.

"My own opinion—" Mr. Ormsby began, but stopped
when Mother raised her finger, the index finger with the scar
from the wart she once had. They stood quiet, and Mrs.
Ormsby listened to the water drip in the sink—the night before he had come down in his bare feet to shut it off. All the
taps dripped now and there was just nothing to do about it
but put a rag or something beneath it to break the ping.

"Thrush!" said Mother. "Next to the nightingale the most
popular of European songbirds."

"Very pretty," he said, although he simply couldn't hear a
thing. Mother walked to the window, folding the collar of her
kimono over her bosom and drawing the tails into a ham-
mock beneath her behind. Mr. Ormsby modestly turned
away. He quick-dipped one hand into the Gold Dust—
drawing it out as he slipped it into the dish pan and worked
up a suds.

As he finished wiping the dishes she came in with a bouquet for Mrs. Dinardo and arranged it, for the moment, in a tall glass.

"According to her letter," Mrs. Ormsby said, "she isn't too sure of having something—"

"Roger!" she said. "You're dripping."

Mr. Ormsby put his hands over the sink and said, "If we're going to be met right at the station I don't see where you're going to see Mrs. Dinardo. You're going to be met at the station and then you're going to sponsor the boat. My own opinion is that after the boat we come on home."

"I know that street of hers," said Mother. "There isn't a wildflower on it!"

On the wall above the icebox was a pad of paper and a blue pencil hanging by a string. As Mother started to write the point broke off, fell behind the icebox.

"Mother," he said, "you ever see my knife?"

"Milkman," said Mother. "If we're staying overnight we won't need milk in the morning."

In jovial tones Mr. Ormsby said, "I'll bet we're right back here before dark." That was all, that was ALL that he said. He had merely meant to call her attention to the fact that Mrs. Dinardo said—all but said—that she didn't have a room for them. But when Mother turned he saw that her mustache was showing, a sure sign that she was mad.

"Well—now," Mother said, and lifting the skirt of her kimono swished around the cabinet and then he heard her on the stairs. From the landing at the top of the stairs she said, "In that case I'm sure there's no need for *my* going. I'm sure the Navy would just as soon have you. After all," she said, "it's *your* name on the boat!"

"Now, Mother," he said, just as she closed the door, *not* slammed it, just closed it as quiet and nice as you'd please. Although he had been through this a thousand times it seemed he was never ready for it, never knew when it would happen, never felt anything but nearly sick. He went into the front room and sat down on the chair near the piano—then got up to arrange the doily at the back of his head. Ordinarily he could leave the house and after three or four days it would blow over, but in all his life—their life—there had been nothing like this. The Government of the United States—he got up again and called, "OHHhhhh Mother!"

No answer.

He could hear her moving around upstairs, but as she often went back to bed after a spat, just moving around didn't mean much of anything. He came back into the front room and sat down on the milk stool near the fireplace. It was the only seat in the room not protected with newspapers. The only thing the boy ever sat on when he had to sit on something. Somehow, thinking about that made him stand up. He could sit in the lawn swing, in the front yard, if Mother hadn't told everybody in town why it was that he, Roger Ormsby, would have to take the day off—not to sit in the lawn swing, not by a long shot. Everybody knew—Captain Sudcliffe's nice letter had appeared on the first page of the *Graphic*, under a picture of Mother leading a bird-lore hike in the Poconos. This picture bore the title LOCAL WOMAN HEADS DAWN BUSTERS, and marked Mother's appearance on the national bird-lore scene. But it was not one of her best pictures—it dated from way back in the twenties and those hipless dresses and round bucket hats were not Mother's type. Until they saw that picture, and the letter beneath it, some people had forgotten that Virgil was missing, and most of them seemed to think it was a good idea to swap him for a boat. The U.S.S. *Ormsby* was a permanent sort of thing. Although he was born and raised in the town hardly anybody knew very much about Virgil, but they all were pretty familiar with his boat. "How's that boat of yours coming along?" they would say, but in more than twenty years nobody had ever asked him about *his* boy. Whose boy? Well, that was just the point. Everyone agreed Ormsby was a fine name for a boat.

It would be impossible to explain to Mother, maybe to anybody for that matter, what this U.S.S. *Ormsby* business meant to him. "The" boy and "The" *Ormsby*—it was a pretty strange thing that they both had the definite article, and gave him the feeling he was facing a monument.

"Oh Rog-gerrr!" Mother called.

"Coming," he said, and made for the stairs.

From the bedroom Mother said, "However I might feel personally, I do have my *own* name to think of. I am not one of these people who can do as they please—Roger, are you listening?"

"Yes, Mother," he said.

"—with their life."

As he went around the corner he found a note pinned to the door.

> Bathroom window up
> Cellar door down
> Is it blue or brown for Navy?

He stopped on the landing and looked up the stairs.

"Did you say something?" she said.

"No, Mother—" he said, then he added, "It's blue. For the Navy, Mother, it's blue.

Barrow Street

Richard Sherman

It was a warm evening in late spring, and the apartment windows were open to the many sounds of the city's roar; but the girl, standing in the center of the living room and nervously twisting a plain gold band around her third finger, heard only two sounds. One was the convulsive throb of the automatic elevator in the corridor outside, and the other was the single chime struck by the mantel clock as its hands marked seven-thirty. For an instant the girl remained motionless, her eyes directed toward the clock's dial. It was a very pretty clock, all gold and ivory. It was, in fact, a very pretty room, spacious and high-ceilinged. The colors were "decorators' colors," the furniture was graceful in design and had the patina of age on it, and wherever one looked there was a combination of comfort and taste. The books lining one wall had the appearance of having been read, and the fireplace, though at present unlighted, was obviously functional. It was a room made warm by much living and much love.

There was a large, silver-framed photograph on the piano between the two windows, and now the girl went slowly toward it and stood gazing meditatively at the handsome and grave face of a dark-mustached young man wearing the uniform of a Navy lieutenant. Her hand went out and touched the photograph, then lifted it. For a moment she glanced around the room, as if seeking a place of concealment. But the somber, appealing eyes below the visored cap seemed to summon her back, and as she looked at them again, she hesitated, and in the end returned the photograph to its original position. Absently and almost as if unconsciously, her hand drifted down to the piano keys and formed a chord, softly. She waited until the last ripple of the chord, washing through the room, had died away, and after that, sighing, she turned toward the hall. But the sigh was not one of sadness. It spoke, rather, of a certain definitiveness, of a chapter closed and a story done. Or another story beginning.

225

In the hall she moved briskly and with assurance. To her left was a small dining room, and she went through it and the swinging door beyond, to the kitchen. She groped for the switch, flicked it, and was confronted by gleaming white walls and stainless steel. In order. Yes, perfectly in order, even to the starched frills of the gay red gingham at the window and to the graduated knives poised bright and pendulous in their wall holder. A dream kitchen, surely, with not even the tell-tale aroma of tonight's dinner to spoil the dream. But the plate of cookies that stood invitingly on the white-enameled table was no dream. The girl picked one up and munched it. As she ate, she noticed a sheet of paper sticking from the re-frigerator door, and bending closer, she read the laboriously penciled scrawl: "Mrs. Ryder. Pls deefrost tonite. Olive." She opened the refrigerator and stood gazing speculatively at its crowded shelves. She pulled out an ice tray, shoved it back. Then, after the customary moment of examination and self-doubt, she turned the knob to "Defrost" and closed the door.

"Okay, Olive," she said aloud. "You're defrosted."

From the kitchen she went into the hall and from there to the nursery. She had left the door partially open, and now she entered the room softly. A small, rose-shaded night light burned in one corner, atop the ivory chest of drawers, and the crib stood in the opposite corner, against the wall. Moving toward the crib, the girl paused by it, looking downward and smiling. A dark fuzz of hair lay against the white satin pillows, and below it was a profiled roundness of cream and pink, bounded by blue blankets. He slept. Mr. Timothy Ry-der, Jr., slept.

"Hello, Tim," whispered the girl, leaning over the rail of the crib. "Hello, Timmy. My baby, my baby, my baby."

The door leading to the adjoining room was open also, and from beyond it now sounded the muffled burr of a telephone ringing. With a final glance at the crib, the girl went toward the sound. The telephone stood on a night table beside the oversize bed, and the girl's hand rested on it for an instant before she picked it up. Then she lifted the instrument. "Hello?" she said.

"Mrs. Ryder, please," said a voice, a once-familiar voice.

"George?" said the girl, and her tone was suddenly light and filled with a thousand secret excitements and enchant-ments. "Is that you, George? Are you really in town? Are you really here?"

"Oh," he said, with a trace of embarrassment. "I guess I

didn't recognize you, did I? Yes, I'm here. I'm at the hotel. Just got in."

"Well, come right on down. I've been waiting and waiting."

There was a small silence at the other end of the line. "Look, Dorothy," said the voice, "when I wired you I was coming, I had no idea you were married. I mean, I wouldn't have bothered you if I'd known that."

"Wouldn't have bothered me?" The girl's tone was a mingling of tender reproof and indignation. "Why, George Hargrave, I'd never have forgiven you if you'd passed through town without looking me up. Never in the world. Now, you stop being silly and get in a taxi and come right down here this very minute. Quick like a rabbit."

"But are you sure it'll be—all right?"

"All right? What on earth do you mean?"

"I mean, how about—your husband?"

"Tim? Oh, George, don't be so difficult. As it happens, Tim isn't here, unfortunately—if that's what's worrying you. He had to go to Boston. But even if he were here, I'd want you to come down anyway. I want to see you. I told you when I wired you back that I wanted to see you. And you've simply got to see the baby."

"Well—"

There was spirit in the girl's voice now, spirit and light sarcasm. "Unless, of course, it would be too dull for a gay young blade like you to sit around and reminisce with an old married woman. Unless it would be too boring. After all, I certainly wouldn't want to bore you."

"Now, Dorothy, please. You know that I—"

She spoke persuasively, and as if to end the discussion. "Enough of this nonsense, George—you ought to be too grown-up for it. Now, you just get on your horse. It's seventeen West Twelfth, the third floor, and all you have to do is get into the elevator and push the button, and I'll be at the door to meet you."

"Okay," he said finally, though with no great enthusiasm. "Okay, I'll be there."

"That's better."

Replacing the phone, the girl regarded it for a moment. She had been sitting on the bed, and now, rising, she smoothed the place where she had sat. She glanced around the room. It was a large room, white, light, and airy. Only one small light was burning, and now she turned on two others, pink-shaded lamps which flanked the dressing table. The girl looked at herself in the dressing-table mirror. Then she went to a mirrored door and looked at herself full length. She was wearing a black dress that could have been called serviceable, though not much more. She frowned. Then she opened the door. A row of dresses met her eyes—a rainbow wall. She tentatively fingered a blue one, a sequined one, and finally settled on one of a chartreuse color. Lifting it from its hanger, she held it up against herself and, looking into the mirror, nodded approvingly. It was a housecoat, long and faintly formal and definitely expensive.

"You'll do," she murmured, and her words might have had reference either to the housecoat or to herself or to both together.

Within the next hour several things happened. Many things, in fact, all of them minor yet all important. The girl was transformed and so, in a sense, was the apartment, which before had had an air of loneliness and desertion about it and which now took on a nervous expectancy. Both the girl and the apartment became illumined, and gayer. Except for the nursery, which remained a shadowy pink, lights went on everywhere. Wearing the chartreuse housecoat, and with her lips freshly rouged, the girl moved busily and efficiently about the kitchen, getting a bottle of Coke from the refrigerator, dumping ice cubes into a silver vacuum bucket, running water into a silver pitcher. Then she placed bottle, bucket, pitcher, and two tall glasses on a tray and carried them to the living room, depositing the tray on a low table in front of the sofa. Her next move was to go to the entrance hall, where she opened the door of the coat closet and, reaching up to the hat shelf, took down an oblong package wrapped in brown paper and tied with string. This she took to the living room, undoing the string and removing the paper as she walked. From a corrugated-cardboard box she lifted out a full and as yet unopened bottle of whisky and, after ripping off the lead foil around its top, put it on the tray on the low table. The string she wound around her finger, the paper she folded and refolded and then pressed flat, and then she dropped both of them, along with the shreds of foil, into a wastebasket. The corrugated-cardboard box she tossed into the wastebasket also.

Her chores completed, she looked at the results—the lamplit room, the laden tray—and moved her head up and down in satisfaction, as if finding them good. Then she lifted the cover of a crystal box on the low table and from it took a cigarette and lighted it. After that she seated herself on the sofa; but almost immediately she rose, to sit in first one and then the other of the two matching modern chairs that stood beside another small table. Then she left those chairs, also, and began to pace up and down the room. Once in her pacing she paused by the radio-phonograph and, lifting its lid, studied the record on the turntable. But she made no effort to play it. Instead, she closed the lid and resumed her pacing.

The gold-and-ivory clock on the mantel struck nine.

Then, at last, she heard the elevator door opening and, an instant later, the sound of the buzzer. She waited a moment, a full moment, and then took a deep breath and went to the door.

The man standing in the corridor was young, blond, handsome, and her first gesture was to extend both hands welcomingly toward his and to cry, "George, how wonderful to see you! How perfectly, perfectly wonderful!"

His reply was somewhat more guarded. He was a highly personable young man, well groomed and well tailored, but at the moment he seemed to be distinctly ill at ease. "Hello, Dorothy," he said. "Well, it's—ah—it's good to see you, too."

She took his hat, and as she placed it on the foyer table and then led him toward the living room, she kept talking. He was looking so well. He really was looking so very, very well, wasn't he? And hadn't he taken on just a little bit of weight? Hadn't he? Just the littlest, littlest bit? Not that it wasn't becoming, because it most definitely was becoming. Anyway, it showed that he was eating well and that the Chicago climate, God forbid, must be agreeing with him.

She had seated herself on the sofa, while he, more cautious and more wary, had chosen one of the matching chairs. Her hands were busy over the tray, and now she interrupted her soliloquy on the fascinating subject of his weight and general condition of health in order to look at him fondly and say, "Why, do you know, George, it just this minute occurred to me. This is actually the first time I've ever seen you in civilian clothes."

"That's right. It is, isn't it?" said the young man. His eyes had been roaming the room. "Nice place," he said appreciatively and with respect and with possibly just a faint note of surprise. "Very nice."

She ignored the tribute, her mind apparently wandering back in gentle nostalgia. "Three years ago," she said, and sighed. "My, it seems a lifetime, doesn't it? And so much has happened since." She held a glass toward him, and he rose to accept it. "Well, here you are. Bourbon and water. See? I remember." She lifted her own glass. "Cheers, darling. And happy days and all that."

He drank. "What's that you've got there? Just a Coke?"

She nodded. "Isn't it ridiculous? Imagine—me, of all people. But I used to get so drunk, and I was such a bad drunk. All that quarreling and those scenes and those awful, awful—" She broke off, and then looked at him with great seriousness. "Tell me, George, how did you ever manage to stand me? I mean, even for as long as you did manage to stand me?"

A sudden flush appeared in the young man's cheeks. "I— ah—" But the rest of his words were lost in the glass, which he again raised to his lips.

"Of course," she said, "I know now why I drank so much. It was because I was so miserable. And now that I'm not miserable—in fact, just the opposite—I don't feel the need of a drink at all."

"Um," said the young man. He cleared his throat. "How long you been married, Dorothy?"

"Two and a half years. It was—let's see—it was just about six months after you went out to Chicago." Her tone seemed to assume a special significance. "You know, when your mother was so sick. Remember?"

"Yeah," said the young man, somewhat uncomfortably. "Yeah, I remember."

"Did your mother ever get well, George?" she asked solicitously.

"Oh, sure. Sure, she got well. She's fine."

She nodded. "I thought she would be," she said. "I was practically certain of it." Smiling, she cradled her glass between her palms, gazed down into it, and then spoke reflectively, though not bitterly. "You know, George, I probably might as well tell you that I really hated you for a while there. I wished you were dead—and I wished I was, too. Just think. There wasn't even a letter. Not one single letter. Not even a post card."

He was silent, and he shifted uneasily in his chair. "I guess it was kind of a lousy trick, wasn't it?" he said then. "But we weren't hitting it off, you know we weren't. And things were getting so—" He stopped, and seemed to grope for the proper word and not find it.

"Complicated, maybe? Messy? Involved?"

"All right. Involved."

"For you, you mean. Not for me. I knew what I wanted. Or at least I thought I did."

He became slightly self-defensive. "I admitted it was a lousy trick, didn't I? I apologized. I—"

She looked at him, and she shook her head. Her manner was friendly, even generous. "Darling, you needn't apologize. I suppose in a way it wasn't the most chivalrous conduct in the world, but for me it turned out to be—well, the most wonderful thing that ever happened, though I didn't realize it at the time. Because it was shortly after that I met Tim. And maybe if you'd still been around, I wouldn't have."

He had got up from his chair and had gone to the two tall windows. Now he stood looking out. From the street below came the cracked treble of a hurdy-gurdy playing one of its many songs of spring. "You're pretty happy, aren't you, Dorothy?" he said.

Her answer came to him like a sigh. "Oh, George, you'll never know." There was a pause, and then she added, "And somehow I have the feeling that you never will know. But—" she shrugged—"you're you, and that's that, and nothing can be done about it."

He had turned, and now he was standing in front of the silver-framed photograph. He indicated it with a gesture. "Is this Tim?"

"Yes," she said. "That's Tim."

"Nice-looking. Quite a guy."

She had risen and was starting toward the hall. "It doesn't half do him justice. He's handsomer than that—much." Turning, she beckoned to the young man. "But if you want to see something really handsome, you just follow me."

He did follow her, and she led him into the nursery, entering stealthily and with a warning finger at her lips. He stood looking down at the sleeping infant. "Fine," he said at last. "Mighty fine."

"Oh, now, George, surely you can do better than that. He's more than just fine." She was engaged in several small maternal operations—the adjustment of a blanket, the straightening of a pillow, the hand held up to detect a possible draft.

"Well, you know I—well, I never can think of anything to say about a baby." And then, inspirationally, he did think of something to say, something brilliant. "How old is he?"

"Ten months." Carelessly, yet with affectionate pressure,

she placed her hand on the young man's sleeve. "George, honey, you really ought to get married. You really, really should."

"Um-hum. I suppose so. I suppose I should, at that."

From the nursery the girl led the young man on a conducted tour of the entire apartment, because, she said it was such a funny old apartment and they had been so lucky to discover it, and she wanted him to see what could be accomplished with these remodeled apartments in old brownstones if you had patience and went at the job properly. Each room called for its own special footnote; but although she displayed a natural pride of ownership, there was no evidence of boastfulness in her manner. Flaws, when there were flaws, were recognized and even emphasized as such. Of the large master bedroom she said, "See—a fireplace. I always wanted a fireplace in my bedroom, and now I've got one. Smoke and all." Of the small room which was mostly filled with a drawing board and scattered blueprints and architect's equipment, she said, "This was intended as a maid's room, but our Olive prefers to sleep out, so Tim decided to fix it up as a place where he could work at home when he wanted to." Of the kitchen she said, "Tim keeps calling it the galley. It's the Navy in him." And of the bath she said, "Isn't it huge? Tim's always saying we ought to give a party in it. But just try to keep it warm. Not all the heaters in Arabia—"

The tour took time, and during it the young man appeared gradually to lose his uneasiness and to become more relaxed. Several times he laughed at the girl's remarks, even though the remarks were not particularly witty. And as she preceded him into this room and into that, he kept his eyes on her slim, chartreuse waistline. The housecoat rustled pleasantly and sibilantly when she moved. The young man's face, which had shown signs of strain, softened and grew thoughtful. It became more than thoughtful. It became admiring. The charms of domesticity had never been revealed more sweetly.

They were back in the living room now, and he had started on his second drink. That is, it was only the second drink he had had since his arrival, but the suddenly accelerated effect it was having on him seemed to indicate that it might have been preceded by others, perhaps by a number of others.

This time he was sitting on the sofa beside the girl, and when she reached for a cigarette from the crystal box, he struck a match for her and cupped the flame as she bent her head toward it. There was a liquid brightness in his eyes, and when he spoke, his voice had a new and almost caressing warmth in it. "Your hair," he said, "I like it that new way. Looks very good."

"Thank you, George," she said. She became the conscientious hostess. "But all we've done ever since you got here is talk about me. Now let's talk about you, for a change. I want to hear all about Chicago. What are you doing out there? Did you go back into advertising again, the way you said you were going to?"

He nodded. "Yup. I'm with an advertising agency."

"Copy?"

Again he nodded. "Mostly. Now and then I do a little selling. Or try to. It hasn't been going too well."

Immediately sympathy welled from her. "Oh, I'm so sorry." She tapped the ash from her cigarette onto a tray and glanced at him with a kind, though detached, benevolence. "And have you got a girl out there, George?"

He hesitated. "Mm, well—yes. Matter of fact, I have."

"That's nice. And is she gay? Is she fun?"

He seemed to consider the question. "Yes, I guess so." Then he set his glass on the low table. His voice was earnest, serious, even moodily philosophical. "But you know, Dorothy, sooner or later the time comes when a man wants more than just fun. You know?"

Her eyes widened in surprise. "But surely not you, George."

"Why not me?"

"No reason, except—well, for instance, when you wired me that you were coming, it was because you wanted just fun, wasn't it?" She was gently reminding. "Wasn't it?" she repeated.

"Well—"

"Of course it was." Leaning back against the sofa pillows, she clasped her hands behind her head, her breasts rounded beneath the chartreuse housecoat. She quoted as if from memory, and ran all the words together without a stop. " 'Lonely and forlorn stranger arriving Thursday evening en route to Washington would appreciate companionship for light wines and dancing please wire reply to University Club love George.' " Turning, she smiled at him, dazzlingly. "Now, if that didn't mean 'just fun,' what did it mean?"

"I wanted to see you," he said stubbornly. "I wanted—old times."

"Undoubtedly." Her arms came down, and her hands

folded themselves placidly in her lap. "And probably it would have been like old times, too. Could have been, anyway. We'd have gone to a bar, and then we'd have gone on to another bar, and then we'd have had dinner—or perhaps we'd even have skipped dinner—and then you'd have picked up a bottle of something, and we'd have gone down to my place on Barrow Street." For the first time there was an edge in her voice, a trace of bite. "And in the morning I'd have got up and gone to the office and you'd have gone to Washington. Exactly as you'll be going to Washington tomorrow." She paused, and added, "Only not quite exactly."

The young man had reached for his glass and was helping himself to more whisky. The portion was generous. "All right," he said. "So I was a heel."

"No, not a heel, George dear. Not a heel at all. Just on the loose. And on the town. And the victim, I think, of certain misconceptions."

He drank. "All right, maybe that was my original plan. I don't say definitely that it was, but it might have been." He looked at her. "But now that I've seen you again, you're— well, you're different. You've changed."

The girl's fingers became less placid. They interlocked. "Changed how?"

He passed a puzzled hand over his brow. "I don't know what it is, exactly. I can't explain it." He gestured at the room. "But look at this place. You never used to have any talent for making a room look like this. You never even had any desire to. Barrow Street always used to be a mess, you know it did. And the baby. I watched you when you were looking at the baby. You were—you were downright beautiful."

"Thank you, George," said the girl. "That's the first time you've ever said that. You used to say I was attractive, sometimes—but never beautiful."

He moved closer to her and leaned forward intently, curiously. "How did you develop it, Dorothy? All this—this serenity you've got. Where did it come from?"

At first she appeared not to understand him, and then she smiled. She spoke as to a child. "But it was there all the time, George. You say I've changed, but I haven't. Really I haven't. It's just that I'm happy, that's all. Basically I'm the same person I always was."

"You're not," he contradicted her. "You don't look the same. You don't act the same."

"Oh," she granted, "I probably needed someone to bring

me out, yes. Someone who had faith in me and who loved me. But that was easy. Tim did that."

"The hell with Tim." He placed his hand on her wrist. "Dot. Dot, honey."

"Yes, George?"

"We made a mistake, didn't we?"

"I didn't."

"Well, then I did. And I admit it." His arm had gone round her, but for the moment he made no attempt to draw her close. "But it's not too late, is it?" Then his arm tightened. "Is it?"

For just a fraction of an instant the girl's arms seemed about to creep up to return his embrace, and then, as he bent his head down and was about to place his lips on hers, her eyes, which had been cast downward, looked up at him. There was no affection in them now, and no warmth. It was a cold, level, contemptuous gaze, and it froze him.

" 'Were' a heel, did you say, George?" she said. And after that, with one swift and agile movement, she had risen from the sofa and was standing looking down at him.

The clock on the mantel struck eleven-thirty.

"I think you'd better go," said the girl. "I think you'd better go right now."

The young man's tie was awry, his coat was mussed, and his face was flushed. "Now, look, Dot," he began. "There's no need to be—"

"I said you'd better go."

He shrugged, and after a moment got up from the sofa. "Okay," he said. "If that's the way you want it."

There was no pretense of a conventionally polite farewell or even of a civil exchange of good nights. She watched him as he walked into the hall, watched him as he picked up his hat. With his hand on the doorknob, he looked back at her. He presented the figure of a very sad, very discomfited, and rather pathetic young man.

"I could have 'brought you out,' too," he said, "just as much as your wonderful Tim did."

"Maybe you could have," she said. "But you didn't. You didn't even want to try."

He opened his mouth as if to speak, and then closed it. Then he went out. Still standing by the sofa, she heard the whine of the elevator ascending, heard the door clang open and clang shut, heard the drone of the car as it started down again. Then and only then did she move. Her first act was to exhale deeply, her shoulders and her whole body slumping. After that she bent to the table and, placing the whisky bottle aside, picked up the tray with the ice bucket and the pitcher and the glasses and the smaller bottle. Methodically she carried the tray to the kitchen and set it on the sink. She put the Coke bottle with other empty bottles in a wooden container under the stove. Then, being careful not to splash the housecoat, she washed and dried the bucket, the pitcher, the glasses. She wiped the sink with the damp dishcloth, hung the dishcloth on the rack. After that, she turned out the light in the kitchen.

She turned out all the other lights, too, all those she previously had turned on. But before turning out the dressing-table lights in the bedroom, she opened the closet door and lifted out the black dress. She took off the chartreuse housecoat and returned it to its hanger, putting it back carefully and adjusting its folds so that they hung straight. Then she got into the black dress again and, after a final look in the full-length mirror, closed the closet door.

From the bedroom she went into the nursery, and for a time she stood looking down at the sleeping child. But she did not look at him long, for from there she went into the living room, emptied the ashtrays, and rubbed her handkerchief over the table to remove the circles left by the glasses. That done, she picked up the whisky bottle and held it to the light, noting that the level of the liquid in it had gone down some three inches. But there was plenty left. Plenty. Stooping to the wastebasket, she retrieved the string, the brown paper, the cardboard box, and the foil. She wadded the foil into a ball and thrust it into one of the pockets in the black dress. She placed the bottle back in the box and skillfully rewrapped and tied it. Then she went to the closet in the hall and put it back on the shelf.

Back in the living room, her final gesture was to remove the plain gold band from her finger and drop it into her pocket. Then she selected a magazine and sat down by the fireplace. But although she opened the magazine, she did not read it. Instead, she looked into the black and empty grate.

She was still seated by the empty grate when there was the sound of a key in the lock, laughter, and voices in the entrance hall. Almost immediately two people entered the room, a man and a woman, and with them there seemed to come a fresh breeze cooling the sluggish night air. Both were young and both were handsome. The man had a dark mustache, and around her head the woman was wearing a silk chartreuse scarf.

"Well," said the man, as the mantel clock chimed once more, "that's timing it. We told you twelve-thirty, and we just made it, right on the button."

"Did everything go all right?" said the young woman pleasantly.

"Everything went fine," said the girl, who had risen from her chair and was placing the magazine on the table. "Just fine."

"No fuss?"

"Not a bit. It was just the way it should be."

"That's good," said the young woman. She turned toward the hall. "Well, I think I'll just go in and have a look at him. Tim, you'd better—ah—"

"Sure," said the young man with the dark mustache. "Sure."

The girl had stepped to the hall and was returning with the paper-wrapped package and a light jacket, which she was draping around her shoulders.

Now the man took out a wallet. "Let's see," he said. "Five hours at ninety cents an hour. That makes it—four-fifty, doesn't it?"

"That's right," she said.

He held out four bills and a coin. "There you are, exactly. And thank you."

"Thank you, Mr. Ryder," she said. The "you" was stressed, but only naturally so.

She moved toward the hall, and as she did so, she met the young woman returning from the nursery. The young woman was smiling. "He's sleeping like a lamb," she said to the girl. "Not a peep."

"He's a very good baby," said the girl. "He's a wonderful baby. I felt as if he were mine. Really mine."

"Did you find the cookies?"

"Yes, thank you. And I took a Coke from the refrigerator. I didn't think you'd mind. There was a note from the maid on the refrigerator door, asking you to defrost. So I did that, too."

"Oh, I'm glad you did," said the young woman. "I might have forgotten." She had taken the scarf from her head and was looping it into loose folds. "Well, I guess that's all, then. Would you be available again if we should need you? What do we do? Call the agency and request Miss—Prescott, is it?"

"That's right," said the girl. "Miss Dorothy Prescott." She hesitated. "But you see, I don't do this regularly. It was—an unusual occasion, a favor. The woman who runs the agency happens to be a friend of mine."

"Oh," said the young woman disappointedly. "I'm sorry. Well, in any case, it was very nice of you to help us out."

"I didn't mind," said the girl. "I loved it. Thank you. Thank you so much."

"Look," said the young man with the dark mustache. "It's late. Do you have far to go?"

"Not far," said the girl, hugging the package more closely and opening the door. "Barrow Street."

Blue Island

J. F. Powers

On the day the Daviccis moved into their house, Ethel was visited by a Welcome Wagon hostess bearing small gifts from local merchants, but after that by nobody for three weeks, only Ralph's relatives and door-to-door salesmen. And then Mrs. Hancock came smiling. They sat on the matching green chairs which glinted with threads of what appeared to be gold. In the picture window, the overstimulated plants grew wild in pots.

Mrs. Hancock had guessed right about Ethel and Ralph, that they were newlyweds. "Am I right in thinking you're of Swedish descent, Mrs. Davicky? You, I mean?"

Ethel smiled, as if taking a compliment, and said nothing.

"I only ask because so many people in the neighborhood are. I'm not, myself," said Mrs. Hancock. She was unnaturally pink, with tinted blue hair. Her own sharp-looking teeth were transparent at the tips. "But you're so fair."

"My maiden name was Taylor," Ethel said. It was, and it wasn't—it was the name she'd got at the orphanage. Wanting a cigarette, she pushed the silver box on the coffee table toward Mrs. Hancock.

Mrs. Hancock used one of her purple claws to pry up the first cigarette from the top layer. "A good old American name like mine."

She was making too much of it, Ethel thought, and wondered about Mrs. Hancock's maiden name.

"Is your husband in business, Mrs. Davicky?"

"Yes, he is." Ethel put the lighter—a simple column of silver, the mate to the box—to Mrs. Hancock's cigarette and then to her own.

"Not here in Blue Island?"

"No." From here on, it could be difficult. Ralph was afraid that people in the neighborhood would disapprove of his business. "In Minneapolis." The Mohawk Inn, where Ethel had worked as a waitress, was first-class—thick steaks, dark

239

lights, an electric organ—but Ralph's other places, for which his brothers were listed as the owners, were cut-rate bars on or near Washington Avenue. "He's a distributor," Ethel said, heading her off. "Non-alcoholic beverages mostly." It was true, Ralph had taken over his family's wholesale wine business, never much in Minneapolis, and got it to pay by converting to soft drinks.

Mrs. Hancock was noticing the two paintings which, because of their size and the lowness of the ceiling, hung two feet from the floor, but she didn't comment on them. "Lovely, lovely," she said, referring to the driftwood lamp in the picture window. A faraway noise came from her stomach. She raised her voice. "But you've been lonely, haven't you? I could see it when I came in. It's this neighborhood."

"It's very nice," said Ethel quickly. Maybe Mrs. Hancock was at war with the neighbors, looking for an ally.

"I suppose you know Mrs. Nilgren," said Mrs. Hancock, nodding to the left.

"No, but I've seen her. Once she waved."

"She's nice. Tied down with children, though." Mrs. Hancock nodded to the right. "How about old Mrs. Mann?"

"I don't think anybody's there now."

"The Manns are away! California. So you don't know anybody yet?"

"No."

"I'm surprised you haven't met some of them at the Cashway."

"I never go there," Ethel said. "Ralph—that's my husband—he wants me to trade at the home-owned stores."

"Oh?" Mrs. Hancock's stomach cut loose again. "I didn't know people still felt that way." Mrs. Hancock looked down the street, in the direction of the little corner store. "Do they do much business?"

"No," said Ethel. The old couple who ran it were suspicious of her, she thought, for buying so much from them. The worst of it was that Ralph had told her to open a charge account, and she hadn't, and she never knew when he'd stop there and try to use it. There was a sign up in the store that said: In God We Trust—All Others Pay Cash.

"I'll bet that's it," Mrs. Hancock was saying. "I'm afraid people are pretty clannish around here—and the Wagners have so many friends. They live one-two-three-five houses down." Mrs. Hancock had been counting the houses across the street. "Mr. Wagner's the manager of the Cashway."

Ethel was holding her breath.

"I'm afraid so," said Mrs. Hancock.

Ethel sighed. It was Ralph's fault. She'd always wanted to trade at the Cashway.

Mrs. Hancock threw back her head, inhaling, and her eyelids, like a doll's, came down. "I'm afraid it's your move, Mrs. Davicky."

Ethel didn't feel that it was her move at all and must have shown it.

Mrs. Hancock sounded impatient. "Invite 'em in. Have 'em in for a morning coffee."

"I couldn't do that," Ethel said. "I've never been to a coffee." She'd only read about coffees in the women's magazines to which Ralph had subscribed for her. "I wouldn't know what to do."

"Nothing to it. Rolls, coffee, and come as you are. Of course nobody really does, not really." Mrs. Hancock's stomach began again. "Oh, shut up," she said to it. "I've just come from one too many." Mrs. Hancock made a face, showing Ethel a brown mohair tongue. She laughed at Ethel. "Cheer up. It wasn't in this neighborhood."

Ethel felt better. "I'll certainly think about it," she said.

Mrs. Hancock rose, smiling, and went over to the telephone. "You'll do it right now," she said, as though being an older woman entitled her to talk that way to Ethel. "They're probably dying to get inside this lovely house."

After a moment, Ethel, who was already on her feet, having thought that Mrs. Hancock was leaving, went over and sat down to telephone. In the wall mirror she saw how she must appear to Mrs. Hancock. When the doorbell had rung, she'd been in too much of a hurry to see who it was to do anything about her lips and hair. "Will they know who I am?"

"Of course." Mrs. Hancock squatted on the white leather hassock with the phone book. "And you don't have to say I'm coming. Oh, I'll come. I'll be more than happy to. You don't need me, though. All you need is confidence."

And Mrs. Hancock was right. Ethel called eight neighbors, and six could come on Wednesday morning, which Mrs. Hancock had thought would be the best time for her. Two of the six even sounded anxious to meet Ethel, and, surprisingly, Mrs. Wagner was one of these.

"You did it all yourself," said Mrs. Hancock.

"With your help," said Ethel, feeling indebted to Mrs.

Hancock, intimately so. It was as if they'd cleaned the house together.

They were saying good-by on the front stoop when Ralph rolled into the driveway. Ordinarily at noon he parked just outside the garage, but that day he drove in—without acknowledging them in any way. "Mr. Daveechee," Ethel commented. For Mrs. Hancock, after listening to Ethel pronounce her name for all the neighbors, was still saying "Davicky."

Mrs. Hancock stayed long enough to get the idea that Ralph wasn't going to show himself. She went down the front walk saying, " 'Bye now."

While Mrs. Hancock was getting into her car, which seemed a little old for the neighborhood, Ralph came out of the garage.

Mrs. Hancock waved and nodded—which, Ethel guessed, was for Ralph's benefit, the best Mrs. Hancock could do to introduce herself at the distance. She drove off. Too late, Ralph's hand moved up to wave. He stared after Mrs. Hancock's moving car with a look that just didn't belong to him, Ethel thought, a look that she hadn't seen on his face until they moved out to Blue Island.

During lunch, Ethel tried to reproduce her conversation with Mrs. Hancock, but she couldn't tell Ralph enough. He wanted to know the neighbors' names, and she could recall the names of only three. Mrs. Wagner, one of them, was very popular in the neighborhood, and her husband . . .

"You go to the Cashway then. Some of 'em sounded all right, huh?"

"Ralph, they all sounded all right, real friendly. The man next door sells insurance. Mr. Nilgren."

Ethel remembered that one of the husbands was a lawyer and told Ralph that. He left the table. A few minutes later Ethel heard him driving away.

It had been a mistake to mention the lawyer to Ralph. It had made him think of the shooting they'd had at the Bow Wow, one of the joints. There had been a mix-up, and Ralph's home address had appeared in the back pages of one of the papers when the shooting was no longer news. Ethel doubted that the neighbors had seen the little item. Ralph might be right about the lawyer, though, who would probably have to keep up with everything like that.

Ralph wouldn't have worried so much about such a little

thing in the old days. He was different now. It was hard to get him to smile. Ethel could remember how he would damn the Swedes for slapping higher and higher taxes on liquor and tobacco, but now, when she pointed out a letter some joker had written to the paper suggesting a tax on coffee, or when she showed him the picture of the wife of the Minnesota senator—the fearless one—christening an ore boat with a bottle of milk, which certainly should've given Ralph a laugh, he was silent.

It just made Ethel sick to see him at the windows, watching Mr. Nilgren, a sandy-haired, dim-looking man who wore plaid shirts and a red cap in the yard. Mr. Nilgren would be raking out his hedge, or wiring up the skinny little trees, or washing his car if it was Sunday morning, and there Ralph would be, behind a drape. One warm day Ethel had seen Mr. Nilgren in the yard with a golf club, and had said, "He should get some of those little balls that don't go anywhere." It had been painful to see Ralph then. She could almost *hear* him thinking. He would get some of those balls and give them to Mr. Nilgren as a present. No, it would look funny if he did. Then he got that sick look that seemed to come from wanting to do a favor for someone who might not let him do it.

A couple of days later Ethel learned that Ralph had gone to an indoor driving range to take golf lessons. He came home happy, with a club he was supposed to swing in his spare time. He'd made a friend, too, another beginner. They were going to have the same schedule and be measured for clubs. During his second lesson, however, he quit. Ethel wasn't surprised, for Ralph, though strong, was awkward. She was better than he was with a hammer and nails, and he mutilated the heads of screws. When he went back the second time, it must have been too much for him, finding out he wasn't any better, after carrying the club around the house for three days. Ethel asked about the other beginner, and at first Ralph acted as though she'd made him up, and then he hotly rejected the word "friend," which she'd used. Finally he said, "If you ask me, that bastard's played before!"

That was just like him. At the coffee, Ethel planned to ask the women to come over soon with their husbands, but she was afraid some of the husbands wouldn't take to Ralph. Probably he could buy insurance from Mr. Nilgren. He would want to do something for the ones who weren't selling anything, though—if there were any like that—and they might misunderstand Ralph. He was used to buying the drinks. He should relax and take the neighbors as they came. Or move.

She didn't know why they were there anyway. It was funny. After they were married, before they left on their honeymoon, Ralph had driven her out to Blue Island and walked her through the house. That was all there was to it. Sometimes she wondered if he'd won the house at cards. She didn't know why they were there when they could just as well be living at Minnetonka or White Bear, where they could keep a launch like the one they'd hired in Florida—and where the houses were far apart and neighbors wouldn't matter so much. What were they waiting for? Some of the things they owned, she knew, were for later. They didn't need sterling for eighteen in Blue Island. And the two big pictures were definitely for later.

She didn't know what Ralph liked about his picture, which was of an Indian who looked all in sitting on a horse that looked all in, but he had gone to the trouble of ordering it from a regular art store. Hers was more cheerful, the palace of the Doge of Venice, Italy. Ralph hadn't wanted her to have it at first. He was really down on anything foreign. (There were never any Italian dishes on the menu at the Mohawk.) But she believed he liked her for wanting that picture, for having a weakness for things Italian, for him—and even for his father and mother, whom he was always sorry to see and hadn't invited to the house. When they came anyway, with his brothers, their wives and children (and wine, which Ralph wouldn't touch), Ralph was in and out, upstairs and down, never long in the same room with them, never encouraging them to stay when they started to leave. They called him "Rock" or "Rocky," but Ralph didn't always answer to that. To one of the little boys who had followed him down into the basement, Ethel had heard him growl, "The name's Ralph"—that to a nine-year-old. His family must have noticed the change in Ralph, but they were wrong if they blamed her, just because she was a little young for him, a blonde, and not a Catholic—not that Ralph went to church. In fact, she thought Ralph would be better off with his family for his friends, instead of counting so much on the neighbors. She liked Ralph's family and enjoyed having them in the house.

And if Ralph's family hadn't come around, the neighbors might even think they weren't properly married, that they

had a love nest going there. Ethel didn't blame the neighbors
for being suspicious of her and Ralph. Mr. Nilgren in his
shirt and cap that did nothing for him, he belonged there, but
not Ralph, so dark, with his dark blue suits, pearl-gray hats,
white jacquard shirts—and with her, with her looks and plati-
num hair. She tried to dress down, to look like an older
woman, when she went out. The biggest thing in their favor,
but it wasn't noticeable yet, was the fact that she was pregnant.

Sometimes she thought Ralph must be worrying about the
baby—as she was—about the kind of life a little kid would
have in a neighborhood where his father and mother didn't
know anybody. There were two pre-school children at the
Nilgrens'. Would they play with the Davicci kid? Ethel didn't
ever want to see that sick look of Ralph's on a child of hers.

That afternoon two men in white overalls arrived from
Minneapolis in a white truck and washed the windows inside
and out, including the basement and garage. Ralph had sent
them. Ethel sat in the dining room and polished silver to the
music of *Carmen* on records. She played whole operas when
Ralph wasn't home.

In bed that night Ralph made her run through the neighbors again. Seven for sure, counting Mrs. Hancock. "Is that
all?" Ethel said she was going to call the neighbor who hadn't
been home. "When?" When she got the number from Mrs.
Hancock. "When's that?" When Mrs. Hancock phoned, if she
phoned . . . And that was where Ralph believed Ethel had
really fallen down. She didn't have Mrs. Hancock's number—or address—and there wasn't a Hancock listed for Blue
Island in the phone book. "How about next door?" Mrs. Nilgren was still coming. "The other side?" The Manns were still
away, in California, and Ralph knew it. "They might come
back. Ever think of that? You don't wanna leave them out."
Them he'd said, showing Ethel what was expected of her. He
wanted those husbands. Ethel promised to watch for the return of the Manns. "They could come home in the night."
Ethel reminded Ralph that a person in her condition needed
a lot of sleep, and Ralph left her alone then.

Before Ralph was up the next morning, Ethel started to
clean the house. Ralph was afraid the house cleaning
wouldn't be done right (*he* spoke of her condition) and
wanted to get another crew of professionals out from Minneapolis. Ethel said it wouldn't look good. She said the neigh-

bors expected them to do their own house cleaning—*and window washing*. Ralph shut up.

When he came home for lunch, Ethel was able to say that Mrs. Hancock had called and that the neighbor who hadn't been home could come to the coffee. Ethel had talked to her, and she had sounded very friendly. "That's three of 'em, huh?" Ethel was tired of that one, but told him they'd *all* sounded friendly to her. "Mrs. Hancock okay?" Mrs. Hancock was okay. More than happy to be coming. Ralph asked if Ethel had Mrs. Hancock's phone number and address. No. "Why not?" Mrs. Hancock would be there in the morning. That was why—and Ralph should get a hold on himself.

In the afternoon, after he was gone, Ethel put on one of her new conservative dresses and took the bus to Minneapolis to buy some Swedish pastry. She wanted something better than she could buy in Blue Island. In the window of the store where they'd bought Ralph's Indian, there were some little miniatures, lovely New England snow scenes. She hesitated to go in when she saw the sissy clerk was on duty again. He had made Ralph sore, asking how he'd like to have the Indian framed in birch bark. The Mohawk was plastered with birch bark, and Ralph thought the sissy recognized him and was trying to be funny. "This is going into my home!" Ralph had said, and ordered the gold frame costing six times as much as the Indian. However, he'd taken the sissy's advice about having a light put on it. Ethel hesitated, but she went in. In his way, the sissy was very nice, and Ethel went home with five little Old English prints. When she'd asked about the pictures in the window, the New England ones, calling them "landscapes," he'd said "snowscapes" and looked disgusted, as if they weren't what she should want.

When she got home, she hung the prints over the sofa where there was a blank space, and they looked fine in their shiny black frames. She didn't say anything to Ralph, hoping he'd notice them, but he didn't until after supper. "Hey, what *is* this?" he said. He bounced off the sofa, confronting her.

"Ralph, they're cute!"

"Not in my home!"

"Ralph, they're humorous!" The clerk had called them that. Ralph called them drunks and whores. He had Ethel feeling ashamed of herself. It was hard to believe that she could have felt they were just fat and funny and just what their living room needed, as the clerk had said. Ralph took them down. "Man or woman sell 'em to you?" Ethel, seeing what he had in mind, knew she couldn't tell him where she'd got them. She lied. "I was in Dayton's . . ."

"A woman—all right, then *you* can take 'em back!"

She was scared. Something like that was enough to make Ralph regret *marrying* her—and to remind her again that she couldn't have made him. If there had been a showdown between them, he would've learned about her first pregnancy. It would've been easy for a lawyer to find out about that. She'd listened to an old doctor who'd told her to go ahead and have it, that she'd love her little baby, who hadn't lived, but there would be a record anyway. She wasn't sorry about going to a regular hospital to have it, though it made it harder for her now, having that record. She'd done what she could for the baby. She hated to think of the whole thing, but when she did, as she did that evening, she knew she'd done her best.

It might have been a bad evening for her, with Ralph brooding on her faults, if a boy hadn't come to the door selling chances on a raffle. Ralph bought all the boy had, over five dollars worth, and asked where he lived in the neighborhood. "I live in Minneapolis."

"Huh? Whatcha doin' way out here then?" The boy said it was easier to sell chances out there. Ethel, who had been doing the dishes, returned to the sink before Ralph could see her. He went back to his *Reader's Digest,* and she slipped off to bed, early, hoping his mind would be occupied with the boy if she kept out of sight.

He came to bed after the ten o'clock news. "You awake?" Ethel, awake, but afraid he wanted to talk neighbors, moaned remotely. "If anybody comes to the door sellin' anything, make sure it's somebody local."

In the morning, Ralph checked over the silver and china laid out in the dining room and worried over the pastry. "Fresh?" Fresh! She'd put it in the deep freeze right away and it hadn't even thawed out yet. "Is that *all?*" That was all, and it was more than enough. She certainly didn't need a whole quart of whipping cream. "Want me to call up for something to go with this?" No. "Turkey or a ham? I maybe got time to go myself if I go right now." He carried on like that until ten o'clock, when she got rid of him, saying, "You wouldn't want to be the only man, Ralph."

Then she was on her own, wishing Mrs. Hancock would come early and see her through the first minutes.

But Mrs. Wagner was the first to arrive. After that, the

neighbors seemed to ring the bell at regular intervals. Ethel met them at the door, hung their coats in the hall closet, returning each time to Mrs. Wagner in the kitchen. They were all very nice, but Mrs. Wagner was the nicest.

"Now let's just let everything be," she said after they'd arranged the food in the dining room. "Let's go in and meet your friends."

They found the neighbors standing before the two pictures. Ethel snapped on the spotlights. She heard little cries of pleasure all around.

"Heirlooms!"

"Is Mr. Divitchy a collector?"

"Just likes good things, huh?"

"I just love this lamp."

"I just *stare* at it when I go by."

"So do I."

Ethel, looking at her driftwood lamp, her plants, and beyond, stood in a haze of pleasure. Earlier, when she was giving her attention to Mrs. Nilgren (who was telling about the trouble "Carl" had with his trees), Ethel had seen Ralph's car cruise by, she thought, and now again, but this time there was no doubt of it. She recognized the rather old one parked in front as Mrs. Hancock's, but where was Mrs. Hancock?

"Hello, everybody!"

Mrs. Hancock had let herself in, and was hanging up her coat.

Ethel disappeared into the kitchen. She carried the coffeepot, which had been on *low,* into the dining room, where they were supposed to come and help themselves. She stood by the pot, nervous, ready to pour, hoping that someone would look in and see that she was ready, but no one did.

She went to see what they were doing. They were still sitting down, listening to Mrs. Hancock. She'd had trouble with her car. That was why she was late. She saw Ethel. "I can see you want to get started," she said, rising. "So do I."

Ethel returned to the dining room and stood by the coffeepot.

Mrs. Hancock came first. "Starved," she said. She carried off her coffee, roll, and two of the little Swedish cookies, and Ethel heard her in the living room rallying the others.

They came then, quietly, and Ethel poured. When all had been served, she started another pot of coffee, and took her cup and a cookie—she wasn't hungry—into the living room.

Mrs. Hancock, sitting on the hassock, had a bottle in her

hand. On the rug around her were some brushes and one copper pan. "Ladies," she was saying, "now here's something new." Noticing Ethel, Mrs. Hancock picked up the pan. "How'd you like to have this for your kitchen? Here."

Ethel crossed the room. She carried the pan back to where she'd been standing.

"This is no ordinary polish," continued Mrs. Hancock, shaking the bottle vigorously. "This is what is known as liquefied ointment. It possesses rare medicinal properties. It renews wood. It gives you a base for polishing—something to shine that simply wasn't there before. There's nothing like it on the market—not in the polish field. It's a Shipshape product, and you all know what that means." Mrs. Hancock opened the bottle and dabbed at the air. "Note the handy applicator." Snatching a cloth from her lap, she rubbed the leg of the coffee table—"remove all foreign matter first"—and dabbed at the leg with the applicator. "This does for wood what liniment does for horses. It relaxes the grain, injects new life, *soothes* the wood. Well, how do you like it?" she called over to Ethel.

Ethel glanced down at the pan, forgotten in her hand.

"Pass it around," said Mrs. Hancock.

Ethel offered the pan to Mrs. Nilgren, who was nearest.

"I've seen it, thanks."

Ethel moved to the next neighbor.

"I've seen it."

Ethel moved on. "Mrs. Wagner, have you?"

"Many times"—with a smile.

Ethel looked back where she'd been standing before she started out with the pan—and went the other way, finally stepping into the hallway. There she saw a canvas duffel bag on the side of which was embossed a pennant flying the word SHIPSHAPE. And hearing Mrs. Hancock—"And this is new, girls. Can you all see from where you're sitting?"—Ethel began to move again. She kept right on going.

Upstairs, in the bedroom, lying down, she noticed the pan in her hand. She shook it off. It hit the headboard of the bed, denting the traditional mahogany, and came to rest in the satin furrow between Ralph's pillow and hers. Oh, God! In a minute, she'd have to get up and go down to them and do *something*—but then she heard the coat hangers banging back empty in the closet downstairs, and the front door opening and, finally, closing. There was a moment of perfect silence in the house before her sudden sob, then another moment before she heard someone coming, climbing the carpeted stairs.

Ethel foolishly thought it would be Mrs. Wagner, but of course it was Mrs. Hancock, after her pan.

She tiptoed into the room, adjusted the venetian blind, and seated herself lightly on the edge of the bed. "Don't think I don't know how you feel," she said. "Not that it shows yet. I wasn't *sure,* dear." She looked into Ethel's eyes, frightening her.

As though only changing positions, Ethel moved the hand that Mrs. Hancock was after.

"My ointment would fix that, restore the surface," said Mrs. Hancock, her finger searching the little wound in the headboard. She began to explain, gently—like someone with a terrible temper warming up: "When we first started having these little Shipshape parties, they didn't tell each other. They do now, oh, yes, or they would if I'd let them. I'm on to them. They're just in it for the mops now. You get one, you know, for having the party in your home. It's collapsible, ideal for the small home or travel. But the truth is you let me down! Why, when you left the room the way you did, you didn't give them any choice. Why, I don't think there's one of that crowd—with the exception of May Wagner—that isn't using one of my free mops! Why, they just walked out on me!"

Ethel, closing her eyes, saw Mrs. Hancock alone, on the hassock, with her products all around her.

"It's a lot of pan for the money," Mrs. Hancock was saying now. She reached over Ethel's body for it. "You'll love your little pan," she said fondling it.

Ethel's eyes were resisting Mrs. Hancock, but her right hand betrayed her.

"Here?" Mrs. Hancock opened a drawer, took out a purse, and handed it over, saying, "Only $12.95."

Ethel found a five and a ten.

"You *do* want the ointment, don't you? The pan and the large bottle come to a little more than this, but it's not enough to worry about."

Mrs. Hancock got up, apparently to leave.

Ethel thought of something. "You do live in Blue Island, don't you?" Ralph would be sure to ask about that—if she had to tell him. And she would!

"Not any more, thank God."

Ethel nodded. She wasn't surprised.

Mrs. Hancock, at the door, peeked out—reminding Ethel of a bored visitor looking for a nurse who would tell her it was time to leave the patient. "You'll find your ointment and mop downstairs," she said. "I just know everything's going to be all right." Then she smiled and left.

When, toward noon, Ethel heard Ralph come into the driveway, she got out of bed, straightened the spread, and concealed the pan in the closet. She went to the window and gazed down upon the crown of his pearl-gray hat. He was carrying a big club of roses.

Beatrice Trueblood's Story

Jean Stafford

When Beatrice Trueblood was in her middle thirties and on the very eve of her second marriage, to a rich and reliable man—when, that is, she was in the prime of life and on the threshold of a rosier phase of it than she had ever known before—she overnight was stricken with total deafness.

"The vile unkindness of fate!" cried Mrs. Onslager, the hostess on whose royal Newport lawn, on a summer day at lunchtime, poor Beatrice had made her awful discovery. Mrs. Onslager was addressing a group of house guests a few weeks after the catastrophe and after the departure of its victim—or, more properly, of its victims, since Marten ten Brink, Mrs. Trueblood's fiancé, had been there, too. The guests were sitting on the same lawn on the same sort of dapper afternoon, and if the attitudes of some of Mrs. Onslager's audience seemed to be somnolent, they were so because the sun was so taming and the sound of the waves was a glamorous lullaby as the Atlantic kneaded the rocks toward which the lawn sloped down. They were by no means indifferent to this sad story; a few of them knew Marten ten Brink, and all of them knew Beatrice Trueblood, who had been Mrs. Onslager's best friend since their girlhood in St. Louis.

"I'm obliged to call it fate," continued Mrs. Onslager. "Because there's nothing wrong with her. All the doctors have reported the same thing to us, and she's been to a battalion of them. At first she refused to go to anyone on the ground that it would be a waste of money, of which she has next to none, but Jack and I finally persuaded her that if she didn't see the best men in the country and let us foot the bills, we'd look on it as unfriendliness. So, from Johns Hopkins, New York Hospital, the Presbyterian, the Leahy Clinic, and God knows

252

where, the same account comes back: there's nothing physical to explain it, no disease, no lesion, there's been no shock, there were no hints of any kind beforehand. And *I'll* not allow the word 'psychosomatic' to be uttered in my presence—not in this connection, at any rate—because I know Bea as well as I know myself and she is not hysterical. Therefore, it has to be fate. And there's a particularly spiteful irony in it if you take a backward glance at her life. If ever a woman deserved a holiday from tribulation, it's Bea. There was first of all a positively hideous childhood. The classic roles were reversed in the family, and it was the mother who drank and the father who nagged. Her brother took to low life like a duck to water and was a juvenile delinquent before he was out of knickers—I'm sure he must have ended up in Alcatraz. They were unspeakably poor, and Bea's aunts dressed her in their hand-me-downs. It was a house of the most humiliating squalor, all terribly genteel. You know what I mean—the mother prettying up her drunkenness by those transparent dodges like 'Two's my limit,' and keeping the gin in a Waterford decanter, and the father looking as if butter wouldn't melt in his mouth when they were out together publicly, although everyone knew that he was a perfectly ferocious tartar. Perhaps it isn't true that he threw things at his wife and children and whipped them with a razor strop—he didn't have to, because he could use his tongue like a bludgeon. And then after all that horror, Bea married Tom Trueblood—really to escape her family, I think, because she couldn't possibly have loved him. I mean it isn't possible to love a man who is both a beast and a fool. *He* was drunker than her mother ever thought of being; he was obscene, he was raucous, his infidelities to that good, beautiful girl were of a vulgarity that caused the mind to boggle. I'll never know how she managed to live with him for seven mortal years. And then at last, after all those tempests, came Marten ten Brink, like redemption itself. There's nothing sensational in Marten, I'll admit. He's rather a stick, he was born rather old, he's rather jokeless and bossy. But, oh, Lord, he's so *safe*, he was so protective of her, and he is so scrumptiously rich! And two months before the wedding *this* thunderbolt comes out of nowhere. It's indecent! It makes me so angry!" And this faithful friend shook her pretty red head rapidly in indignation, as if she were about to hunt down fate with a posse and hale it into court.

"Are you saying that the engagement has been broken?"

asked Jennie Fowler, who had just got back from Europe and to whom all this was news.

Mrs. Onslager nodded, closing her eyes as if the pain she suffered were unbearable. "They'd been here for a week, Marten and Bea, and we were making the wedding plans, since they were to be married from my house. And the very day after this gruesome thing happened, she broke the engagement. She wrote him a note and sent it in to his room by one of the maids. I don't know what she said in it, though I suppose she told him she didn't want to be a burden, something like that—much more gracefully, of course, since Bea *is* the soul of courtesy. But whatever it was, it must have been absolutely unconditional, because he went back to town before dinner the same night. The letter I got from him afterward scarcely mentioned it—he only said he was sorry his visit here had ended on 'an unsettling note.' I daresay he was still too shocked to say more."

"Hard lines on ten Brink," said Harry McEvoy, who had never married.

"What do you mean, 'hard lines on *ten Brink?*' " cried Mrs. Fowler, who had married often, and equally often had gone, livid with rage, to Nevada.

"Well, if he was in love with her, if he counted on this . . . Not much fun to have everything blow up in your face. Lucky in a way, I suppose, that it happened before, and not afterward."

The whole party glowered at McEvoy, but he was entirely innocent of their disapproval and of his stupidity that had provoked it, since he was looking through a pair of binoculars at a catboat that seemed to be in trouble.

"If he was in love with her," preached Mrs. Fowler rabidly, "he would have stuck by her. He would have refused to let her break the engagement. He would have been the one to insist on the specialists, he would have moved heaven and *earth,* instead of which he fled like a scared rabbit at the first sign of bad luck. I thought he was only a bore—I didn't know he was such a venomous pill."

"No, dear, he isn't that," said Priscilla Onslager. "Not the most sensitive man alive, but I'd never call him a venomous pill. After all, remember it was *she* who dismissed *him.*"

"Yes, but if he'd had an ounce of manliness in him, he would have put up a fight. No decent man, no manly man, would abandon ship at a time like that." Mrs. Fowler hated men so passionately that no one could dream why she married so many of them.

"Has it occurred to any of you that she sent him packing because she didn't want to marry him?" The question came from Douglas Clyde, a former clergyman, whose worldliness, though it was very wise, had cost him his parish and his cloth.

"Certainly not," said Priscilla. "I tell you, Doug, I know Bea. But at the moment the important thing isn't the engagement, because I'm sure it could be salvaged if she could be cured. And how's she to be cured if nothing's wrong? I'd gladly have the Eumenides chase me for a while if they'd only give her a rest."

Jack Onslager gazed through half-closed eyes at his wholesome, gabbling wife—he loved her very much, but her public dicta were always overwrought and nearly always wrong—and then he closed his eyes tight against the cluster of his guests, and he thought how blessed it would be if with the same kind of simply physical gesture one could also temporarily close one's ears. One could decline to touch, to taste, to see, but it required a skill he had not mastered to govern the ears. Those stopples made of wax and cotton would be insulting at a party; besides, they made him claustrophobic, and when he used them, he could hear the interior workings of his skull, the boiling of his brains in his brainpan, a rustling behind his jaws. He would not like to go so far as Beatrice had gone, but he would give ten years of his life (he had been about to say he would give his eyes and changed it) to be able, when he wanted, to seal himself into an impenetrable silence.

To a certain extent, however, one could insulate the mind against the invasion of voices by an act of will, by causing them to blur together into a general hubbub. And this is what he did now; in order to consider Mrs. Trueblood's deafness, he deafened himself to the people who were talking about it. He thought of the day in the early summer when the extraordinary thing had taken place.

It had been Sunday. The night before, the Onslagers and their houseparty—the young Allinghams, Mary and Leon Herbert, Beatrice and ten Brink—had gone to a ball. It was the kind of party to which Onslager had never got used, although he had been a multimillionaire for twenty years and not only had danced through many such evenings but had

been the host at many more, in his own houses or in bla-
zoned halls that he had hired. He was used to opulence in
other ways, and took for granted his boats and horses and
foreign cars. He also took for granted, and was bored by,
most of the rites of the rich: the formal dinner parties at
which the protocol was flawlessly maneuvered and conversation moved on stilts and the food was platitudinous; evenings
of music to benefit a worthy cause (How papery the turkey
always was at the buffet supper after the Grieg!); the tea parties to which one went obediently to placate old belles who
had lost their looks and their husbands and the roles that, at
their first assembly, they had assumed they would play forever. Well-mannered and patient, Onslager did his duty
suavely, and he was seldom thrilled.

But these lavish, enormous midsummer dancing parties in
the fabulous, foolish villas on Bellevue Avenue and along the
Ocean Drive did make his backbone tingle, did make him
glow. Even when he was dancing, or proposing a toast, or
fetching a wrap for a woman who had found the garden air
too cool, he always felt on these occasions that he was static,
looking at a colossal *tableau vivant* that would vanish at the
wave of a magic golden wand. He was bewitched by the
women, by all those *soignée* or demure or jubilant or saucy
or dreaming creatures in their caressing, airy dresses and
their jewels whose priceless hearts flashed in the light from
superb chandeliers. They seemed, these dancing, laughing, in-
candescent goddesses, to move in inaccessible spheres; indeed,
his wife, Priscilla, was transfigured, and, dancing with her, he
was moon-struck. No matter how much he drank (the champagne of those evenings was invested with a special
property—one tasted the grapes, and the grapes had come
from celestial vineyards), he remained sober and amazed
and, in spite of his amazement, so alert that he missed nothing
and recorded everything. He did not fail to see, in looks and
shrugs and the clicking of glasses, the genesis of certain adul-
teries, and the demise of others in a glance of contempt or an
arrogant withdrawal. With the accuracy of the uninvolved by-
stander, he heard and saw among these incredible women
moving in the aura of their heady perfume their majestic passions—tragic heartbreak, sublime fulfillment, dangerous jealousy, the desire to murder. When, on the next day, he had
come back to earth, he would reason that his senses had
devised a fiction to amuse his mind, and that in fact he had

witnessed nothing grander than flirtations and impromptu pangs as ephemeral as the flowers in the supper room.

So, at the Paines' vast marble house that night, Onslager, aloof and beguiled as always, had found himself watching Beatrice Trueblood and Martenten Brink with so much interest that whenever he could he guided his dancing partner near them, and if they left the ballroom for a breath of air on a bench beside a playing fountain, or for a glass of champagne, he managed, if he could do so without being uncivil to his interlocutor and without being observed by them, to excuse himself and follow. If he had stopped to think, this merciful and moral man would have been ashamed of his spying and eavesdropping, but morality was irrelevant to the spell that enveloped him. Besides, he felt invisible.

Consequently, he knew something about that evening that Priscilla did not know and that he had no intention of telling her, partly because she would not believe him, partly because she would be displeased at the schoolboyish (and parvenu) way he put in his time at balls. The fact was that the betrothed were having a quarrel. He heard not a word of it—not at the dance, that is—and he saw not a gesture or a grimace of anger, but he nevertheless knew surely, as he watched them dance together, that ten Brink was using every ounce of his strength not to shout, and to keep in check a whole menagerie of passions—fire-breathing dragons and bone-crushing serpents and sabertoothed tigers—and he knew also that Beatrice was running for dear life against the moment when they would be unleashed, ready to gobble her up. Her broad, wide-eyed, gentle face was so still it could have been a painting of a face that had been left behind when the woman who owned it had faded from view, and Bea's golden hand lay on ten Brink's white sleeve as tentatively as a butterfly. Her lover's face, on the other hand, was—Onslager wanted to say "writhing," and the long fingers of the hand that pressed against her back were splayed out and rigid, looking grafted onto the sunny flesh beneath the diaphanous blue stuff on her dress. He supposed that another observer might with justification have said that the man was animated and that his fiancée was becomingly engrossed in all he said, that ten Brink was in a state of euphoria as his wedding approached, while Beatrice moved in a wordless haze of happiness. He heard people admiringly remark on the compatibility of their good looks; they were said to look as if they were "dancing on air"; women thanked goodness that

Mrs. Trueblood had come at last into a safe harbor, and men said that ten Brink was in luck.

As soon as the Onslagers and their guests had driven away from the ball and the last echo of the music had perished and the smell of roses had been drowned by the smell of the sea and the magic had started to wane from Onslager's blood, he began to doubt his observations. He was prepared to elide and then forget his heightened insights, as he had always done in the past. The group had come in two cars, and the Allinghams were with him and Priscilla on the short ride home. Lucy Allingham, whose own honeymoon was of late and blushing memory, said, with mock petulance, 'I thought *young* love was supposed to be what caught the eye. But I never saw anything half so grand and wonderful as the looks of those two." And Priscilla said, "How true! How magnificently right you are, Lucy! They were radiant, both of them."

Late as it was, Priscilla proposed a last drink and a recapitulation of the party—everyone had found it a joy—but ten Brink said, "Beatrice and I want to go down and have a look at the waves, if you don't mind," and when no one minded but, on the contrary, fondly sped them on their pastoral way, the two walked down across the lawn and presently were gone from sight in the romantic mist. Their friends watched them and sighed, charmed, and went inside to drink a substitute for nectar.

Hours later (he looked at his watch and saw that it was close on five o'clock), Jack woke, made restless by something he had sensed or dreamed, and, going to the east windows of his bedroom to look at the water and see what the sailing would be like that day, he was arrested by the sight of Beatrice and Marten standing on the broad front steps below. They were still in their evening clothes. Beatrice's stance was tired; she looked bedraggled. They stood confronting each other beside the balustrade; ten Brink held her shoulders tightly, his sharp, handsome (but, thought Onslager suddenly, Mephistophelean) face bent down to hers.

"You mustn't think you can shut your mind to these things," he said. "You can't shut your ears to them." Their voices were clear in the hush of the last of the night.

"I am exhausted with talk, Marten," said Beatrice softly. "I will not hear another word."

An hour afterward, the fairest of days dawned on Newport, and Jack Onslager took out his sloop by himself in a perfect breeze, so that he saw none of his guests until just before lunch, when he joined them for cocktails on the lawn. Everyone was there except Beatrice Trueblood, who had slept straight through the morning but a moment before had called down from her windows that she was nearly ready. It was a flawless day to spend beside the sea: the chiaroscuro of the elm trees and the sun on the broad, buoyant lawn shifted as the sea winds disarrayed the leaves, and yonder, on the hyacinthine water, the whitecaps shuddered and the white sails swelled; to the left of the archipelago of chairs and tables where they sat, Mrs. Onslager's famous rosary was heavily in bloom with every shade of red there was and the subtlest hues of yellow, and her equally famous blue hydrangeas were at their zenith against the house, exactly the color of this holiday sky, so large they nodded on their stems like drowsing heads.

The Allinghams, newly out of their families' comfortable houses in St. Louis and now living impecuniously in a railroad flat in New York that they found both adventurous and odious, took in the lawn and seascape with a look of real greed, and even of guile, on their faces, as if they planned to steal something or eat forbidden fruit.

In its pleasurable fatigue from the evening before and too much sleep this morning, the gathering was momentarily disinclined to conversation, and they all sat with faces uplifted and eyes closed against the sun. They listened to the gulls and terns shrieking with their evergreen gluttony; they heard the buzz-saw rasp of outboard motors and the quick, cleaving roar of an invisible jet; they heard automobiles on the Ocean Drive, a power mower nasally shearing the grass at the house next door, and from that house they heard, as well, the wail of an infant and the panicky barking of an infant dog.

"I wish this day would never end," said Lucy Allingham. "This is the kind of day when you want to kiss the earth. You want to have an affair with the sky."

"Don't be maudlin, Lucy," said her husband. "And above all, don't be inaccurate." He was a finicking young cub who had been saying things like this all weekend.

Onslager's own wife, just as foolishly given to such figures of speech but with a good deal more style, simply through being older, said, "Look, here comes Beatrice. She looks as if her eyes were fixed on the Garden of Eden before the Fall and as if she were being serenaded by angels."

Marten ten Brink, an empiricist not given to flights of fancy, said, "Is that a depth bomb I hear?"

No one answered him, for everyone was watching Beatrice as she came slowly, smiling, down the stone steps from the terrace and across the lawn, dulcifying the very ground she walked upon. She was accompanied by Mrs. Onslager's two Siamese cats, who cantered ahead of her, then stopped, forgetful of their intention, and closely observed the life among the blades of grass, then frolicked on, from time to time emitting that ugly parody of a human cry that is one of the many facets of the Siamese cat's scornful nature. But the insouciant woman paid no attention to them, even when they stopped to fight each other, briefly, with noises straight from Hell.

"You look as fresh as dew, dear," said Priscilla. "Did you simply sleep and sleep?"

"Where on earth did you get that fabric?" asked Mrs. Herbert. "Surely not here. It must have come from Paris. Bea, I do declare your clothes are always the ones I want for myself."

"Sit here, Beatrice," said ten Brink, who had stood up and was indicating the chair next to himself. But Beatrice, ignoring him, chose another chair. The cats, still flirting with her, romped at her feet; one of them pretended to find a sporting prey between her instep and her heel, and he pounced and buckjumped silently, his tail a fast, fierce whip. Beatrice, who delighted in these animals, bent down to stroke the lean flanks of the other one, momentarily quiescent in a glade of sunshine.

"What do you think of the pathetic fallacy, Mrs. Trueblood?" said Peter Allingham, addressing her averted head. "Don't you think it's pathetic?" By now, Onslager was wishing to do him bodily harm for his schoolmasterish teasing of Lucy.

"Monkeys," murmured Beatrice to the cats. "Darlings."

"Beatrice!" said Marten ten Brink sharply, and strode across to whisper something in her ear. She brushed him away as if he were a fly, and she straightened up and said to Priscilla Onslager, "Why is everyone so solemn? Are you doing a charade of a Quaker meeting?"

"Solemn?" said Priscilla, with a laugh. "If we seem solemn, it's because we're all smitten with this day. Isn't it supreme? Heaven can't possibly be nicer."

"Is this a new game?" asked Beatrice, puzzled, her kind eyes on her hostess's face.

"Is what a new game, dear?"

"What *is* going on?" She had begun to be ever so slightly annoyed. "Is it some sort of silence test? We're to see if we can keep still till teatime? Is it that? I'd be delighted—only, for pity's sake, tell me the rules and the object."

"Silence test! Sweetheart, you're still asleep. Give her a martini, Jack," said Priscilla nervously, and to divert the attention of the company from her friend's quixotic mood she turned to ten Brink. "I believe you're right," she said, "I believe they're detonating depth bombs. Why on Sunday? I thought sailors got a day of rest like everybody else."

A deep, rumbling subterranean thunder rolled, it seemed, beneath the chairs they sat on.

"It sounds like ninepins in the Catskills," said Priscilla.

"I never could abide that story," said Mary Herbert. "Or the Ichabod Crane one, either."

Jack Onslager, his back toward the others as he poured a drink for Beatrice, observed to himself that the trying thing about these weekends was not the late hours, not the overeating and the overdrinking and the excessive batting of tennis balls and shuttlecocks; it was, instead, this kind of aimless prattle that never ceased. There seemed to exist, on weekends in the country, a universal terror of pauses in conversation, so that it was imperative for Mary Herbert to drag in Washington Irving by the hair of his irrelevant head. Beatrice Trueblood, however, was not addicted to prattle, and he silently congratulated her on the way, in the last few minutes, she had risen above their fatuous questions and compliments. That woman was as peaceful as a pool in the heart of a forest. He turned to her, handing her the drink and looking directly into her eyes (blue and green, like an elegant tropic sea), and he said, "I have never seen you looking prettier."

For just a second, a look of alarm usurped her native and perpetual calm, but then she said, "So you're playing it, too. I don't think it's fair not to tell me—unless this is a joke on me. Am I 'it'?"

At last, Jack was unsettled; Priscilla was really scared; ten Brink was angry, and, getting up again to stand over her like a prosecuting attorney interrogating a witness of bad character, he said, "You're not being droll, Beatrice, you're being tiresome."

Mrs. Onslager said, "Did you go swimming this morning, lamb? Perhaps you got water in your ears. Lean over—see, like this," and she bent her head low to the left and then to the right while Beatrice, to whom these calisthenics were inexplicable, watched her, baffled.

Beatrice put her drink on the coffee table, and she ran her forefingers around the shells of her ears. What was the look that came into her face, spreading over it as tangibly as a blush? Onslager afterward could not be sure. At the time he had thought it was terror; he had thought this because, in the confusion that ensued, he had followed, sheeplike with the others, in his wife's lead. But later, when he recaptured it for long reflection, he thought that it had not been terror, but rather that Priscilla in naming it that later was actually speaking of the high color of her own state of mind, and that the look in Beatrice's eyes and on her mouth had been one of revelation, as if she had opened a door and had found behind it a new world so strange, so foreign to all her knowledge and her experience and the history of her senses, that she had spoken only approximately when, in a far, soft, modest voice, she said, "I am deaf. That explains it."

When Onslager had come to the end of his review of those hours of that other weekend and had returned to the present one, he discovered that he had so effectively obliterated the voices around him that he now could not recall a single word of any of the talk, although he had been conscious of it, just as some part of his mind was always conscious of the tension and solution of the tides.

"But you haven't told us yet how she's taking it now," Mrs. Fowler was saying.

"I can't really tell," replied Priscilla. "I haven't been able to go to town to see her, and she refuses to come up here— the place probably has bad associations for her now. And I'm no good at reading between the lines of her letters. She has adjusted to it, I'll say that." Priscilla was thoughtful, and her silence commanded her guests to be silent. After a time, she went on, "I'll say more than that. I'll say she has adjusted too well for my liking. There is a note of gaiety in her letters— she is almost jocose. For example, in the last one she said that although she had lost Handel and music boxes and the purring of my Siamese, she had gained a valuable immunity to the voices of professional Irishmen."

"Does she mention ten Brink?" asked someone.

"Never," said Priscilla. "It's as if he had never existed. There's more in her letters than the joking tone. I wish I could put my finger on it. The closest I can come is to say she sounds *bemused*."

"Do you think she's given up?" asked Jennie Fowler. "Or has she done everything there is to be done?"

"The doctors recommended psychiatry, of course," said Priscilla, with distaste. "It's a dreary, ghastly, humiliating thought, but I suppose—"

"I should think you *would* suppose!" cried Mrs. Fowler. "You shouldn't leave a stone unturned. Plainly someone's got to *make* her go to an analyst. They're not that dire, Priscilla. I've heard some very decent things about several of them."

"It won't be I who'll make her go," said Priscilla, sighing. "I disapprove too much."

"But you don't disapprove of the medical people," persisted Jennie. "Why fly in the face of their prescription?"

"Because . . . I *couldn't* do it. Propose to Beatrice that she is mental? I can't support the thought of it."

"Then Jack must do it," said the managerial divorcée. "Jack must go straight down to town and get her to a good man and then patch up things with Marten ten Brink. I still detest the sound of him, but *de gustibus*, and I think she ought to have a husband."

The whole gathering—even the cynical ex-pastor—agreed that this proposal made sense, and Onslager, while he doubted his right to invade Bea's soft and secret and eccentric world, found himself so curious to see her again to learn whether some of his conjectures were right that he fell in with the plan and agreed to go to New York in the course of the week. As, after lunch, they dispersed, some going off for *boccie* and others to improve their shining skin with sun, Douglas Clyde said sotto voce to Onslager, "Why doesn't it occur to anyone but you and me that perhaps she doesn't *want* to hear?"

Startled, the host turned to his guest. "How did you know I thought that?"

"I watched you imitating deafness just now," said the other. "You looked beatific. But if I were you, I wouldn't go too far."

"Then you believe . . . contrary to Priscilla and her Eumenides . . . ?"

"I believe what you believe—that the will is free and very strong," Clyde answered, and he added, "I believe further that it can cease to be an agent and become a despot. I suspect hers *has*."

Mrs. Trueblood lived in the East Seventies, in the kind of apartment building that Jack Onslager found infinitely more melancholy than the slum tenements that flanked and faced it in the sultry city murk of August. It was large and new and commonplace and jerry-built, although it strove to look as solid as Gibraltar. Its brick façade was an odious mustardy brown. The doorman was fat and choleric, and when Onslager descended from his cab, he was engaged in scolding a band of vile-looking little boys who stood on the curb doubled up with giggles, now and again screaming out an unbelievable obscenity when the pain of their wicked glee abated for a moment. A bum was lying spread-eagled on the sidewalk a few doors down; his face was bloody but he was not dead, for he was snoring fearsomely. Across the street, a brindle boxer leaned out a window, his forepaws sedately crossed on the sill in a parody of the folded arms of the many women who were situated in other windows, irascibly agreeing with one another at the tops of their voices that the heat was hell.

But the builders of the house where Mrs. Trueblood lived had pretended that none of this was so; they had pretended that the neighborhood was bourgeois and there was no seamy side, and they had commemorated their swindle in a big facsimile of rectitude. Its square foyer was papered with a design of sanitary ferns upon a field of hygenic beige; two untruthful mirrors mirrored each other upon either lateral wall, and beneath them stood love seats with aseptic green plastic cushions and straight blond legs. The slow self-service elevator was an asphyxiating chamber with a fan that blew a withering sirocco; its tinny walls were embossed with a meaningless pattern of fleurs-de-lis; light, dim and reluctant, came through a fixture with a shade of some ersatz material made esoterically in the form of a starfish. As Onslager ascended to the sixth floor at a hot snail's pace, hearing alarming *râles* and exhalations in the machinery, he was fretful with his discomfort and fretful with snobbishness. He deplored the circumstances that required Beatrice, who was so openhearted a woman, to live in surroundings so mean-minded; he could not help thinking sorrowfully that the ideal place for her was Marten ten Brink's house on Fifty-fifth Street, with all its depths of richness and its sophisticated planes. The bastard, he thought, taking Jennie Fowler's line—why did he let her down? And then he shook his head, because, of course, he knew it hadn't been like that.

This was not his first visit to Beatrice. He and Priscilla had been here often to cocktail parties since she had lived in New York, but the place had made no impression on him; he liked cocktail parties so little that he went to them with blinders on and looked at nothing except, furtively, his watch. But today, in the middle of a hostile heat wave and straight from the felicities of Newport, he was heavyhearted thinking how her apartment was going to look; he dreaded it; he wished he had not come. He was struck suddenly with the importunity of his mission. How had they *dared* be so possessive and dictatorial? And why had *he* been delegated to urge her to go to a psychiatrist? To be sure, his letter to her had said only that since he was going to be in the city, he would like to call on her, but she was wise and sensitive and she was bound to know that he had come to snoop and recommend. He was so embarrassed that he considered going right down again and sending her some flowers and a note of apology for failing to show up. She could not know he was on his way, for it had not been possible to announce himself over the house telephone—and how, indeed, he wondered, would she know when her doorbell rang?

But when the doors of the elevator slid open, he found her standing in the entrance of her apartment. She looked at her watch and said, "You're punctual." Her smiling, welcoming face was cool and tranquil; unsmirched by the heat, and the dreariness of the corridor and, so far as he could judge, by the upheaval of her life, she was as proud and secret-living as a flower. He admired her and he dearly loved her. He cherished her as one of life's most beautiful appointments.

"That you should have to come to town on such a day!" she exclaimed. "I'm terribly touched that you fitted me in."

He started to speak; he was on the point of showering on her a cornucopia of praise and love, and then he remembered that she would not hear. So, instead, he kissed her on either cheek and hoped the gesture, mild and partial, obscured his turmoil. She smelled of roses; she seemed the embodiment of everything most pricelessly feminine, and he felt as diffident as he did at those lovely summer balls.

Her darkened, pretty sitting room—he should not have been so fearful, he should have had more faith in her—smelled of roses, too, for everywhere there were bowls of them from Priscilla's garden, brought down by the last week-end's guests.

"I'm terribly glad you fitted me in," repeated Beatrice when she had given him a drink, and a pad of paper and a pencil, by means of which he was to communicate with her (she did this serenely and without explanation, as if it were the most natural thing in the world), "because yesterday my bravura began to peter out. In fact, I'm scared to death."

He wrote, "You shouldn't be alone. Why not come back to us? You know nothing would please us more." How asinine, he thought. What a worthless sop.

She laughed. "Priscilla couldn't bear it. Disaster makes her cry, good soul that she is. No, company wouldn't make me less scared."

"Tell me about it," he wrote, and again he felt like a fool.

It was not the deafness itself that scared her, she said—not the fear of being run down by an automobile she had not heard or violated by an intruder whose footfall had escaped her. These anxieties, which beset Priscilla, did not touch Beatrice. Nor had she yet begun so very much to miss voices or other sounds she liked; it was a little unnerving, she said, never to know if the telephone was ringing, and it was strange to go into the streets and see the fast commotion and hear not a sound, but it had its comic side and it had its compensations—it amused her to see the peevish snapping of a dog whose bark her deafness had forever silenced, she was happy to be spared her neighbors' vociferous television sets. But she was scared all the same. What had begun to harry her was that her wish to be deaf had been granted. This was exactly how she put it, and Onslager received her secret uneasily. She had not bargained for banishment, she said; she had only wanted a holiday. Now, though, she felt that the Devil lived with her, eternally wearing a self-congratulatory smile.

"You are being fanciful," Onslager wrote, although he did not think she was at all fanciful. "You can't wish yourself deaf."

But Beatrice insisted that she *had* done just that.

She emphasized that she had *elected* to hear no more, would not permit of accident, and ridiculed the doting Priscilla's sentimental fate. She had done it suddenly and out of despair, and she was sorry now. "I am ashamed. It was an act of cowardice," she said.

"How cowardice?" wrote Onslager.

"I could have broken with Marten in a franker way. I could simply have told him I had changed my mind. I didn't have to make him mute by making myself deaf."

"Was there a quarrel?" he wrote, knowing already the question was superfluous.

"Not *a* quarrel. An incessant wrangle. Marten is jealous and he is indefatigably vocal. I wanted terribly to marry him—I don't suppose I loved him very much but he seemed good, seemed safe. But all of a sudden I thought, I cannot and I will not listen to another word. And now I'm sorry because I'm so lonely here, inside my skull. Not hearing makes one helplessly egocentric."

She hated any kind of quarrel, she said—she shuddered at raised voices and quailed before looks of hate—but she could better endure a howling brawl among vicious hoodlums, a shrill squabble of shrews, a degrading jangle between servant and mistress, than she could the least altercation between a man and a woman whose conjunction had had as its origin tenderness and a concord of desire. A relationship that was predicated upon love was far too delicate of composition to be threatened by cross-purposes. There were houses where she would never visit again because she had seen a husband and wife in ugly battle dress; there were restaurants she went to unwillingly because in them she had seen lovers in harsh dispute. How could things ever be the same between them again? How could two people possibly continue to associate with each other after such humiliating, disrobing displays?

As Beatrice talked in discreet and general terms and candidly met Jack Onslager's eyes, in another part of her mind she was looking down the shadowy avenue of all the years of her life. As a girl and, before that, as a child, in the rambling, shambling house in St. Louis, Beatrice in her bedroom doing her lessons would hear a rocking chair on a squeaking board two flights down; this was the chair in which her tipsy mother seesawed, dressed for the street and wearing a hat, drinking gin and humming a Venetian barcarole to which she had forgotten the words. Her mother drank from noon, when, with lamentations, she got up, till midnight, when, the bottle dry, she fell into a groaning, nightmare-ridden unconsciousness that resembled the condition immediately preceding death. This mortal sickness was terrifying; her removal from reality was an ordeal for everyone, but not even the frequent and flamboyant threats of suicide, the sobbed proclamations that she was the chief of sinners, not all the excruciating embarrassments that were created by that interminable and joyless spree, were a fraction as painful as the daily quarrels that commenced as soon as Beatrice's father came home, just before six, and continued, unmitigated, until he—a methodical man, despite his unfathomable spleen—went to bed, at ten. Dinner, nightly, was a hideous experience for a child, since the parents were not inhibited by their children or the maid and went on heaping atrocious abuse upon each other, using sarcasm, threats, lies—every imaginable expression of loathing and contempt. They swam in their own blood, but it was an ocean that seemed to foster and nourish them; their awful wounds were their necessities. Freshly appalled each evening, unforgiving, disgraced, Beatrice miserably pushed her food about on her plate, never hungry, and often she imagined herself alone on a desert, far away from any human voice. The moment the meal was finished, she fled to her schoolbooks, but even when she put her fingers in her ears, she could hear her parents raving, whining, bullying, laughing horrible, malign laughs. Sometimes, in counterpoint to this vendetta, another would start in the kitchen, where the impudent and slatternly maid and one of her lovers would ask *their* cross questions and give crooked answers.

In spite of all this hatefulness, Beatrice did not mistrust marriage, and, moreover, she had faith in her own even temper. She was certain that sweetness could put an end to strife; she believed that her tolerance was limitless, and she vowed that when she married there would be no quarrels.

But there were. The dew in her eyes as a bride gave way nearly at once to a glaze when she was a wife. She left home at twenty, and at twenty-one married Tom Trueblood, who scolded her for seven years. Since she maintained that it took two to make a quarrel, she tried in the beginning, with all the cleverness and fortitude she had, to refuse to be a party to the storms that rocked her house and left it a squalid shambles, but her silence only made her husband more passionately angry, and at last, ripped and raw, she had to defend herself. Her dignity trampled to death, her honor mutilated, she fought back, and felt estranged from the very principles of her being. Like her parents, Tom Trueblood was sustained by rancor and contentiousness; he really seemed to love these malevolent collisions which made her faint and hot and ill, and he seemed, moreover, to regard them as essential to the married state, and so, needing them, he would not let

Beatrice go but tricked and snared her and strewed her path with obstacles, until finally she had been obliged to run away and melodramatically leave behind a note.

Beatrice was a reticent woman and had too much taste to bare all these grubby secret details, but she limned a general picture for Onslager and, when she had finished, she said, "Was it any wonder, then, that when the first blush wore off and Marten showed himself to be cantankerous my heart sank?"

Onslager had listened to her with dismay. He and Priscilla were not blameless of the sin she so deplored—no married people were—but their differences were minor and rare and guarded, their sulks were short-lived. Poor, poor Beatrice, he thought. Poor lamb.

He wrote, "Have you heard from Marten?"

She nodded and closed her eyes in a dragging weariness. "He has written me volumes," she said. "In the first place, he doesn't believe that I am deaf but thinks it's an act. He says I am indulging myself, but he is willing to forgive me if I will only come to my senses. Coming to my senses involves, among other things, obliterating the seven years I lived with Tom—I told you he was madly jealous? But how do you amputate experience? How do you eliminate what intransigently *was?*"

"If that's Marten's line," wrote Onslager, revolted by such childishness, "obviously you can't give him a second thought. The question is what's to be done about *you?*"

"Oh, I don't know, I *do* not know!" There were tears in her voice, and she clasped her hands to hide their trembling. "I am afraid that I am too afraid ever to hear again. And you see how I speak as if I had a choice?"

Now she was frankly wringing her hands, and the terror in her face was sheer. "My God, the mind is diabolical!" she cried. "Even in someone as simple as I."

The stifling day was advancing into the stifling evening, and Jack Onslager, wilted by heat and unmanned by his futile pity, wanted, though he admired and loved her, to leave her. There was nothing he could do.

She saw this, and said, "You must go. Tomorrow I am starting with an analyst. Reassure Priscilla. Tell her I know that everything is going to be all right. I know it not because I am naïve but because I *still* have faith in the kindness of life." He could not help thinking that it was will instead of faith that put these words in her mouth.

And, exteriorly, everything was all right for Beatrice. Almost at once, when she began treatment with a celebrated man, her friends began to worry less, and to marvel more at her strength and the wholeness of her worthy soul and the diligence with which she and the remarkable doctor hunted down her troublesome quarry. During this time, she went about socially, lent herself to conversation by reading lips, grew even prettier. Her analysis was a dramatic success, and after a little more than a year she regained her hearing. Some months later, she married a man, Arthur Talbot, who was far gayer than Marten ten Brink and far less rich; indeed, a research chemist, he was poor. Priscilla deplored this aspect of him, but she was carried away by the romance (he looked like a poet, he adored Beatrice) and at last found it in her heart to forgive him for being penniless.

When the Talbots came to Newport for a long weekend not long after they had married, Jack Onslager watched them both with care. No mention had ever been made by either Jack or Beatrice of their conversation on that summer afternoon, and when his wife, who had now become a fervent supporter of psychiatry, exclaimed after the second evening that she had never seen Beatrice so radiant, Onslager agreed with her. Why not? There would be no sense in quarreling with his happy wife. He himself had never seen a face so drained of joy, or even of the memory of joy; he had not been able to meet Bea's eyes.

That Sunday—it was again a summer day beside the sea—Jack Onslager came to join his two guests, who were sitting alone on the lawn. Their backs were to him and they did not hear his approach, so Talbot did not lower his voice when he said to his wife, "I have told you a thousand times that my life has to be exactly as I want it. So stop these hints. *Any* dedicated scientist worth his salt is bad-tempered."

Beatrice saw that her host had heard him; she and Onslager travailed in the brief look they exchanged. It was again an enrapturing day. The weather overhead was fair and bland, but the water was a mass of little wrathful whitecaps.

The Condemned Librarian

Jessamyn West

Louise McKay, M.D., the librarian at Beaumont High School, sent me another card today. It was on the wickerwork table, where Mother puts my snack, when I got home from teaching. This afternoon the snack was orange juice and graham crackers, the orange juice in a plain glass, so that the deepness, the thickness of the color was almost like a flame inside a hurricane lamp. The graham crackers were on a blue willowware plate, and it just so happened that Dr. McKay's card was Van Gogh's "Sunflowers." It was a perfect still life, the colors increasing in intensity through the pale sand of the wickerwork table to the great bong (I want to say), for I swear I could hear it, of Van Gogh's flaming sunflowers. I looked at the picture Mother had composed for me (I don't doubt) for some time before I read Dr. McKay's card.

Dr. McKay sends me about four cards a year—not at any particular season, Christmas, Easter, or the like. Her sentiments are not suited to such festivals. Usually her message is only a line or two: "Why did you do it?" or "Condemned, condemned, condemned." Something very dramatic and always on a post card, so that the world at large can read it if it chooses. Mother shows her perfect tact by saying nothing if she does read. Perhaps she doesn't; though a single sentence in a big masculine hand is hard to miss. Except for her choice of the Van Gogh print, which showed her malice, Dr. McKay's message this afternoon was very mild—for her. "I am still here, which will no doubt make you happy."

Apart from the fact that anyone interested in the welfare of human beings generally would want her there (or at least not practicing in a hospital), it does make me happy. This evening when I pulled down the flag, I was somehow reassured, standing there in the schoolyard with the cold north wind blowing the dust in my face, to think that over there on

271

the other side of the mountains Louise McKay was ending her day, too. Take away the mountains and fields and we might be gazing into each other's eyes.

I sat down in my room with the juice my mother had squeezed—we hate substitutes—and looked at the card and remembered when I had first seen that marching handwriting. Everything else about her has changed, but not that. I saw it first on the card she gave me telling me of my next date with her. From the moment I arrived at Oakland State, I started hearing about Dr. Louise McKay. She was a real campus heroine, though for no real reason. Except that at a teachers college, with no football heroes, no faculty members with off-campus reputations, the craving for superiority must satisfy itself on the material at hand, however skimpy. And for a student body made up of kids and middle-aged teachers come to Oakland from the lost little towns of mountain and desert, I suppose it was easy to think of Dr. McKay as heroic or fascinating or accomplished.

I was different, though. I was neither middle-aged nor a kid. I was twenty-six years old and I had come to Oakland expecting something. I had had choices. I had made sacrifices to get there, sacrifices for which no "heroic" lady doctor, however "fascinating," "well dressed" (I can remember all the phrases used about her now), could be a substitute.

I had a very difficult time deciding to go to Oakland State. I had taught at Liberty School for six years and I loved that place. It was "beautiful for situation," as the Bible says, located ten miles out of town in the rolling semi-dry upland country where the crop was grain, not apricots and peaches. It was a one-room school, and I was its only teacher. It stood in the midst of this sea of barley and oats like an island. In winter and spring this big green sea of ripening grain rolled and tossed about us—all but crested and broke—all but, though never quite. In a way, this was irritating.

For half the year at Liberty there were no barley waves to watch, only the close-cut stubble of reaped fields and the enormous upthrust of the San Jacinto Mountains beyond. Color was my delight then. I used to sit out in the schoolyard at noon or recess and paint. A former teacher had discarded an old sleigh-back sofa, had it put out in the yard halfway between the school and the woodshed. It stood amidst the volunteer oats and mustard like a larger growth. It seemed planted in earth. In the fall when Santa Anas blew, tumbleweeds piled up about it. I don't know how long it had

been there when I arrived, but it had taken well to its life in
the fields; its legs balanced, its springs stayed inside the
upholstery, and the upholstery itself still kept some of its
original cherry tones. There I sat—when I wasn't playing ball
with the kids—like a hunter, hidden in a game blind; only
my game wasn't lions and tigers, it was the whole world, so
to speak: the mountains, the grain fields, the kids, the schoolhouse itself. I sat there and painted.

Oh, not well. I've never said that, ever. Never claimed that
for a minute. And it's easy to impress children and country
people who think it's uncanny if you can draw an apple that
looks like an apple. And I could do much more than that. I
could make mountains that looked like mountains, children
who looked like children. How that impressed the parents! So
I had gotten in the habit of being praised, though from no
one who counted, no one who knew. I had been sensibly
brought up by my mother, taught to evaluate these plaudits
rightly. I understood that my schoolyard talent didn't make
me a Bonheur or Cassatt. Even so, there was nothing else I
had ever wanted to do. This schoolteaching was just a way of
making money, of helping my mother, who was a widow.

So, because of the time I had for painting and because of
the gifts Liberty School had for my eyes, I had six happy
years. I sat like a queen on that sofa in the grass while the
meadowlarks sang and the butcherbirds first caught their
lunches, then impaled their suppers, still kicking, on the
barbed-wire fence. I didn't paint all the time, of course. Kids
learned to read there. At the end of the sixth year there was
only one eighth grader who could beat me in mental arithmetic. I was the acknowledged champion at skin-the-cat and
could play adequately any position on the softball team.

There was not much left to learn at Liberty, and I began, I
don't know how, to feel that learning, not teaching, was my
business.

In the middle of my sixth year I had to put a tarpaulin
over the sofa. A spring broke through the upholstery, a leg
crumbled. After that I had to prop it on a piece of stove
wood. That spring I noticed for the first time that the babies
of age six I had taught my first year were developing Adam's
apples or busts. Girls who had been thirteen and fourteen my
first year came back to visit Liberty School, married and with
babies in their arms.

"You haven't changed," they would tell me. "Oh, it's a real
anchor to find you here, just the same."

Their husbands, who were often boys my own age, twenty-four or twenty-five, treated me like an older woman. I might have been their mother, or mother-in-law. I was the woman who had taught their wives. I don't think I looked so much old then as ageless. I've taken out some of the snaps of that year, pictures taken at school. My face, in a way, looks as young as my pupils; in other ways, as old as Mt. Tahquitz. It looks back at me with the real stony innocence of a face in a coffin—or cradle.

At Thanksgiving time I was to be out of school three days before the holiday, so that I could have a minor operation. When I left school on Friday, Mary Elizabeth Ross, one of my fourth graders, clasped me fondly and said, "May I be the first to hold your baby when you get back from the hospital?"

She wouldn't believe it when I told her I was going to the hospital because I was sick, not to get a baby, and she cried when I came back to school empty-armed.

That I noticed these things showed my restlessness. It might have passed, I might have settled into a lifetime on that island, except that at Christmas I hung some of my paintings with my pupils' pictures at the annual Teachers' Institute exhibit. They caused a stir, and I began foolishly to dream of painting full time, of going to a big city, Los Angeles or San Francisco, where I would take a studio and have lessons. I didn't mention the idea to anyone, scarcely to myself. When anyone else suggested such a thing to me, I pooh-poohed it. "Me, paint? Don't be funny."

But I dreamed of it; the less I said, the more I dreamed; and the more I dreamed, the less possible talking became. I didn't paint much that winter, but I moved through those months with the feel of a paintbrush in my hand. I could feel, way up in my arm, the strokes I would need to make to put Tahquitz, dead white against the green winter sky, on canvas, put it there so people could see how it really floated, that great peak, was hung aloft there like a giant ship against the sky. But I didn't say a word to anyone about my plans, not even to the School Board when I handed in my resignation at Easter. I hadn't lost my head entirely. I told them I was going to "study." I didn't say what. They thought education, of course.

The minute I had resigned, I was filled with fear. I sat on my three-legged sofa amidst the waves of grain that never crested and shivered until school was out. I had undoubtedly been a fool; not only was I without money, but where would

I find anything as good as what I had? Everything began to say "stay." I would enter my room at night (the one in which I now write), which my mother kept so exquisitely, books ranged according to size and color, the white bedspread at once taut and velvety, the blue iris in a fan-shaped arc in a brown bowl—and I was a part of that composition. If I walked out, the composition collapsed. And outside, I, too, was a fragment. I would stand there asking myself, "Where will you find anything better?"

There was never any answer.

I could only find something different, and possibly worse. So why go? I had seen myself as a lady Sherwood Anderson, locking the factory door behind me and walking down the tracks toward freedom and self-expression. I could dream that dream but I was afraid to act it. I would stand in my perfectly neat bedroom and frighten myself with pictures of my next room, far away, sordid, with strangers on each side. Fear was in my chest like a stone that whole spring. I had no talent, I was gambling everything on an egotistical attention-seeking whim. It was perfectly natural to have done so, but my misery finally drove me to talking with my mother. It was perfectly natural, she assured me, to want a change of scene and occupation. Who didn't occasionally? But why run away to big cities and studios? Why wouldn't the perfectly natural, perfectly logical thing (since I'd already resigned) be to go to Oakland State and study for my Secondary Credential? The minute I, or Mother—I don't remember which of us—thought of this way out, I was filled with bliss, real bliss. I would get away, go to a real city, be surrounded with people devoted to learning, but not risk everything.

I heard about Dr. Louise McKay from the minute I arrived on the campus. She was, as I've said, a kind of college heroine, though it was hard to understand why. What had she done that was so remarkable? She had been a high-school librarian, and had become a doctor. What's so extraordinary about that? The girls, and by that I mean the women students—for many of them were teachers themselves, well along in their thirties and forties, or even fifties—the girls always spoke about Louise McKay's change of profession as if it were a Lazaruslike feat; as if she had practically risen from the dead. People are always so romantic about doctors, and it's understandable, I suppose, dealing as they do with life and death. But Louise McKay! The girls talked about her as if what she'd done had been not only romantic, but also heroic.

In the first place, they emphasized her age. Forty-two! To me at twenty-six that didn't, of course, seem young. Still, it was silly to go on about her as if she were a Grandma Moses of medicine—and as if medicine itself were not, quite simply, anything more than doctoring people; saying, "This ails you" and "I think this pill will help you." They spoke of doctoring as if it were as hazardous as piloting a jet plane. And they spoke of Louise McKay's size, "that tiny, tiny thing," as if she'd been a six-year-old, praising her for her age and her youth at one and the same time. Her size, they said, made it seem as if the child-examining-doll game were reversed; as if doll took out stethoscope and examined child. She was that tiny and dainty, they said, that long-lashed and pink-cheeked. They exclaimed over her clothes, too. They were delightful in themselves, but particularly so because they emphasized the contrast between her profession and her person. She was a scientist and might have been expected to wear something manly and practical—or something dowdy. She did neither. They'd all been to her for their physical examinations—somehow I'd never been scheduled for that—and could give a complete inventory of her chic wardrobe. I saw her only once before I called on her professionally in December. I didn't see many people, as a matter of fact, at Oakland State, in any capacity, except professional.

True, I was studying. Not that the work was difficult—or interesting either. History of Education, Principles of Secondary Education, Classroom Management, Curriculum Development. But the books were better than the people. Had I lived out there on my three-legged sofa with children and nature too long? Or was there something really wrong with the people in teachers colleges? Anyway, I had no friends, and the nearer I got to a Secondary Credential, the less I wanted it. But I wanted something—miserably, achingly, wretchedly. I wanted something. Whether or not this longing, this sense of something lost, had anything to do with the illness that came upon me toward the end of December, I don't know. I attributed this illness at first to the raw damp bay weather after my lifetime in the warmth and dryness of the inland foothills; I thought that my lack of routine, after days of orderly teaching, might be responsible, and, finally, after I had adopted a routine and had stayed indoors out of the mists and fogs and the discomfort persisted, I told myself that everyone as he grew older lost some of his early exuberant health. I was no longer in my first youth, and thus, "when my health began to fail"—I thought of it in that way rather than as having any specific ailment—accounted for my miseries. I had always been impatient with the shufflings and snuffings, the caution on stairs and at the table of the no-longer-young. I thought they could do better if they tried. Now I began to understand that they couldn't do better and that they probably were trying. I was trying. I couldn't do better. I panted on the hills and puffed on the library steps. I leaned against handrails, I hawked and spat and harrumphed like any oldster past his prime. I did what I could to regain the well-being of my youth. I took long walks to get back my lost wind, ate sparingly, plunged under tingling showers.

By the end of December I felt so miserable I decided to see Dr. MaKay at the infirmary. So many new things had been discovered about glands and vitamins, about toxins and antitoxins, that one pill a day was possibly all that stood between me and perfect health. I had the feeling, as people do who have always been well, that a doctor commands a kind of magic—can heal with a glance. Even Dr. McKay, this little ex-librarian, a doll of a woman, with her big splashy earrings and high-heeled shoes and expensive perfumes, could cast a spell of health upon me.

That was the first time I'd ever seen Louise McKay close. My first thought was, She looks every inch her age. She had dark hair considerably grayed, there were lines about her eyes, and her throat muscles were somewhat slack. My second thought was, Why doesn't she admit it? I was dressed more like a middle-aged woman than she. Of course, since she had on a white surgeon's coat, all that could be seen of her "personal attire" was the three or four inches of brown tweed skirt beneath it. But she wore red, very high-heeled shell pumps. Her hair was set in a modified page boy, ends turned under in a soft roll, with a thick, rather tangly fringe across her forehead. It was a somewhat advanced hair style for that year—certainly for a middle-aged doctor. Her eyebrows, which were thick and dark, had been obviously shaped by plucking, and her fingernails were painted coral. She was smiling when I came in. She had considerable color in her face for a dark-haired woman, and she sat at a desk with flowers and pictures on it—not family pictures, but little prints of famous paintings.

She said, looking at her appointment calendar, which had my name on it, "Miss McCullars?"

I said, "Yes."

Then she said, "I see we have something in common." She meant our Scotch names of course, but out of some contrariness which I find hard to explain now, I pretended not to understand, so that she had to explain her little joke to me. But then, it wasn't very funny. She discovered, in looking through her files, that I hadn't had the usual physical examination on entering college.

"Why not?" she asked.

"I didn't get a notice to come," I said, "so I just skipped it."

"It would've helped," she told me, "to have that record now to check against. Just what seems to be the trouble?"

"It's probably nothing. I'm probably just the campus hypochondriac."

"That role's already filled."

I didn't feel well even then, though the stimulation of the talk and of seeing the famous Dr. McKay did make me forget some of my miseries. So I began that afternoon what I always continued in her office—an impersonation of high-spirited, head-tossing health. I don't know why. It wasn't a planned or analyzed action. It just happened that the minute I opened her office door I began to act the part of a person bursting with vitality and health. There I was, practically dying on my feet, as it was later proved, but hiding the fact by every device I could command. What did I think I was doing? The truth is, I wasn't thinking at all.

"I must say you don't look sick," she admitted. Then she began to ask me about my medical history.

"I don't have any medical history. Except measles at fifteen."

"Was there some specific question you wanted to ask me? Some problem?"

So she thought I was one of those girls? Or one of her worshipers just come in to marvel.

"I don't feel well."

"What specifically?"

"Oh—aches and pains."

"Where?"

"Oh—here, there, and everywhere."

"We'll run a few tests, and I'll examine you. The nurse will help you get undressed."

When it was over, she said, "Is your temperature ordinarily a little high?"

"I don't know. I never take it."

"You have a couple of degrees now."

"Above or below normal?"

A little of her school-librarian manner came out. "Are you trying to be funny?"

I wasn't in the least.

"A fever is always above normal."

"What does it mean to have a fever?"

"An infection of some sort."

"It could be a tooth? A tonsil?"

"Yes, it could be. I want to see you tomorrow at ten."

I remember my visit next morning very well. The acacia trees were in bloom, and Dr. McKay's office was filled with their dusty honeybee scent. Dr. McKay was still in street clothes—a blouse, white, high-necked, but frothy with lace and semitransparent, so that you saw more lace beneath. As if she were determined to have everything, I thought: age and youth, practicality and ornamentation, science and femininity. You hero of the campus, I thought, ironically. But she rebuked us schoolteachers by the way she dressed and held herself—and lived, I expected; she really did. And I, I rebuked her in turn, for our hurt honor.

"How do you feel this morning?" she asked.

What did she think to uncover in me? A crybaby and complainer, she standing there in her lovely clothes and I in my dress sun-faded from the Liberty schoolyard?

"Fine," I told her, "I feel fine."

How I felt was her business to discover, wasn't it, not mine to tell? If I knew exactly how I felt, and why, what would've been the use of seeing a doctor? Besides, once again in her office I was stimulated by her presence so that my miseries when not there seemed quite possibly something I had imagined.

"I wanted to check your temperature this morning," she told me.

She sat down on a white stool, put a thermometer in my mouth, then, while we waited, asked me questions which she thought I could answer with a nod of the head.

"You like teaching? You want to go on with it? You have made friends here?"

She was surprised when she took the thermometer from my mouth. After looking at it thoughtfully, she shook it down and said, "Morning temperature, too."

"You didn't expect that?"

"No, frankly, I didn't."

"Why not?"

"In the kind of infection I suspected you had, a morning temperature isn't usual."

I didn't ask what infection she suspected. I had come to her office willing to be thumped, X-rayed, tested in any way she thought best. I was willing to give her samples of sputum or urine, to cough when told to cough, say ahhh or hold my breath while she counted ten. Whatever she told me to do I would do. But she had turned doctor, not I. If she was a doctor, not a librarian, now was her chance to prove it. Here I was with my fever, come willingly to her office. Let her tell me its cause.

For the next month, Dr. McKay lived, so far as I was concerned, the life of a medical detective, trying to find the villain behind the temperature. The trouble was that the villain's habits differed from day to day. It was as if a murderer had a half-dozen different thumbprints, and left now one, now another, behind him. One day much temperature, the next day none. Dr. McKay eliminated villain after villain: malaria, tonsillitis, rheumatic fever, infected teeth. And while she found disease after disease which I did not have, I grew steadily worse. By May about the only time I ever felt well was while I was in Dr. McKay's office. Entering it was like going onto a stage. However near I might have been to collapse before that oak door opened, once inside it I was to play with perfect ease my role of health. I was unable, actually, to do anything else. I assumed health when I entered her office, as they say Dickens, unable to stand without support, assumed health when he walked out before an audience.

It was nothing I planned. I couldn't by an act of will have feigned exuberance and well-being, gone to her office day after day consciously to play the role of Miss Good Health of 1940, could I? No, something unconscious happened the minute I crossed that threshold, something electric—and ironic. I stood, sat, stooped, reclined, breathed soft, breathed hard, answered questions, flexed my muscles, exposed my reflexes for Dr. McKay with vigor and pleasure—and irony. Especially irony. I was sick, sick, falling apart, crumbling dying on my feet, and I knew it. And this woman, this campus hero whose province it was to know it, was ignorant of the fact. I didn't know what ailed me and wasn't supposed to. She was. It was her business to know.

In the beginning, tuberculosis had been included among the other suspected diseases. But the nontubercular fever pattern, the absence of positive sputum, the identical sounds of the lungs when percussed all had persuaded Dr. McKay that the trouble lay elsewhere. I did not speculate at all about my sickness. I had never been sick before, or even, for that matter, known a sick person. For all I knew, I might have elephantiasis or leprosy, and when Dr. McKay began once again to suspect tuberculosis, I was co-operative and untroubled. She was going to give me what she called a "patch test." Whether this is still used, I don't know. The test then consisted of the introduction of a small number of tubercle bacilli to a patch of scraped skin. If, after a day or two, there was no "positive" reaction, no inflammation of the skin, one was thought to have no tubercular infection.

On the day Dr. McKay began this test she used the word "tuberculosis" for the first time. I had experienced when I entered her office that afternoon my usual heightening of well-being, what amounted to a real gaiety.

"So you still don't give up?" I asked when she announced her plan for the new test. "Still won't admit that what you have on your hands is a hypochondriac?"

It was a beautiful afternoon in late May. School was almost over for the year. Students drifted past the window walking slowly homeward, relishing the sunshine and the blossoming hawthorn, their faces lifted to the light. Cubberly and Thorndyke and Dewey given the go-by for an hour or two. Some of this end-of-the-year, lovely-day quiet came into my interview with Dr. McKay. Though it had started with my usual high-spirited banter, I stopped that. It seemed inappropriate. I experienced my usual unusual well-being, but there was added to it that strange, quiet, listening tenderness which marks the attainment of a pinnacle of some kind.

Dr. McKay stood before her window, her surgeon's jacket off—I was her last patient for the day—in her usual frothy blouse, very snow-white against the rose-red of the hawthorn trees.

She turned away from the window and said to me, "You aren't a hypochondriac."

She shook her head. "I don't know." Then she explained the patch test to me.

"Tuberculosis?" I asked. "And no hectic flush, no graveyard cough, no skin and bones?"

The words were still bantering, possibly, but the tone had changed, tender, tender, humorous, and fondling; the battle—if there had been one—over; and the issue, whatever it was, settled. "In spite of all that, this test?"

"In spite of all that," she said.

She did the scraping deftly. I watched her hands, and while I doubt that there is any such thing as a "surgeon's hands," Dr. McKay's didn't look like a librarian's either, marked by fifteen years of mucilage pots, library stamps, and ten-cent fines. I could smell her perfume and note at close range the degree to which she defied time and the expected categories.

"Come back Monday at the same time," she told me when she had finished.

"What do you expect Monday?" I asked.

"I'm not a prophet," she answered. "If I were . . ." She didn't finish her sentence.

We parted like comrades who have been together on a long and dangerous expedition, I don't know what she felt or thought—that she had really discovered, at last, the cause of my illness, perhaps. What I felt is difficult to describe. Certainly my feelings were not those of the usual patient threatened with tuberculosis. Instead, I experienced a tranquility I hadn't known for a long time. I felt like a lover and a winner, triumphant but tranquil. I knew there would be no positive reaction to the skin test. Beyond that I didn't think.

I was quite right about the reaction. Dr. McKay was completely professional Monday afternoon; buttoned up in her jacket, stethoscope hanging about her neck. I entered her office feeling well, but strange. My veins seemed bursting with blood or triumph. I looked out the window and remembered where I had been a year ago. Breathing was difficult, but in the past months I had learned to live without breathing. I wore a special dress that afternoon because I thought the occasion special. I wouldn't be seeing Dr. McKay again. It was made of white men's-shirting Madras and had a deep scooped neckline, bordered with a ruffle.

"How do you feel?" Dr. McKay asked, as she always did, when I entered.

"Out of this world," I told her.

"Don't joke," she said.

"I wasn't. It's the truth. I feel wonderful."

"Let's have a look at the arm."

"You won't find anything."

"How do you know? Did you peek?"

"No, I didn't, but you won't find anything."

"I'll have a look anyway."

There was nothing, just as I'd known. Not a streak of pink even. Nothing but the marks of the adhesive tape to distinguish one arm from the other. Dr. McKay looked and looked. She touched the skin and pinched it.

"Okay," she said, "you win."

"What do you mean I win? You didn't want me to be infected, did you?"

"Of course not."

"I told you all along I was a hypochondriac."

"Okay, Miss McCullars," she said again, "you win." She sat down at her desk and wrote something on my record sheet.

"What's the final verdict?" I asked.

She handed the sheet to me. What she had written was "TB patch test negative. Fluctuating temperature due to neurotic causes."

"So I won't need to come back?"

"No."

"Nor worry about my lungs?"

"No."

Then with precise timing, as if that were the cue for which for almost six months I had been waiting, I had, there in Dr. McKay's office, my first hemorrhage. A hemorrhage from the lungs is always frightening, and this was a very bad one and my first. They got me to the infirmary at once, but there behind me in Dr. McKay's office was the card stained with my blood and saying that nothing ailed me. I was not allowed to speak for twenty-four hours, and my thought, once the hemorrhage had stopped, was contained in two words, which ran through my mind, over and over again. "I've won. I've won." What had I won? Well, for one thing, I'd won my release from going on with my work for that Secondary Credential. All that could be forgotten, and forgotten also the need to leave Liberty at all. I could go back there, back to my stranded sofa and the school library and the mountains, blue over the green barley.

When at the end of twenty-four hours I was permitted to whisper, Dr. Stegner, the head physician at Oakland State, came to see me.

"When did you first see Dr. McKay?" he asked.

"In December."

"What course of treatment did she prescribe?"

"Not any. She didn't know what was wrong with me."

"Did she ever X-ray you?"

"No."

This, I began to learn, was the crux of the case against Dr. McKay. For there was one. She should have X-rayed me. She should have known that in cases of far advanced tuberculosis, and that was what I had, the already deeply infected system pays no attention to the introduction of one or two more bacilli. All of its forces are massed elsewhere—there are no guards left to repulse border attacks of unimportant skirmishers. But by this time my mother had arrived, alert, knowledgeable, and energetic.

"My poor little girl," she said, "this woman doctor has killed you."

I wasn't dead yet, but as I heard the talk around me I began to understand that in another year or two I might very well be so. And listening to my mother's talk, I began to agree with her. Dr. McKay had robbed me not only of health, but also of a promising career—I had been poised upon the edge of something unusual. I was training myself for service. I had remarkable talents. And now all was denied me, and for this denial I could blame Dr. McKay. I did. She had cut me down in mid-career through her ignorance. What did the campus think of its hero now? For the campus had heard of Dr. McKay's mistake. And the Board of Regents! My mother said it was her duty; that she owed the steps she was taking to some other poor girl who might suffer as I had through Dr. McKay's medical incompetence. I thought it was a matter for her to decide, and besides, I was far too ill to have or want any say in such decisions. I was sent, as soon as I was able to be moved, to a sanatorium near my home in Southern California.

I had been there four months when I saw Dr. McKay again. At the beginning of the visiting hour on the first Saturday in October, the nurse on duty came to my room.

"Dr. McKay to see you," she said.

I had no chance to refuse to see her—though I don't know that I would have refused if I'd had the chance—for Dr. McKay followed the nurse into the room and sat down by my bed.

She had changed a good deal; she appeared little, nondescript, and mousy. She had stopped shaping her eyebrows and painting her nails. I suppose I had changed, too. With the loss of my fever, I had lost also all my show of exuberance and life. I lay there in the hospital bed looking, I knew, as sick as I really was. We stared at each other without words for a time.

Then I said, to say something, for she continued silent, "How are things at Oakland State this year?"

"I'm not at Oakland State. I was fired."

I hadn't known it. I was surprised and dismayed, but for a heartbeat—in a heartbeat—I experienced a flash of that old outrageous exultation I had known in her office. I was, in spite of everything, for a second, well and strong and tender in victory. Though what my victory was, I sick and she fired, I couldn't have told.

"I'm sorry," I said. I was. It is a pitiful thing to be out of work.

"Don't lie," she said.

"I am not lying," I told her.

She didn't contradict me. "Why did you do it?" she asked me.

"Do what?" I said, at first really puzzled. Then I remembered my mother's threats. "I had nothing to do with it. Even if I'd wanted to, I was too sick. You know that. I had no idea you weren't in Oakland this year."

"I don't mean my firing—directly. I mean that long masquerade. I mean that willingness to kill yourself, if necessary, to punish me. I tell you a doctor of fifty years' experience would've been fooled by you. Why? I'd never seen you before. I wanted nothing but good for you. Why did you do it? Why?"

"I don't know what you mean."

"What had I ever done to you? Lost there in that dark library, dreaming of being a doctor, saving my money and finally escaping. How had I harmed or threatened you that you should be willing to risk your life to punish me?"

Dr. McKay had risen and was walking about the room, her voice, for one so small, surprisingly loud and commanding. I was afraid a nurse would come to ask her to be quiet. Yet I hesitated myself to remind her to speak more quietly.

"Well," she said, "you have put yourself in a prison, a fine narrow prison. Elected it of your own free will. And that's all right for you, if you wanted a prison. But you had no right to elect it for me, too. That was murderous. Really murderous." I began to fear that she was losing control of herself, and tried to ask questions that would divert her mind from the past.

"Where are you practicing, now?" I asked.

She stopped her pacing and stood over me. "I am no longer in medicine," she said. "I'm the librarian in the high school at Beaumont."

"That's not where you were before?"

"No, it's much smaller and hotter."

"It's only thirty miles—as the crow flies—from Liberty, where I used to teach. I'm going back there as soon as I'm well. It was a mistake to leave it." She said nothing.

"I really love Liberty," I said, "and teaching. The big fields of barley, the mountains. There was an old sofa in the schoolyard, where I used to sit. It was like a throne. I thought for a while I wanted to get away from there and try something else. But that was all a crazy dream. All I want to do now is get back."

"I wish you could have discovered that before you came to Oakland."

I ignored this. "Don't you love books?"

"I had better love books," she said, and left the room.

As it happened, I've never seen her again, though I get these cards. I didn't go back to Liberty four years later—when I was able again to teach. I got this other school, but somehow the magic I had felt earlier with the children, I felt no longer. An outdated little schoolroom with the windows placed high so that neither teacher nor pupils could see out; a dusty schoolyard; and brackish water. The children I teach now look so much like their predecessors that I have the illusion of living in a dream, of being on a treadmill teaching the same child the same lesson through eternity. Outside on the school grounds, my erstwhile throne, the sofa, does not exist. The mountains, of course, are still there—a great barrier at the end of the valley.

Just across the mountains are Beaumont and Dr. McKay; and I am sometimes heartened, standing on the packed earth of the schoolyard in the winter dusk, as she suggested, to think of her reshelving her books, closing the drawer of her fine-till, at the same hour. We can't all escape; some of us must stay home and do the homely tasks, however much we may have dreamed of painting or doctoring. "You have company," I tell myself, looking toward her across the mountains. Then I get into my car to drive into town, where my mother has all this loveliness waiting for me; a composition, once again, that really includes me.

The Pocketbook Game

Alice Childress

Marge . . . day's work is an education! Well, I mean workin' in different homes you learn much more than if you was steady in one place. . . . I tell you, it really keeps your mind sharp tryin' to watch for what folks will put over on you.

What? . . . No, Marge, I do not want to help shell no beans, but I'd be more than glad to stay and have supper with you, and I'll wash the dishes after. Is that all right? . . .

Who put anything over on who? . . . Oh yes! It's like this. . . . I been working for Mrs. E . . . one day a week for several months and I notice that she has some peculiar ways. Well, there was only one thing that really bothered me and that was her pocketbook habit. . . . No, not those little novels. . . . I mean her purse—her handbag.

Marge, she's got a big old pocketbook with two long straps on it . . . and whenever I'd go there, she'd be propped up in a chair with her handbag double wrapped tight around her wrist, and from room to room she'd roam with that purse hugged to her bosom. . . . Yes, girl! This happens every time! No, there's *nobody* there but me and her. . . . Marge, I couldn't say nothin' to her! It's her purse, ain't it? She can hold onto it if she wants to!

I held my peace for months, tryin' to figure out how I'd make my point. . . . Well, bless Bess! *Today was the day*! . . . Please, Marge, keep shellin' the beans so we can eat! I know you're listenin', but you listen with your ears, not your hands. . . . Well, anyway, I was almost ready to go home when she steps in the room hangin' onto her bag as usual and says, "Mildred, will you ask the super to come up and fix the kitchen faucet?" "Yes, Mrs. E . . ." I says, "as soon as I leave." "Oh, no," she says, "he may be gone by then. Please go now." "All right," I says, and out the door I went, still wearin' my Hoover apron.

I just went down the hall and stood there a few minutes

. . . and then I rushed back to the door and knocked on it as hard and frantic as I could. She flung open the door sayin', "What's the matter? Did you see the super?" . . . "No," I says, gaspin' hard for breath, "I was almost downstairs when I remembered . . . *I left my pocketbook!*"

With that I dashed in, grabbed my purse and then went down to get the super! Later, when I was leavin' she says real timid-like, "Mildred, I hope that you don't think I distrust you because . . ." I cut her off real quick. . . . "That's all right, Mrs. E. . ., I understand. 'Cause if I paid anybody as little as you pay me, I'd hold my pocketbook too!"

Marge, you fool . . . lookout! . . . You gonna drop the beans on the floor!

Rima the Bird Girl

Rona Jaffe

I don't remember the day we first met, but my first
memory of her is of a wraithlike dark-haired girl sitting in
the corner of the living room of our dormitory at college, re-
citing poetry—no, almost shouting it—she and a friend in
unison. And it seemed to me then as if poetry should always
be shouted in this inspired, almost orgiastic, way, for it was
really music. "O love is the crooked thing,/-There is nobody
wise enough/To find out all that is in it, . . . Ah, penny,
brown penny, brown penny,/-One cannot begin it too soon."

Her name was Rima Allen, and she came from a small
town in Pennsylvania which had neither the distinction of
being a grimy coal town nor Main Line, but just a town. Her
mother had been reading *Green Mansions* when her daughter
was born, and she felt it would give her child some individuality to be named Rima. Her father was a tax accountant, a
vague man who spent his life bent over records of other
people's lives. He thought Rima was a silly name, but his
wife overruled him, and later it was she who chose Radcliffe
for Rima, and so we met.

There was a fireplace at one end of the living room in our
dormitory, and beside it a nook, wood paneled and cushioned
in velvet. Rima was sitting in that nook with her temporary
friend, a lumpy debutante from New York who powdered
her face like a Kabuki dancer and had once brought a copy
of the Social Register into dinner to point out her own name
in it. This frightened and graceless snob (whose registered
name I have forgotten) was the last person on earth you
would expect to find chanting Yeats with such obvious joy,
yet Rima had made her memorize dozens of his poems. I
knew at once that Rima was a special girl, a girl people grav-
itated toward to find their dream, their opposite, whatever it
was they could not find alone.

"An aged man is but a paltry thing,/A tattered coat upon

289

a stick, unless/Soul clap its hands and sing, and louder sing/For every tatter in its mortal dress."

Rima was a tall girl who always looked very small and fragile, until you noticed her standing next to someone else and realized with surprise that she was big. She had narrow shoulders and small bones, a delicate way of moving, and a soft, child's voice. Her face, in those years of our late teens, was a white blur, as I suppose all our faces were, for we did not yet know who we were. I have a photograph of her sitting on the library steps, a pretty, pale, no-face child of seventeen, all wonder, her arms held out to the wan New England sun.

Every one of us owned several bottles of cologne; Rima had none, but she had one bottle of perfume. We all had many party dresses; Rima had only one, but it was orange, with a swirly skirt, and it had cost a hundred dollars. I remember her always hiding in her room, the shades down, studying, or reading the poetry she loved, and then the sound of the phone bell . . . and ten minutes later she emerged—a swirl of orange skirt, a cloud of Arpege drifting after her, as if she had suddenly been told she existed.

That's all I remember of her from those days; it was, after all, fifteen years ago, and her story had not begun. When we graduated, four of us went to Washington to work in offices, share a house, and find husbands. I had been a zoology major in college, studying such unfeminine things as mollusks, but when we went to Washington I decided to become a secretary along with the others, because we were almost twenty-one and not getting any younger. Everyone knew you found nothing among the mollusks but shells and a lot of ugly old men. We had decided on Washington instead of New York because the other two girls said that was where the bright young men were. A few months after the four of us settled in rooms in a Greek Revival style mansion turned into a rooming house, the two who had brought us to this city of romance began going steady with two boys they had known back at Harvard, and I realized why we had come.

I missed zoology and hated typing and filing; but missing one's work takes an odd form in girls, I think—I was less conscious of the loss than I was of what replaced it, a ferocious need to be loved. I needed someone to inflict all that creative energy on, it didn't matter much who. Of the four of us, it was only Rima who seemed to enjoy being a secretary; who preferred staying home and listening to old Noel Cow-

ard records to going out with a new prospect; who went to
bed early and got up early, eagerly, without resentment; and
who went to the office in her prettiest clothes. I soon discovered it was because she was in love with someone she had
met at work.

It was one of those impossibly romantic meetings that occur only in bad movies and real life. The man was attached
to the State Department, one of those career diplomats whose
work is so important and confidential that you can talk to
him for an hour at a cocktail party and realize afterward he
has not said a word about himself. He was American, forty-
five years old, very attractive, totally sophisticated and, of
course, married. Rima had been dispatched to take some papers to his office. There she was, in the doorway—his secretary was in the powder room—and he was alone behind the
largest desk she had ever seen. She looked at him, knowing
only vaguely who he was and how important he was, thinking
only that he was a grownup and extraordinarily attractive.
She was wearing her neat little college-girl suit, her hair tied
back with a ribbon, her face all admiration and awe. She
thought as girls do in the darkness of movie theaters without
any sense of further reality: I'd love to go out with him! No
one knows what he thought. But the next day he took her to
the country for lunch.

She did not tell me who her mysterious lover was for
several months, and she never told our other two roommates
at all. She saved newspaper clippings about glittering Washington parties he had attended, but because diplomatic
amours are very diplomatic in Washington, she had little else
in the way of souvenirs, not even a matchbook from a restaurant. I did not know how they managed to meet during those
first few months, but I always knew when she was meeting
him because again, as in our college days, there was a swirl
of brightly colored skirt running down the stairs, a faint
cloud of perfume (Joy this time instead of Arpege), and the
air around her was charged with life. When she finally told
me his name, it was only after they had both decided they
were in love.

Rima had had crushes on boys at Harvard, had even cried
over a few missed phone calls, but it was nothing like this. As
for him, he had played around with little interest with a few
predatory wives, but he had never had a real love affair with
anyone since his marriage. Rima was so young, so full of
confidence in a future in which she would always be young

and he would always care for her, that she never even thought of asking him to get a divorce. It was a courtship. They planned how they would meet, when they would meet, how she could see him most often, how she could get along. He could not bear for her to be poor; even the thought that she was spending part of her $60 salary on taxis to meet him appalled him, he wanted to make everything up to her, but how? She refused to go out with any of the boys (we still called them that) who phoned, and he knew it. Suddenly, one day, our freezer was full of steaks, the refrigerator was filled with splits of champagne, and our house was so filled with flowers I thought someone had died.

I went with Rima one day to help her sell her jewelry so that she could buy him a birthday present. Her charm bracelet with the gold disk that said "Sweet Sixteen," her college ring . . . whatever she could not sell she pawned. None of it meant anything to her. "I want to get him gold cuff links," she said. "He wears French cuffs." I thought of the O. Henry story about the gift of the Magi, but it was not the same, because he was not giving up anything for her, and what she was giving up for him was only bits of metal and chips of gems that belonged to an already fading past.

That summer, when our first year of independence drew to a close, our two roommates married the boys they had come to Washington to pursue, and Rima and I had two whole rooms to ourselves. Summers in Washington are very hot. An air conditioner mysteriously appeared in our bedroom window, installed by a man from the air-conditioning company whom neither of us had sent for. On the first cool fall day, for the first time, I was allowed to meet the diplomat. He came to our house for tea and sat on the edge of one of our frayed chairs, very elegant in his hand-tailored suit and Sulka tie. He even wore a vest. I thought he looked like our uncle; not our father—he was too young, too glamorous, too much from another world. But there was something fatherly in the way he looked around at our landlady's furniture with amusement and yet a little annoyance—was it clean enough, good enough, for his child?—the way he smiled with adult pride at everything Rima said, as if she were a precious being from another planet. I could hardly believe any of this was happening; I think, in a way, neither could he. Yet they were obviously in love with each other.

He went to New York on several business trips that fall and winter and took Rima with him, meeting her as if by ac-

dent on the train, where he had taken a private bedroom
or the short trip and Rima had a ticket in the parlor car.
hey had rooms in the same hotel on different floors. At Buc-
ellati's he bought her a gold and emerald ring, which she
ore on her left hand, but they entered and left the shop by
e back door. When they returned to Washington after the
st trip, his wife met him at the station, and Rima alighted
om a different car and stood staring on the station platform
s her love drove off in a silver-gray foreign automobile with
omeone who was suddenly flesh and blood, an actuality, a
orce, a monster.

"I saw her, the old hag," Rima said to me that night, almost in tears. "I wish I could kill her. She's very sophisticated
. . she was wearing a real Chanel suit, and the Chanel
hoes and bag too . . . she's too thin, she chain-smokes and
ses a holder . . . she's one of those terribly chic, tense
women who knows everybody and always says and does the
ight things. You could tell. She's unhappy, though . . . she
must know he loves someone else. Women as nervous as that
always know they aren't loved. He told me he doesn't love
her any more. He'd leave her if it weren't for his career; a
scandal—zip!" She drew her finger across her throat. "He's so
proper and old-fashioned in his way, nobody is like him any
more. If it weren't for her he could marry me and we'd both
e happy. I hate her, the old hag."

"She doesn't sound like an old hag," I said.

"She is!"

"All right, she is."

"And ugly, too."

"Well, at least she's ugly."

"No, she's not ugly," Rima said. "I wish she were. She
must have something if he won't leave her for me. If he real-
y didn't love her, he'd leave her, no matter what he says.
How could he marry me? I couldn't be a hostess, I couldn't
un two homes the way she does. I don't know anything
about being a diplomat's wife. I *know* he loves me, but he
won't leave *her*. . . ."

So she did want to marry him after all. It had been inevi-
able. The courtship had been beautiful; the five-minute meet-
ngs in hallways, the stolen afternoons and weekends—all had
een part of the discovery and wonder of love. But after a
year and a half the champagne of secrecy had gone flat. I
uspected that Rima had wanted to marry him long before
his but had never dared say the words until she saw his wife

and realized bitterly that someone had married him, someone was sharing all of his life except those stolen afternoons; for someone it was possible.

All lovers make near-fatal mistakes in their relationships; it is part of the pleasure of love, illicit or not, to tempt providence. So when, one weekend when his wife was away, the diplomat took Rima to his home, it seemed to me merely one of the fatal mistakes some lovers have to make. It was not fatal in any immediate sense, for they were not caught, no one saw them, the servants were away, his wife did not return unexpectedly with a detective or a gun. On his part, it was only a further avowal of his love for Rima; he wanted her to see where and how he lived, he didn't want her to be an outsider. He wanted her to approve of him, of the beautiful things with which he filled his life. He wanted to give her a setting to picture when she dreamed of him, a background for her lonely fantasies; perhaps he also wanted to be able to imagine her in his home when she was no longer there and he was sitting through a dull diplomatic dinner party. The mistake was fatal because Rima did approve of his home . . . she approved of it too much.

She told me about it that night in detail, and I could picture her scampering through those huge rooms like a child, touching each piece of antique furniture as her lover told her what famous person might have sat in this chair, dined from that plate (now an ashtray), or what skill distinguished the weaving of this piece of cloth from any other. She peered into every closet, learning about the heirloom silver, the china, the crystal; she even tried on some of his wife's clothes. To him, Rima was a child, wistful, amusing, and filled with amazement, so he let her try on the Chanels, the Diors, stroke the furs, wave the lapis cigarette holder in the air as if it held a cigarette and she were a grownup at the ball. When she returned home to the Greek Revival rooming house, the photographic mind that had gotten A's at Radcliffe was a living archive of memorabilia.

The bulging scrapbooks of souvenirs and photographs from our college days, which still amused us on Sunday afternoons, were shipped home to her parents. In their place appeared glossy magazines that looked more like books, with names like "Antiquaries," and "A History of Battersea Boxes." One of them was even in French. The diplomat collected Battersea boxes, and also tiny silver boxes with crests on them, so Rima began to scour back street antique shops for a collection ex-

ctly like his. Real Battersea boxes were too expensive, but
n her twenty-third birthday the diplomat gave her one,
opped with white china, on which was written in fine script:
A Trifle From a Friend."

"He wanted to give me a coat," she told me, "but this coat
will go another year. I just had to have a real Battersea box."

There was a one-of-a-kind pair of Louis XV chairs in the
diplomat's living room. But there turned out to be, surprisingly, an identical pair, for Rima discovered it on a trip to
New York, and she began putting away part of her salary ev-
ry month to buy them. "A hundred dollars a month for-
ver. . . ." Our landlady's frayed chairs were sent to the
asement, and the two Louis XV chairs took their place in
ront of our fireplace that December, for the diplomat had
dded the frighteningly large difference for a Christmas
resent. But he seemed disappointed with the gift she had
hosen for him to give her, because he surprised her with an
dditional present, a beige and white fox fur coat. She looked
oung and rich and daring in the coat, but as for the chairs, I
was afraid to sit on them.

One night Rima packed all her career-girl clothes in a
arge box and sent them to charity, for she was the new
wner of a real Chanel suit with the shoes and bag to match.
he bought a cigarette holder and began to smoke; she said it
would help her lose weight, for she had suddenly decided she
was too fat. When her lover told her she was getting too thin,
he cried all night, but she did not stop smoking, for the ex-
use was it would help her stop biting her nails. The collec-
on of tiny silver boxes with crests grew larger and covered
he entire top of a spindly-legged antique table Rima had
ound, which was by coincidence exactly like the one in the
edroom of the diplomat and his wife. The real Chanel suit
was joined, in a few months, by another, and a white Dior
vening gown, which Rima wore at home in the evening,
lone, while she sipped sherry from a certain crystal
wineglass, chain-smoked, and wrote letters to a certain firm in
aris asking if it was possible to obtain ten yards of a certain
rocaded fabric which had been specially made at one time
or another American client, and a tiny sample of which she
appened to have snipped from the underside of that client's
ofa.

When the fabric finally arrived, the sofa it would cover
ad arrived too, a gift for Rima's twenty-fourth birthday. I
eminded her we were still paying rent for a furnished apart-

ment, although it now looked like a museum, and our land
lady's basement looked like a warehouse. Rima looked at me
with the nervous, near-tearful look she had acquired during
the past year, which somehow made her look rather tragic
and mysterious. "We're too old to live like pigs anymore,"
she said. "Don't you want a real home?"

I did, and I wanted something more, something elusive but
wonderful, which I felt must surely be beyond the next corner, or at the next party, or on the threshold of our front
door tomorrow night. . . . It had to be, or I felt I would disappear. So one fall evening, when the doorbell rang, announcing the arrival of perhaps the hundredth blind date I
would have had in Washington, I decided: If he's anything
better than a monster, whoever he is, *this one* I will fall in
love with.

He was far from a monster, and he had green eyes and a
sense of humor—my two fatal weaknesses—so while he sat in
my living room talking and trying to make me like him he
never knew he needn't have bothered, because I already loved
him. He talked all night, and at dawn, when he remembered
he had invited me to his apartment after dinner to make a
pass at me, and now it was too late because it was day and
we had to go to our offices, he decided he was in love with
me, too.

"How could I not love you?" he asked (this young man
who was already destined to become my first husband). "You
are me. If I didn't love you, it would be like not loving myself."

My decision to marry him seemed as mad and romantic as
my decision to fall in love with him. We were in his car at
the curb in front of a restaurant. It was that first night, before his apartment, at our first restaurant together, the first
time I had been in his car. I wanted to invent some test for
destiny, something simple, arbitrary and irrevocable, therefore
magic. "If he comes around to my side to open the door, I'll
marry him. If he doesn't, he'll never know." He came around
to open the door.

Rima gave a cocktail party for us when we announced our
engagement, one of many parties she had begun to give. She
had become a polished hostess, entertaining a mélange of
people: minor politicians, intellectuals, an artist, a writer, an
actress, a few foreigners who spoke no English at all but
whose languages Rima had studied in college and perfected
during the past few years of her diplomatic education. Her

diplomat was not there, of course, and she had hidden her half-dozen tiny framed photographs of him in the dresser drawer, but his presence hovered in the rooms thoughout the party, for it was now his home, done in his taste, filled with the objects of his pleasures, and the hostess who presided over it all with infinite charm might as well have been his wife. I had a brief irreverent fantasy of the diplomat coming here one night by accident, and panicking, not knowing which home he had come to.

At the party there was a visitor from New York, a young advertising executive. He was thirty-four, married twelve years to his high school sweetheart, and had two children. He was in Washington on business and obviously had never seen anyone like Rima at such close range. He was almost childishly infatuated with her after ten minutes. She flirted with him, named him Heathcliff (for that was rather whom he resembled), and although she obviously enjoyed playing with him, she seemed unaware of her new power. When she was moving about the room talking to her other guests he did not take his eyes off her.

"You need some more champagne, Heathcliff," Rima said, touching his arm lightly as she drifted past. "I want you to get good and drunk. 'Wine comes in at the mouth and love comes in at the eye; That's all we shall know for truth before we grow old and die.' "

" 'I lift the glass to my mouth,' " he finished, " 'I look at you, and I sigh.' "

She stopped dead and stared at him.

He smiled. There was something about him both boyish and wire-strong, a man who would piously refuse to deceive anyone and yet who was destined to deceive many people throughout his life because they would mistake him for some-one simple. He raised his champagne glass at Rima. " 'A mermaid found a swimming lad, picked him for her own, pressed her body to his body, laughed; and plunging down forgot in cruel happiness that even lovers drown.' "

"I don't think anyone could drown you," she said. "Heath-cliff. . . ."

"Lady Brett Ashley. . . ." he said, transfixed.

"Me?" Rima laughed. *"Me?"*

He asked her to have dinner with him, as he was alone in this city, but she refused, explaining that she was in love with someone and never went out with anyone else.

"Where is he?" the advertising man asked, looking around the crowded room.

"He's not here."

"Oh. Married."

"Aren't you?" she replied sweetly, and drifted away to her guests.

My husband's work took him to New York, where we lived in a three-room apartment that I cleaned carefully every day. I went to the grocery store, read his magazines, his books, played his records, and waited for him to come home to eat the dinners I cooked. He did not like his work very much, and I did not work at all, so in the evenings we talked about the past, our childhoods, our friends; and when we were bored with that we talked about the future, although that seemed more like a game than reality. Sometimes we talked about Rima, who he said was neurotic. He said her life was going to end badly. "If I weren't married to you, I would save her from that man."

"Really? What makes you think she'd want you?" And at that moment, only six months after we had vowed to stay together forever, I wondered why I wanted him, either. I was beginning to look the way Rima had: nervous, lost, a bird girl who appeared out of a tree in the jungle to answer someone's dream and then disappeared at dawn . . . or was it he who disappeared, back into the real world, while the bird girl waited, invisible, for his return, for his summons, for her moments of reality?

Rima wrote to me quite regularly during those months. She had nothing else to do in the evenings, for the decorating job on her apartment was completed, and for some reason the diplomat was not seeing her as often as he used to. He was overworked, she wrote to me, and when he did manage a little time with her he usually spent it falling asleep.

"For the first time in my life," she wrote, "I feel old. I feel like a wife. But I want to marry him, and I know this isn't what our life would be like if I were really his wife. Then we'd share everything. But now he acts as if it isn't a romance any more. I don't know why. Do you remember in the beginning, when the house was full of flowers? He hasn't taken me out to lunch in four months."

They had their first serious fight. "He called me extravagant, said I cared too much about clothes," Rima wrote. "He used to tell me she was extravagant (the old hag) and I told him never to dare compare me with her. He said, 'In some vays you are like her,' and the way he said it was like an insult. He refused to explain. What more does he want from me? I can't be perfect, I need love, I can't help that. Why can't he love me enough to leave her? What's wrong with me that he can't love me enough to choose me over someone he doesn't love at all?"

The day after her fifth anniversary with the diplomat, Rima arrived at my apartment in New York. It seems they had been planning their fifth anniversary celebration for months; she had saved for and bought a new white Dior gown, had had her hair done at eight in the morning in order to be at the office on time, and then at five o'clock—an hour before they were to meet to celebrate—he had phoned to say he had to go to an important dinner party, his wife would not understand if she had to attend alone, there was nothing he could do. Rima had gotten tremendously drunk on the bottle of Taittinger Blanc de Blancs 1953 she had been chilling in her refrigerator, given the Malossol caviar to the cleaning woman, thrown the white Dior on the closet floor, and taken the morning train to New York. He had promised to make it up to her, perhaps even a whole weekend away somewhere . . . but she could not wait.

"Wait!" she cried to me, tears pouring down her face as if she were a marble statue in a fountain. "Wait! Wait! All I have ever done is wait."

When my husband came home he flirted with Rima all evening—to save her?—as if I were invisible, and she took an instant dislike to it. When he started to talk about a girl he had known before he met me, Rima stood up. "If I ever get married," she said coldly, "my husband will never talk about other women in my presence. Nor will he ever flirt with other women when I am in the room. It's insulting. I am going to be the first in his life, not just something that's *there*, and if I ever find there's someone else I'm going to leave."

"Isn't that a little too much to ask of a man?" I said, wishing I had her courage.

"It's what I will ask," Rima said.

"Well, Rima," he said, cheerfully nasty, "you ought to know."

I don't remember her ever speaking to my husband again, for that was the way Rima was. She drifted in and out of rooms during the two days she stayed with us, graceful and silent as a cat, always pleasant, but whenever he began to talk she suddenly wasn't there. The afternoon of the second day, when she was feeling repentant toward the diplomat, who did not know where she had gone, I went with Rima to Gucci's where she bought him a wallet. It was elegant, expensive, and impersonal—no, thank you, she would not wait to have it initialed—the kind of gift one had to give a man whose wife noticed all his personal possessions. Coming out of the store we saw the advertising man who had been at Rima's party, or rather, he saw us, for she did not recognize him.

He was so excited he called out to stop us; he shook her gloved hand with both his hands, and then he blushed, as if he had attacked her in my presence. Rima laughed, and then he laughed, too, and invited us both for a drink.

We went to the Plaza (Rima's choice), where Heathcliff had one Scotch (his limit, he told us) and Rima had champagne. She was wearing the beige and white fox coat over a pale wool dress, she had a long gold cigarette holder, her beige alligator handbag and the little package from Gucci were on the table, and she did indeed look like Lady Brett Ashley, or someone equally golden and fictional. We sat in the dark wood-paneled room, watching the sunset through the windows that overlooked the park, laughing, happy; and I thought that people from out of town who saw her here must be thinking she was a real New Yorker, on her way somewhere exciting for the evening. The advertising man evidently thought so, too, when he got up reluctantly, almost jealously, to catch his train to Old Greenwich.

There was a row of taxis at the curb. He helped us into the first, gave her a mischievous look and kissed her hand. When their eyes met, I had the feeling he had done some investigating about her friend in Washington. As we watched him walk away to the second taxi he seemed to change, grow firmer, more stubborn, as if preparing himself for an everyday life he had momentarily forgotten.

"He makes me feel young," Rima said wistfully. She smiled. "He makes me want to go to the country and throw snowballs."

She went back to Washington that night, and we did not see each other again until spring. In the meantime I had gotten what is known as a friendly divorce, and custody of the three-room apartment. There had been only two short letters from Rima during the intervening months. The first said, "I'm too depressed to write, everything is lousy."

The second said, "I have begun to realize that people don't

break up because of one unforgivable incident, but rather, because of hopelessness. I used to think love could be killed with a mortal blow, but that's not true. Love goes on and on, until one day you wake up and realize that the hopelessness is stronger than the love. I've done everything I could think of, and it was not enough. He sees me once a week, for twenty minutes. How many more ways can I change? He says he loves me, but somehow that doesn't mean anything any more; they're just words. I hear them and I don't remember what they used to mean."

One morning Rima packed all her clothes and the collection of tiny antique boxes, and left Washington forever. She did not say goodbye to the diplomat, she simply disappeared into the dawn. She left every stick of antique furniture—his, hers, theirs, whatever it was—and I imagine the rooms in the Greek Revival style mansion must have looked very strange, as if the occupant had only gone out for a walk. She came to stay with me, and the first thing she did was give me her precious collection.

"I remember you used to admire them. Just consider them a house gift."

The second thing she did was get another secretarial job, because she insisted on paying half the rent. I had decided to go back to zoology and was taking a Master's degree at night and working days as a receptionist so I could study my textbooks behind the potted plant that stood on my glossy desk. I was much happier than I had expected to be. Rima surprised me by her resiliency. I had resigned myself nervously to having to nurse a potential suicide, but what I found was a convalescent who was grateful to have survived.

We went to a few cocktail parties, to dinner with a few old friends, and introduced each other to the few single men we found in our respective offices who were not nineteen. It was a restful existence, and the weeks drifted by almost without notice. Then, one afternoon, Rima rushed back early from the office, and when I came home the scent of bath oil filled the entire apartment. She had put her newest Chanel suit on the bed and was washing her emerald ring with a nail brush.

"Guess what I did today! I just felt like doing something crazy, like we used to do when we were at college, so I called Heathcliff at his office and said, 'Here I am in New York!' He had a moment of conscience—I could hear it over the phone, almost like a gulp—and then he asked me to dinner."

"Dinner? Where's his wife?"

"Evidently she's a Den Mother, whatever that is, and they have a meeting. He was going to stay and work late at the office. He says he works late at the office once or twice a week anyway, and he has to eat somewhere, so—oh, you should have heard the stammering, the excuses. He's terrified of me. Of *me*, the girl who never got anybody in her life!"

They went to an Italian restaurant where Rima had often gone with the diplomat, and where the advertising man had never been in his life. The headwaiter recognized her, with obvious respect. The menu was not only in Italian but in handwriting, and Rima took pains to explain innocently to the old Italian waiter what a certain simple dish consisted of, so that Heathcliff could stammer, "Make it two."

He missed the nine-o'clock train, and before the nine-forty-two he had bought her a white orchid. "An orchid," Rima laughed, showing it to me. "An *orchid!* I haven't had an orchid since the Senior Prom. I didn't think they made them any more."

But she put it carefully into a glass of champagne in the refrigerator, the alchemy that we had believed in our Senior Prom days would keep an orchid fresh for a week.

She had been almost silent about her affair with the diplomat, as if the gravity of first love had stunned her, but she bubbled over with her delight in Heathcliff, and I knew she had fallen in love with him before she did. "He's so square," she would say, laughing, and then add, "But he's a fox—oh, smart—watch out! I really think I'm the only one who sees the other side of him, the humor. In the advertising business they're just afraid of him, because he's so young and shrewd and on the way up. His wife's name is Dorlee—can you imagine?—and she's the same age he is, of course, because they've known each other all their lives. The old hag."

One of Rima's casual beaus, a plump young man who was also in advertising, took her to a cocktail party where Heathcliff appeared with Dorlee. "She just stood in the corner and talked to the wives," Rima told me afterward. "She looks as if she has steel fillings in her teeth. I don't think she ever shortened a dress in her life; she just wears them the way they come from the store. I heard her telling somebody that in Old Greenwich she has a TV room decorated like the inside of a ship. When she started talking about how they had to have plastic covers on everything I had to run out of the room because I nearly choked."

Heathcliff's commuting hours were irregular, for he often

worked late and his two children were old enough to stay up in the TV room decorated like a ship until the captain came home to say good night. He met Rima after work several times a week. He seemed to have a calming effect on her in one way, for she stopped smoking and gave her long gold cigarette holder to our cleaning woman, who had admired it. It was a romance confined to furtive handholding, for he was consumed by guilt and told Rima often that she was "dangerous."

"Dangerous!" she told me in delight. "Dangerous! Me, the failure, dangerous! Isn't he beautiful?"

A letter arrived from our former Washington landlady informing Rima she was not running a storage company, and then several huge crates arrived, Railway Express collect. Rima and I stared at them with dismay. "It's either storage or my own apartment," she said, "and I think at this point, an apartment of my own might be a good idea."

She found an apartment in a new, modern building, a block from Grand Central Station. "And believe me," she said, "an apartment a block from Grand Central is not easy to find." The choice of this location was logical to her— Heathcliff could stop by for a drink every evening on his way to his train. It seems several times he had mentioned, as if he were talking about an impossible dream, that such an arrangement would be the height of bliss.

The beautiful old furniture took some of the coldness away from the boxlike rooms of this glass-and-steel monstrosity, whose only redeeming feature was that it had a working fireplace; and when I went to visit her I found the rooms once again filled with flowers. The only strange note was a small bottle with a ship inside it, which perched on the center of her spindly-legged table.

"He collects them," she said. "He gave it to me. It's kind of pretty, don't you think?"

The next time I visited Rima's apartment a block from Grand Central it was a month later. There was a man's bathrobe hanging on the hook on the bathroom door, and a can of shaving cream on the tole shelf next to the sink. A small photograph of Heathcliff stood on the table beside her bed, framed in rope.

"It's so wonderful being in love with a man near my own age," she said. "He's thirty-four, I'm twenty-six—that means when I'm seventy, he'll be only seventy-eight."

"And commuting?"

"No, of course not," she said, touching his photograph reverently. "He's never been in love before, he never cheated on her in all those years, and do you know they were both virgins when they got married? Him, too. He has a very strong sense of honor. He said he wished she would find out about us so she would do something terrible to him, because he feels he deserves it; and then he said I ought to leave him, because he deserves that; and then he said if I did leave him he might as well be dead."

"He sounds happy," I said.

"It's just his sense of honor," Rima said. "It's a man like that who makes decisions. Men *do* leave their wives, you know, but only because of great love or great guilt. And he has both. I'm glad I didn't get married last time, because I was so young I mistook romance for love. This is real love: planning a life together, being able to help someone, making someone feel alive for the first time. Before he met me, his whole life was encased in plastic, just like that horrible chintz furniture of his in the country."

Men did leave their wives, as I well knew, and lovers left lovers, but it was neither for great love nor great guilt. Rima had been right the first time, in her letter to me: people part because of hopelessness. The death of love leads to the rebirth of another love, for love is a phoenix. A greater love does not kill a small one; it only adds pomp to the funeral.

During the following year, Rima and her advertising man tried to break up three times, but each time he came back to her, vowing he loved her more than ever and felt guiltier. She had already proposed to him several times, pretending it was only a joke, but at the end of their second year of afternoons before the train, she proposed to him seriously, and he answered her.

"How could I marry you?" he asked, tears in his eyes. "I'd bore you. You'd get tired of me. You're my elusive golden girl, and I'm just a husband and father."

"But that's what I *want*," Rima said.

"No. . . . I see you in front of the fire on a snowy night . . . I see you in that white fur coat, your eyes shining, going into the Plaza to meet an ambassador or a movie star. . . . I just don't see you in a gingham dress at the supermarket."

"Where do you think I get my food, out of flowers?"

"Yes," he answered. "And I will always bring them to you."

The transformation of Rima began that night. The next

day, printed cotton slipcovers appeared on the Louis XV chairs. She bought a huge Early American object she informed me was called an Entertainment Center, containing a 19-inch television set, a stereo phonograph with four speakers, and a radio, with a long flat surface on top that was soon covered with a collection of ships in bottles. Her Chanels and Diors were sent to a thrift shop (tax deductible) and she replaced them with tweed skirts, cashmere sweater sets, and flowered, sleeveless cotton blouses. She had pawned her emerald ring to buy the Entertainment Center, and now she wore a single strand of imitation pearls. She learned to cook tuna fish casserole with potato chips on top, and in time even a peanut butter soufflé. She saved trading stamps and redeemed them for a hobnail glass lamp with a ruffly shade, and gave her 1850 tole lamp to the cleaning woman, who ventured she'd just as soon have had the nice new one.

She washed and set her hair herself, because it was obvious Dorlee had, and she used the money thus saved to buy books called *The Sexually Satisfied Housewife*, and *The Problems of the Adolescent Stepchild*, which she piled on top of the spindly-legged antique table until it broke and she replaced it with something that had formerly been a butter churn.

Her triumph came on Heathcliff's birthday. He had left his office early, and a light snow had begun to fall. At four-thirty, in the winter's early darkness, he arrived at Rima's apartment. There was snow on his coat, and he was carrying a gold-wrapped package that later turned out to contain champagne. Rima was sitting in front of the roaring fire, wearing blue jeans and toasting marshmallows.

He looked around the room as if he had never really noticed it before, still wearing his coat, still clutching the bottle of champagne in his arms. The air was fragrant with the scent of detergent and meat loaf.

"Happy birthday, honey," Rima said.

"Thank you. . . ." he murmured. "I'd better hang my coat in the bathroom; it's wet."

"Wait till you see your present! I made it."

When he came out of the bathroom he seemed more composed. He opened his present: a ship in a bottle. Rima had put the ship inside, herself. "You see," she said, "to get it in, the sails lie flat, and then I pull the string . . ."

"I know."

"Look at the marshmallow," she said. "When it's burned black like that, with the little red lights inside, it looks the way New York used to look to me at night, when I first came here—all dark and mysterious, with just those millions of little lights."

"Oh, Rima," Heathcliff whispered, holding the two bottles in his hands, the one with the ship and the one with the champagne, "I wish you had written me a poem."

She did write him a poem, the following summer, but she never gave it to him. Instead, she read it to me on the telephone. I had not seen very much of her during the winter and spring, because I had gotten a new job doing research (and my Master's degree), and she had spent most of her time in her apartment waiting for him to visit her, although the visits were fewer and farther between. We were both going to be thirty, but now it no longer seemed to matter that when Rima was thirty Heathcliff would be only thirty-eight.

"Send him the poem," I told her. "It's beautiful."

"No," she said. "I'm going to push it into one of his revolting little bottles and I'm going to toss it into the Greenwich Sound, or whatever the name is of that river he lives on. Then when he's walking in front of his split-level saying *Yo-Ho-Ho* he can find it, and see what he lost. Four years. . . . Well, last time it was five, so you can't say I'm not improving. At least it doesn't take me as long to find out I'm doomed. I am doomed, you know. I'm the girl they recite poetry to, and then in the mornings they always go back to their wives. It must be me, because I fell in love with two completely different men and neither of them wanted to stay with me."

"It's not you," I said. "Neither of them really knew what you were like. If they had, they would have loved you."

I don't know if she ever threw the bottle into the Sound, but she might have tossed it into the lake in Central Park, because all that summer Rima was addicted to long, lonely walks. Perhaps she was trying to figure things out; perhaps she was only still in her fantasy of the country wife, and the streets of the summer city were her Old Greenwich roads. I felt guilty not spending more time with her, but this time I had met someone I loved. I had not met him among the mollusks and the octogenarians; I had met him at a cocktail party. He was a producer, but he did not think lady zoologists were freaks, and I certainly did not think producers were freaks, although I had never met one before, either.

While I was occupied with the extraordinary miracle of my second (and present) love, Rima became involved in what, to her, seemed only an ordinary meeting. She had been on a long walk, it was about midnight, and she was passing Grand Central Station on her way back to her apartment when she saw a man fall down in the street. The few passers-by thought he was drunk and avoided him, but Rima went closer to see if he was ill, and discovered that he was indeed drunk. She also discovered, with delight and dismay, that he was one of her favorite authors.

"What are you doing, lying there on the curb?" she said sternly. "A great writer does not lie on the curb."

"He does if he's drunk," the author answered. He was trying to go to sleep, his cheek nestled on the sidewalk.

"You get up this minute." Rima pulled him to his feet, which was not too difficult as he was a short, wiry man, about her height, quite undernourished from too much wine, women and song. He was, she remembered reading, only four years older than she was, and she felt maternal toward him.

"Have to go to Bennington," he murmured. "Where the hell is Bennington?   Have to be there in the morning."

"Bennington, Vermont?"

"Little girls' school . . . college. Lecture. Where's my train?"

"You can't lecture at Bennington like this," Rima said. She inspected his soiled clothing and bleary face with distaste. "Those girls idolize you. If they see you like this, it might ruin the rest of their lives."

"I'm . . . going to be sick."

"Good."

He decided not to be sick. "Who are you?"

"A former English major at Radcliffe, and an admirer of yours—although not at the moment. Come with me, I live around the corner." She was already leading him, his arm about her shoulders.

The writer stared at the sleeveless flowered cotton blouse, the chino walking skirt, the little strand of pearls. "Funniest-looking streetwalker I ever saw . . ." Rima slapped him.

She then took him to her apartment, a block from Grand Central, where she forced him to eat scrambled eggs and drink three cups of black coffee, and then spot-cleaned and pressed his suit while he cursed at her from a cold shower. She scanned the timetable while the writer looked around her apartment.

"You in the Waves?"

"Very funny. You can take the two-thirty train to Boston, and then there's probably a connection."

"You've even got a timetable."

"Purely for sentimental reasons," Rima said. "Here, take this aspirin and these vitamins; you'll need them later."

"You have any children?"

"No. Do you?"

"I'm not married," he said.

Suddenly, he became more than an idol or an invalid—he became a person. "You're *not?*"

"Divorced," he said.

"So am I," Rima said, "sort of."

"That's too bad. You'd make a wonderful wife. Very homey apartment. It reminds me of my mother's. You wouldn't think I had a mother, would you? Well, I do."

"You need her," Rima said. "Or a nurse. How could you possibly have gotten so drunk when you have an appointment tomorrow—or today, I should say?"

"Oh!" he said, looking wildly for his jacket. "Where's the train?"

"At the station. Where are your lecture notes? Good. Your aspirin? Good. Now, take these cookies, in case you get tempted on the way."

The writer took hold firmly of Rima's arm. "You're coming with me."

"Are you crazy?"

"Yes. Come with me. I need you. I'll only be there one day, and then we'll go to St. Thomas. I live in St. Thomas; you'll like it."

Rima looked around her apartment, the cozy, chintzy, friendly room filled with its memories of love and failure. " 'Be not afeard. The isle is full of noises, sounds and sweet airs, that give delight and hurt not.' "

"Come with Caliban," he said.

"No," Rima said, following him docilely to the door, "no, not Caliban . . . Shakespeare."

When she came back from Bennington she came to visit me, to bring me her collection of ships in bottles and to say goodbye. "When you marry that divine man you're going with, you'll have a little boy someday, and he'll like these."

"Are you really going away with him?" I asked stupidly.

"Imagine—St. Thomas! He can write his books, and I can keep house. I'll walk on the beach, and I'll send you shells if you like, if I find anything they don't have anywhere else.

magine—he's not married—at last! He's so brilliant; I've always adored his work. I've read everything he ever wrote and o you know what? Once, when we were in college and he ad his first story published, I cut his picture out of the magzine and kept it for a year."

"Listen," I said, hating myself for it, "I read in *Time* magaine that he travels around with a Great and Good Friend. he lives in St. Thomas with him. What happened to her?"

"Oh, her!" Rima said. "He hates her. She just happens to ive in St. Thomas, that's all. He says she's not a girlfriend, he's a friend girl. I saw that picture in *Time*; she looks like a quaw. She's got a braid down her back and she had this eather thong around her neck with a big tooth attached to it. 'll bet it came out of her mouth. No wonder he drank before e met me."

"He's stopped drinking?"

"One Scotch before dinner, like Heathcliff used to. Oh, I'm a reformer now." She laughed at herself, the reformer, and I wondered if life would at last be kind to her, she who could never be kind to herself.

She left the apartment, the furniture, her winter clothes, everything, and she and the writer went to St. Thomas. I went to her apartment two days before my wedding, suddenly taken by the absurdly sentimental thought that I must sell that Early American Entertainment Center and get Rima's emerald ring out of the pawn shop, if it was still there, and send it to her. I don't know why that ring seemed so important to me—perhaps because I was going to be married and I was happy, and I couldn't bear the thought of a ring Rima had worn for five years on the third finger of her left hand being misused by some stranger. But the landlord had taken possession of all the furniture in lieu of the rent she had never sent from St. Thomas, and the apartment had been sublet. Well, I thought, caught up again in my own happiness, we've both learned enough from the past, and that ring doesn't mean anything any more.

So I was married, and two years later we did have a little boy who will like the collection of ships in bottles, when he's old enough not to break them to get the ships out. Our apartment is filled with scripts, books, records, theatrical posters, an aquarium, shells, textbooks, toys; but still there is room on the piano for Rima's collection of Battersea boxes. She had written me two happy postcards the first year, and then, nothing. I wondered if she was still in St. Thomas. Five years after she had left New York, I took a chance and wrote to her at her last address to tell her that my husband and I were going to take a winter vacation in St. Thomas, and was she still alive? She wrote back immediately.

"Yes," her letter said. "I'm still alive. Alive and single. Surprise. Look for me in the bar at your hotel any night at about ten o'clock. I'll be the one seated at the right hand of the Bard."

We arrived in St. Thomas in the afternoon. When we went down to the hotel bar that night at ten, Rima was not there. There were some pink-broiled American tourists, and a party of Italians from a large yacht that was moored in the harbor: the owner, very rich, very clean in a blue blazer, two teen-aged starlets who sat toying with the speared fruit in their drinks, two rather sinister-looking young men, and two contessas with streaks in their hair and a lot of diamonds. The Calypso trio played on a small bandstand, and the starlets got up to do whatever dance it was teen-aged starlets were doing that winter in the jet set. The contessas and their escorts looked bored because they were supposed to, and the Italian millionaire looked bored because he was. I was afraid Rima wasn't going to show up after all.

Then, at half past twelve, she arrived. She was, indeed at the right hand of the Bard, and the Bard was very, very drunk. At the left hand of the Bard, helping to support him, was a young woman the same age as Rima, with a long black braid down her back, a turtleneck T-shirt, a peasant skirt, no makeup, and a silver-and-turquoise ornament the size of a breast-plate dangling from a chain around her neck. Rima had let her hair grow to her waist and braided it, her face was scrubbed and tanned, she was dressed in an almost identical village outfit, and the only difference between the two Squaw Twins was that Rima was the prettier one.

Rima let go the writer's hand and ran over to our table. Liberated, he pulled free of the other lady and went to the bar.

"Oh, I'm so glad to see you!" Rima said. "Look how pale you are—you'll have to come to the beach with me." She held her arm, the color of glistening walnut, against mine.

My husband was transfixed by the object dangling from a thong around Rima's neck. "Whose tooth is that?"

She shrugged. "I don't know. It's Olive's; we trade."

"How is everything?" I asked lamely.

"Don't ask that. I want to be happy tonight. No, it's all

ight, really. I'm content; I mean, I'm over him, I just stay
vith him because he needs me."

"Who's Olive?"

Rima glanced at her Squaw Twin. "Remember the
irlfriend he said was only a friend girl? That's her. Actually,
'd go insane if I didn't have her to talk to. He's so drunk
ately. And, do you know, in the beginning I really hated
ter? She has great individuality, though, and a crystalline in-
ellect. She's above such things as jealousy and animosity, she
eally believes in the purity of non-thought. . . . oh, hell, she
tores me to death."

The writer had taken the sticks away from the Calypso
lrummer and was crashing them on every cymbal, drum, and
tny surface in sight. The musicians and waiters ignored him
ts if he was a nightly fixture. Olive was watching him inscru-
ably. The Italians from the yacht looked amused.

"If I had his talent . . ." Rima said. "If I had *any*
alent. . . . Tell me about New York! Tell me about the
vorld, is it still there?"

We ordered drinks and told her about people she had
known, and then we ordered more drinks and she made us
tell her about people she didn't know. She was insatiable. The
world, the world, what was happening outside this tiny island,
this paradisiacal prison? The American tourists went up to
bed, the Calypso trio disappeared, the writer and Olive were
now sitting with the party of Italians from the yacht. The
millionaire glanced over at us and bent toward him to whisper a question; the writer shook his head.

"How old is your baby?" Rima asked suddenly.

"Three years old."

"I'm thirty-five," Rima said. "Do I look it? Don't answer.
Look—the sun's coming up, I'm going to walk on the beach."

She ran out of the bar, across the patio, across the sand,
and was gone. I was afraid she might be going to drown herself and was going to run after her, but then I saw her again,
wandering among the sea-grape trees, sad and alone. The
writer had fallen asleep at the table, his head between the
empty glasses. Olive was watching over him, totally still, a
little smile at the corner of her mouth. The Italian millionaire
excused himself to the group and went out to the beach.

I could see his silhouette in the pink-and-gold dawn,
bowing slightly to Rima's silhouette, and then, after a moment, walking slowly beside it through the silhouettes of the
sea-grape trees. The sea was all blue and gold and silver now,

and in the distance the Italian's yacht rocked gently at anchor, all white.

We went up to our room. Then, suddenly, I felt one of those obsessive, extrasensory calls that are like a shout in the mind. "I'll be right back," I said, and ran down the stairs to the lobby.

The bar was closed, chairs piled on top of the tables. The Italians had all gone, and in a corner of the lobby Olive was asleep in a big chair. A yawning porter handed me a hotel envelope with my name on it, and went back behind the desk. The writer, despite his hangover, was milling around like twelve people. "Where is she? Where is she? *Rima...*!"

I tore open the envelope, and the tooth on the leather thong fell into my hand. There was a note, in Rima's impeccable script: " 'When such as I cast out remorse so great a sweetness flows into the breast we must laugh and we must sing, We are blest by everything. Everything we look upon is blest.' *La donna é mobile.* Goodbye, and love."

I looked out to sea, where the yacht was only a tiny toy ship on the horizon, and then I went up to our room.

So she was gone again, with the Italian millionaire, and his starlets, and his contessas with the streaked hair. Soon, I knew, she would fall in love, and cut her braid, and toss her pueblo jewelry into the sea. She would paint her eyelids and enamel her toenails, and disappear. Once again, as always, a man who had fallen in love with a fantasy that had been created for another man would lose that fantasy, consuming it in the fire of his love. I remembered that the Rima of *Green Mansions,* for whom Rima Allen had been named, had been killed in a fire that destroyed her hiding-tree. It seemed to me, that lonely morning in St. Thomas, that the Rima I knew had been killed in many fires, rising again from the ashes of each one like a bright bird to sing the song of some wanderer's need. Had there ever been a real Rima? Born and reborn to a splendid image, she had never looked for her self, nor had anyone else. Being each man's dream of love, she had eventually failed him, and so he had failed her, and so, finally, she had failed herself.

Tell Me a Riddle

Tillie Olsen

1

For forty-seven years they had been married. How deep back the stubborn, gnarled roots of the quarrel reached, no one could say—but only now, when tending to the needs of others no longer shackled them together, the roots swelled up visible, split the earth between them, and the tearing shook even to the children, long since grown.

Why now, why now? wailed Hannah.

As if when we grew up weren't enough, said Paul.

Poor Ma. Poor Dad. It hurts so for both of them, said Vivi. They never had very much; at least in old age they should be happy.

Knock their heads together, insisted Sammy; tell 'em: you're too old for this kind of thing; no reason not to get along now.

Lennie wrote to Clara: They've lived over so much together; what could possibly tear them apart?

Something tangible enough.

Arthritic hands, and such work as he got, occasional. Poverty all his life, and there was little breath left for running. He could not, could not turn away from this desire: to have the troubling of responsibility, the fretting with money, over and done with; to be free, to be *care*free where success was not measured by accumulation, and there was use for the vitality still in him.

There was a way. They could sell the house, and with the money join his lodge's Haven, cooperative for the aged. Happy communal life, and was he not already an official; had he not helped organize it, raise funds, served as a trustee?

But she—would not consider it.

"What do we need all this for?" he would ask loudly, for

313

her hearing aid was turned down and the vacuum was shrilling. "Five rooms" (pushing the sofa so she could get into the corner) "furniture" (smoothing down the rug) "floors and surfaces to make work. Tell me, why do we need it?" And he was glad he could ask in a scream.

"Because I'm use't."

"Because you're use't. This is a reason, Mrs. Word Miser? Used to can get unused!"

"Enough unused I have to get used to already. . . . Not enough words?" turning off the vacuum a moment to hear herself answer. "Because soon enough we'll need only a little closet, no windows, no furniture, nothing to make work, but for worms. Because now I want room. . . . Screech and blow like you're doing, you'll need that closet even sooner. . . . Ha, again!" for the vacuum bag wailed, puffed half up, hung stubbornly limp. "This time fix it so it stays; quick before the phone rings and you get too important-busy."

But while he struggled with the motor, it seethed in him. Why fix it? Why have to bother? And if it can't be fixed, have to wring the mind with how to pay the repair? At the Haven they come in with their own machines to clean your room or your cottage; you fish, or play cards, or make jokes in the sun, not with knotty fingers fight to mend vacuums.

Over the dishes, coaxingly: "For once in your life, to be free, to have everything done for you, like a queen."

"I never liked queens."

"No dishes, no garbage, no towel to sop, no worry what to buy, what to eat."

"And what else would I do with my empty hands? Better to eat at my own table when I want, and to cook and eat how I want."

"In the cottages they buy what you ask and cook it how you like. *You* are the one who always used to say: better mankind born without mouths and stomachs than always to worry for money to buy, to shop, to fix, to cook, to wash, to clean."

"How cleverly you hid that you heard. I said it then because eighteen hours a day I ran. And you never scraped a carrot or knew a dish towel sops. Now—for you and me—who cares? A herring out of a jar is enough. But when *I* want, and nobody to bother." And she turned off her ear button, so she would not have to hear.

But as *he* had no peace, juggling and rejuggling the money

o figure: how will I pay for this now?; prying out the storm
windows (there they take care of this); jolting in the streetcar
on errands (there I would not have to ride to take care of this
or that); fending the patronizing relatives just back from
Florida (at the Haven it matters what one is, not what one
can afford), he gave *her* no peace.

"Look! In their bulletin. A reading circle. Twice a week it
meets."

"Haumm," her answer of not listening.

"A reading circle. Chekhov they read that you like, and
Peretz. Cultured people at the Haven that you would enjoy."

"Enjoy!" She tasted the word. "Now, when it pleases you,
you find a reading circle for me. And forty years ago when
the children were morsels and there was a Circle, did you
stay home with them once so I could go? Even once? You
rained me well. I do not need others to enjoy. Others!" Her
voice trembled. "Because *you* want to be there with others.
Already it makes me sick to think of you always around others. Clown, grimacer, floormat, yesman, entertainer, whatever
they want of you."

And now it was he who turned on the television loud so he
need not hear.

Old scar tissue ruptured and the wounds festered anew.
Chekhov indeed. She thought without softness of that young
wife, who in the deep night hours while she nursed the current baby, and perhaps held another in her lap, would try to
stay awake for the only time there was to read. She would
feel again the weather of the outside on his cheek when, coming late from a meeting, he would find her so, and stimulated
and ardent, sniffing her skin, coax: "I'll put the baby to bed,
and you—put the book away, don't read, don't read."

That had been the most beguiling of all the "don't read,
put your book away" her life had been. Chekhov indeed!

"Money?" She shrugged him off. "Could we get poorer
than once we were? And in America, who starves?"

But as still he pressed:

"Let me alone about money. Was there ever enough?
Seven little ones—for every penny I had to ask—and sometimes, remember, there was nothing. But always *I* had to
manage. Now *you* manage. Rub your nose in it good."

But from those years she had had to manage, old humilia-
tions and terrors rose up, lived again, and forced her to relive
them. The children's needings; that grocer's face or this mer-
chant's wife she had had to beg credit from when credit was

a disgrace; the scenery of the long blocks walked around
when she could not pay; school coming, and the desperate
going over the old to see what could yet be remade; the soups
of meat bones begged "for-the-dog" one winter. . . .

Enough. Now they had no children. Let *him* wrack his
head for how they would live. She would not exchange her
solitude for anything. *Never again to be forced to move to
the rhythms of others.*

For in this solitude she had won to a reconciled peace.

Tranquillity from having the empty house no longer an enemy, for it stayed clean—not as in the days when it was her
family, the life in it, that had seemed the enemy: tracking,
smudging, littering, dirtying, engaging her in endless defeating
battle—and on whom her endless defeat had been spewed.

The few old books, memorized from rereading; the pictures to ponder (the magnifying glass superimposed on her
heavy eyeglasses). Or if she wishes, when he is gone, the phonograph, that if she turns up very loud and strains, she can
hear: the ordered sounds and the struggling.

Out in the garden, growing things to nurture. Birds to be
kept out of the pear tree, and when the pears are heavy and
ripe, the old fury of work, for all must be canned, nothing
wasted.

And her one social duty (for she will not go to luncheons
or meetings) the boxes of old clothes left with her, as with a
life-practised eye for finding what is still wearable within the
worn (again the magnifying glass superimposed on the heavy
glasses) she scans and sorts—this for rag or rummage, that
for mending and cleaning, and this for sending away.

*Being able at last to live within, and not move to the
rhythms of others,* as life had helped her to: denying; removing; isolating; taking the children one by one; then deafening,
half-blinding—and at last, presenting her solitude.

And in it she had won to a reconciled peace.

Now he was violating it with his constant campaigning:
Sell the house and move to the Haven. (You sit, you sit—
there too you could sit like a stone.) He was making of her a
battleground where old grievances tore. (Turn on your ear
button—I am talking.) And stubbornly she resisted—so that
from wheedling, reasoning manipulation, it was bitterness he
now started with.

And it came to where every happening lashed up a quarrel.

"I will sell the house anyway," he flung at her one night. "I am putting it up for sale. There will be a way to make you sign."

The television blared, as always it did on the evenings he stayed home, and as always it reached her only as noise. She did not know if the tumult was in her or outside. Snap! she turned the sound off. "Shadows," she whispered to him, pointing to the screen, "look, it is only shadows." And in a scream: "Did you say that you will sell the house? Look at me, not at that. I am no shadow. You cannot sell without me."

"Leave on the television. I am watching."

"Like Paulie, like Jenny, a four-year-old. Staring at shadows. *You cannot sell the house.*"

"I will. We are going to the Haven. There you would not hear the television when you do not want it. I could sit in the social room and watch. You could lock yourself up to smell your unpleasantness in a room by yourself—for who would want to come near you?"

"No, no selling." A whisper now.

"The television is shadows. Mrs. Enlightened! Mrs. Cultured! A world comes into your house—and it is shadows. People you would never meet in a thousand lifetimes. Wonders. When you were four years old, yes, like Paulie, like Jenny, did you know of Indian dances, alligators, how they use bamboo in Malaya? No, you scratched in your dirt with the chickens and thought Olshana was the world. Yes, Mrs. Unpleasant, I will sell the house, for there better can we be rid of each other than here."

She did not know if the tumult was outside, or in her. Always a ravening inside, a pull to the bed, to lie down, to succumb.

"Have you thought maybe Ma should let a doctor have a look at her?" asked their son Paul after Sunday dinner, regarding his mother crumpled on the couch, instead of, as was her custom, busying herself in Nancy's kitchen.

"Why not the President too?"

"Seriously, Dad. This is the third Sunday she's lain down like that after dinner. Is she that way at home?"

"A regular love affair with the bed. Every time I start to talk to her."

Good protective reaction, observed Nancy to herself. The workings of hos-til-ity.

"Nancy could take her. I just don't like how she looks. Let's have Nancy arrange an appointment."

"You think she'll go?" regarding his wife gloomily. "All right, we have to have doctor bills, we have to have doctor bills." Loudly: "Something hurts you?"

She startled, looked to his lips. He repeated: "Mrs. Take It Easy, something hurts?"

"Nothing. . . . Only you."

"A woman of honey. That's why you're lying down?"

"Soon I'll get up to do the dishes, Nancy."

"Leave them, Mother, I like it better this way."

"Mrs. Take It Easy, Paul says you should start ballet. You should go to see a doctor and ask: how soon can you start ballet?"

"A doctor?" she begged. "Ballet?"

"We were talking, Ma," explained Paul, "you don't seem any too well. It would be a good idea for you to see a doctor for a checkup."

"I get up now to do the kitchen. Doctors are bills and foolishness, my son. I need no doctors."

"At the Haven," he could not resist pointing out, "a doctor is *not* bills. He lives beside you. You start to sneeze, he is there before you open up a Kleenex. You can be sick there for free, all you want."

"Diarrhea of the mouth, is there a doctor to make you dumb?"

"Ma. Promise me you'll go. Nancy will arrange it."

"It's all of a piece when you think of it," said Nancy, "the way she attacks my kitchen, scrubbing under every cup hook, doing the inside of the oven so I can't enjoy Sunday dinner, knowing that half-blind or not, she's going to find every speck of dirt. . . ."

"Don't, Nancy, I've told you—it's the only way she knows to be useful. What did the *doctor* say?"

"A real fatherly lecture. Sixty-nine is young these days. Go out, enjoy life, find interests. Get a new hearing aid, this one is antiquated. Old age is sickness only if one makes it so. Geriatrics, Inc."

"So there was nothing physical."

"Of course there was. How can you live to yourself like she does without there being? Evidence of a kidney disorder, and her blood count is low. He gave her a diet, and she's to come back for follow-up and lab work. . . . But he was

clear enough: Number One prescription—start living like a
human being. . . . When I think of your dad, who could
really play the invalid with that arthritis of his, as active as a
teenager, and twice as much fun. . . ."

"You didn't tell me the doctor says your sickness is in you,
how you live." He pushed his advantage. "Life and enjoyments you need better than medicine. And this diet, how can
you keep it. To weigh each morsel and scrape away each bit
of fat, to make this soup, that pudding. There, at the Haven,
they have a dietician, they would do it for you."
   She is silent.
   "You would feel better there, I know it," he says gently.
"There there is life and enjoyments all around."
   "What is the matter. Mr. Importantbusy, you have no card
game or meeting you can go to?"—turning her face to the
pillow.

   For a while he cut his meetings and going out, fussed over
her diet, tried to wheedle her into leaving the house, brought
in visitors:

   "I should come to a fashion tea. I should sit and look at
pretty babies in clothes I cannot buy. This is pleasure?"
   "Always you are better than everyone else. The doctor said
you should go out. Mrs. Brem comes to you with goodness
and you turn her away."
   "Because *you* asked her to, she asked me."

   "They won't come back. People you need, the doctor said.
Your own cousins I asked; they were willing to come and
make peace as if nothing had happened. . . ."
   "No more crushers of people, pushers, hypocrites, around
me. No more in *my* house. You go to them if you like."

   "Kind he is to visit. And you, like ice."
   "A babbler. All my life around babblers. Enough!"

   "She's even worse, Dad? Then let her stew a while," ad-
vised Nancy. "You can't let it destroy you; it's a psychologi-
cal thing, maybe too far gone for any of us to help."
   So he let her stew. More and more she lay silent in bed,
and sometimes did not even get up to make the meals. No
longer was the tongue-lashing inevitable if he left the coffee

cup where it did not belong, or forgot to take out the garbage or mislaid the broom. The birds grew bold that summer and for once pocked the pears, undisturbed.

A bellyful of bitterness and every day the same quarrel in a new way and a different old grievance the quarrel forced her to enter and relive. And the new torment: I am not really sick, the doctor said it, then why do I feel so sick?

One night she asked him: "You have a meeting tonight? Do not go. Stay . . . with me."

He had planned to watch "This Is Your Life," but half sick himself from the heavy heat, and sickening therefore the more after the brooks and woods of the Haven, with satisfaction he grated:

"Hah, Mrs. Live Alone And Like It wants company all of a sudden. It doesn't seem so good the time of solitary when she was a girl exile in Siberia. 'Do not go. Stay with me.' A new song for Mrs. Free As A Bird. Yes, I am going out, and while I am gone chew this aloneness good, and think how you keep us both from where if you want people, you do not need to be alone."

"Go, go. All your life you have gone without me."

After him she sobbed curses he had not heard in years, old-country curses from their childhood: Grow, oh shall you grow like an onion, with your head in the ground. Like the hide of a drum shall you be, beaten in life, beaten in death. Oh shall you be like a chandelier, to hang, and to burn. . . .

She was not in their bed when he came back. She lay on the cot on the sun porch. All week she did not speak or come near him; nor did he try to make peace or care for her.

He slept badly, so used to her next to him. After all the years, old harmonies and dependencies deep in their bodies; she curled to him, or he coiled to her, each warmed, warming, turning as the other turned, the nights a long embrace.

It was not the empty bed or the storm that woke him, but a faint singing. *She* was singing. Shaking off the drops of rain, the lightning riving her lifted face, he saw her so; the cot covers on the floor.

"This is a private concert?" he asked. "Come in, you are wet."

"I can breathe now," she answered; "my lungs are rich." Though indeed the sound was hardly a breath.

"Come in, come in." Loosing the bamboo shades. "Look

how wet you are." Half helping, half carrying her, still faint-breathing her song.

A Russian love song of fifty years ago.

He had found a buyer, but before he told her, he called to-gether those children who were close enough to come. Paul, of course, Sammy from New Jersey, Hannah from Connecti-cut, Vivi from Ohio.

With a kindling of energy for her beloved visitors, she ar-rayed the house, cooked and baked. She was not prepared for the solemn after-dinner conclave, they too probing in and tearing. Her frightened eyes watched from mouth to mouth as each spoke.

His stories were eloquent and funny of her refusal to go back to the doctor; of the scorned invitations; of her stubborn silence or the bile "like a Niagara"; of her contrariness: "If I clean it's no good how I cleaned; if I don't clean, I'm still a master who thinks he has a slave."

(Vinegar he poured on me all his life; I am well mar-inated; how can I be honey now?)

Deftly he marched in the rightness for moving to the Haven; their money from social security free for visiting the children, not sucked into daily needs and into the house; the activities in the Haven for him; but mostly the Haven for *her*: her health, her need of care, distraction, amusement, friends who shared her interests.

"This does offer an outlet for Dad," said Paul; "he's al-ways been an active person. And economic peace of mind isn't to be sneezed at, either. I could use a little of that my-self."

But when they asked: "And you, Ma, how do you feel about it?" could only whisper:

"For him it is good. It is not for me. I can no longer live between people."

"You lived all your life *for* people," Vivi cried.

"Not with." Suffering doubly for the unhappiness on her children's faces.

"You have to find some compromise," Sammy insisted. "Maybe sell the house and buy a trailer. After forty-seven years there's surely some way you can find to live in peace."

"There is no help, my children. Different things we need."

"Then live alone!" He could control himself no longer. "I have a buyer for the house. Half the money for you, half for

me. Either alone or with me to the Haven. You think I can
live any longer as we are doing now?"

"Ma doesn't have to make a decision this minute, however
you feel, Dad," Paul said quickly, "and you wouldn't want
her to. Let's let it lay a few months, and then talk some
more."

"I think I can work it out to take Mother home with me
for a while," Hannah said. "You both look terrible, but especially you, Mother. I'm going to ask Phil to have a look at
you."

"Sure," cracked Sammy. "What's the use of a doctor husband if you can't get free service out of him once in a while
for the family? And absence might make the heart . . . you
know."

"There was something after all," Paul told Nancy in a
colorless voice. "That was Hannah's Phil calling. Her gall
bladder. . . . Surgery."

"Her *gall* bladder. If that isn't classic. 'Bitter as gall'—talk
of psychosom—"

He stepped closer, put his hand over her, mouth, and said
in the same colorless, plodding voice. "We have to get Dad.
They operated at once. The cancer was everywhere, sur-
rounding the liver, everywhere. They did what they could
. . . at best she has a year. Dad . . . we have to tell him."

2

Honest in his weakness when they told him, and that she
was not to know. "I'm not an actor. She'll know right away by
how I am. Oh that poor woman. I am old too, it will break me
into pieces. Oh that poor woman. She will spit on me: 'So my
sickness was how I live.' Oh Paulie, how she will be, that poor
woman. Only she should not suffer. . . . I can't stand
sickness, Paulie, I can't go with you."

But went. And play-acted.

"A grand opening and you did not even wait for me. . . .
A good thing Hannah took you with her."

"Fashion teas I needed. They cut out what tore in me; just
in my throat something hurts yet. . . . Look! so many flowers, like a funeral. Vivi called, did Hannah tell you? And
Lennie from San Francisco, and Clara; and Sammy is coming." Her gnome's face pressed happily into the flowers.

It is impossible to predict in these cases, but once over the immediate effects of the operation, she should have several months of comparative well-being.

The money, where will come the money?

Travel with her, Dad. Don't take her home to the old associations. The other children will want to see her.

The money, where will I wring the money?

Whatever happens, she is not to know. No, you can't ask her to sign papers to sell the house; nothing to upset her. Borrow instead, then after. . . .

I had wanted to leave you each a few dollars to make life easier, as other fathers do. There will be nothing left now. (Failure! you and your "business is exploitation." Why didn't you make it when it could be made?—Is that what you're thinking, Sammy?)

Sure she's unreasonable, Dad—but you have to stay with her; if there's to be any happiness in what's left of her life, it depends on you.

Prop me up, children, think of me, too. Shuffled, chained with her, bitter woman. No Haven, and the little money going. . . . How happy she looks, poor creature.

The look of excitement. The straining to hear everything (the new hearing aid turned full). Why are you so happy, dying woman?

How the petals are, fold on fold, and the gladioli color. The autumn air.

Stranger grandsons, tall above the little gnome grandmother, the little spry grandfather. Paul in a frenzy of picture-taking before going.

She, wandering the great house. Feeling the books; laughing at the maple shoemaker's bench of a hundred years ago used as a table. The ear turned to music.

"Let us go home. See how good I walk now." "One step from the hospital," he answers, "and she wants to fly. Wait till Doctor Phil says."

"Look—the birds too are flying home. Very good Phil is and will not show it, but he is sick of sickness by the time he comes home."

"Mrs. Telepathy, to read minds," he answers; "read mine what it says: when the trunks of medicines become a suitcase, then we will go."

The grandboys, they do not know what to say to us. . . .

Hannah, she runs around here, there, when is there time for herself?

Let us go home. Let us go home.

Musing; gentleness—*but for the incidents of the rabbi in the hospital, and of the candles of benediction.*

Of the rabbi in the hospital:

Now tell me what happened, Mother.

From the sleep I awoke, Hannah's Phil, and he stands there like a devil in a dream and calls me by name. I cannot hear. I think he prays. Go away, please, I tell him, I am not a believer. Still he stands, while my heart knocks with fright.

You scared *him,* Mother. He thought you were delirious.

Who sent him? Why did he come to me?

It is a custom. The men of God come to visit those of their religion they might help. The hospital makes up the list for them—race, religion—and you are on the Jewish list.

Not for rabbis. At once go and make them change. Tell them to write: Race, human; Religion, none.

And of the candles of benediction:

Look how you have upset yourself, Mrs. Excited Over Nothing. Pleasant memories you should leave.

Go in, go back to Hannah and the lights. Two weeks I saw candles and said nothing. But she asked me.

So what was so terrible? She forgets you never did, she asks you to light the Friday candles and say the benediction like Phil's mother when she visits. If the candles give her pleasure, why shouldn't she have the pleasure?

Not for pleasure she does it. For emptiness. Because his family does. Because all around her do.

That is not a good reason too? But you did not hear her. For heritage, she told you. For the boys, from the past they should have tradition.

Superstition! From the savages, afraid of the dark, of themselves: mumbo words and magic lights to scare away ghosts.

She told you: how it started does not take away the goodness. For centuries, peace in the house it means.

Swindler! does she look back on the dark centuries? Candles bought instead of bread and stuck into a potato for a candlestick? Religion that stifled and said: in Paradise, woman, you will be the footstool of your husabnd, and in life—poor chosen Jew—ground under, despised, trembling in cellars. And cremated. And cremated.

This is religion's fault? You think you are still an orator of the 1905 revolution? Where are the pills for quieting? Which are they?

Heritage. How have we come from the savages, how no longer to be savages—this to teach. To look back and learn what humanizes man—this to teach. To smash all ghettos that divide us—not to go back, not to go back—this to teach. Learned books in the house, will humankind live or die, and she gives to her boys—superstition.

Hannah that is so good to you. Take your pill, Mrs. Excited For Nothing, swallow.

Heritage! But when did I have time to teach? Of Hannah I asked only hands to help.

Swallow.

Otherwise—musing; gentleness.

Not to travel. To go home.

The children want to see you. We have to show them you are as thorny a flower as ever.

Not to travel.

Vivi wants you should see her new baby. She sent the tickets—airplane tickets—a Mrs. Roosevelt she wants to make of you. To Vivi's we have to go.

A new baby. How many warm, seductive babies. She holds him stiffly, *away* from her, so that he wails. And a long shudder begins, and the sweat beads on her forehead.

"Hush, shush," croons the grandfather, lifting him back. "You should forgive your grandmamma, little prince, she has never held a baby before, only seen them in glass cases. Hush, shush."

"You're tired, Ma," says Vivi. "The travel and the noisy dinner. I'll take you to lie down."

(A long travel from, to, what the feel of a baby evokes.)

In the airplane, cunningly designed to encase from motion (no wind, no feel of flight), she had sat severely and still, her face turned to the sky through which they cleaved and left no scar.

So this was how it looked, the determining, the crucial sky, and this was how man moved through it, remote above the dwindled earth, the concealed human life. Vulnerable life, that could scar.

There was a steerage ship of memory that shook across a

great, circular sea: clustered, ill human beings: and through the thick-stained air, tiny fretting waters in a window round like the airplane's—sun round, moon round. (The round thatched roofs of Olshana.) Eye round—like the smaller window that framed distance the solitary year of exile when only her eyes could travel, and no voice spoke. And the polar winds hurled themselves across snows trackless and endless and white—like the clouds which had closed together below and hidden the earth.

Now they put a baby in her lap. Do not ask me, she would have liked to beg. Enough the worn face of Vivi, the remembered grandchildren. I cannot, cannot. . . .

Cannot what? Unnatural grandmother, not able to make herself embrace a baby.

She lay there in the bed of the two little girls, her new hearing aid turned full, listening to the sound of the children going to sleep, the baby's fretful crying and hushing, the clatter of dishes being washed and put away. They thought she slept. Still she rode on.

It was not that she had not loved her babies, her children. The love—the passion of tending—had risen with the need like a torrent; and like a torrent drowned and immolated all else. But when the need was done—oh the power that was lost in the painful damming back and drying up of what still surged, but had nowhere to go. Only the thin pulsing left that could not quiet, suffering over lives one felt, but could no longer hold nor help.

On that torrent she had borne them to their own lives, and the riverbed was desert long years now. Not there would she dwell, a memoried wraith. Surely that was not all, surely there was more. Still the springs, the springs were in her seeking. Somewhere an older power that beat for life. Somewhere coherence, transport, meaning. If they would but leave her in the air now stilled of clamor, in the reconciled solitude, to journey to her self.

And they put a baby in her lap. Immediacy to embrace, and the breath of *that* past: warm flesh like this that had claims and nuzzled away all else and with lovely mouths devoured; hot-living like an animal—intensely and now; the turning maze; the long drunkenness; the drowning into needing and being needed. Severely she looked back—and the shudder seized her again, and the sweat. Not that way. Not there, not now could she, not yet. . . .

And all that visit, she could not touch the baby.

"Daddy, is it the . . . sickness she's like that?" asked Vivi. "I was so glad to be having the baby—for her. I told Tim, it'll give her more happiness than anything, being around a baby again. And she hasn't played with him once."

He was not listening, "Aahh little seed of life, little charmer," he crooned, "Hollywood should see you. A heart of ice you would melt. Kick, kick. The future you'll have for a ball. In 2050 still kick. Kick for your grandaddy then."

Attentive with the older children; sat through their performances (command performance; we command you to be the audience); helped Ann sort autumn leaves to find the best for a school program; listened gravely to Richard tell about his rock collection, while her lips mutely formed the words to remember: *igneous, sedimentary, metamorphic;* looked for missing socks, books, and bus tickets; watched the children whoop after their grandfather who knew how to tickle, chuck, lift, toss, do tricks, tell secrets, make jokes, match riddle for riddle (Tell me a riddle, Grammy. I know no riddles, child.) Scrubbed sills and woodwork and furniture in every room; folded the laundry; straightened drawers; emptied the heaped baskets waiting for ironing (while he or Vivi or Tim nagged: You're supposed to rest here, you've been sick) but to none tended or gave food—and could not touch the baby.

After a week she said: "Let us go home. Today call about the tickets."

"You have important business, Mrs. Inahurry? The President waits to consult with you?" He shouted, for the fear of the future raced in him. "The clothes are still warm from the suitcase, your children cannot show enough how glad they are to see you, and you want home. There is plenty of time for home. We cannot be with the children at home."

"Blind to around you as always: the little ones sleep four in a room because we take their bed. We are two more people in a house with a new baby, and no help."

"Vivi is happy so. The children should have their grandparents a while, she told to me. I should have my mommy and daddy. . . ."

"Babbler and blind. Do you look at her so tired? How she starts to talk and she cries? I am not strong enough yet to help. Let us go home."

(To reconciled solitude.)

For it seemed to her the crowded noisy house was listening to her, listening for her. She could feel it like a great ear pressed under her heart. And everything knocked: quick constant raps: let me in, let me in.

How was it that soft reaching tendrils also became blows that knocked?

C'mon, Grandma, I want to show you. . . .
Tell me a riddle, Grandma. (*I know no riddles.*)
Look, Grammy, he's so dumb he can't even find his hands. (Dody and the baby on a blanket over the fermenting autumn mould.)
I made them—for you. (Ann) (Flat paper dolls with aprons that lifted on scalloped skirts that lifted on flowered pants; hair of yarn and great ringed questioning eyes.)
Watch me, Grandma. (Richard snaking up the tree, hanging exultant, free, with one hand at the top. Below Dody hunching over in pretend-cooking.) (*Climb too, Dody, climb and look.*)
Be my nap bed, Grammy. (The "No!" too late.) Morty's abandoned heaviness, while his fingers ladder up and down her hearing-aid cord to his drowsy chant: eentsiebeentsie-spider. (*Children trust.*)
It's to start off your own rock collection, Grandma. That's a trilobite fossil, 200 million years old (millions of years on a boy's mouth) and that one's obsidian, black glass.

Knocked and knocked.

Mother, I *told* you the teacher said we had to bring it back all filled out this morning. Didn't you even ask Daddy? Then tell *me* which plan and I'll check it: evacuate or stay in the city or wait for you to come and take me away. (Seeing the look of straining to hear.) It's for Disaster, Grandma. (*Children trust.*)

Vivi in the maze of the long, the lovely drunkenness. The old old noises: baby sounds; screaming of a mother flayed to exasperation; children quarreling; children playing; singing; laughter.

And Vivi's tears and memories, spilling so fast, half the words not understood.

She had started remembering out loud deliberately, so her mother would know the past was cherished, still lived in her.

Nursing the baby: My friends marvel, and I tell them, oh

it's easy to be such a cow. I remember how beautiful my mother seemed nursing my brother, and the milk just flows. . . . Was that Davy? It must have been Davy. . . .

Lowering a hem: How did you ever . . . when I think now you made everything we wore . . . Tim, just think, seven kids and Mommy sewed everything . . . do I remember you sang while you sewed? That white dress with the red apples on the skirt you fixed over for me, was it Hannah's or Clara's before it was mine?

Washing sweaters: Ma, I'll never forget, one of those days so nice you washed clothes outside; one of the first spring days it must have been. The bubbles just danced while you scrubbed, and we chased after, and you stopped to show us how to blow our own bubbles with green onion stalks . . . you always. . . .

"Strong onion, to still make you cry after so many years," her father said, to turn the tears into laughter.

While Richard bent over his homework: Where is it now, do we still have it, the Book of the Martyrs? It always seemed so, well—exalted, when you'd put it on the round table and we'd all look at it together; there was even a halo from the lamp. The lamp with the beaded fringe you could move up and down; they're in style again, pulley lamps like that, but without the fringe. You know the book I'm talking about, Daddy, the Book of the Martyrs, the first picture was a bust of Socrates? I wish there was something like that for the children. Mommy, to give them what you. . . . (And the tears splashed again.)

(What I intended and did not? Stop it, daughter, stop it, leave that time. And he, the hypocrite, sitting there with tears in his eyes—it was nothing to you then, nothing.)

. . . The time you came to school and I almost died of shame because of your accent and because I knew you knew I was ashamed; how could I? . . . Sammy's harmonica and you danced to it once, yes you did, you and Davy squealing in your arms. . . . That time you bundled us up and walked us down to the railway station to stay the night 'cause it was heated and we didn't have any coal, that winter of the strike, you didn't think I remembered that, did you, Mommy? . . . How you'd call us out to see the sunsets. . . .

Day after day, the spilling memories. Worse now, questions, too. Even the grandchildren: Grandma, in the olden days, when you were little. . . .

It was the afternoons that saved.

While they thought she napped, she would leave the mosaic on the wall (of children's drawings, maps, calendars, pictures, Ann's cardboard dolls with their great ringed questioning eyes) and hunch in the girls' cupboard, on the low shelf where the shoes stood, and the girls' dresses covered.

For that while she would painfully sheathe against the listening house, the tendrils and noises that knocked, and Vivi's spilling memories. Sometimes it helped to braid and unbraid the sashes that dangled, or to trace the pattern on the hoop slips.

Today she had jacks and children under jet trails to forget. Last night, Ann and Dody silhouetted in the window against a sunset of flaming man-made clouds of jet trail, their jacks ball accenting the peaceful noise of dinner being made. Had she told them, yes she had told them of how they played jacks in her village though there was no ball, no jacks. Six stones, round and flat, toss them out, the seventh on the back of the hand, toss, catch and swoop up as many as possible, toss again. . . .

Of stones (repeating Richard) there are three kinds: earth's fire jetting; rock of layered centuries; crucibled new out of the old (*igneous, sedimentary, metamorphic*). But there was that other—frozen to black glass, never to transform or hold the fossil memory . . . (let not my seed fall on stone). There was an ancient man who fought to heights a great rock that crashed back down eternally—eternal labor, freedom, labor . . . (stone will perish, but the word remain). And you, David, who with a stone slew, screaming: Lord, take my heart of stone and give me flesh

Who was screaming? Why was she back in the common room of the prison, the sun motes dancing in the shafts of light, and the informer being brought in, a prisoner now, like themselves. And Lisa leaping, yes, Lisa, the gentle and tender, biting at the betrayer's jugular. Screaming and screaming.

No, it is the children screaming. Another of Paul and Sammy's terrible fights?

In Vivi's house. Severely: you are in Vivi's house.

Blows, screams, a call: "Grandma!" For her? Oh please not for her. Hide, hunch behind the dresses deeper. But a trembling little body hurls itself beside her—surprised, smothered laughter, arms surround her neck, tears rub dry on her cheek, and words too soft to understand whisper into her ear

(Is this where you hide too, Grammy? It's my secret place, we have a secret now).

And the sweat beads, and the long shudder seizes.

It seemed the great ear pressed inside now, and the knocking. "We have to go home," she told him. "I grow ill here."

"It's your own fault, Mrs. Busybody, you do not rest, you do too much." He raged, but the fear was in his eyes. "It was a serious operation, they told you to take care. . . . All right, we will go to where you can rest."

But where? Not home to death, not yet. He had thought to Lennie's, to Clara's; beautiful visits with each of the children. She would have to rest first, be stronger. If they could but go to Florida—it glittered before him, the never-realized promise of Florida. California: of course. (The money, the money, dwindling!) Los Angeles first for sun and rest; then to Lennie's in San Francisco.

He told her the next day. "You saw what Nancy wrote: snow and wind back home, a terrible winter. And look at you—all bones and a swollen belly. I called Phil: he said: 'A prescription, Los Angeles sun and rest.'"

She watched the words on his lips. "You have sold the house," she cried, "that is why we do not go home. That is why you talk no more of the Haven, why there is money for travel. After the children you will drag me to the Haven."

"The Haven! Who thinks of the Haven any more? Tell her, Vivi, tell Mrs. Suspicious: a prescription, sun and rest, to make you healthy. . . . And how could I sell the house without *you?*"

At the place of farewells and greetings, of winds of coming and winds of going, they say their good-byes.

They look back at her with the eyes of others before them: Richard with her own blue blaze; Ann with the nordic eyes of Tim; Morty's dreaming brown of a great-grandmother he will never know; Dody with the laughing eyes of him who had been her springtide love (who stands beside her now); Vivi's, all tears.

The baby's eyes are closed in sleep.

Good-bye, my children.

3

It is to the back of the great city he brought her, to the dwelling places of the cast-off old. Bounded by two lines of amusement piers to the north and to the south, and between a long straight paving rimmed with black benches facing the sand—sands so wide the ocean is only a far fluting.

In the brief vacation season, some of the boarded stores fronting the sands open, and families, young people and children, may be seen. A little tasselled tram shuttles between the piers, and the lights of roller coasters prink and tweak over those who come to have sensation made in them.

The rest of the year it is abandoned to the old, all else boarded up and still; seemingly empty, except the occasional days and hours when the sun, like a tide, sucks them out of the low rooming houses, casts them onto the benches and sandy rim of the walk—and sweeps them into decaying enclosures once again.

A few newer apartments glint among the low bleached squares. It is in one of these Lennie's Jeannie has arranged their rooms. "Only a few miles north and south people pay hundreds of dollars a month for just this gorgeous air, Grandaddy, just this ocean closeness."

She had been ill on the plane, lay ill for days in the unfamiliar room. Several times the doctor came by—left medicine she would not take. Several times Jeannie drove in the twenty miles from work, still in her Visiting Nurse uniform, the lightness and brightness of her like a healing.

"Who can believe it is winter?" he asked one morning. "Beautiful it is outside like an ad. Come, Mrs. Invalid, come to taste it. You are well enough to sit in here, you are well enough to sit outside. The doctor said it too."

But the benches were encrusted with people, and the sands at the sidewalk's edge. Besides, she had seen the far ruffle of the sea: "there take me," and though she leaned against him, it was she who led.

Plodding and plodding sitting often to rest, he grumbling. Patting the sand so warm. Once she scooped up a handful, cradling it close to her better eye; peered, and flung it back. And as they came almost to the brink and she could see the glistening wet, she sat down, pulled off her shoes and stockings, left him and began to run. "You'll catch cold," he screamed, but the sand in his shoes weighed him down—he who had always been the agile one—and already the white spray creamed her feet.

He pulled her back, took a handkerchief to wipe off the wet and the sand. "Oh no," she said, "the sun will dry," seized the square and smoothed it flat, dropped on it a mound of sand, knotted the kerchief corners and tied it to a bag—"to look at with the strong glass" (for the first time in years explaining an action of hers)—and lay down with the little bag against her cheek, looking toward the shore that nutured life as it first crawled toward consciousness the millions of years ago.

He took her one Sunday in the evil-smelling bus, past flat miles of blister houses, to the home of relatives. Oh what is this? she cried as the light began to smoke and the houses to dim and recede. Smog, he said, everyone knows but you. . . . Outside he kept his arms about her, but she walked with hands pushing the heavy air as if to open it, whispered: who has done this? sat down suddenly to vomit at the curb and for a long while refused to rise.

One's age as seen on the altered face of those known in youth. Is this they he has come to visit? This Max and Rose, smooth and pleasant, introducing them to polite children, disinterested grandchildren, "the whole family, once a month on Sundays. And why not? We have the room, the help, the food."

Talk of cars, of houses, of success: this son that, that daughter this. And *your* children? Hastily skimped over, the intermarriages, the obscure work—"my doctor son-in-law, Phil"—all he has to offer. She silent in a corner. (Car-sick like a baby, he explains.) Years since he has taken her to visit anyone but the children, and old apprehensions prickle: "no incidents," he silently begs, "no incidents." He itched to tell them. "A very sick woman," significantly, indicating her with his eyes, "a very sick woman." Their restricted faces did not react. "Have you thought maybe she'd do better at Palm Springs?" Rose asked. "Or at least a nicer section of the beach, nicer people, a pool." Not to have to say "money" he said instead: "would she have sand to look at through a magnifying glass?" and went on, detail after detail, the old habit betraying of parading the queerness of her for laughter.

After dinner—the others into the living room in men- or women-clusters, or into the den to watch TV—the four of them alone. She sat close to him, and did not speak. Jokes, stories, people they had known, beginning of reminiscence, Russia fifty-sixty years ago. Strange words across the Duncan Phyfe table: *hunger; secret meetings; human rights; spies; betrayals; prison; escape*—interrupted by one of the grandchildren: "Commercial's on; any Coke left? Gee, you're missing a real hair-raiser." And then a granddaughter (Max proudly: "look at her, an American queen") drove them home on her way back to U.C.L.A. No incident—except that there had been no incidents.

The first few mornings she had taken with her the magnifying glass, but he would sit only on the benches, so she rested at the foot, where slatted bench shadows fell, and unless she turned her hearing aid down, other voices invaded.

Now on the days when the sun shone and she felt well enough, he took her on the tram to where the benches ranged in oblongs, some with tables for checkers or cards. Again the blanket on the sand in the striped shadows, but she no longer brought the magnifying glass. He played cards, and she lay in the sun and looked towards the waters; or they walked—two blocks down to the scaling hotel, two blocks back—past chili-hamburger stands, open-doored bars. Next to New and Perpetual Rummage Sale stores.

Once, out of the aimless walkers, slow and shuffling like themselves, someone ran unevenly towards them, embraced, kissed, wept: "dear friends, old friends." A friend of *hers*, not his: Mrs. Mays who had lived next door to them in Denver when the children were small.

Thirty years are compressed into a dozen sentences; and the present, not even in three. All is told: the children scattered; the husband dead; she lives in a room two blocks up from the sing hall—and points to the domed auditorium jutting before the pier. The leg? phlebitis; the heavy breathing? that, one does not ask. She, too, comes to the beaches each day to sit. And tomorrow, tomorrow, are they going to the community sing? Of course he would have heard of it, everybody goes—the big doings they wait for all week. They have never been? She will come to them for dinner tomorrow and they will all go together.

So it is that she sits in the wind of the singing, among the thousand various faces of age.

*She had turned off her hearing aid at once they came into
the auditorium—as she would have wished to turn off sight.*

*One by one they streamed by and imprinted on her—and
though the savage zest of their singing came voicelessly soft
and distant, the faces still roared—the faces densened the
air—chorded into*

children-chants, mother-croons, singing of the chained love
serenades, Beethoven storms, mad Lucia's scream drunken
joy-songs, keens for the dead, work-singing

*while from floor to balcony to dome a bare-footed sore-
covered little girl threaded the sound-thronged tumult,
danced her ecstasy of grimace to flutes that scratched at a
cross-roads village wedding*

*Yes, faces became sound, and the sound became faces; and
faces and sound became weight—pushed, pressed*

"Air"—her hands claw his.

"Whenever I enjoy myself. . . ." Then he saw the gray
sweat on her face. "Here. Up. Help me, Mrs. Mays," and
they support her out to where she can gulp the air in sob after sob.

"A doctor, we should get for her a doctor."

"Tch, it's nothing," says Ellen Mays, "I get it all the time.
You've missed the tram; come to my place. Fix your hearing
aid, honey . . . close . . . tea. My view. See, she *wants* to
come. Steady now, that's how." Adding mysteriously:
"Remember your advice, easy to keep your head above
water, empty things float. Float."

The singing a fading march for them, tall woman with a
swollen leg, weaving little man, and the swollen thinness they
help between.

The stench in the hall: mildew? decay? "We sit and rest
then climb. My gorgeous view. We help each other and
here we are."

The stench along into the slab of room. A washstand for a
sink, a box with oilcloth tacked around for a cupboard, a
three-burner gas plate. Artificial flowers, colorless with dust.
Everywhere pictures foaming: wedding, baby, party, vacation, graduation, family pictures. From the narrow couch un-

der a slit of window, sure enough the view: lurching rooftops and a scallop of ocean heaving, preening, twitching under the moon.

"While the water heats. Excuse me . . . down the hall." Ellen Mays has gone.

"You'll live?" he asks mechanically, sat down to feel his fright: tried to pull her alongside.

She pushed him away. "For air," she said; stood clinging to the dresser. Then in a terrible voice:

After a lifetime of room. Of many rooms.

Shhh.

You remember how she lived. Eight children. And now one room   like a coffin.

She pays rent!

Shrinking the life of her   into one room   like a coffin
Rooms and rooms like this   I lie on the quilt and hear them talk

Please, Mrs. Orator-without-Breath.

Once you went for coffee   I walked   I saw   A Balzac   a Chekhov to write it   Rummage   Alone   On scraps

Better old here than in the old country!

On scraps   Yet they sang like   like Wondrous!   *Humankind   one has to believe*   So strong for what?   To rot   not grow?

Your poor lungs beg you. They sob between each word.

Singing.   Unused   the life in them. She in this poor room   with her   pictures Max   You   The children Everywhere unused the life. And who has meaning? Century after century   still all in us   not   to grow?

Coffins, rummage, plants: sick woman. Oh lay down. We will get for you the doctor.

"And when will it end. Oh, *the end.*" *That* nightmare thought, and this time she writhed, crumpled against him, seized his hand (for a moment again the weight, the soft distant roaring of humanity) and on the strangled-for breath, begged: "Man . . . we'll destroy ourselves?"

And looking for answer—in the helpless pity and fear for her (for *her*) that distorted his face—she understood the last months, and knew that she was dying.

4

"Let us go home," she said after several days.

"You are in training for a cross-country trip? That is why

you do not even walk across the room? Here, like a prescription Phil said, till you are stronger from the operation. You want to break doctor's orders?"

She saw the fiction was necessary to him, was silent; then: "At home I will get better. If the doctor here says?"

"And winter? And the visits to Lennie and to Clara? All right," for he saw the tears in her eyes, "I will write Phil, and talk to the doctor."

Days passed. He reported nothing. Jeannie came and took her out for air, past the boarded concessions, the hooded and tented amusement rides, to the end of the pier. They watched the spent waves feeding the new, the gulls in the clouded sky; even up where they sat, the wind-blown sand stung.

She did not ask to go down the crooked steps to the sea.

Back in her bed, while he was gone to the store, she said: "Jeannie, this doctor, he is not one I can ask questions. Ask him for me, can I go home?"

Jeannie looked at her, said quickly: "Of course, poor Granny. You want your own things around you, don't you? I'll call him tonight. . . . Look, I've something to show you," and from her purse unwrapped a large cookie, intricately shaped like a little girl. "Look at the curls—can you hear me well, Granny?—and the darling eyelashes. I just came from a house where they were baking them."

"The dimples, there in the knees," she marveled, holding it to the better light, turning, studying, "like art. Each singly they cut, or a mold?"

"Singly," said Jeannie, "and if it is a child only the mother can make them. Oh Granny, it's the likeness of a real little girl who died yesterday—Rosita. She was three years old. *Pan del Muerto*, the Bread of the Dead. It was the custom in the part of Mexico they came from."

Still she turned and inspected. "Look, the hollow in the throat, the little cross necklace. . . . I think for the mother it is a good thing to be busy with such bread. You know the family?"

Jeannie nodded. "On my rounds. I nursed. . . . Oh Granny, it is like a party; they play songs she liked to dance to. The coffin is lined with pink velvet and she wears a white dress. There are candles. . . ."

"In the house?" Surprised. "They keep her in the house?"

"Yes," said Jeannie, "and it is against the health law. I think she is . . . prepared there. The father said it will be sad to bury her in this country; in Oaxaca they have a feast night with candles each year; everyone picnics on the graves of those they loved until dawn."

"Yes, Jeannie, the living must comfort themselves." And closed her eyes.

"You want to sleep, Granny?"

"Yes, tired from the pleasure of you. I may keep the Rosita? There stand it, on the dresser, where I can see; something of my own around me."

In the kitchenette, helping her grandfather unpack the groceries, Jeannie said in her light voice:

"I'm resigning my job, Grandaddy."

"Ah, the lucky young man. Which one is he?"

"Too late. You're spoken for." She made a pyramid of cans, unstacked, and built again.

Something is wrong with the job?"

"With me. I can't be"—she searched for the word—"What they call professional enough. I let myself feel things. And tomorrow I have to report a family. . . ." The cans clicked again. "It's not that, either. I just don't know what I want to do, maybe go back to school, maybe go to art school. I thought if you went to San Francisco I'd come along and talk it over with Momma and Daddy. But I don't see how you can go. She wants to go home. She asked me to ask the doctor."

The doctor told her himself. "Next week you may travel, when you are a little stronger." But next week there was the fever of an infection, and by the time that was over, she could not leave the bed—a rented hospital bed that stood beside the double bed he slept in alone now.

Outwardly the days repeated themselves. Every other afternoon and evening he went out to his newfound cronies, to talk and play cards. Twice a week, Mrs. Mays came. And the rest of the time, Jeannie was there.

By the sickbed stood Jeannie's FM radio. Often into the room the shapes of music came. She would lie curled on her side, her knees drawn up, intense in listening (Jeannie sketched her so, coiled, convoluted like an ear), then thresh her hand out and abruptly snap the radio mute—still to lie in her attitude of listening, concealing tears.

Once Jeannie brought in a young Marine to visit, a friend from high-school days she had found wandering near the empty pier. Because Jeannie asked him to, gravely, without self-consciousness, he sat himself cross-legged on the floor and performed for them a dance of his native Samoa.

Long after they left, a tiny thrumming sound could be heard where, in her bed, she strove to repeat the beckon, flight, surrender of his hands, the fluttering footbeats, and his low plaintive calls.

Hannah and Phil sent flowers. To deepen her pleasure, he placed one in her hair. "Like a girl," he said, and brought the hand mirror so she could see. She looked at the pulsing red flower, the yellow skull face; a desolate, excited laugh shuddered from her, and she pushed the mirror away—but let the flower burn.

The week Lennie and Helen came, the fever returned. With it the excited laugh, and incessant words. She, who in her life had spoken but seldom and then only when necessary (never having learned the easy, social uses of words), now in dying, spoke incessantly.

In a half-whisper: "Like Lisa she is, your Jeannie. Have I told you of Lisa who taught me to read? Of the highborn she was, but noble in herself. I was sixteen; they beat me; my father beat me so I would not go to her. It was forbidden, she was a Tolstoyan. At night, past dogs that howled, terrible dogs, my son, in the snows of winter to the road, I to ride in her carriage like a lady, to books. To her, life was holy, knowledge was holy, and she taught me to read. They hung her. Everything that happens one must try to understand why. She killed one who betrayed many. Because of betrayal, betrayed all she lived and believed. In one minute she killed, before my eyes (there is so much blood in a human being, my son), in prison with me. All that happens, one must try to understand.

"The name?" Her lips would work. "The name that was their pole star; the doors of the death houses fixed to open on it; I read of it my year of penal servitude. Thuban!" very excited, "Thuban, in ancient Egypt the pole star. Can you see, look out to see it, Jeannie if it swings around *our* pole star that seems to *us* not to move.

"Yes, Jeannie, at your age my mother and grandmother had already buried children . . . yes, Jeannie, it is more than oceans between Olshana and you . . . yes, Jeannie, they danced, and for all the bodies they had they might as well be chickens, and indeed, they scratched and flapped their arms and hopped.

"And Andrei Yefimitch, who for twenty years had never

known of it and never wanted to know, said as if he wanted to cry: but why my dear friend this malicious laughter?" Telling to herself half-memorized phrases from her few books. "Pain I answer with tears and cries, baseness with indignation, meanness with repulsion . . . for life may be hated or wearied of, but never despised."

Delirious: "Tell me, my neighbor, Mrs. Mays, the pictures never lived, but what of the flowers? Tell them who ask: no rabbis, no ministers, no priests, no speeches, no ceremonies: ah, false—let the living comfort themselves. Tell Sammy's boy, he who flies, tell him to go to Stuttgart and see where Davy has no grave. And what?" A conspirator's laugh. "And what? Where millions have no graves—save air."

In delirium or not, wanting the radio on; not seeming to listen, the words still jetting, wanting the music on. Once, silencing it abruptly as of old, she began to cry, unconcealed tears this time. "You have pain, Granny?" Jeannie asked.

"The music," she said, "still it is there and we do not hear; knocks, and our poor human ears too weak. What else, what else we do not hear?"

Once she knocked his hand aside as he gave her a pill, swept the bottles from her bedside table: "no pills, let me feel what I feel," and laughed as on his hands and knees he groped to pick them up.

Nighttimes her hand reached across the bed to hold his.

A constant retching began. Her breath was too faint for sustained speech now, but still the lips moved:

When no longer necessary   to injure others
Pick   pick pick   Blind chicken
As a human being   responsibility

"David!" imperious, "Basin!" and she would vomit, rinse her mouth, the wasted throat working to swallow, and begin the chant again.

She will be better off in the hospital now, the doctor said.

He sent the telegrams to the children, was packing her suitcase, when her hoarse voice startled. She had roused, was pulling herself to sitting.

"Where now?" she asked. "Where now do you drag me?"

"You do not even have to have a baby to go this time," he soothed, looking for the brush to pack. "Remember, after Davy you told me—worthy to have a baby for the pleasure of the hospital?"

"Where now? Not home yet?" Her voice mourned. "Where *is* my home?"

He rose to ease her back. "The doctor, the hospital," he started to explain, but deftly, like a snake, she had slithered out of bed and stood swaying, propped behind the night table.

"Coward," she hissed, "runner."

"You stand," he said senselessly.

"To take me there and run. Afraid of a little vomit."

He reached her as she fell. She struggled against him, half slipped from his arms, pulled herself up again.

"Weakling," she taunted, "to leave me there and run. Betrayer. All your life you have run."

He sobbed, telling Jeannie. "A Marilyn Monroe to run for her virtue. Fifty-nine pounds she weighs, the doctor said, and she beats at me like a Dempsey. Betrayer, she cries, and I running like a dog when she calls; day and night, running to her, her vomit, the bedpan. . . ."

"She needs you, Grandaddy," said Jeannie. "Isn't that what they call love? I'll see if she sleeps, and if she does, poor worn-out darling, we'll have a party, you and I: I brought us rum babas."

They did not move her. By her bed now stood the tall hooked pillar that held the solutions—blood and dextrose—to feed her veins. Jeannie moved down the hall to take over the sickroom, her face so radiant, her grandfather asked her once: "you are in love?" (Shameful the joy, the pure overwhelming joy from being with her grandmother; the peace, the serenity that breathed.) "My darling escape," she answered incoherently, "my darling Granny"—as if that explained.

Now one by one the children came, those that were able. Hannah, Paul, Sammy. Too late to ask: and what did you learn with your living, Mother, and what do we need to know?

Clara, the eldest, clenched:

Pay me back, Mother, pay me back for all you took from me. Those others you crowded into your heart. The hands I needed to be for you, the heaviness, the responsibility.

Is this she? Noises the dying make, the crablike hands crawling over the covers. The ethereal singing.

She hears that music, that singing from childhood; forgotten sound—not heard since, since. . . . And the hardness breaks like a cry: Where did we lose each other, first mother, singing mother?

Annulled: the quarrels, the gibing, the harshness between; the fall into silence and the withdrawal.

I do not know you, Mother. Mother, I never knew you.

Lennie, suffering not alone for her who was dying, but for that in her which never lived (for that which in him might never live). From him too, unspoken words: *good-bye Mother who taught me to mother myself.*

Not Vivi, who must stay with her children; not Davy, but he is already here, having to die again with *her* this time, for the living take their dead with them when they die.

Light she grew, like a bird, and, like a bird, sound bubbled in her throat while the body fluttered in agony. Night and day, asleep or awake (though indeed there was no difference now) the songs and the phrases leaping.

And he, who had once dreaded a long dying (from fear of himself, from horror of the dwindling money) now desired her quick death profoundly, for *her* sake. He no longer went out, except when Jeannie forced him; no longer laughed, except when, in the bright kitchenette, Jeannie coaxed his laughter (and she, who seemed to hear nothing else, would laugh too, conspiratorial wisps of laughter).

Light, like a bird, the fluttering body, the little claw hands, the beaked shadow on her face; and the throat, bubbling, straining.

He tried not to listen, as he tried not to look on the face in which only the forehead remained familiar, but trapped with her the long nights in that little room, the sounds worked themselves into his consciousness, with their punctuation of death swallows, whimpers, gurglings.

Even in reality (swallow) *life's lack of it*
Slaveships   deathtrains   clubs   eeenough
The bell   summons what enables
78,000 in one minute (whisper of a scream) *78,000 human beings   we'll destroy ourselves?*

"Aah, Mrs. Miserable," he said, as if she could hear, "all your life working, and now in bed you lie, servants to tend, you do not even need to call to be tended, and still you work. Such hard work it is to die? Such hard work?"

The body threshed, her hand clung in his. A melody, ghost-thin, hovered on her lips, and like a guilty ghost, the vision of her bent in listening to it, silencing the record instantly he was near. Now, heedless of his presence, she floated the melody on and on.

"Hid it from me," he complained, "how many times you listened to remember it so?" And tried to think when she had first played it, or first begun to silence her few records when he came near—but could reconstruct nothing. There was only this room with its tall hooked pillar and its swarm of sounds.

No man one   except through others
Strong   with the not yet   in the now
Dogma dead   war dead   one country

"It helps, Mrs. Philosopher, words from books? It helps?" And it seemed to him that for seventy years she had hidden a tape recorder, infinitely microscopic, within her, that it had coiled infinite mile on mile, trapping every song, every melody, every word read, heard, and spoken—and that maliciously she was playing back only what said nothing of him, of the children, of their intimate life together.

"Left us indeed, Mrs. Babbler," he reproached, "you who called others babbler and cunningly saved your words. A lifetime you tended and loved, and now not a word of us, for us. Left us indeed? Left me."

And he took out his solitaire deck, shuffled the cards loudly, slapped them down.

Lift high banner of reason (tatter of an orator's voice)
justice   freedom   light
Humankind   life   worthy   capacities
Seeks (blur of shudder) *belong   human being*

"Words, words," he accused, "and what human beings did *you* seek around you, Mrs. Live Alone, and what humankind think worthy?"

Though even as he spoke, he remembered she had not always been isolated, had not always wanted to be alone (as he knew there had been a voice before this gossamer one; before the hoarse voice that broke from silence to lash, make incidents, shame him—a girl's voice of eloquence that spoke their holiest dreams). But again he could reconstruct, image, nothing of what had been before, or when, or how, it had changed.

Ace, queen, jack. The pillar shadow fell, so, in two tracks; in the mirror depths glistened a moonlike blob, the empty solution bottle. And it worked in him: *of reason and justice and freedom . . . Dogma dead:* he remembered the full quotation, laughed bitterly. "Hah, good you do not know what you say; good Victor Hugo died and did not see it, his twentieth century."

Deuce, ten, five. Dauntlessly she began a song of their youth of belief:

> *These things shall be, a loftier race*
> *than e'er the world hath known shall rise*
> *with flame of freedom in their souls*
> *and light of knowledge in their eyes*

King, four jack. "In the twentieth century, hah!"

> *They shall be gentle, brave and strong*
> *to spill no drop of blood, but dare*
>
> > *earth and fire and sea and air*

"To spill no drop of blood, hah! So, cadaver, and you too, cadaver Hugo, 'in the twentieth century ignorance will be dead, dogma will be dead, war will be dead, and for all mankind one country—of fulfilment?' Hah!"

> *And every life* (long strangling cough) *shall*
> *be a song*

The cards fell from his fingers. Without warning, the bereavement and betrayal he had sheltered—compounded through the years—hidden even from himself—revealed itself,
> uncoiled,
> released,
> *sprung*

and with it the monstrous shapes of what had actually happened in the century.

A ravening hunger or thirst seized him. He groped into the kitchenette, switched on all three lights, piled a tray—"you have finished your night snack, Mrs. Cadaver, now I will have mine." And he was shocked at the tears that splashed on the tray.

"Salt tears. For free. I forgot to shake on salt?"

Whispered: "Lost, how much I lost."

Escaped to the grandchildren whose childhoods were childish, who had never hungered, who lived unravaged by disease in warm houses of many rooms, had all the school for which they cared, could walk on any street, stood a head taller than their grandparents, towered above—beautiful skins, straight backs, clear straightforward eyes. "Yes, you in Olshana," he said to the town of sixty years ago, "they would be nobility to you."

And was this not the dream then, come true in ways undreamed? he asked.

And are there no other children in the world? he answered, as if in her harsh voice.

And the flame of freedom, the light of knowledge?

And the drop, to spill no drop of blood?

And he thought that at six Jeannie would get up and it would be his turn to go to her room and sleep, that he could press the buzzer and she would come now; that in the afternoon Ellen Mays was coming, and this time they would play cards and he could marvel at how rouge can stand half an inch on the cheek; that in the evening the doctor would come, and he could beg him to be merciful, to stop the feeding solutions, to let her die.

To let her die, and with her their youth of belief out of which her bright, betrayed words foamed; stained words, that on her working lips came stainless.

Hours yet before Jeannie's turn. He could press the buzzer and wake her to come now; he could take a pill, and with it sleep; he could pour more brandy into his milk glass, though what he had poured was not yet touched.

Instead he went back, checked her pulse, gently tended with his knotty fingers as Jeannie had taught.

She was whimpering; her hand crawled across the covers for his. Compassionately he enfolded it, and with his free hand gathered up the cards again. Still was there thirst or hunger ravening in him.

That world of their youth—dark, ignorant, terrible with hate and disease—how was it that living in it, in the midst of corruption, filth, treachery, degradation, they had not mistrusted man nor themselves; had believed so beautifully, so . . . falsely?

"Aaah, children," he said out loud, "how we believed, how we belonged." And he yearned to package for each of the children, the grandchildren, for everyone, *that joyous cer-*

tainty, that sense of mattering, of moving and being moved, of being one and indivisible with the great of the past, with all that freed, ennobled man. Package it, stand on corners, in front of stadiums and on crowded beaches, knock on doors, give it as a fabled gift.

"And why not in cereal boxes, in soap packages?" he mocked himself. "Aah. You have taken my senses, cadaver."

Words foamed, died unsounded. Her body writhed; she made kissing motions with her mouth. (Her lips moving as she read, poring over the Book of the Martyrs, the magnifying glass superimposed over the heavy eyeglasses.) *Still she believed?* "Eva!" he whispered. "Still you believed? You lived by it? These Things Shall Be?"

"One pound soup meat," she answered distinctly, "one soup bone."

"My ears heard you. Ellen Mays was witness: 'Humankind . . . one has to believe.'" Imploringly: "Eva!"

"Bread, day-old." She was mumbling. "Please, in a wooden box . . . for kindling. The thread, hah, the thread breaks. Cheap thread"—and a gurgling, enormously loud, began in her throat.

"I ask for stone; she gives me bread—day-old." He pulled his hand away, shouted: "Who wanted questions? Everything you have to wake?" Then dully, "Ah, let me help you turn, poor creature."

Words jumbled, cleared. In a voice of crowded terror:

"Paul, Sammy, don't fight.

"Hannah, have I ten hands?

"How can I give it, Clara, how can I give it if I don't have?"

"You lie," he said sturdily, "there was joy too." Bitterly: "Ah how cheap you speak of us at last."

As if to rebuke him, as if her voice had no relationship with her flailing body, she sang clearly, beautifully, a school song the children had taught her when they were little; begged:

"Not look   my hair   where they cut. . . ."

(The crown of braids shorn.) And instantly he left the mute old woman poring over the Book of the Martyrs; went past the mother treading at the sewing machine, singing with the children; past the girl in her wrinkled prison dress, hiding her hair with scarred hands, lifting to him her awkward, shamed, imploring eyes of love; and took her in his arms, dear, personal, fleshed, in all the heavy passion he had loved to rouse from her.

"Eva!"

Her little claw hand beat the covers. How much, how much can a man stand? He took up the cards, put them down, circled the beds, walked to the dresser, opened, shut drawers, brushed his hair, moved his hand bit by bit over the mirror to see what of the reflection he could blot out with each move, and felt that at any moment he would die of what was unendurable. Went to press the buzzer to wake Jeannie, looked down, saw on Jeannie's sketch pad the hospital bed, with *her;* the double bed alongside, with him; the tall pillar feeding into her veins, and their hands, his and hers, clasped, feeding each other. And as if he had been instructed he went to his bed, lay down, holding the sketch (as if it could shield against the monstrous shapes of loss, of betrayal, of death) and with his free hand took hers back into his.

So Jeannie found them in the morning.

That last day the agony was perpetual. Time after time it lifted her almost off the bed, so they had to fight to hold her down. He could not endure and left the room; wept as if there never would be tears enough.

Jeannie came to comfort him. In her light voice she said: Grandaddy, Grandaddy don't cry. She is not there, she promised me. On the last day, she said she would go back to when she first heard music, a little girl on the road of the village where she was born. She promised me. It is a wedding and they dance, while the flutes so joyous and vibrant tremble in the air. Leave her there. Grandaddy, it is all right. She promised me. Come back, come back and help her poor body to die.

For two of that generation
Seevya and Genya

Death deepens the wonder

Wife-Wooing

John Updike

Oh my love. Yes. Here we sit, on warm broad floorboards, before a fire, the children between us, in a crescent, eating. The girl and I share one half-pint of French fried potatoes; you and the boy share another; and in the center, sharing nothing, making simple reflections within himself like a jewel, the baby, mounted in an Easybaby, sucks at his bottle with frowning mastery, his selfish, contemplative eyes stealing glitter from the center of the flames. And you. You. You allow your skirt, the same black skirt in which this morning you with woman's soft bravery mounted a bicycle and sallied forth to play hymns in difficult keys on the Sunday school's old piano—you allow this black skirt to slide off your raised knees down your thighs, slide *up* your thighs in your body's absolute geography, so the parallel whiteness of their undersides is exposed to the fire's warmth and to my sight. Oh. There is a line of Joyce. I try to recover it from the legendary, imperfectly explored grottoes of *Ulysses:* a garter snapped, to please Blazes Boylan, in a deep Dublin den. What? Smackwarm. That was the crucial word. Smacked smackwarm on her smackable warm woman's thigh. Something like that. A splendid man, to feel that. Smackwarm woman's. Splendid also to feel the curious and potent, inexplicable and irrefutably magical life language leads within itself. What soul took thought and knew that adding "wo" to man would make a woman? The difference exactly. The wide w, the receptive o. Womb. In our crescent the children for all their size seem to come out of you toward me, wet fingers and eyes, tinted bronze. Three children, five persons, seven years. Seven years since I wed wide warm woman, white-thighed. Wooed and wed. Wife. A knife of a word that for all its final bite did not end the wooing. To my wonderment.

We eat meat, meat I wrestled warm from the raw hands of the hamburger girl in the diner a mile away, a ferocious place, slick with savagery, wild with chrome; young predators

348

snarling dirty jokes menaced me, old men reached for me with coffee-warmed paws; I wielded my wallet, and won my way back. The fat brown bag of buns was warm beside me in the cold car; the smaller bag holding the two tiny cartons of French-fries emitted an even more urgent heat. Back through the black winter air to the fire, the intimate cave, where halloos and hurrahs greeted me, the deer, mouth agape and its cotton throat gushing, stretched dead across my shoulders. And now you, beside the white O of the plate upon which the children discarded with squeals of disgust the rings of translucent onion that came squeezed into the hamburgers—you push your toes an inch closer to the blaze, and the ashy white of the inside of your deep thigh is lazily laid bare, and the eternally elastic garter snaps smackwarm against my hidden heart.

Who would have thought, wide wife, back there in the white tremble of the ceremony (in the corner of my eye I held, despite the distracting hall of ominous vows, the vibration of the cluster of stephanotis clutched against your waist), that seven years would bring us no distance, through all those warm beds, to the same trembling point, of beginning? The cells change every seven years and down in the atom, apparently, there is a strange discontinuity; as if God wills the universe anew every instant. (Ah God, dear God, tall friend of my childhood, I will never forget you, though they say dreadful things. They say rose windows in cathedrals are vaginal symbols.) Your legs, exposed as fully as by a bathing suit, yearn deeper into the amber wash of heat. Well: begin. A green jet of flame spits out sideways from a pocket of resin in a log, crying, and the orange shadows on the ceiling sway with fresh life. Begin.

"Remember, on our honeymoon, how the top of the kerosene heater made a great big rose window on the ceiling?"

"Vnn." Your chin goes to your knees, your shins draw in, all is retracted. Not much to remember, perhaps, for you; blood badly spilled, clumsiness of all sorts. "It was cold for June."

"Mommy, what was cold? What did you say?" the girl asks, enunciating angrily, determined not to let language slip on her tongue and tumble her so that we laugh.

"A house where Daddy and I stayed one time."

"I don't like dat," the boy says, and throws a half bun painted with chartreuse mustard onto the floor.

You pick it up and with beautiful sombre musing ask, "Isn't that funny? Did any of the others have mustard on them?"

"I *hate* dat," the boy insists; he is two. Language is to him thick vague handles swirling by; he grabs what he can.

"Here. He can have mine. Give me his." I pass my hamburger over, you take it, he takes it from you, there is nowhere a ripple of gratitude. There is no more praise of my heroism in fetching Sunday supper, saving you labor. Cunning, you sense, and sense that I sense your knowledge, that I had hoped to hoard your energy toward a more ecstatic spending. We sense everything between us, every ripple, existent and nonexistent; it is tiring. Courting a wife takes tenfold the strength of winning an ignorant girl. The fire shifts, shattering fragments of newspaper that carry in lighter gray the ghost of the ink of their message. You huddle your legs and bring the skirt back over them. With a sizzling noise like the sighs of the exhausted logs, the baby sucks the last from his bottle, drops it to the floor with its distasteful hoax of vacant suds, and begins to cry. His egotist's mouth opens; the delicate membrane of his satisfaction tears. You pick him up and stand. You love the baby more than me.

Who would have thought, blood once spilled, that no barrier would be broken, that you would be each time healed into a virgin again? Tall, fair, obscure, remote, and courteous.

We put the children to bed, one by one, in reverse order of birth. I am limitlessly patient, paternal, good. Yet you know. We watch the paper bags and cartons ignite on the breathing pillow of embers, read, watch television, eat crackers, it does not matter. Eleven comes. For a tingling moment you stand on the bedroom rug in your underpants, untangling your nightie; oh, fat white sweet fat fatness. In bed you read. About Richard Nixon. He fascinates you; you hate him. You know how he defeated Jerry Voorhis, martyred Mrs. Douglas, how he played poker in the Navy despite being a Quaker, every fiendish trick, every low adaptation. Oh my Lord. Let's let the poor man go to bed. We're none of us perfect. "Hey let's turn out the light."

"Wait. He's just about to get Hiss convicted. It's very strange. It says he acted honorably."

"I'm sure he did." I reach for the switch.

"No. Wait. Just till I finish this chapter. I'm sure there'll be something at the end."

"Honey, Hiss was guilty. We're all guilty. Conceived in concupiscence, we die unrepentant." Once my ornate words wooed you.

I lie against your filmy convex back. You read sideways, a sleepy trick. I see the page through the fringe of your hair, sharp and white as a wedge of crystal. Suddenly it slips. The book has slipped from your hand. You are asleep. Oh cunning trick, cunning. In the darkness I consider. Cunning. The headlights of cars accidentally slide fanning slits of light around our walls and ceiling. The great rose window was projected upward through the petal-shaped perforations in the top of the black kerosene stove, which we stood in the center of the floor. As the flame on the circular wick flickered, the wide soft star of interlocked penumbrae moved and waved as if it were printed on a silk cloth being gently tugged or slowly blown. Its color soft blurred blood. We pay dear in blood for our peaceful homes.

In the morning, to my relief, you are ugly. Monday's wan breakfast light bleaches you blotchily, drains the goodness from your thickness, makes the bathrobe a limp stained tube flapping disconsolately, exposing sallow décolletage. The skin between your breasts a sad yellow. I feast with the coffee on your drabness. Every wrinkle and sickly tint a relief and a revenge. The children yammer. The toaster sticks. Seven years have worn this woman.

The man, he arrows off to work, jousting for right-of-way, veering on the thin hard edge of the legal speed limit. Out of domestic muddle, softness, pallor, flaccidity: into the city. Stone is his province. The winning of coin. The maneuvering of abstractions. Making heartless things run. Oh the inanimate, adamant joys of job!

I return with my head enmeshed in a machine. A technicality it would take weeks to explain to you snags my brain; I fiddle with phrases and numbers all the blind evening. You serve me supper as a waitress—as less than a waitress, for I have known you. The children touch me timidly, as they would a steep girder bolted into a framework whose height they don't understand. They drift into sleep securely. We survive their passing in calm parallelity. My thoughts rework in chronic right angles the same snagging circuits on the same professional grid. You rustle the book about Nixon; vanish upstairs into the plumbing; the bathtub pipes cry. In my head I seem to have found the stuck switch at last: I push at it; it

jams; I push; it is jammed. I grow dizzy, churning with cigarettes. I circle the room aimlessly.

So I am taken by surprise at a turning when at the meaningful hour of ten you come with a kiss of toothpaste to me
moist and girlish and quick; the momentous moral of this
story being, An expected gift is not worth giving.

Gloss on a Decision of the Council of Nicaea

Joanne Greenberg

The major schisms of the Church. A list of the Bishops of
Sarum. She knew a great deal about medieval church politics.
With luck and God's help, knowledge would save her. Be-
cause the jail was so terrifying.

She had seen the demonstrators out there in front of the library, and she had watched them for a few minutes, unemo-
tionally, and then she had gone into her little office and
scratched out some words on a piece of cardboard for a sign.
Then she had walked out of the library and down the steps to
stand with the demonstrators. She had made no conscious decision to do this. Her heart was exploding its blood in rhythmic spasms of panic, but she paid no attention to it; and this
frightened Myra, because she had always weighed her choices
carefully and measured feeling against propriety.

Now she was standing in a jail cell. What was there to be
afraid of? Jails haven't changed much since the Middle
Ages; the properties of a jail—the dirt, discomfort, lack of
privacy, and ugliness—were the same. Being a student of history, she had pondered many imprisonments. Except for the
electric lights, Tugwell's county jail might have been anywhere at any time; and for Myra, who had always respected
fighters for a cause, prison had meant Boethius' great hour,
Gottschalk, the Albigensian teachers, and John of the Cross.
She now understood that the worst, the most horrifying feature of their imprisonment had eluded her; and in her own
moment, its sudden presence was almost too much to stand.
Captors hate. How could she have missed so plain a fact?
Captors hate. When the sheriff had come to "protect" them
from the hecklers, she had started forward, trying to get to
him. "These Negroes and I are protesting an unjust . . ."

But he had turned, reaching to take her and the girl next
to her, and he had looked at them with a look that stopped

the words in her mouth. At the jail, as they went past him into the cell, she saw the look again, a loathing, an all-pervading contempt. Before the wave of fear and sickness had passed, the door was closed and he was gone.

There were no statements taken, no charges made. She had wasted the first hours mustering answers from an array of imprisoned giants, the brilliant, searing words of men whose causes, once eclipsed and darkened, were now the commonplace truths of our civilization.

After a while Myra had looked around and counted. There are eight of us. The young men had been taken somewhere else. Eight girls, two beds—an upper and lower bunk—one spigot, two slop buckets, one bare wall, and two square yards of floor to sit on. That was all. The girls had gone to the bunks in an order that seemed natural: two rested or slept on the lower, four sat on the upper bunk, leaving the floor for the remaining two. When anyone had sat or rested enough, she would move and a girl on the floor would take her place.

She had expected choices. There were none, not even a list of rules that they could obey or refuse to obey. It underlined the sheriff's look. One doesn't give choices to an animal; the sheriff, giving such choices, would be recognizing the humanity of his prisoners and their right to make some disposition of their own lives. So, Miss Myra, the careful librarian of Tugwell, who walked in the crosswalks and did not spit where it said *No Spitting*, was forced to put her own boundaries to her day. She decided to spend the mornings mentally recounting history, braiding popes and synods and the heresies they sifted. Perhaps they would shed light on the evolution of secular law, in which she had done a good deal of reading. In the afternoon she would have to find a way to get some exercise, to get a letter out, to wash her clothes. . . . The girls talked a little now and then, the random exchanges of people waiting. Myra sensed that they didn't have her need for formed, measured bits of time, for routines and categories. They seemed to hang free within the terms of imprisonment, simply waiting.

On the evening of the second day Matilda Jane asked her, "Miss Myra, how you come to be with us?"

The others looked over at her, some smiling, no doubt remembering the scene of themselves as they stood and sang in front of the library, hoping they could keep their voices from quavering. They had watched the door, certain of the nose of a gun or the tip of a firehose as it slowly opened. Instead, there had grown only the tiny white edge of Myra's quickly lettered sign, giving them a word at a time: OPEN LIBRARY TO ALL! IGNORANCE IS NOT BLISS. Then, Myra herself had come, slowly, very much alone. It was as if in the expectation of a cannon, they had been shocked by a pop gun. Some of them had even laughed.

"I'd never thought about it, I mean about colored people not using the library, not until Roswell Dillingham came. After that, I had to—well—to protest."

"*Roswell?*" And the other girls sat up, surprised, interested, waiting for something rich. "Heber's little brother?"

"Hey, she mean Sailor."

They laughed.

"What Sailor done now?"

"I didn't know his nickname," Myra said, and Lalie, who was sitting on the bed beside her, guffawed. "Lord, yes! Great big mouth, blowin' an' goin' all the time, two big ears a-flappin', ma'am; you be with Sailor, you ain' need no boat!" And they all wanted to know what Sailor had done now. They were all eager to hear Roswell's latest, all except Delphine, who was stretched out on the bed dozing.

"Well," Myra said, "there's not much to tell, really. You see, when Mrs. Endicott left and I took over as county librarian, she simply told me that you—I mean that Negroes—just didn't use the library, but that when a Negro needed to look something up, why he would come to me and I would take the book out myself. I know it will seem odd to you—it does to me now—but before that it had never occurred to me that there were no Negroes coming into the library. Anyway, one day this spring, I was locking up and Roswell came and asked me for a book. I just followed Mrs. Endicott's instructions—I got it for him on my card. In three days he was back. Soon he started asking me to recommend books for him to read, the more foolish it seemed not to have him come and browse around and pick out the books for him to read. Two or three books every week. I started combing lists for things I thought he would like, and the more he read, the more foolish it seemed not to have him come and browse around and pick out the books for himself. When I told him to come, he looked at me as if I had told him to fly like a bird. Negroes were forbidden to use the library.

"*The library!* That business of my getting the books for him had been designed to make me ask him why he wanted them, and then to decide that he wasn't responsible! I wrote an inquiry to the county commission and never got an answer. I never dreamed of demonstrating. I have to be honest and say that, but *the library*—well—I just couldn't consent to that. So, I suppose it was Roswell who got me to come out."

M.J. looked away and there was silence while everyone groped for a new, less dangerous subject.

Loretta whistled softly and said, "Kin you beat that damn Roswell?"

No getting away now; there it was. "What's the trouble?" Myra asked.

"You in here with us, Miss Myra," M.J. said, "so I'm gonna tell you truly what Roswell been doin'. He been makin' money offa them books."

"I don't see how. They were returned on time and in good shape."

"Ma'am, he been liftin' offa them books."

"I'm sorry, M.J., I just don't understand . . ."

"I'm in here in this jail, an' I got to be ashame' for that bigmouth! He takes them books, an' he reads 'em, an' then he take an' make 'em into a play. Then he go an' puts up a sign down to Carters' store an' he an' Fernelle an' one or two of 'em, they acts it out, see. Ten cents a person. He get almost everyone to come an' bring the kids an' make a night out. He ain' stop there. I know there's whole parts of the play that he have just graff right out of the book. I could tell it. Don't shake your head, Lalie, you know good as I do, ain' no words like that come out o' Roswell bigmouth! He lays them words down so nice—an' *powerful!* Miss Myra, he been gettin' maybe five, six dollars clear every Saturday, just showin' *your* books in the meetin' hall of the Hebron Funeral Home!"

Echo of Boethius, calling out of a sixth century cell, "Come, Goddess Wisdom, Come, Heart-ravishing Knowledge . . ." Roswell Dillingham, bootlegger of knowledge, echoed that day when knowledge was an absolute and its conquest as sure as the limits of a finite heaven. Myra wished she could tell them about Boethius, broken and condemned, and crying in his agony: "Earth conquered gives the stars!" It would only embarrass them. She said, "Do the people like the plays?"

"Well—yes, they do. See, Roswell's plays—they're about us, about colored people. It's a' interestin' play, an' folks don' have to go all the way in to Winfiel' Station, sit in the balcony. My granmaw say, she gets to see a play she understan', an' they's nobody drinkin', swearin', runnin' aroun' in they

underwear. Roswell plays—I mean *your* plays—they about
what happen to our people. Like las' week, he had one call
Oliver Twiss. Everybody cry in that one. Before that he had
one called *Two Cities*."

Myra heard Dickens' story about how Sydney Carton gave
himself up to the sheriff, back in the thirties, when the
K.K.K. rode patrol out of Tugwell.

"Kite my books, will he . . . I wish I'd known. There's a
fine one about a Civil Rights worker who got too rich and
comfortable, name of Julius Caesar; one about a girl named
Antigone, the freedom play of all time."

There was a snort from the bed. Delphine stretched and
then swung her legs over the side and grunted again. "*Miss*
Myra, we don't need white stories made over for black
people."

"I wasn't patronizing. The books I gave Roswell were good
books. They weren't 'white' stories. They were about people—
any people . . ."

"No, *ma'am*, Miss Myra, *ma'am*, not while you got 'em
piled up and stored away in the white-only library."

"That's why I was glad about Roswell." Myra looked down
at Delphine. The two girls on the floor shifted a little, ready
to use their bed places. Delphine got up slowly, and Myra got
down, and they stood together in the cell.

From the beginning Delphine was the only one with whom
Myra knew she could have no more than an armed truce.
Delphine knew it too, probably. They seldom spoke to one
another directly; when they had to speak, they used an ago-
nizingly elaborate etiquette, which Myra noted had just gone
over into parody. Delphine had a hard, absolute way of
speaking that Myra found irritating; but Myra knew that Delphine must find life in the cramped cell more difficult with
her there. Delphine was their leader. She had been in protests
and sit-ins, and jailed four times. She spoke with hard-won,
frightening knowledge.

"Next time, wear pedal-pushers like I got on, plaid or
check. They hold up good an' they don't show the dirt."

"When they're going to hit you, the muscles by their eyes
cinch up. You can always tell. Never take the smack, let the
smack take you. Go with it."

If she had been an Albigensian under the Question, Myra
knew that Delphine would wake great admiration in her. She
was strong and intelligent; she could duck a blow, parry a
question, and make her silence ring with accusation. Some-

how, the heroine was also an arrogant bitch. Myra wondered if some straying grain of her own prejudice made Delphine's virtues seem so much like faults. As the pressures built up in the shares of water, slop bucket, and stench, Myra could see, from her neatly labeled and scheduled mental busy-work, that Delphine was trying to separate her from the rest of the girls.

They waited for three days. On the morning of the fourth, the sheriff came around with his notebook. As he stopped on the other side of the bars, Myra spoke to him. They had been arrested and jailed without being given their legal rights, she said. Would this be remedied?

The sheriff looked up slowly from his book, feigning a courteous confusion. "Why you're the little lady works over to the library, ain't you?" Then he let his gaze sift slowly over the others in the cell and come back to her, the expression now one of sympathetic reproof. (Now, look at what you have caused to happen to you.)

She had a sudden, terrifying vision of him in all his genial Southern courtesy cutting away their justice, their law, their lives.

"Oh, ma'am, it's a shame! The commissioners only decided last week that we got to do Comminists the same as we do niggers. Comminist wants to live with niggers, why we ain't gonna stop 'em. But, ma'am, I seen you over in church on Sunday, an' all the bazaars, an' you was servin' donuts at the Legion parade." He looked at her earnestly. "It must be a mistake. I'm sure you ain' one of them Comminists."

Myra had never thought of herself as being a perceptive person. A narrow and careful life had never made it a necessity. Sensitivity can be a frightening gift. It was better to depend on more tangible things: hard work, reasonableness, and caution. Now, in the quiet, fear-laced minute, she suddenly knew that this contemptuously play-acting man was offering her a way out. She had only to weep and tell him how confused she was, to ask for his protection. (Lonely spinster-woman—everybody knows how notional they get. A woman, being more took up with the biological part of things, why, if she don't get to realize that biological part of her nature, it's a scientific fact she'll go to gettin' frusterated. Women, why they're *cows!*) It was as if she heard his mind form words. When he did speak, the words were so close that she was dumfounded.

"I guess you kinda got turned around here, all this niggers rights business. I guess you just got confused for a bit. I sure hate to see you in here like this. It sure is a pity." White women are ladies, the code said. You crush ladies not with violence but with pleasant contempt.

She didn't want to leave the girls in the cell. She looked at the sheriff, but she did not speak. The "lady" dealt with, he turned his attention to the others, and his voice hardened and coarsened as the code demanded when speaking to Them.

"We got a list here. You answer to your name when I call it." Then he read the names, stopping between each syllable to allow for their slow black wits to apprehend his meaning. The girls answered in the way Delphine had taught them: their voices cool and level, their eyes straight on him. Myra had been in Tugwell for only three years, having come in answer to a wildly exaggerated ad in the *Library Journal*, and staying because she had liked the town. She had never had any dealings with Tugwell's Negroes, except for Roswell; but she knew somehow that this was not the usual way for Negroes to react to authority in Tugwell. She couldn't trace this knowledge—she had never seen it directly or heard mention of it—it was just there, a certitude that their look was treason and would damn them. She also knew that from that judgment anyway, she was exempt. She might face down the sheriff and be called an old maid eccentric, but she wouldn't be hurt. Another line of difference had been drawn, excluding her; and for a long moment of the sheriff's passing by, she was overwhelmed with a loneliness so keen that she found herself shivering and on the verge of tears.

She tried to close this separation. To do it, she had to appeal to Delphine. "Four days!" she said. "There must be a way we can get hold of a lawyer . . ."

But Delphine stepped back from the line that the sheriff had helped to set between them. "You aren't Miss Myra here; you aren't ma'am. Not with us. Not for giving us white-man heroes or white-man lawyers either. *You* get *your* lawyer. Let him get *you* out."

"Look, Delphine, I don't know anything about the struggle between the races. I know about the library and the books that are in the library; and I know that it is wrong for the library to deny its treasures to those who want them. I know about books and reading. That's what I know about, where I am strong and where I will fight."

But Delphine had turned her back and gone toward a space on the bed which Myra realized shouldn't have been there. It was there for Delphine. She was the complete leader now.

She would always have a seat on the bed or a space to lie down on the bed when she wanted it. Having measured the sheriff, the others had chosen his adversary—tyrant for tyrant. Delphine went to rest on "her" bunk, to claim her compensation. "Her" places would now be offered to others only at her discretion. It was wrong. Myra saw it denying the very equality for which they were risking so much; because Myra now knew that her cellmates were facing the sons of the men who had broken Gottschalk's bones. If only she could give them some of his or Boethius' passionate and simple poetry to have when the time came. They might be strengthened by the words of great prisoners whose causes had been so much like their own. The would need grandeur. That sheriff was one who, to the end, would follow the Customs of the Country.

Later, she was sitting next to M.J. on the floor and they were talking quietly about wonderful food they had eaten. After Myra had dismembered a large, delicately broiled lobster and dipped the red claw carapace full of its vulnerable meat into a well of butter, M.J. leaned close and whispered, "Hey, Myra—uh—you ain' a Comminist or nothin', are you?"

Myra turned in wonder from the fading lobster. "What? Whatever gave you that idea?" Some words scurried across her mind in a disorderly attempt to escape being thought.

"I didn' mean to hurt your feelin's," M.J. murmured, "but, see, Delphine don' trust you, because if you was another kind of different person—well—it wouldn' be like it was one of the regular whites comin' over to our side; it would be like you was arguin' for your own difference, see?"

"M.J., you tell Delphine that all I want is to have the Tugwell library open to everybody, regardless of race, creed, color, or national origin."

"I don' think Delphine is really agains' you."

"Where does she come from?" Myra asked, and M.J. said quickly, "Oh, she from here . . ." And then she looked down. "It's the schoolin' make her talk so much nicer, that's all. Her folks don't live but a street away from us. Her daddy work on the railroad, though, made steady money."

"It's not the way she talks," Myra said, stumbling over that other barrier between them. How could she have read the sheriff so well that his predicted words followed like footprints, and yet not be able to show herself to this girl who had the face and voice of a friend? "Delphine is different from you other girls, she . . ."

"It's the same with us as with the white," M.J. said, and she fingered her torn sleeve in a little nervous gesture that Myra had seen her begin to use after the sheriff's visit. "Some people, you fit 'em in with the rest; it don't bother 'em none. Some, they got to be just one an' the mold broke. Delphine, she like that. She always did feel sharp for things that was done wrong to her. I think she felt hurts more, say, than me. It's cause she's smarter; she got more person to hurt. You know, she went up North to the college."

"I didn't know that."

"I can remember her sayin' all the time how learnin' and education was goin' to get her free. Our grade school here in Tugwell, it ain' hardly one-legged to the white school; an' our high school ain' but a butt-patch to the white. Oh, Myra, an' we didn' know it! Delphine come out of Booker T. Washington High all proud an' keen. She made the straight A. Then she went up North to the college. An' all of a sudden, here she was, bein' counted by white folks measure—an' put down, put way low. It shamed her. The white-school diploma she got cost her a extra year just to fill in on what ol' Booker T. High didn' think a Negro had to know."

"But she did succeed . . ."

"That's what I wonder at—why she come back afterward, here to Tugwell, where she ain't no different from any of us that never done what she did. I can't see how anybody that got the college degree would come back here to be put down low again."

"The fight and the fighter have to be close to each other," Myra murmured.

"What?"

Myra felt a gnawing in her mind that was strange to her. She had to wait until it became plain, and then she recognized that it was her mind moving, feeling blindly toward one of its own motives. It came bumping against something, won the shape from the darkness, and with the shape, a meaning. "Not pretty or smart or gifted, but I had one thing that was mine. The pretty and smart ones had the future; the rich ones had the present. I had the past. In a way, in 'having,' I 'owned.' The history and literature were mine to give when I opened that library door every morning. . . . When Roswell told me that Negroes couldn't use the library, I was mad because the town had no right, no right to deny what wasn't

theirs to give or withhold. In a way, Delphine and I are alike."
Then she said to M.J., "Delphine has a calling; there's no
doubt about that."

Why can't I like her? Myra looked at the leader over the
soggy bread in her dinner plate. She has everything I've always reverenced. Watching Delphine at the spigot. . . . not
running away, standing, as Boethius stood, and Gottschalk
and John. The courage is in knowing exactly what will happen, where the wound will gall most cruelly, and still, standing. . . . But the arrogance in Delphine, who was beginning
to posture like Savonarola silhouetted by the light of his own
fire, made Myra wince. Delphine's arrogance reached into
Myra's thoughts and began to move toward all of the heroes
Myra had stored there. She began to worry for the giants she
venerated, for years of her pity and love. Was courage only
the arrogance used to an enemy?

The next morning the sheriff began.

Tactical blunder: He took Delphine first. She came back
sick, the brown color of her face grayed. She was bloody and
puffy-faced and harder than ever. Now, anyone who followed
would have to come to Delphine before and after, and would
be judged. When Loretta went in the afternoon and returned
still retching, she was greeted by Delphine's wry smile and
the slow unfolding of Delphine's bones, one by one, to make
a place for her on the bunk throne of honor. The next day
Dilsey and Lalie went. They came back trembling and exhausted, embarrassed at where their hurts were, and with a
rumor that things were going to be speeded up because the
legal machinery was slowly lumbering in to help. In the
night, counting the heretics she knew, burned between 890
and 1350 in France, Myra could hear M.J. quietly sobbing
with fear.

It had been hardest for M.J., who had seen all the hurts and
heard the accumulating voices in their nightmares. Now
the untried ones had the floor all the time. Myra crawled
over to M.J. and put a hand on her thin back in a forlorn
gesture of comfort. M.J.'s back stopped heaving and the crying stopped or, rather, retreated inward. Myra began to feel
that someone was observing her; another silence was there,
one that seemed to fill its space instead of being there by de-
fault of sound. She turned and saw Delphine looking at them
from a seat on the top bunk, her face showing nothing in the
dimness. She was awake, all right, watching, listening, as if
she were waiting to pounce. It made Myra feel guilty of

something. She looked down at M.J., who hadn't moved and was pretending to be asleep, and then she stood up. It was painfully slow; she grunted with the effort and the pain; her legs had been bent against the concrete floor for a long time. When she finally stood, her eyes were at the level of Delphine's kneecaps.

"Help M.J. You know, Delphine, we can't all be as tough as you." She realized immediately that such a plea for M.J. was wrong and stupid.

Crying weakness to Delphine was like asking sympathy from a tornado. Were all heroes so frighteningly impersonal? Damn her! Why couldn't that precious martyrs' firelight extend its warmth and radiance to cover M.J., who had waited all these days while the terror grew?

"Listen, Delphine, I know something about you."

Delphine's impassive face did not move. Damn her, I'll make it move.

"I know, for instance," she continued slowly, whispering, a word at a time, "that whatever you took from the sheriff, it didn't hurt as much as theirs did . . ." And she gestured around the cell at the sleepers who were shielding their ugly dreams from the forty-watt light that burned in the corridor outside the cell. "Maybe you didn't feel it at all."

"How come?" Delphine said, fastidiously disinterested.

"You knew it before you went in," Myra went on. "It's a nice secret, too, Delphine, because the welts are real and no one can prove they didn't hurt. Maybe they don't even hurt now."

"No!" Delphine hissed. "Nothing hurts! It's the black skin. Makes you immune. Tougher than the white! Less sensitive!"

"Come off it. It's the anger or the hate that makes you immune. Your anger and hate are better than morphine for shielding you from pain. You were dressed up to the eyes in hate, and you walked in with it to the sheriff and took your licks and came back bleeding. You didn't even have to lie. Did it make you feel superior to the other girls who had to take it raw, without hate?"

That hit. Myra could see it going in to burn behind Delphine's slowly blinking eyes. She was standing close to Delphine, whispering, but they were both aware that M.J. and maybe others were awake and would hear them if their voices got any louder.

Delphine began to negotiate. "What are you going to do about it?"

"You help M.J. to take what she's going to have to take or I'll tell what I know about you."

Delphine laughed, a silent mouth-laugh, whose mirth died long before it reached her eyes.

"I know they won't believe me," Myra said, "but maybe there'll be a minute of doubt, just enough to force you to come right out and claim that bed space and that first drink in the morning."

Delphine sat there, surprised, and Delphine's surprise was a source of pain to Myra. She had no style and she knew it. Her courage looked silly. Nevertheless, she had gotten to Delphine, and Delphine wasn't used to being gotten to.

"I don't want you here!" she hissed. "I don't want what you have to give us! Get your white face out of this cell and let us, for once, do something all by ourselves!"

"I'm here and my white face is here, and you can either like it or lump it."

Where had the words and the strength come from? She had always been a sheltered person, and three years as Miss Myra, the toy librarian in this toy white town of antimacassars and mint tea hadn't done any more than confirm her opinion. Who had she been a week ago that she could be so far from that self right now? Like a rocket, she thought, that had veered a millionth of a degree from the center of its thrust. She had, on the 14th of April, asked a question of a boy named Roswell Dillingham. It was only the smallest shift, a millionth of a degree, and that smallest change was measuring her path at tangent, thousands of miles into strange darkness, to end lost, perhaps in uncharted spaces that she could not imagine.

Delphine was muttering curses, and Myra turned back to her place on the floor and sat down. Delphine didn't want her, and she had said so. Why not? What did Myra, and by extension white people, have that Delphine couldn't accept? If Delphine hadn't been to college up North, it might have been a falsely exalted picture of American history, a Parson Weems history that no Negro in slave-holding country could take seriously. It wasn't that. Delphine had read enough and learned enough to know that white men also searched their souls occasionally. Myra knew that she had to get at it, whatever it was, because she needed everything she could use against Delphine's arrogance. She found herself staring at the slop bucket, riveted on it. Exhausted, she thought.

Hard floors and groping, needs and angers, mine and hers,

and barely knowing where to separate mine and hers. Why *is*
she in this cell? Then she found herself staring at Lalie's back
as if to bore through it, and Lalie shifted and moaned so that
Myra pulled her eyes away. I have the past. . . . I have the
past and two enemies, who both seem to say "nothing personal." It really isn't, I suppose. They are enemies to my history. What a couple they would make: the sheriff, with his
fake past, and Delphine, with her fake . . .

It was there, somewhere near, elusive but near, in Delphine's idea of a future. She became alert, groping to more purpose now. It was in a future of which Delphine dreamed, a
world that made "white" history irrelevant and Myra a danger. She looked over the sleeping girls. Delphine had given up
too, and was curled in a ball, her arm protectively over her
face. The only ones who merely pretended to sleep were the
two whose turn it would be to go with the sheriff tomorrow.
Myra knew that she would not be beaten, and that the law
was slowly lumbering toward her. If only Delphine had let it
happen, she might have given them a thousand years of
prison humor and two thousand years of resistance to the
tyrant, eloquent, proud resistance, face to face, as Delphine
would have liked it.

And *I* wanted to be in the history too! She thought. Oh,
my God, it was as simple as that! I wanted to be in the history even more than I wanted to fight over Roswell's reading.
I wanted to come forward where the fire was, feeling that in
the fire, I would not be so alone. . . . The thoughts that she
had sent out walking for Delphine's weakness had found hers
instead. Does it hurt and sear and shatter, that thought? Is it
as hard as the sheriff's blows? no, not so hard as that. She
wasn't going to be in the history, even though she was in the
fire. In the fire, but no less alone. Delphine had fixed that. A
segregated fire. She would have to work at not hating Delphine. This cause was right and the cause should take prece-
dence over its leaders. Heaven knows it was an old argument.
It showed up at the Montanist Controversy; and it was put to
a rule in 325 A.D.: Decision of the Nicene Council, valid
sacraments by a lapsed bishop. Very good. It was a comfort
to know that the early Church had ruled on Delphine's case.

M.J. rolled over, but her eyes were closed, and she was still
pretending to be asleep. She was a nice girl. If Delphine had
allowed it, they could have been, all of them, friends together
in this cause. Her mind yearned toward M.J. in the night.
There were thousands of men and women before you in that

room, a thousand rooms, acts, moments. Don't be afraid. You are neighbored all around by people who have screamed or been silent, wept or been brave—all the nations are represented, all the colors of man. Don't be afraid of pleading, of weeping. You are with some shining names.

At the window there was a little gray light coming. The window was almost hidden by the bunks which had been pushed against its bars, but from where Myra sat on the floor, she could see up into a tiny square of the changing sky. The cell looked even worse in the muddy yellow of the electric bulb.

I suppose I shouldn't stop at the heroes of the Middle Ages. There are more recent slaves and conquerers. Dachau and Belsen—they, too, had men who stood in their moment and said, "I am a person; you must not degrade me." Her eye wandered around the cell and fixed on the slop bucket again, and she tried to ease her aching body on the floor. Dachau and Belsen.

In 1910, technology was going to make everybody free and freedom was going to make everybody good. The new cars had rolled up to the gates of death camps. Dreams of the perfecting of man ended in the gas chambers and behind the cleverly devised electric fences. Didn't everybody dream that dream? Didn't we *all?*

Maybe all but one. Is man imperfect by nature? Maybe only white man? There it was. Delphine was answering to everyone who had ever told her that she and hers were outside the elm-street-and-steeple dream of democracy. If the black heroes weren't in the history books, then they were also not included in the Albigensian Crusade and the ride to Belsen. The possibility of perfection—that was being girded all right. If Delphine took her blows in hate and in the belief that *her* people could be perfect, not in some millennium but soon, and by her own good efforts, what would be, could be given her, what pain could she endure that wasn't worth it? Not for freedom, not for friendship, certainly not for the right of ingress to the Tugwell library. Oh, God, who will help M.J. take her hurting now, when all that M.J. wants is to include in her God-blesses before bed all the misery-running, sorrow-spawning world of white and black?

It was morning. M.J. was trembling quietly on the floor. She looked exhausted and ill, and she hadn't even gone yet. Myra got up, and the aching numbed to her every bone. She went to where Delphine was perched, sleeping.

"Delphine?"

"What-do-you-want?" It was the too-clear enunciation of an educated Negro to a white who will call him Rastus if he slurs a letter.

"You've got to do something to help M.J."

"I bet you're happy, white gal. If it wasn't for your people putting us down, she wouldn't *be* scared now!"

So it was true. The blind would see and the halt would rejoice. No cowards, no sinners, no wrongs. In the jubilee. In the great jubilee. "Help her, Delphine. The sheriff is looking for weakness. If he finds it, he might kill her with his hands or with her own shame. Help her, or I'm going to start talking about you, Delphine. I'm going to start asking questions that the others have never asked."

Myra could see the gains and losses ticking off in Delphine's head. Her eyes were clinical and her expression detached as an Egyptian funerary statue. Delphine, at the height of her concentration, was intensely, breathtakingly beautiful. She stayed in her place for a minute, two. Then she stretched and the odds and possibilities arranged themselves before her. With elaborate, lithe ease she swung down to the floor, yawning, and bent to where M.J. lay. They began to whisper. Myra was glad she couldn't hear them. For a moment her eye strayed to the vacant place, Delphine's place on the bed. She had a sudden urge to climb up and take it and make Delphine fight to get it back. The place would be comfortable for a little nap; she was sore all over from the floor. The place would be dark against the back wall; she could sleep for a while.

No, Delphine was the leader, the place was her place. Only Delphine, however fanatical and blind, could lead the girls through all the questions, the licks and the lawyers. She found her eyes fixed again. What was so fascinating about that slop bucket! We're both on the floor, she thought.

"I wish to record an opinion," she said to it quietly. "In 325 the Council of Nicaea decided that sacraments at the hands of a lapsed bishop were valid where the intent of the communicant was sincere. The baptisms of these bishops stood. I always wondered about that decision. It smacked too much of ends justifying means. I hereby make my statement to the estimable theologians of the Council of Nicaea: '*Avé*, fellas, *Salvé*, fellas, Congratulations and greetings from the Tugwell jail.' "

The Star Blanket

Shirley Schoonover

They had walked miles that day. They walked miles every day that they changed grazing land. The man and woman followed the sheep silently, the only conversation was that of the sheep as they flowed down the hills. The dogs were merely extensions of the man's will, moving to his short whistles, guiding the woolly mass down from the summer grazing lands to the winter flatlands. The man raised his right hand and the dogs fell to the ground, allowing the sheep to stop and graze.

The man threw his pack to the ground and sat next to it.

"Ought to be good grazing farther on down." He pulled tobacco from his shirt and bit off a corner.

The woman remained standing, looking up the side of the mountain they had descended and down the foothills.

"All the steps it took for us to get down here. All the steps it'll take for us to reach winter pasture. Who'd think there were that many steps to a mountain?" She shook her head and eased one booted foot against the other.

"You sure waste your time thinking about steps in mountains. If you want to get from one place to another it always takes steps." He rolled the tobacco around his tongue, savoring the fresh flavor, the bite on his tongue.

"And when we go back up the mountain again, what a waste of steps. We don't even leave marks to remember from one spring to another. Or even spring to fall."

"Don't worry about it, we don't need marks, we find the best grass, that's enough." He stood up and whistled the dogs into action.

The rest of the day they spent following the sheep down the shallow hills, down to a valley that would hold them all the California winter.

As they went the man kept his eyes to the ground remarking the grass and the dryness. "It's going to be a hard winter

368

in the mountains." From time to time he would spit brown
juice onto the gray grass.

The woman walked behind him, carrying her pack, looking
at the sky and the progress of the sun and clouds. She
watched the man ahead of her, thinking, He never looks at
the sky unless it's going to rain or snow. He doesn't notice
the sheep-clouds or the feather-clouds, just the rain clouds.
She stumbled over a hummock of grass and the man turned
and laughed at her.

"Get your nose out of the clouds, they won't save you any
steps."

"I was just watching the sky, and the clouds running down
it."

"No use watching the sky, it'll be there tonight and tomorrow. It's not good for anything except weather."

"Sometimes I think a thing doesn't always have to be used
to be good. The sky is good to look at." She spoke softly to
herself, not seeing the land around her; rather seeing into the
land and sky in dimensions she could not explain, but merely
sense.

"What?" The man called back, then, watching her unseeing
progress down the hillside. He turned, grinned, and walked
on, head down.

That night they bedded the sheep down in an outcropping
of gray boulders and sandy ledges. The dogs gathered the
sheep like needles gathering beads, and scolded them into a
bumping, blatting, woolly scuffle of bodies.

The man and woman sat beside their fire, drinking black
sour coffee from tin cups. The man threw small shards of
wood into the fire, and thought about the sheep and the dogs,
and his need for another dog.

The woman lay on her back, half dozing, lying against the
earth, feeling its outward thrust against her back.

"Do you suppose the mountains are growing?" she asked
her husband.

"I don't suppose anything so crazy. These mountains have
been here all my life, never grew an inch that I saw." He
squinted at her through the fire. His pale eyes took on a
white cast from the flames; and as he looked, his face
changed, becoming cunning and sensual. He arose and went
to her. He lay beside her, taking her body with his hard
hands, gripping her rather than caressing her. She lay passive,
looking at him with mildly wondering eyes. When he was

through he left her and rolled up in his blanket to sleep. She
continued to stare up into the sky, past the stars.

She had come to him from her father in exchange for
three pregnant ewes. She had been thirteen then, and a plain,
quiet girl. Her father had been a sheep rancher who had
fallen into difficulty, and with a large family of girls, it was
expedient to bestow his middle daughter upon a wandering
sheepherder who promised to keep her. She had been a good
wife to the shepherd, having a quiet gentleness with the
lambing ewes, and a quickness of foot when needed to herd
the sheep. She had lived these two years with him in the
mountains and the flat lands, wearing levis and flannel shirts,
cropping her hair once a year like the sheep, and had pleased
him in the secret moments of their life together. He had
taken her with him into the small town that was their outside
world every spring during the shearing time, until a vagrant
cowboy had noticed her feminine form under the heavy shirt.

"I'd sure like to take your daughter into the dance
tonight." His eyes had spoken more than the words, and understanding flashed between the men.

"My wife ain't free to go dancing. We're going back to the
sheep tonight."

"Sheepherder!" The cowboy narrowed his eyes at them. He
mounted his horse and, looking tall and arrogant, he said,
"Maybe we could wash the smell off your woman, but right
now it would be like bedding a lousy sheep."

The man never took her into town again; instead he left
her to tend the sheep when he made trading trips. She was no
more lonely during these trips than when he was with her.

The next day they reached their small cabin which was
their winter shelter. It was adequate for shelter and no more.
The man had built it ten years before, and owned the acres
that surrounded it. They established themselves in it, the
sheep in a large pen, the woman cooked supper in the iron
stove. The man dozed while the woman folded blankets into
the bed and pushed the table and chairs into a new design
against the wall. She heated water and bathed herself, washing her hair and body over and over with yellow soap until
she felt clean of the sheep dust and grit of the trail.

"You going into town tomorrow?" she asked.

"Yeah. I'm taking some of the lambs for selling. We need

stock for the winter, so clear out the shelves for whatever I can pick up." He turned noisily onto his side.

"Bring me something from town," she spoke softly to his back; hands brushing through her hair, drying it, twisting it into a knot at the back of her neck.

"What like? I can't spend money on foolishness."

"Just something little for me to look at. I saw a picture card when we were at the cowboy's camp. That was pretty. I could look at that and think of what other places there are."

"You want that card? I'll bring you a new shirt and pants, they're pretty when they're new."

"No, something for me to look at and hold. I don't want to use everything. Remember that fair we saw that first trip? They had cards and pretty boxes with shells. Bring me a pretty box with shells. I could look at it and touch the shells . . ."

"I'll see what there is to bring that doesn't cost too dear. Come to bed now so we can sleep."

When he had gone into town with the lambs she shook out the blankets and swept the floor.

All the day long and night that he was gone she thought about the town and the rushing cattle in the stockyard, the lighted cafés, and the pretty goods in the store and the town women who wore colorful dresses.

If he brings me the box I'll keep it on the table all winter. I can see the watermarks on the shells and think of all the miles they've come to be here. She hummed to herself and tended the sheep.

When he came home she waited, breathless, while he unpacked the borrowed mule. He unloaded a package of wadded shirts and denim pants, wool socks, and a pair of boots for her. She watched him, and put away the sacked flour, coffee, sugar, tobacco, and tins of food. She dug through the sacks looking for the thing she had asked for.

"Did you bring me something pretty?" She hugged her arms to her chest.

"I spent all I could on things we need. I can't see what you needed that box for." He unwrapped a dozen tins of snuff and stacked them on the table. "Here's something you like, lump sugar for your coffee." He handed her a box of sugar.

She took the sugar from him and put it on the shelf.

"No thanks, hey? Well, I can get my thanks in bed." He touched her shirt front with a hard, accustomed hand.

"Look outside in the sheep pen. There's something else I got in town."

She went slowly outside. In the gray mass of sheep stood a large, dark shape, It was a horse, standing solemnly in the half dark, looking toward her with mysterious black eyes. A fringe of forelock covered its eyes so that it seemed to look at her from a shadow. She entered the pen and pushed the sheep aside to walk to the horse. It stood unmoving when she touched its nose. She ran her hand up between its ears and stroked its neck. Its head drooped and it sighed. It neither welcomed her nor rejected her, but stood accepting her attention without resistance.

The man buffeted his way through the sheep and stood before her. "I got him free from that cowboy we saw last spring. He was going to shoot the horse because it's wind broke and can't keep up with the cattle."

The woman looked at them both. He put his arm possessively around the horse's neck. "I can use him for packing our stuff up mountain next spring. One thing's sure, he won't be running away from us, he's too windbroken."

"He's a pretty thing," she said.

"Well, see, I brought you something to look at. He isn't much good for anything but looking at right now, but come spring he can be used." He slapped the horse's shoulder and turned away. The horse looked at the woman and closed its eyes.

During the winter the dogs herded the sheep into nearby valleys for pasture. The horse grazed with the sheep, following them listlessly from spot to spot. The dogs nipped its heels and made it trot, causing it to breathe heavily in a wheezing, whuffling shortness of breath. The woman, seeing this, would call the dogs to stop; but they, listening to the man, would loll their tongues at her and dart at the horse until the man whistled them down.

At night, when the sheep were penned, the horse would stand at the fence looking off into the mountains. The man would sit beside the stove oiling his rifle, splicing tanned hides into a rope. The woman would sit on the floor staring into the grated opening of the stove, listening to the nightsounds. It was during one of these nights that she said: "I think I'm starting a baby."

"Well, that's good." He stopped his work to touch her hair. "When did this happen?"

"I think three months ago. I haven't had any woman signs for that long, and my belt's too tight."

She stood while he felt her belly and sides.

"A baby, hey?" He thrust his hand within her shirt to her breasts. "You are fattening up and filling out. Next time I go into town, I'll bring you some more sugar and some canned fruit. You feel all right?"

"Oh, yes. I think it'll be born in the summer. Could you bring me some cloth to make it some clothes?"

"Yeah, I guess I could. Flannel, I expect, and some pins and thread. You'll have to pack it with you when we go up mountain." He held her to him and kissed her head. "Give me a boy. He'd be a big help and we could keep more sheep."

That night when they were in bed and he lay against her he repeated, "Give me a boy. Give me a boy."

When he slept she rose to one elbow and watched him. In sleep his face was the tender version of the day face, the pale eyes were hidden beneath a short run of lashes, the animal cunning mouth was relaxed into softer lines, tinted by tobacco juice and perpetual windburn. In sleep his face allowed no more knowledge of him than did his day face, it was so utterly expressionless. Whatever imagination or feeling he might have had was covered by the continuous need for material satisfaction. He had been orphaned at six years and had herded sheep for other men until he had begun his own flock. Since he had lost his parents, he had lost all identity except as a shepherd in the mountains. His dreams were of wool and sheep and the steadily increasing roll of money in a tin container under the floor. Some nights he panted like a dog in his sleep, dreaming of the heights and slow unwinding of the pasture lands up into the emptiness of the sky.

He had first seen his wife while she was tending her father's sheep on a winter pasture, sitting in the scrubby grass bent over some knitting. She was thirteen, just budding from a youth into womanliness. Her small, round head bent so seriously over woman's work touched some memory of his dead mother; her brown boyish hands knitting steadily and her yet unformed, unmarred face struck him in the groin with a kind of sad desire both to possess her and father her. In his late thirties, he had had few dealings with women, and so instead of courting her, he spoke with her father.

"She's a little bit strange," said the father. "She reads books and wanders off alone into the hills and we never know when she'll come back. But if you want her and figure you can put up with her ways, take her."

The girl had stood silently watching from the doorway of her father's house. For the exchange of three sheep she was given to the man. Her mother had spoken to her, bidding: "I never had time to tell you what to expect from a man. I can't tell you now except to be good to him. When he comes to you at night, take him." The girl had looked at her mother with mute eyes. "There's no way to find out about men and their ways except by doing. In ten years you'll not remember what it was like not to know a man. It seems to have been going on forever, and it will go on that way until he's too old." The mother held her daughter for the last time. "If you can take joy from his man's ways, that's good. If you can't, try to give him what you can, there's some joy in that too." She kissed her daughter's round forehead. "Now go to him, he seems to be kind, and you'd have to marry someone someday."

The man had taken her away with him into the cabin he had built. He watched her arrange her small store of clothing on the high shelf. She walked about the room, touching the table and the chairs. She looked into the cupboard at the supplies, patted the dogs and touched the window ledge. Her presence in the room made it a less lonely place for the man and he smiled at her hands when they touched the dogs.

The room was a new and lonely place for the girl. The smells of the man and dogs, wet fur and wool, the low flickering fire in the stove, the absence of her mother made her aware of being pitched out into an alien world. The presence of the man, his physical urge toward her, made her feel shut in and apprehensive. She had some knowledge of what her mother had meant, but only enough to keep her nerves tense. She remembered the rams in mating season, their arrogant, almost cruel way of commanding the ewes; the ewes falling to their knees under the onslaught of the rams, the heavy odors of life regenerating itself. She tried to think if her father had ever looked at her mother that way, and the patience of her mother's eyes when night came.

"Come now, you've seen all the things I have." The man took her arm and held her close against his chest, stroking her hair and back gently. He took her to the bed and watched her undress to the pale baby skin. She lay beneath the wool blanket, eyes closed.

If I must learn man's ways, let it be now. Don't let it hurt.
Don't let him hurt me.

When the man touched her shoulder she flinched and
opened her eyes. She stared at him and clasped her hands
over her breasts, hiding them and herself from his maleness.

"Ah, now, I won't hurt you," he said. "Let me hold your
hand and we'll talk a bit."

She gave her hand to him and pulled the cover up to her
chin.

"You're still afraid, hey? I won't hurt you." He leaned over
her and touched her face with his. "You're so small, more
like my child than my wife." He touched her body under the
blanket, gently, as if plucking a fragile plant. She turned her
face to his shoulder and closed her eyes. He stroked her body
carefully, she sensing the rushing of his passion, he building
his desire slowly so as not to frighten her.

"Will you let me?" he asked her. She had fallen into a
musing state. She nodded.

When he was through he turned her head and looked at
her.

"Well, now, it didn't hurt, did it?" She looked at him with
patient eyes and shook her head. He took her hand and rested
with her until they both fell asleep.

During the years before she became pregnant her figure
filled out into feminine contours. Her waist lengthened and
diminished to a fitting slimness, her breasts lost the baby
roundness and drooped slightly, her hips and buttocks rounded to firm, earth-round lines. Her walk changed from a girl's
gait to a purposeful stride, although she still walked as if paying no attention to the earth, but walked slightly above it.

She and the man spoke little, they shared all their activities, but his mind rested on the sheep while hers mused over
the eternally silent mountains and the dimension of sound
and color.

In the spring of her pregnancy and after the lambing, they
made their way back over the foothills and into the mountain
pasturelands.

The woman had become fond of the horse, feeling that it
and she shared the same state of uselessness. The horse had
recovered some of its broken wind and moved more alertly.
Daily it was packed with their supplies and carried them
silently after the sheep. The man walked ahead, whistling the
dogs into the familiar patterns of action, watching the new
grasses come up before them. The woman stepped behind

him watching the rain mists climb higher up the mountain each day, seeing the horse move ahead of her, flicking its tail against the constant flies, reaching for the short grasses along the way. She drew pleasure from the horse's grace and its increasing strength and wildness. At night when the horse was unpacked, it would roll on the earth, rubbing its skin against the sharp strength of the mountain side, rising and kicking itself into the air. At these times she would clasp her hands and laugh while the horse nickered to her and coaxed her for the secret lumps of sugar she kept for it. The time came when she would ride the horse around the camp, calling the dogs to romp with her and the horse. She and the horse would pick their way from the camp to sudden ledges of the mountain and look down through the ground fog to the foothills, catching glimpses of occasional rivers and lights from other campfires. She would always return with the horse running and snorting, both looking wild and fresh from mysterious journeys in the night. The man would wait for her return and she would prepare the supper.

"What do you find in the night to look so happy about?"

"Oh, we look for the different stars. We saw camplights down east of us. We smelled the pines up mountain. It's all so different from the day. The stars are different up here from downland."

"The stars are always the same. No matter where you are." He drank his coffee and sat back. "You're getting as strange now as you were when I first brought you home."

"Strange? No, I'm not." She looked at him anxiously.

"It's that horse. You ride him too much, and you're away from me too much. You need to settle down to thinking about regular things like the sheep and the camp. You're going to have a baby soon, you should think about that."

"I do. Everytime he moves, I think about him. I made up a song to him." She began humming to herself.

"Songs." The man grunted. "I mean the sewing of clothes, that thread and cloth cost too dear to be wasted."

She looked at him and smiled. "I have been sewing. But my mind keeps straying to the other things he'll need."

"What else will he need? Plenty of flannel there."

"Oh, I meant the sun to shine on him, the stars to sparkle at him at night. I hear little voices in the wind singing for him. I want him to have flowers to look at and pull apart."

The man looked at her and shook his head. He settled into his blankets for the night.

The woman continued sewing straight white seams up and down squares of flannel. She threaded and rethreaded the needle dreaming of her child.

That night while she was sewing she saw stars falling, running down the hill of the skies and disappearing behind the mountain. She wondered to herself, If the stars never change, why do some fall out of the sky? She watched hard for some minutes to see if certain stars would lose their place and fall. But they didn't. Rather, as if from some place beyond the familiar stars, the falling stars appeared and then began their descent. The idea of familiar and new stars held her breathless, and she spoke to the child within her.

Did you know that there are old stars and new ones? Or maybe the old ones are those that fall out of the sky, and we just see their ending. She fell asleep and dreamed of the falling stars.

The next morning she was struck with the idea of making a blanket for the baby with stars on it. "I remember when I was little, ma had a blanket with patches and designs on it. I want to make the same kind of blanket, but with stars on it."

The man looked at her and jostled her arm. "Stars on a blanket, hey? Well, if you've got any of that cloth left you could make it, I suppose. But what's the use of it?"

She smiled, "There doesn't have to be a use for it except for me to look at. I look at the stars at night, and this way, I can carry the baby in them when he's born. And he can look at them when it's cloudy."

They walked many strenuous miles that day and came to a camp of cowboys and cattle. They settled near it and walked to the campfire. The cowboys greeted them with jokes and glances at her burdened figure. They sat around the campfire and shared supper and coffee.

"Yeah, this is as high as we'll take the cattle. You're welcome to the rest of this mountain," the foreman said.

"We'll go up to the broken pass and summer graze there," the man said, offering the cowboys his tobacco, and accepting a handrolled cigarette.

"Your wife going to have that baby soon?" the foreman asked.

"In about two months, she figures."

"You'd better send her down the mountain then. She'll need help with it." The foreman was father to seven children, and knew of the difficulties of childbirth.

"Oh, could I go down to a ranch?" she asked.

"You figure she'll need help? I'll be with her when the baby comes." Her husband exhaled cigarette smoke and glanced at his wife.

"Bringing babies is woman's work. You never know what might happen. Bring her down to our ranch, we have an old woman there who brings lots of babies."

"Well, I guess I can spare her for a couple of weeks." He took his wife's hand and held it on his knee.

"Why don't you let her stay at the ranch until you come back down mountain? She can pay her way by helping the cook. And she'll need the rest. You don't want her bringing the baby back up mountain."

"Oh, I'd like that." The woman sat back thinking about the society of other women, the talk she missed, and the help she'd have when the baby came. "I could make the star blanket then, if somebody would help me."

"Star blanket?" The foreman looked at her and then at her husband.

"Yeah. She got a notion the other night she wants to make a blanket for the baby with stars on it. No use in it, though."

"What kind of blanket is that, Missus?" the foreman spoke kindly.

"I thought I'd make a white blanket with blue stars on it. The baby could look at them when it's cloudy, and it could know what stars are right off."

"I have an old blanket like that." He stood and went to his pack, pulling out a small saddle blanket of some Indian design. He held it out to her. "You can have it if you want."

She took it in her hands and smiled at him. The blanket was white bordered with bands of black and blue and with blue stars and lightning shapes. It was heavy, coarsely woven wool. "That's pretty. I take it with many thanks." She smiled again at him and stroked the stars.

"You don't have to give my wife anything like that." Her husband frowned in gratitude.

"No, no, take it. You can keep it for the baby, and it will be warm for him in the winter."

The foreman turned to the husband, "I mean what I say about sending her down mountain when her time comes. You've got that horse, it'll carry her down in a couple of days."

"I'll have to think about it."

"Mister, don't take this unkindly. I've watched the two of you go up and down the mountain these years, and I know you're tight with a dollar. But don't be tight with your wife or your baby. You can't ever get them back when they're dead. So just risk the sheep for that last month and send her down to the ranch." He turned to the woman. "When you feel your time coming, ma'am, you just start down the mountain. If you need help down, I'll be glad to ride down with you."

"Thank you. I'll try to come down without help." She touched her stomach and sighed. "But how will I know when it's time?"

"My wife says when the baby moves down so you can breathe again, that's the time to get ready. So you just get on that horse and start down."

That night the cowboys talked and told stories about their lives with the cattle. The man and woman watched and listened. As it is with all lonely men they sang the melancholy songs and played handmade guitars. The woman saw them as beautiful and kindly strangers who shared her loneliness on the mountain. She saw the glint of their saddle decorations in the night light and watched their dark figures slump in the darkening, star-filled night. They spoke of towns she had never seen; one spoke of the ocean and its strangeness. He showed her some shells he had brought from the ocean shore. She held them and touched the water-etched designs. The cowboy had linked the shells together on a hand-braided cord. The shells tinkled together and shone blue and white under the stars.

"See, ma'am, the inside is shiny and smooth. The outside is rougher and dull." He turned the shells over and over. "Folks say that they've found shells like this up here in the mountains."

"What? Shells in the mountains?" She looked at him for the joke.

"Ma'am, I'm not fooling you. When I was down on the coast last year, I ran into a fellow who told me so. He said if we keep our eyes open in the raw parts of the mountain, sometime we might spot marks of shells and plants that live under the water. I've been looking ever since then. But I haven't seen any." He poured the last of the coffee into her cup. "If you get up higher you might just keep your eyes open. You might find some. This fellow told me these mountains are still young. And that they've hardly finished growing."

"I never heard of such a thing." She looked at him sharply to see if he was making fun of her.

"The way he tells it, the mountains grew up out of ocean water, pushing and shoving each other, and carrying the shells and plants with them." He looked at her earnestly.

"I've heard some tall stories in my day, but this takes them all." Her husband rolled into his blanket and eyed the cowboy. "Don't fill her head up with any stranger ideas than she already has."

"Tell me the rest. How young are these mountains?" She leaned forward to hear every word.

"Ma'am, they're way older than we are. They've been here before white men or Indians ever came, but this fellow said that they are babies compared to mountains in other parts of the world."

She looked away from him to the mountain looming over them. "Could we tell if they were still growing?"

"I figure if this mountain ever starts to grow again, we can forget about getting off. I don't think a mountain's growing pains would be easy to take. This man said that when mountains grow they grow from the inside out, and parts break off." He smiled at her and said, "He didn't think they'd be growing any more for years, so don't you worry about it, ma'am."

"Thank you for telling me about it. My husband thinks I'm strange for thinking such things." She looked apprehensively at her sleeping husband.

"No, ma'am, you're not strange. There's a lot to be known about this world, and the only way I figure you can find out anything is to wonder about it and ask somebody. I've got some books back at the ranch, you're welcome to read them and look at the pictures."

"Thank you, I look forward to reading them. How did you get them?"

"Every winter when we're in slow times I go out to the towns and look around. There's ways to find books and ways to learn things. All you have to do is go out and hunt for them."

"Why do you look for books?"

"Ma'am, I guess I'm just part cat. When I see something I've got to know all I can about it. That star blanket you wanted. I think you're smart to give it to your baby. He'll grow up looking at the stars and maybe be a better or smarter man than his dad. I don't mean disrespect toward your husband, but every little shove we can give to another person, means they'll go a lot farther than we did."

He stood up and moved away from her. "I'd better let you get some sleep now. You listen to Jake and go down mountain when your time comes. And you read all the books you want. When winter comes, if you want, I'll bring you some more."

She lay rolled up in her blanket looking into the darkness where the cowboy had disappeared. Her mind hummed and murmured with the things he had told her. And he hadn't thought her strange for her thought and questions. She hugged the star blanket to her and fell into a deep sleep.

The sounds of men moving and the barking of dogs woke her. She lay for minutes watching the men in the dawnlight squatting over their coffee cups and tin plates. When her husband leaned over her, she smiled and struggled to her feet. They shared breakfast with the cowboys and left the camp. They had walked a mile when they heard a horse coming behind. They stopped and saw the cowboy riding up the slope. When he reached them, he stopped his horse and handed the woman the string of shells.

"I thought you might like these for the baby, ma'am. I'll be going down to the ocean again in a couple of years, and I'll get more." He saluted her with his hat and turned his horse.

"Thank you! Thank you!" she called after him.

"Well, he's a strange one. You forget all that fooling with shells and books." Her husband turned up the mountain and whistled at the dogs. She followed him, holding the string of shells and wondering at the cowboy's goodness.

That summer as they followed the sheep higher into the mountain she looked for marks in the raw sections of the ledges. She wandered from the sheep trail onto ledges and shelves, scratching into the sliding shale for the shell marks. But she found none.

She gazed into the side of the mountain as if willing it to disclose its hidden shells. As her size and awkwardness increased she was forced to ride the horse for the major part of the day, or stay in camp while her husband took the sheep to new grazing. When she was left alone she sewed more garments for the child or took slow walks with the horse, talking to it about the cowboy and what he had said to her. The horse had become doglike in its devotion to her and followed her, nuzzling her pockets for the sugar. She sat long hours on the mountainside, making bouquets of the spring flowers, garlanding the horse's mane with them, and laughing when he ate them indiscriminately.

The man changed with the summer, growing more irritable. He would watch her while she turned the shells over in her hands, or take out the star blanket and count the stars on it. He watched her find things on the mountain and rejoice over them, things that he had seen, unseeing, for years. What new dimensions she found and lived in were not of his liking, and he grew to dislike and then hate the mountain and her preoccupation with it.

"Next spring," he said, "we're going up another mountain. This one's been overgrazed, and it's too crowded."

She glanced at him and then up at the ledged peak.

"We'll find new places on the next mountain. Maybe it will have shells like the cowboy said."

"You're wasting time looking for shells on a mountain. That kind of talk is for kids and old folks, we're looking for grazing land." He frowned at her and held her arm tightly. "You forget that kind of talk. And forget that cowboy."

"I won't. You always think I'm strange. But I'm not. I can wonder about anything I want to." She pulled away from him.

"You're thinking about that cowboy. I heard you talking to him, and looking at him." He raged at her, suddenly jealous, suddenly aware that she was more than a convenience.

He took her by the shoulders and shook her. She glared at him and ground her teeth. He released her and went to the fire. They had supper and lay down to sleep. After a few minutes he went to her and took her body fiercely to his. She lay passive, looking at him with a fresh awareness of his body. She felt the coarse hairs of his body and the perspiration running down his face. At once she remembered his kindness to her on that first night. What had made him change over the years? She felt the thrusting of his body and a quick discomfort about the child. She tried to push him away, saying, "Stop. The baby. You're hurting me."

He continued to thrust against her, determined to reclaim her from the mountain, to bring her back to the docile wife she had been. Through the haze of desire and his own loneliness he finally heard her words and their meaning. He stopped, resting heavily against her, looking into her eyes. She resisted him now not only with her body, but with her will. He turned away from her body and lay beside her. They lay side by side on the mountain slope, he gazing at her with a lonely despair, she lying silent, no longer resisting him, but mute and aloof, part of the mountain, removed utterly from his grasp, eyes turned inward to the remote workings of her own mind and body.

She lay resting softly against the mountain, listening somehow to the silent workings of the child within her, feeling the kicking and stretching of the unborn, sensing a rebellious anger in its movements. She touched her stomach, marvelling at the fruitful fullness that jutted imperiously against the black night sky.

"Mountains grow from the inside out." It was that way with her. The vigorous, active wonder within her was pushing her body out of shape to accommodate its own demands, lying heavily against her spine. She stretched a hand out against the peaceful tilting mountain slope, feeling the roundness of it, imagining the massed bones and structure beneath. She nestled against the curve of the mountain and slept.

The next day they reached the summer grazing land. The mountain here was open for miles to flats of grassland and small ponds filled with ice water from underground springs. The sheep would graze for weeks before exhausting the ground cover. The man and woman set up a tent against a windfall of trees, gathered the broken, sun-dried wood into stacks for their small summer fire, and prepared for the weeks of wandering after the sheep during the day and returning at night to the same spot.

The woman continued her search for shells, although aware that none would be found in the grass-grown flats. She walked with the sheep and the horse, disappearing into the alleys that led up and into the mountain. From time to time she saw deer and rabbits staring out from the mountain's secret avenues, heard birds calling above her and felt the silence of the mountain. She walked daily higher through the trees and ledges, following dead stream beds into echoing chambers of the mountain's interior. As she picked her way deeper into the mountain she lost track of what she was looking for, listening to the stillness of the mountain and the creak of trees. She followed the mysterious silent voice of the mountain as it led her farther from her husband and his sheep to some invisible, lost, unspeaking essence that beckoned her and charmed her senses with a provocative, almost sensual desire. When night fell on the mountain she would drift down through the ground mists to the camp, lost in the wanderings of her mind, to prepare supper.

Her nights were filled with the campfire, her husband and his talk of the sheep, the alien duties of cooking and eating. She cooked and ate in silence, looking at the pots and plates, trying to recognize some familiar quality about them. Her husband's face, once so involved with herself as to be her own identity, now was foreign and harsh.

He would look at her over his plate, wondering at her silence. He spoke to her and received no answer.

"I shot a deer today," he'd say. "We'll have meat every day now and dry the rest." He'd pause and wait for her reply. None came.

"How's your sewing? You finish all that flannel?" He stoked his mouth with tobacco and closed the tin.

"Hey! Answer me!" He threw a stick at her.

She turned her head in his direction, inquiringly.

"Talk to me!" He threw another stick at her.

"Yes." She smiled in his direction, her eyes looking through him into the dark beyond.

"You are queerer now than you used to be." He rolled the tobacco in his mouth. "Is it the baby?"

"The baby is fine. We walked into the mountain today. There's something up there." She took out the star blanket and unrolled it over her knees.

"What's up there? I suppose there's deer and a few bear. You be careful when you go alone." He peered at her, watching her hands stroking the stars on the blanket.

"No, there's something up there that I can't find. I can almost hear it. Sometimes when I come around the corner of a ravine I think it will be standing there. But it never is."

"You take a dog with you tomorrow. And take the rifle."

"No. The dogs might frighten it away. And I don't want to shoot it. I want to find it and see what it is."

Her husband stood up, throwing the remaining coffee into the fire. "Well, you better stay close to camp. Your time is almost here and you don't figure that thing in the mountain is going to help you any, do you?"

"No, I just want to find it." She opened her blankets for the night. "I feel like the baby is moving down. When can I start for the ranch?"

"I don't figure on letting you go. You talk so strange they might not let you come back." He lay next to her, holding her head in his hands. "You going crazy on me?"

She shook her head. "No, can't you tell there's something waiting in the mountain?"

"There isn't anything in that mountain but deer and bear." He pulled her down to his chest. "Now you just forget that crazy talk and think about how you're going to have that baby here in camp."

"You promised I could go to the ranch and have a woman help me."

She huddled beside him, her distended abdomen pushing him away from her as his arms tightened about her.

"No, I've been thinking. You go down mountain to that ranch and read those books about shells and growing mountains and you'll get so crazy you won't come back."

"I will come back. Oh, let me go down. I'm afraid of being alone when the baby comes."

"What help you need, I'll give you. If I can bring sheep, I can bring a baby." He looked at her cunningly, "If you stay here you can hunt for that thing."

She looked levelly at him. "You are breaking your promise."

"Promises are for people who can use them. This promise is better used broken. I'll take care of you and the boy when he comes."

Her eyes flickered and she looked away toward the horse.

"I'll be taking the horse with me every day from now on, so you won't be trying to sneak out on him." He spoke with his eyes closed.

"I don't like you for this," she said. "If the baby is hurt by your keeping me here, it's all your blame."

"No blame will be coming. I'll take care of that." He slept leaning against her, holding her body as if to keep her with him even in sleep.

During the rest of her time, the woman walked restlessly through the mountain's interiors. She spoke to the mountain and the thing that haunted her. "Let me have the baby easily and quickly, don't let the baby be hurt." The listening air around her echoed upon the mountain walls: *Hurt*.

Early in the morning her labor began. She went into the tent and lay on the blankets. Her husband watched her face and said, "I'll just take the sheep out to the grazing and come right back." She nodded and he left.

When he didn't return when she expected him, she crept out of the tent to watch for him. She lay on her side against the yielding slope, resting between pains, holding the star blanket to her, twisting it between her hands when the pains reached their peak, relaxing when the pains subsided.

She watched the sun climb the hill of the sky and descend. At times it seemed as if she must fall off the shoulder of the earth and down into the sky. Moments went by that she clung to the side of the mountain, feeling a pulsebeat under her, hearing a beating in the air as if the mountain were heaving with her and falling out from under her. She was sweating heavily, her body sliding within her clothes, her hands were slippery in the grass and on the blanket. The pains increased in rapidity and strength until she was constantly knotted with them, breathing harshly through her mouth. She was swept from the side of the mountain at one second, and pushed back into it at the next. Then, suddenly, the child was forced from her body into the air, and the mountain stopped twisting beneath her. She lay spent, watching the mountain fall back into place above her. Then she sat up and reached for the child. Its face turned up to hers, utterly lifeless. The cord between the child and the afterbirth had strangled it, choking off its first cry. She looked down at it dumbly, hearing a forlorn wail from beyond her ken. She held the dead child to her, rocking it. She twisted the cord from its neck, and covered the child and all in the star blanket.

When the man returned he found her sitting on the slope, holding the dead child wrapped in its bloodied star blanket.

"I lost my way in those ravines. How's the boy?"

"He's dead. choked on the cord." She smoothed the blanket over the child.

"Let me see. Huh. He never got his breath." The man turned the child about in the blanket, touching the round, puckered face, the blunt features, the scruff of hair.

"Well, you rest. I'll bury him in the trees." He walked away with the child.

"No, don't bury him up here. Let me take him down so he can have a mark on his grave." She went after the man, reaching for the child.

"No need in that. He died here and he can stay here." He laid the baby under a tree and dug a shallow grave. She stood, leaning against the tree, eyes averted. He buried the child and covered the small enclosure with branches and stones. "This tree can be his mark. He never needed more than that."

The woman sat beside the grave and dropped leaves gently on it, seeming to hear a heartbeat from the buried child. She laid her head down on the branches and closed her eyes. "I'll stay here with him until morning. He might be lonely and afraid all alone."

The man nodded and walked to the camp.

That night, lying next to her child's grave she listened to the sounds of the mountain and dreamed about the child.

In the morning the man prepared to take the sheep away to the grazing. The woman went to the fire and cleaned herself. When the man spoke to her she said: "You take the sheep today. I want the horse."

The man looked at her. She found her string of shells and put them into a pocket. "I'm going down mountain."

"What for, you don't need help any more."

"I'm going down mountain," she said stubbornly. "I let you strangle my baby with your ideas of keeping and using."

"I didn't strangle the baby." He stepped toward her, hands out.

"No, not likely, but it's the same." She called the horse and turned down the mountain.

"You figure you're going to find some shells?" He called at her, running after the horse. "You won't find any. Ever. There's no use looking!"

"I want to look. I want to see what it's like to look."

"You'll be back. You'll see. There's no use in it at all!"

"No, no use at all." She looked at him for the last time and rode down the mountain.

Accomplished Desires

Joyce Carol Oates

There was a man she loved with a violent love, and she spent much of her time thinking about his wife.

No shame to it, she actually followed the wife. She followed her to Peabody's Market, which was a small, dark crowded store, and she stood in silence on the pavement as the woman appeared again and got into her station wagon and drove off. The girl, Dorie, would stand as if paralyzed, and even her long fine blond hair seemed paralyzed with thought—her heart pounded as if it too was thinking, planning—and then she would turn abruptly as if executing one of the steps in her modern dance class and cross through Peabody's alley and out to the Elks' Club parking lot and so up toward the campus, where the station wagon was bound.

Hardly had the station wagon pulled into the driveway when Dorie, out of breath, appeared a few houses down and watched. How that woman got out of a car!—you could see the flabby expanse of her upper leg, white flesh that should never be exposed, and then she turned and leaned in, probably with a grunt, to get shopping bags out of the back seat. Two of her children ran out to meet her, without coats or jackets. They had nervous, darting bodies—Dorie felt sorry for them—and their mother rose, straightening, a stout woman in a colorless coat, either scolding them or teasing them, one bag in either muscular arm—and so—so the mother and children went into the house and Dorie stood with nothing to stare at except the battered station wagon, and the small snowy wilderness that was the Arbers' front yard, and the house itself. It was a large, ugly, peeling Victorian home in a block of similar homes, most of which had been fixed up by the faculty members who rented them. Dorie, who had something of her own mother's shrewd eye for hopeless, cast-off things, believed that the house could be remodeled and made presentable—but as long as he remained married to *that woman* it would be slovenly and peeling and ugly.

She loved that woman's husband with a fierce love that was itself a little ugly. Always a rather stealthy girl, thought to be simply quiet, she had entered his life by no accident—had not appeared in his class by accident—but every step of her career, like every outfit she wore and every expression on her face, was planned and shrewd and desperate. Before her twenties she had not thought much about herself; now she thought about herself continuously. She was leggy, long-armed, slender, and had a startled look—but the look was stylized now, and attractive. Her face was denuded of make-up and across her soft skin a galaxy of freckles glowed with health. She looked like a girl about to bound onto the tennis courts—and she did play tennis, though awkwardly. She played tennis with *him*. But so confused with love was she that the game of tennis, the relentless slamming of the ball back and forth, had seemed to her a disguise for something else, the way everything in poetry or literature was a disguise for something else—for love?—and surely he must know, or didn't he know? Didn't he guess? There were many other girls he played tennis with, so that was nothing special, and her mind worked and worked while she should have slept, planning with the desperation of youth that has never actually been young—planning how to get him, how to get him, for it seemed to her that she would never be able to overcome her desire for this man.

The wife was as formidable as the husband. She wrote narrow volumes of poetry Dorie could not understand and he, the famous husband, wrote novels and critical pieces. The wife was a big, energetic, high-colored woman; the husband, Mark Arber, was about her size though not so high-colored—his complexion was rather putty-colored, rather melancholy. Dorie thought about the two of them all the time, awake or asleep, and she could feel the terrible sensation of blood flowing through her body, a flowing of desire that was not just for the man but somehow for the woman as well, a desire for her accomplishments, her fame, her children, her ugly house, her ugly body, her very life. She had light, frank blue eyes and people whispered that she drank; Dorie never spoke of her.

The college was a girls' college, exclusive and expensive, and every girl who remained there for more than a year understood a peculiar, even freakish kinship with the place—as if she had always been there and the other girls, so like herself with their sleepy unmade-up faces, the skis in winter and the bicycles in good weather, the excellent expensive professors, and the excellent air—everything, everything had always been there, had existed for centuries. They were stylish and liberal in their cashmere sweaters with soiled necks; their fingers were stained with ballpoint ink; and like them, Dorie understood that most of the world was wretched and would never come to this college, never, would be kept back from it by armies of helmeted men. She, Dorie Weinheimer, was not wretched but supremely fortunate, and she must be grateful always for her good luck, for there was no justification for her existence any more than there was any justification for the wretched lots of the world's poor. And there would flash to her mind's eye a confused picture of dark-faced starving mobs, or emaciated faces out of an old-fashioned Auschwitz photograph, or something—some dreary horror from the *New York Times'* one hundred neediest cases in the Christmas issue— She had, in the girls' soft, persistent manner, an idealism-turned·pragmatism under the influence of the college faculty, who had all been idealists at Harvard and Yale as undergraduates but who were now in their forties, and as impatient with normative values as they were with their students' occasional lockets-shaped-into-crosses; Mark Arber was the most disillusioned and the most eloquent of the Harvard men.

In class he sat at the head of the seminar table, leaning back in his leather-covered chair. He was a rather stout man. He had played football once in a past Dorie could not quite imagine, though she wanted to imagine it, and he had been in the war—one of the wars—she believed it had been World War II. He had an ugly, arrogant face and discolored teeth. He read poetry in a raspy, hissing, angry voice. "Like Marx, I believe that poetry has had enough of love; the hell with it. Poetry should now cultivate the whip," he would say grimly, and Dorie would stare at him to see if he was serious. There were four senior girls in this class and they sometimes asked him questions or made observations of their own, but there was no consistency in his reaction. Sometimes he seemed not to hear, sometimes he nodded enthusiastically and indifferently, sometimes he opened his eyes and looked at them, not distinguishing among them, and said: "A remark like that is quite characteristic." So she sat and stared at him and her heart seemed to turn to stone, wanting him, hating his wife and envying her violently, and the being that had been Dorie

Weinheimer for twenty-one years changed gradually through the winter into another being, obsessed with jealousy. She did not know what she wanted most, this man or the victory over his wife.

She was always bringing poems to him in his office. She borrowed books from him and puzzled over every annotation of his. As he talked to her he picked at his fingernails, settled back in his chair, and he talked on in his rushed, veering, sloppy manner, as if Dorie did not exist or were a crowd, or a few intimate friends, it hardly mattered, as he raved about frauds in contemporary poetry, naming names, "that bastard with his sonnets," "that cow with her daughter-poems," and getting so angry that Dorie wanted to protest, no, no, why are you angry? Be gentle. Love me and be gentle.

When he failed to come to class six or seven times that winter the girls were all understanding. "Do you think he really is a genius?" they asked. His look of disintegrating, decomposing recklessness, his, shiny suit and bizarre loafer shoes, his flights of language made him so different from their own fathers that it was probable he was a genius; these were girls who believed seriously in the existence of geniuses. They had been trained by their highly paid, verbose professors to be vaguely ashamed of themselves, to be silent about any I.Q. rated under 160, to be uncertain about their talents within the school and quite confident of them outside it—and Dorie, who had no talent and only adequate intelligence, was always silent about herself. Her talent perhaps lay in her faithfulness to an obsession, her cunning patience, her smile, her bared teeth that were a child's teeth and yet quite sharp. . . .

One day Dorie had been waiting in Dr. Arber's office for an hour, with some new poems for him. He was late but he strode into the office as if he had been hurrying all along, sitting heavily in the creaking swivel chair, panting; he looked a little mad. He was the author of many reviews in New York magazines and papers and in particular the author of three short, frightening novels, and now he had a burned-out, bleached-out look. Like any of the girls at this college, Dorie would have sat politely if one of her professors set fire to himself, and so she ignored his peculiar stare and began her rehearsed speech about—but what did it matter what it was about? The poems of Emily Dickinson or the terrible yearning of Shelley or her own terrible lust, what did it matter? He let his hand fall onto hers by accident. She stared at the hand, which was like a piece of meat—and she stared at him and was quite still. She was pert and long-haired, in the chair facing him, an anonymous student and a minor famous man, and every wrinkle of his sagging, impatient face was bared to her in the winter sunlight from the window—and every thread of blood in his eyes—and quite calmly and politely she said, "I guess I should tell you, Dr. Arber, that I'm in love with you. I've felt that way for some time."

"You what, you're what?" he said. He gripped her feeble hand as if clasping it in a handshake. "What did you say?" He spoke with an amazed, slightly irritated urgency, and so it began.

II

His wife wrote her poetry under an earlier name, Barbara Scott. Many years before she had had a third name, a maiden name—Barbara Cameron—but it belonged to another era about which she never thought except under examination from her analyst. She had a place cleared in the dirty attic of her house and she liked to sit up there, away from the children, and look out the small octagon of a window, and think. People she saw from her attic window looked bizarre and helpless to her. She herself was a hefty, perspiring woman, and all her dresses—especially her expensive ones—were stained under the arms with great lemon-colored half-moons no dry cleaner could remove. Because she was so large a woman, she was quick to see imperfections in others, as if she used a magnifying glass. Walking by her window on an ordinary morning were an aged tottering woman, an enormous Negro woman—probably someone's cleaning lady—and a girl from the college on aluminum crutches, poor brave thing, and the white-blond child from up the street who was precocious and demonic. Her own children were precocious and only slightly troublesome. Now two of them were safe in school and the youngest, the three-year-old, was asleep somewhere.

Barbara Scott had won the Pulitzer Prize not long before with an intricate sonnet series that dealt with the "voices" of many people; her energetic, coy line was much imitated. This morning she began a poem that her agent was to sell, after Barbara's death, to the *New Yorker:*

What awful wrath
what terrible betrayal
and these aluminum crutches, rubber-tipped. . . .

She had such a natural talent that she let words take her anywhere. Her decade of psychoanalysis had trained her to hold
nothing back; even when she had nothing to say, the very authority of her technique carried her on. So she sat that morning at her big, nicked desk—over the years the children had
marred it with sharp toys—and stared out the window and
waited for more inspiration. She felt the most intense kind of
sympathy when she saw someone deformed—she was anxious, in a way, to see deformed people because it released
such charity in her. But apart from the girl on the crutches
she saw nothing much. Hours passed and she realized that
her husband had not come home; already school was out and
her two boys were running across the lawn.

When she descended the two flights of stairs to the kitchen,
she saw that the three-year-old, Geoffrey, had opened a white
plastic bottle of ammonia and had spilled it on the floor and
on himself; the stench was sickening. The two older boys
bounded in the back door as if spurred on by the argument
that raged between them, and Barbara whirled upon them
and began screaming. The ammonia had spilled onto her
slacks. The boys ran into the front room and she remained in
the kitchen, screaming. She sat down heavily on one of the
kitchen chairs. After half a hour she came to herself and
tried to analyze the situation. Did she hate these children, or
did she hate herself? Did she hate Mark? Or was her hysteria
a form of love, or was it both love and hate together . . . ?
She put the ammonia away and made herself a drink.

When she went into the front room she saw that the boys
were playing with their mechanical inventors' toys and had
forgotten about her. Good. They were self-reliant. Slight,
cunning children, all of them dark like Mark and prema-
turely aged, as if by the burden of their prodigious intelli-
gences, they were not always predictable: they forgot things,
lost things, lied about things, broke things, tripped over themselves and each other, mimicked classmates, teachers, and
their parents, and often broke down into pointless tears. And
yet sometimes they did not break down into tears when Barbara punished them, as if to challenge her. She did not always know what she had given birth to: they were so remote,
even in their struggles and assaults, they were so fictional, as

if she had imagined them herself. It had been she who'd imagined them, not Mark. Their father had no time. He was always in a hurry, he had three aged typewriters in his study and paper in each one, an article or a review or even a novel in progress in each of the machines, and he had no time for the children except to nod grimly at them or tell them to be quiet. He had been so precocious himself, Mark Arber, that after his first, successful novel at the age of twenty-four he had had to whip from place to place, from typewriter to typewriter, in a frantic attempt to keep up with—he called it keeping up with his "other self," his "real self," evidently a kind of alter ego who was always typing and creating, unlike the real Mark Arber. The real Mark Arber was now forty-five and he had made the transition from "promising" to "established" without anything in between, like most middle-aged critics of prominence.

Strachey, the five-year-old, had built a small machine that was both a man and an automobile, operated by the motor that came with the set of toys. "This is a modern centaur," he said wisely, and Barbara filed that away, thinking perhaps it would do well in a poem for a popular, slick magazine. . . . She sat, unbidden, and watched her boys' intense work with the girders and screws and bolts, and sluggishly she thought of making supper, or calling Mark at school to see what had happened . . . that morning he had left the house in a rage and when she went into his study, prim and frowning, she had discovered four or five crumpled papers in his wastebasket. It was all he had accomplished that week.

Mark had never won the Pulitzer Prize for anything. People who knew him spoke of his slump, familiarly and sadly; if they disliked Mark they praised Barbara, and if they disliked Barbara they praised Mark. They were "established" but it did not mean much, younger writers were being discovered all the time who had been born in the mid- or late forties, strangely young, terrifyingly young, and people the Arbers' age were being crowded out, hustled toward the exits. . . . Being "established" should have pleased them, but instead it led them to long spiteful bouts of eating and drinking in the perpetual New England winter.

She made another drink and fell asleep in the chair. Sometime later her children's fighting woke her and she said, "Shut up," and they obeyed at once. They were playing in the darkened living room, down at the other end by the big brick fireplace that was never used. Her head ached. She got to her feet and went out to make another drink.

Around one o'clock Mark came in the back door. He stumbled and put the light on. Barbara, in her plaid bathrobe, was sitting at the kitchen table. She had a smooth, shiny, bovine face, heavy with fatigue. Mark said, "What the hell are you doing here?"

She attempted a shrug of her shoulders. Mark stared at her. "I'm getting you a housekeeper," he said. "You need more time for yourself, for your work. For your work," he said, twisting his mouth at the word to show what he thought of it. "You shouldn't neglect your poetry so we're getting in a housekeeper, not to do any heavy work, just to sort of watch things—in other words—a kind of external consciousness. You should be freed from ordinary considerations."

He was not drunk but he had the appearance of having been drunk, hours before, and now his words were muddled and dignified with the air of words spoken too early in the morning. He wore a dirty tweed overcoat, the same coat he'd had when they were married, and his necktie had been pulled off and stuffed somewhere, and his puffy, red face looked mean. Barbara thought of how reality was too violent for poetry and how poetry, and the language itself, shimmered helplessly before the confrontation with living people and their demands. "The housekeeper is here. She's outside," Mark said. "I'll go get her."

He returned with a college girl who looked like a hundred other college girls. "This is Dorie, this is my wife Barbara, you've met no doubt at some school event, here you are," Mark said. He was carrying a suitcase that must have belonged to the girl. "Dorie has requested room and board with a faculty family. The Dean of Women arranged it. Dorie will babysit or something—we can put her in the spare room. Let's take her up."

Barbara had not yet moved. The girl was pale and distraught; she looked about sixteen. Her hair was disheveled. She stared at Barbara and seemed about to speak.

"Let's take her up, you want to sit there all night?" Mark snarled.

Barbara indicated with a motion of her hand that they should go up without her. Mark, breathng heavily, stomped up the back steps and the girl followed at once. There was no indication of her presence because her footsteps were far too light on the stairs. She said nothing, and only a slight change in the odor of the kitchen indicated something new—a scent of cologne, hair scrubbed clean, a scent of panic. Barbara sat listening to her heart thud heavily inside her and she recalled how, several years before, Mark had left her and had turned up at a friend's apartment in Chicago—he'd been beaten up by someone on the street, an accidental event—and how he had blackened her eye once in an argument over the worth of Samuel Richardson, and how—there were many other bitter memories—and of course there had been other women, some secret and some known—and now this—

So she sat thinking with a small smile of how she would have to dismiss this when she reported it to their friends: *Mark has had this terrible block for a year now, with his novel, and so . . .*

She sat for a while running through phrases and explanations, and when she climbed up the stairs to bed she was grimly surprised to see him in their bedroom, asleep, his mouth open and his breath raspy and exhausted. At the back of the house, in a small oddly shaped maid's room, slept the girl; in their big dormer room slept the three boys, or perhaps they only pretended to sleep; and only she, Barbara, stood in the dark and contemplated the bulk of her own body, wondering what to do and knowing that there was nothing she would do, no way for her to change the process of events any more than she could change the heavy fact of her body itself. There was no way to escape what the years had made her.

III

From that time on they lived together like a family. Or it was as Mark put it: "Think of a babysitter here permanently. Like the Lunt girl, staying on here permanently to help, only we won't need that one any more." Barbara made breakfast for them all, and then Mark and Dorie drove off to school and returned late, between six and six-thirty, and in the evenings Mark worked hard at his typewriters, going to sit at one and then the next and then the next, and the girl, Dorie, helped Barbara with the dishes and odd chores and went up to her room, where she studied . . . or did something, she must have done something.

Of the long afternoons he and the girl were away Mark

said nothing. He was evasive and jaunty; he looked younger. He explained carefully to Dorie that when he and Mrs. Arber were invited somewhere she must stay home and watch the children, that she was not included in these invitations; and the girl agreed eagerly. She did so want to help around the house! She had inherited from her background a dislike for confusion—so the mess of the Arber house upset her and she worked for hours picking things up, polishing tarnished objects Barbara herself had forgotten were silver, cleaning, arranging, fixing. As soon as the snow melted she was to be seen outside, raking shyly through the flower beds. How to explain her to the neighbors? Barbara said nothing.

"But I didn't think we lived in such a mess. I didn't think it was so bad," Barbara would say to Mark in a quiet, hurt voice, and he would pat her hand and say, "It isn't a mess, she just likes to fool around. *I* don't think it's a mess."

It was fascinating to live so close to a young person. Barbara had never been young in quite the way Dorie was young. At breakfast—they ate crowded around the table—everyone could peer into everyone else's face, there were no secrets, stale mouths and bad moods were inexcusable, all the wrinkles of age or distress that showed on Barbara could never be hidden, and not to be hidden was Mark's guilty enthusiasm, his habit of saying, "*We* should go to . . . ," *We* are invited . . ." and the "we" meant either him and Barbara, or him and Dorie, but never all three; he had developed a new personality. But Dorie was fascinating. She awoke to the slow gray days of spring with a panting, wondrous expectation, her blond hair shining, her freckles clear as dabs of clever paint on her heartbreaking skin, her teeth very, very white and straight, her pert little lips innocent of lipstick and strangely sensual . . . yes, it was heartbreaking. She changed her clothes at least twice a day while Barbara wore the same outfit—baggy black slacks and a black sweater—for weeks straight. Dorie appeared downstairs in cashmere sweater sets that were the color of birds' eggs, or of birds' fragile legs, and white trim blouses that belonged on a genteel hockey field, and bulky pink sweaters big as jackets, and when she was dressed casually she wore stretch slacks that were neatly secured by stirrups around her long, narrow, white feet. Her eyes were frankly and emptily brown, as if giving themselves up to every observer. She was so anxious to help that it was oppressive; "No, I can manage, I've been making breakfast for eight years by myself," Barbara would say angrily, and

Dorie, a chastised child, would glance around the table not only at Mark but at the children for sympathy. Mark had a blackboard set up in the kitchen so that he could test the children's progress in languages, and he barked out commands for them—French or Latin or Greek words—and they responded with nervous glee, clacking out letters on the board, showing off for the rapt, admiring girl who seemed not to know if they were right or wrong.

"Oh, how smart they are—how wonderful everything is," Dorie breathed.

Mark had to drive to Boston often because he needed his prescription for tranquillizers refilled constantly, and his doctor would not give him an automatic refill. But though Barbara had always looked forward to these quick trips, he rarely took her now. He went off with Dorie, now his "secretary," who took along a notebook decorated with the college's insignia to record his impressions in, and since he never gave his wife warning she could not get ready in time, and it was such an obvious trick, so crudely cruel, that Barbara stood in the kitchen and wept as they drove out. . . . She called up friends in New York but never exactly told them what was going on. It was so ludicrous, it made her seem such a fool. Instead she chatted and barked with laughter; her conversations with these people were always so witty that nothing, nothing seemed very real until she hung up the receiver again; and then she became herself, in a drafty college-owned house in New England, locked in this particular body.

She stared out the attic window for hours, not thinking. She became a state of being, a creature. Downstairs the children fought, or played peacefully, or rifled through their father's study, which was forbidden, and after a certain amount of time something would nudge Barbara to her feet and she would descend slowly, laboriously, as if returning to the real world where any ugliness was possible. When she slapped the boys for being bad, they stood in meek defiance and did not cry. "Mother, you're out of your mind," they said. "Mother, you're losing control of yourself."

"It's your father who's out of his mind!" she shouted.

She had the idea that everyone was talking about them, everyone. Anonymous, worthless people who had never published a line gloated over her predicament; high-school baton twirlers were better off than Barbara Scott, who had no dignity. Dorie, riding with Mark Arber on the expressway to Boston, was at least young and stupid, anonymous though she was, and probably she too had a slim collection of poems that Mark would manage to get published . . . and who knew what would follow, who could tell? Dorie Weinheimer was like any one of five hundred or five thousand college girls and was no one, had no personality, and yet Mark Arber had somehow fallen in love with her, so perhaps everyone would eventually fall in love with her . . . ? Barbara imagined with panic the parties she knew nothing about to which Mark and his new girl went: Mark in his slovenly tweed suits, looking like his own father in the thirties, and Dorie chick as a Vogue model in her weightless bones and vacuous face.

"Is Dorie going to stay here long?" the boys kept asking.

"Why, don't you like her?"

"She's nice. She smells nice. Is she going to stay long?"

"Go ask your father that," Barbara said angrily.

The girl was officially boarding with them; it was no lie. Every year certain faculty families took in a student or two, out of generosity or charity, or because they themselves needed the money, and the Arbers themselves had always looked down upon such hearty liberalism. But now they had Dorie, and in Peabody's Market Barbara had to rush up and down the aisles with her shopping cart, trying to avoid the wives of other professors who were sure to ask her about the new boarder; and she had to buy special things for the girl, spinach and beets and artichokes, while Barbara and Mark liked starches and sweets and fat, foods that clogged up the blood vessels and strained the heart and puffed out the stomach. While Barbara ate and drank hungrily, Dorie sat chaste with her tiny forkfuls of food, and Barbara could eat three platefuls to Dorie's one; her appetite increased savagely just in the presence of the girl. (The girl was always asking politely, "Is it the boys who get the bathroom all dirty?" or "Could I take the vacuum cleaner down and have it fixed?" and these questions, polite as they were, made Barbara's appetite increase savagely.)

In April, after Dorie had been boarding with them three and a half months, Barbara was up at her desk when there was a rap on the plywood door. Unused to visitors, Barbara turned clumsily and looked at Mark over the top of her glasses. "Can I come in?" he said. "What are you working on?"

There was no paper in her typewriter. "Nothing," she said.

"You haven't shown me any poems lately. What's wrong?"

He sat on the window ledge and lit a cigarette. Barbara felt a spiteful satisfaction to see how old he looked—he hadn't her fine, fleshed-out skin, the smooth complexion of an overweight woman; he had instead the bunched, baggy complexion of an overweight man whose weight keeps shifting up and down. Good. Even his fingers shook as he lit the cigarette.

"This is the best place in the house," he said.

"Do you want me to give it up to Dorie?"

He stared at her. "Give it up—why? Of course not."

"I thought you might be testing my generosity."

He shook his head, puzzled. Barbara wondered if she hated this man or if she felt a writer's interest in him. Perhaps he was insane. Or perhaps he had been drinking again; he had not gone out to his classes this morning and she'd heard him arguing with Dorie. "Barbara, how old are you?" he said.

"Forty-three. You know that."

He looked around at the boxes and other clutter as if coming to an imporant decision. "Well, we have a little problem here."

Barbara stared at her blunt fingernails and waited.

"She got herself pregnant. It seems on purpose."

"She what?"

"Well," Mark said uncomfortably, "she did it on purpose."

They remained silent. After a while, in a different voice he said, "She claims she loves children. She loves our children and wants some of her own. It's a valid point, I can't deny her her rights . . . but . . . I thought you should know about it in case you agree to help."

"What do you mean?"

"Well, I have something arranged in Boston," he said, not looking at her, "and Dorie has agreed to it . . . though reluctantly . . . and unfortunately I don't think I can drive her myself . . . you know I have to go to Chicago. . . ."

Barbara did not look at him.

"I'm on this panel at the University of Chicago, with John Ciardi. You know, it's been set up for a year, it's on the state of contemporary poetry—you know—I can't possibly withdraw from it now—"

"And so?"

"If you could drive Dorie in—"

"If I could drive her in?"

"I don't see what alternative we have," he said slowly.

"Would you like a divorce so you can marry her?"

"I have never mentioned that," he said.

"Well, would you?"

"I don't know."

"Look at me. Do you want to marry her?"

A nerve began to twitch in his eye. It was a familiar twitch—it had been with him for two decades. "No, I don't think so. I don't know—you know how I feel about disruption."

"Don't you have any courage?"

"Courage?"

"If you want to marry her, go ahead. I won't stop you."

"Do you want a divorce yourself?"

"I'm asking you. It's up to you. Then Dorie can have her baby and fulfill herself," Barbara said with a deathly smile. "She can assert her rights as a woman twenty years younger than I. She can become the third Mrs. Arber and become automatically envied. Don't you have the courage for it?"

"I had thought," Mark said with dignity, "that you and I had an admirable marriage. It was different from the marriages of other people we know—part of it is that we don't work in the same area, yes, but the most important part lay in our understanding of each other. It has taken a tremendous generosity on your part, Barbara, over the last three months and I appreciate it," he said, nodding slowly, "I appreciate it and I can't help asking myself whether . . . whether I would have had the strength to do what you did, in your place. I mean, if you had brought in—"

"I know what you mean."

"It's been an extraordinary marriage. I don't want it to end on an impulse, anything reckless or emotional," he said vaguely. She thought that he did look a little mad, but quietly mad; his ears were very red. For the first time she began to feel pity for the girl who was, after all, nobody, and who had no personality, and who was waiting in the ugly maid's room for her fate to be decided.

"All right, I'll drive her to Boston," Barbara said.

IV

Mark had to leave the next morning for Chicago. He would be gone, he explained, about a week—there was not only the speaking appearance but other things as well. The three of them had a kind of farewell party the night before. Dorie sat with her frail hand on her flat, child's stomach and drank listlessly, while Barbara and Mark argued about the comparative merits of two English novelists—their literary arguments were always witty, superficial, rapid, and very enjoyable. At two o'clock Mark woke Dorie to say good-by and Barbara, thinking herself admirably discreet, went upstairs alone.

She drove Dorie to Boston the next day. Dorie was a mother's child, the kind of girl mothers admire—clean, bright, passive—and it was a shame for her to be so frightened. Barbara said roughly, "I've known lots of women who've had abortions. They lived."

"Did you ever have one?"

"No."

Dorie turned away as if in reproach.

"I've had children and that's harder, maybe. It's thought to be harder," Barbara said, as if offering the girl something.

"I would like children, maybe three of them," Dorie said.

"Three is a good number, yes."

"But I'd be afraid . . . I wouldn't know what to do. . . . I don't know what to do now. . . ."

She was just a child herself, Barbara thought with a rush of sympathy; of all of them it was Dorie who was most trapped. The girl sat with a scarf around her careless hair, staring out the window. She wore a camel's hair coat like all the girls and her fingernails were colorless and uneven, as if she had been chewing them.

"Stop thinking about it. Sit still."

"Yes," the girl said listlessly.

They drove on. Something began to weigh at Barbara's heart, as if her flesh were aging moment by moment. She had never liked her body. Dorie's body was so much more prim and chaste and stylish, and her own body belonged to another age, a hearty nineteenth century where fat had been a kind of virtue. Barbara thought of her poetry, which was light and sometimes quite clever, the poetry of a girl, glimmering with half-seen visions and echoing with peculiar off-rhymes—and truly it ought to have been Dorie's poetry and not hers. She was not equal to her own writing. And, on the highway like this, speeding toward some tawdry destination, she had the sudden terrible conviction that language itself did not matter and that nothing mattered ultimately except the body, the human body and the bodies of other creatures and objects: what else existed?

Her own body was the only real fact about her. Dorie, huddled over in her corner, was another real fact and they were going to do something about it, defeat it. She thought of Mark already in Chicago, at a cocktail party, the words growing like weeds in his brain and his wit moving so rapidly through the brains of others that it was, itself, a kind of lie. It seemed strange to her that the two of them should move against Dorie, who suffered because she was totally real and helpless and gave up nothing of herself to words.

They arrived in Boston and began looking for the street. Barbara felt clumsy and guilty and did not dare to glance over at the girl. She muttered aloud as they drove for half an hour, without luck. Then she found the address. It was a small private hospital with a blank gray front. Barbara drove past it and circled the block and approached it again. "Come on, get hold of yourself," she said to Dorie's stiff profile, "this is no picnic for me either."

She stopped the car and she and Dorie stared out at the hospital, which looked deserted. The neighborhood itself seemed deserted. Finally Barbara said, with a heaviness she did not yet understand, "Let's find a place to stay tonight first. Let's get that settled." She took the silent girl to a motel on a boulevard and told her to wait in the room, she'd be back shortly. Dorie stared in a drugged silence at Barbara, who could have been her mother—there flashed between them the kind of camaraderie possible only between mother and daughter—and then Barbara left the room. Dorie remained sitting in a very light chair of imitation wood and leather. She sat so that she was staring at the edge of the bureau; occasionally her eye was attracted by the framed picture over the bed, of a woman in a red evening gown and a man in a tuxedo observing a waterfall by moonlight. She sat like this for quite a while, in her coat. A nerve kept twitching in her thigh but it did not bother her; it was a most energetic, thumping twitch, as if her very flesh were doing a dance. But it did not bother her. She remained there for a while, waking to the morning light, and it took her several panicked moments to remember where she was and who had brought her here. She had the immediate thought that she must be safe—if it was morning she must be safe—and someone had taken care of her, had seen what was best for her and had carried it out.

V

And so she became the third Mrs. Arber, a month after the second one's death. Barbara had been found dead in an elegant motel across the city, the Paradise Inn, which Mark thought was a brave, cynical joke; he took Barbara's death with an alarming, rhetorical melodrama, an alcoholic melancholy Dorie did not like. Barbara's "infinite courage" made Dorie resentful. The second Mrs. Arber had taken a large dose of sleeping pills and had died easily, because of the strain her body had made upon her heart; so that was that. But somehow it wasn't—because Mark kept talking about it, speculating on it, wondering: "She did it for the baby, to preserve life. It's astonishing, it's exactly like something in a novel," he said. He spoke with a perpetual guilty astonishment.

She married him and became Mrs. Arber, which surprised everyone. It surprised even Mark. Dorie herself was not very surprised, because a daydreamer is prepared for most things and in a way she had planned even this, though she had not guessed how it would come about. Surely she had rehearsed the second Mrs. Arber's suicide and funeral already a year before, when she'd known nothing, could have guessed nothing, and it did not really surprise her. Events lost their jagged edges and became hard and opaque and routine, drawing her into them. She was still a daydreamer, though she was Mrs. Arber. She sat at the old desk up in the attic and leaned forward on her bony elbows to stare out the window, contemplating the hopeless front yard and the people who strolled by, some of them who—she thought—glanced toward the house with a kind of amused contempt, as if aware of her inside. She was almost always home.

The new baby was a girl, Carolyn. Dorie took care of her endlessly and she took care of the boys; she hadn't been able to finish school. In the evening when all the children were at last asleep Mark would come out of his study and read to her in his rapid, impatient voice snatches of his new novel, or occasionally poems of his late wife's, and Dorie would stare at him and try to understand. She was transfixed with love for him and yet—and yet she was unable to locate this love in this particular man, unable to comprehend it. Mark was invited everywhere that spring; he flew all the way out to California to take part in a highly publicized symposium with George Steiner and James Baldwin, and Dorie stayed home. Geoffrey was seeing a psychiatrist in Boston and she had to drive him in every other day, and there was her own baby, and Mark's frequent visitors who arrived often without notice and stayed a week—sleeping late, staying up late, drinking, eating, arguing—it was exactly the kind of life she had known would be hers, and yet she could not adjust to it. Her baby was somehow mixed up in her mind with the other wife, as if it had been that woman's and only left to her, Dorie, for safekeeping. She was grateful that her baby was a girl because wasn't there always a kind of pact or understanding between women?

In June two men arrived at the house to spend a week, and Dorie had to cook for them. They were long, lean, gray-haired young men who were undefinable, sometimes very fussy, sometimes reckless and hysterical with wit, always rather insulting in a light, veiled manner Dorie could not catch. They were both vegetarians and could not tolerate anyone eating meat in their presence. One evening at a late dinner Dorie began to cry and had to leave the room, and the two guests and Mark and even the children were displeased with her. She went up to the attic and sat mechanically at the desk. It did no good to read Barbara Scott's poetry because she did not understand it. Her understanding had dropped to tending the baby and the boys, fixing meals, cleaning up and shopping, and taking the station wagon to the garage perpetually . . . and she had no time to go with the others to the tennis courts, or to accompany Mark to New York . . . and around her were human beings whose lives consisted of language, the grace of language, and she could no longer understand them. She felt strangely cheated, a part of her murdered, as if the abortion had taken place that day after all and something had been cut permanently out of her.

In a while Mark climbed the stairs to her. She heard him coming, she heard his labored breathing. "Here you are," he said, and slid his big beefy arms around her and breathed his liquory love into her face, calling her his darling, his beauty. After all, he did love her, it was real and his arms were real, and she still loved him although she had lost the meaning of that word. "Now will you come downstairs and apologize, please?" he said gently. "You've disturbed them and it can't be left like this. You know how I hate disruption."

She began weeping again, helplessly, to think that she had disturbed anyone, that she was this girl sitting at a battered desk in someone's attic, and no one else, no other person who might confidently take upon herself the meaning of this man's words—she was herself and that was a fact, a final fact she would never overcome.

Sandra

George P. Elliott

A few years ago I inherited a handsome, neo-Spanish house in a good neighborhood in Oakland. It was much too large for a single man, as I knew perfectly well; if I had behaved sensibly I would have sold it and stayed in my bachelor quarters; I could have got a good price for it. But I was not sensible; I liked the house very much; I was tired of my apartment-house life; I didn't need the money. Within a month I had moved in and set about looking for a housekeeper.

From the moment I began looking, everyone assured me that I should get a domestic slave. I was reluctant to get one, not so much because of the expense as because of my own inexperience. No one in my family had ever had one, and among my acquaintances there were not more than three or four who had any. Nevertheless, the arguments in favor of my buying a slave were too great to be ignored. The argument that irritated me most was the one used by the wives of my friends. "When you marry," they would say, "think how happy it would make your wife to have a domestic slave." Then they would offer, zealously, to select one for me. I preferred to do my own selecting. I began watching the classified ads for slaves for sale.

Some days there would be no slaves listed for sale at all; on Sundays there might be as many as ten. There would be a middle-aged Negro woman, twenty-two years' experience, best recommendations, $4500; or a thirty-five-year-old Oriental, speaks English, excellent cook, recommendations, $5000; or a middle-aged woman of German descent, very neat, no pets or vices, good cook, recommendations, $4800. Sensible choices, no doubt, but none of them appealed to me. Somewhere in the back of my mind there was the notion of the slave I wanted. It made me restless, looking; all I knew about it was that I wanted a female. I was hard to satisfy. I took to dropping by the Emeryville stores, near where my plant was

407

located, looking for a slave. What few there were in stock
were obviously of inferior quality. I knew that I would have
to canvass the large downtown stores to find what I wanted. I
saw the ads of Oakland's Own Department Store, announcing
their January white sale; by some quirk, they had listed seven
white domestic slaves at severely reduced prices. I took off a
Wednesday, the first day of the sale, and went to the store at
opening time, nine forty-five, to be sure to have the pick of
the lot.

Oakland's Own is much the largest department store in the
city. It has seven floors and two basements, and its quality
runs from $1498 consoles to factory-reject cotton work socks.
It has a good, solid merchandising policy, and it stands behind its goods in a reassuring, old-fashioned way. The wives
of my friends were opposed to my shopping in Oakland's
Own, because, they said, second-hand slaves were so much
better trained than new, and cost so little more. Nevertheless,
I went.

I entered the store the moment the doors opened, and went
straight up to the sixth floor on the elevator. All the same I
found a shapeless little woman in the slave alcove ahead of
me picking over the goods—looking at their teeth and hair,
telling them to bend over, to speak so she could hear the
sound of their voices, stick out their tongue, like an army
doctor. I was furious at having been nosed out by the
woman, but I could not help admiring the skill and authority
with which she inspected her merchandise. She told me something about herself. She maintained a staff of four, but what
with bad luck, disease, and her husband's violent temper she
was always having trouble. The Federal Slave Board had
ruled against her twice—against her husband, really, but the
slaves were registered in her name—and she had to watch her
step. In fact she was on probation from the FSB now. One
more adverse decision and she didn't know what she'd do.
Well, she picked a strong, stolid-looking female, ordered two
sets of conventional domestic costumes for her, signed the
charge slip, and left. The saleswoman came to me.

I had made my decision. I had made it almost the moment
I had come in, and I had been in agonies for fear the dumpy
little shopper would choose my girl. She was not beautiful exactly, though not plain either, nor did she look especially
strong. I did not trouble to read her case-history card; I did
not even find out her name. I cannot readily explain what
there was about her that attracted me. A certain air of in-

souciance as she stood waiting to be looked over—the bored way she looked at her fingernails and yet the fearful glance she cast from time to time at us shoppers, the vulgarity of her make-up and the soft charm of her voice—I do not know. Put it down to the line of her hip as she stood waiting, a line girlish and womanly at once, dainty and strong, at ease but not indolent. It's what I remember of her best from that day, the long pure line from her knee to her waist as she stood staring at her nails, cocky and scared and humming to herself.

I knew I should pretend impartiality and indifference about my choice. Even Oakland's Own permits haggling over the price of slaves; I might knock the price down as much as $300, particularly since I was paying for her cash on the line. But it wasn't worth the trouble to me. After three weeks of dreary looking I had found what I wanted, and I didn't feel like waiting to get it. I asked the saleswoman for the card on my slave. She was the sixth child of a carpenter in Chico. Chico is a miserable town in the plains of the San Joaquin Valley; much money is spent each year teaching the people of Chico how to read and write; "chico" means greasewood. Her father had put her up for sale, with her own consent, at the earliest legal age, eighteen, the year of graduation from high school. The wholesaler had taught her the rudiments of cooking, etiquette, and housecleaning. She was listed as above average in cleanliness, intelligence, and personality, superb in copulation, and fair in versatility and sewing. But I had known as much from just looking at her, and I didn't care. Her name was Sandra, and in a way I had known that too. She had been marked down from $3850 to $3299. As the saleswoman said, how could I afford to pass up such a bargain? I got her to knock the price down the amount of the sales taxes, wrote out my check, filled out the FSB forms, and took my slave Sandra over to be fitted with clothes.

And right there I had my first trouble as a master, right on the fifth floor of Oakland's Own in the Women's Wear department. As a master, I was supposed to say to Sandra, or even better to the saleswoman about Sandra, "Plain cotton underwear, heavyweight nylon stockings, two dark-blue maid's uniforms and one street dress of conservative cut," and so on and so on. *The slave submits to the master:* I had read it in the FSB manual for domestic slave owners. Now I find it's all very well dominating slaves in my office or my factory. I am chief engineer for the Jergen Calculating

Machine Corporation, and I had had no trouble with my in-
dustrial and white-collar slaves. They come into the plant
knowing precisely where they are, and I know precisely
where I am. It's all cut and dried. I prefer the amenities when
dealing with, say, the PBX operator. I prefer to say, "Miss
Persons, will you please call Hoskins of McKee Steel?" rather
than "Persons, get me Hoskins of McKee." But this is merely
a preference of mine, a personal matter, and I know it and
Persons knows it. No, all that is well set, but this business of
Sandra's clothes quite threw me.

I made the blunder of asking her her opinion. She was
quick to use the advantage I gave her, but she was very careful not to go too far. "Would you like a pair of high heels for
street wear?" I asked her.

"If it is agreeable with you, sir."

"Well, now, let's see what they have in your size. . . .
Those seem sturdy enough and not too expensive. Are they
comfortable?"

"Quite comfortable, sir."

"There aren't any others you'd rather have?"

"These are very nice, sir."

"Well, I guess these will do quite well, for the time being
at least."

"I agree with you, sir."

I agree with you: that's a very different matter from *I submit to you.* And though I didn't perceive the difference at the
moment, still I was anything but easy in my mind by the time
I had got Sandra installed in my house. Oh, I had no trouble
preserving the proper reserve and distance with her, and I
could not in the slightest detail complain of her behavior. It
was just that I was not to the manner bred; that I was alone
in the house with her, knowing certain external things to do,
but supported by no customs and precedents as I was at the
plant; that I found it very uncomfortable to order a woman,
with whom I would not eat dinner at the same table, to come
to my bed for an hour or so after she had finished washing
the dishes. Sandra was delighted with the house and with her
quarters, with the television set I had had installed for her
and with the subscription to *Cosmopolitan* magazine that I
had ordered in her name. She was delighted and I was glad
she was delighted. That was the bad thing about it—I was
glad. I should have provided these facilities only as a heavy
industry provides half-hour breaks and free coffee for its
workers—to keep her content and to get more work out of

her. Instead I was as glad at her pleasure in them as though
she were an actual person. She was so delighted that tears
came to her eyes and she kissed my feet; then she asked me
where the foot basin was kept. I told her I had none. She said
that the dishpan would do until we got one. I told her to order a foot basin from Oakland's Own the next day, along
with any other utensils or supplies she felt we needed. She
thanked me, fetched the dishpan, and washed my feet. It embarrassed me to have her do it; I knew it was often done, I
enjoyed the sensuous pleasure of it, I admired the grace and
care with which she bent over my feet like a shoeshine, but
all the same I was embarrassed. Yet she did it every day
when I came home.

I do not think I could describe more economically the earlier stages of my connection to Sandra than by giving an account of the foot washing.

At first, as I have said, I was uneasy about it, though I
liked it too. I was not sure that as a slave she had to do it,
but she seemed to think she had to and she certainly wanted
to. Now this was all wrong of me. It is true that domestic
slaves usually wash their master's feet, but this is not in any
sense one of the slave's rights. It is a matter about which the
master decides, entirely at his own discretion. Yet, by treating
it as a set duty, a duty like serving me food in which she had
so profound an interest as to amount to a right, Sandra had
from the outset made it impossible for me to will not to have
her wash my feet. She did it every day when I came home;
even when I was irritable and told her to leave me alone, she
did it. Of course, I came to depend upon it as one of the
pleasures and necessary routines of the day. It was, in fact,
very soothing; she spent a long time at it and the water was
always just lukewarm, except in cold weather when it was
quite warm; as they do in good restaurants, she always
floated a slice of lemon in the water. The curve of her back,
the gesture with which she would shake the hair out of her
eyes, the happy, private smile she wore as she did it, these
were beautiful to me. She would always kiss, very lightly, the
instep of each foot after she had dried them—always, that is,
when we were alone.

If I brought a friend home with me, she would wash our
feet all right, but matter-of-factly, efficiently, with no little in-
timacies as when I was alone. But if it was a woman who
came with me, or a man and wife, Sandra would wash none
of our feet. Nor did she wash the feet of any callers. I

thought this was probably proper etiquette. I had not read my *Etiquette for Slaves* as well as Sandra obviously had, I let it go. During the first few weeks, all my friends, and particularly all my women friends, had to come to observe Sandra. She behaved surely and with complete consistency toward them all. I was proud of her. None of the women told me that Sandra was anything less than perfect, not even Helen, who would have been most likely to, being an old friend and sharp-tongued. After the novelty had worn off, I settled down with her into what seemed to be a fine routine, as one does with a mistress. To be sure, it was not long before I would think twice about bringing someone home for dinner with me; if there was much doubt in my mind about it, the difference in Sandra's foot washing alone would sway me not to bring my friend along, especially if my friend was a woman.

When I would come home late at night she would be waiting for me, with a smile and downcast eyes. I went, in October, to a convention in St. Louis for a week. When I came back, I think she spent an hour washing my feet, asking me to tell her about the physical conditions of my trip, nothing personal or intimate but just what I had eaten and what I had seen and how I had slept; but the voice in which she asked it. One night I came home very late, somewhat high, after a party. I did not want to disturb her, so I tried to go to my room noiselessly. But she heard me and came in in her robe to wash my feet; she helped me to bed, most gently. Not by a glance did she reproach me for having disturbed her sleep. But then, she never reproached me.

I did not realize fully how much I had come to depend on her until she fell sick. She was in the hospital with pneumonia for three days and spent six days convalescing. It was at Thanksgiving time. I declined invitations out to dinner, in order to keep Sandra company—to tend to her, I said to myself, though she tended to herself very nicely. I was so glad to have her well again that the first time she could come to me I kept her in my bed all night—so that she might not chill herself going back to her own bed, I told myself. That was the first time, yet by Christmas we were sleeping together regularly, though she kept her clothes in her own room. She still called me sir, she still washed my feet; according to the bill of sale I owned her; I thought her a perfect slave. I was uneasy no longer.

In fact, of course, I was making a fool of myself, and it took Helen to tell me so.

"Dell," she said over the edge of her cocktail glass, "you're in love with this creature."

"In love with Sandra!" I cried. "What do you mean?"

And I was about to expostulate hotly against the notion, when it occurred to me that too much heat on my part would confirm her in her opinion. Therefore, seeming to study the problem, I relapsed into a brown study—under Helen's watchful eye—and tried to calculate the best out for myself.

I rang for Sandra.

"More Manhattans," I said to her.

She bowed, took the shaker on her tray, and left. She was impeccable.

"No, Helen," I said finally, "she does not make my pulses race. The truth is, I come a lot closer to being in love with you than with Sandra."

"How absurd. You've never even made a pass at me."

"True."

But Sandra returned with the drinks, and after she had left we talked about indifferent matters.

As I was seeing Helen to the door, she said to me, "All the same, Dell, watch out. You'll be marrying this creature next. And who will drop by to see you then?"

"If I ever marry Sandra," I said, "it will not be for love. If I have never made a pass at you, my dear, it has not been for lack of love."

I looked at her rather yearningly, squeezed her hand rather tightly, and with a sudden little push closed the door behind her. I leaned against the wall for a moment and offered up a short prayer than Helen would never lose her present husband and come looking in my part of the world for another. I could have managed to love her all right, but she scared me to death.

I thought about what she had told me. I knew that I was not in love with Sandra—there were a thousand remnants of Chico in her that I could not abide—but I could not deny that I needed her very much. What Helen had made me see clearly was the extent to which I had failed to keep Sandra a slave. I did not know whether it was her scheming that had brought it about, or my slackness, or whether, as I suspected, something of both. Some of the more liberal writers on the subject say, of course, that such development is intrinsic in the situation for anyone in our cultural milieu. It is a problem recognized by the FSB in its handbook. But the handbook advises the master who finds himself in my predicament to trade his slave for another, preferably some stodgy, uninteresting number or one who is deficient in the proper qualities—in my case, as I thought, copulating. The trouble with this sound advice was that I didn't want to get rid of Sandra. She made me comfortable.

In fact, she made me so comfortable that I thought I was happy. I wanted to show my gratitude to her. After she had straightened up the kitchen that evening I called her into the living room where I was sitting over the paper.

"Yes, sir?" she said, standing demurely on the other side of the coffee table.

"Sandra," I began, "I'm very proud of you. I would like to do something for you."

"Yes, sir."

"Sit down."

"Thank you, sir."

As she sat, she took a cigarette from the box, without asking my permission, and lighted it. The way she arched her lips to smoke it, taking care not to spoil her lipstick, annoyed me, and the coy way she batted her eyelids made me regret I had called her in. Still, I thought, the Chico in her can be trained out. She's sound.

"What can I give you, Sandra?"

She did not answer for a moment. Every slave knows the answer to that question, and knows it is the one answer for which he won't be thanked.

"Whatever you wish to give me, sir, would be deeply appreciated."

I couldn't think of a thing to buy for her. Magazines, movies, television, clothes, jewelry, book club books, popular records, a permanent wave every four months, what else could I get her? Yet I had started this offer; I had to follow up with something. In my uneasiness and annoyance with myself, and knowing so well what it was she wanted, I went too far.

"Would you like freedom, Sandra?"

She dropped her eyes and seemed to droop a little. Then tears rolled down her cheeks, real mascara-stained tears of sadness, of profound emotion.

"Oh yes, sir," she said. "Oh my God, yes. Don't tease me about it. Please don't tease me."

So I promised her her freedom. I myself was moved, but I did not want to show it.

"I'm going for a short walk," I said. "You may go to your room."

I went for my walk, and when I came back she had prepared my foot bath. She had burned two pine boughs in the fireplace so that the room smelled wonderful. She had put on her loveliest dress, and had brushed her hair down as I liked it best. She did not speak as she washed my feet, nor even look up at my face. All her gratitude she expressed in the tenderness with which she caressed my feet and ankles. When she had finished drying them, she kissed them and then pressed them for a time against her breast. I do not think either of us, during these past few years, has ever been happier than at that moment.

Well, I had my lawyer draw up a writ of substantial manumission, and Sandra took the brass ring out of her left ear, and that was that. And that was about all of that, so far as I could see. She was free to go as she wanted, but she didn't want. She got wages now, it is true, but all she did with them was to buy clothes and gewgaws. She continued to take care of the house and me, to sleep in my bed and keep her own personal possessions in her own room, and to wash my feet as before. The manumission was nothing in itself, only a signpost that there had been some changes made. Continually and slowly changes kept being made.

For one thing, we began to eat together, unless I had guests in to dinner. For another, she began to call me Mr. Oakes. It seemed strange to have her go where she wanted, without asking me about it, on her nights out. I became so curious about what she could be doing that finally I asked her where she went. To night school, she said, learning how to type. I was delighted to hear that she had not been wasting her time at public dances, but I could not imagine why she wanted to learn typing. She had even bought a portable typewriter which she practiced on in her room when I was away. "Why?" she said. "My mother always said to me, 'Sandra, they can't fire slaves.' Well, I'm not a slave any longer. That was one nice thing about it, I wasn't ever afraid you'd fire me."

"But, my darling," I cried, "I'm never going to fire you. I couldn't possibly get along without you."

"I know it," she replied, "and I never want to leave either. All the same, I'm going to learn how to type." She had her own friends in to visit her; she even gave a bridge party one evening when I was not at home. But she never called me by my first name, she never checked up on me, she never asked me the sort of intrusive, prying question which a man hates answering. She kept her place.

Then she discovered she was pregnant. I immediately said I would assume all the financial responsibilities of her pregnancy and of rearing the child. She thanked me, and did not mention the subject again. But she took to sleeping in her own bed most of the time. She would serve breakfast while still in her robe and slippers. Her eyes were often red and swollen, though she always kept some sort of smile on her face. She mentioned something about going back to Chico. She began serving me canned soup at dinner. I drove her off to Reno and married her.

Helen had been right, I had married Sandra; but I had been right too, it wasn't for love. Oh, I loved her, some way or other, I don't know just how. But I married her simply because it was the next thing to do; it was just another milestone.

Nothing much happened for a while after we were married, except that she called me Dell and didn't even take the curlers out of her hair at breakfast. But she hadn't got to be free and equal overnight. That was to take some months of doing.

First of all, as a wife, she was much frailer than she had been as a slave. I had to buy all sorts of things for her, automatic machines to wash the clothes and the dishes, a cooking stove with nine dials and two clocks, an electric ironer that could iron a shirt in two minutes, a vacuum cleaner, one machine to grind the garbage up and another to mix pancake batter, a thermostatic furnace, an electric floor waxer, and a town coupe for her to drive about to do her errands in. She had to get other people to wash her hair now, and shave her legs and armpits, and polish her toenails and fingernails for her. She took out subscriptions to five ladies' magazines, which printed among them half a million words a month for her to read, and she had her very bathrobe designed in Paris. She moved the television set into the living room and had a teardrop chandelier hung from the center of the ceiling. When she had a miscarriage in her sixth month, she had a daily bouquet of blue orchids brought to her room; she had to rest, and pale blue orchids are so restful. She became allergic to the substance of which my mattress and pillows were composed, and I had to get a foam rubber mattress and foam rubber pillow, which stank. She finally insisted that we go to visit her

family in Chico, so we finally did, and that we go to visit my
family in Boston, so we finally did. The visits were equally
painful. We began to go to musical comedies and night clubs.
Helen had been right: my friends did not drop by to see us,
and they were apt to be sick when I invited them to dinner.
Still we weren't all the way.

One night I came home late from work, tired and hungry.
Dinner was not yet started, because Sandra had been delayed
by her hairdresser. She fixed pork chops, frozen green beans,
and bread and butter, with canned apricots for dessert. I had
done better myself. After dinner, after the machine had
washed the dishes, I asked her if she would bathe my feet. I
was so tired, I told her, my feet were so tired; it would be
very soothing to me. But she said, in an annoyed voice, that
she was feeling nervous herself. She was going to go to bed
early. Besides, the silence she left behind her said, besides I
am your wife now. She went to bed and I went to bed. She
was restless; she twisted and turned. Every time I would shift
my position or start to snore a little, she would sigh or poke
me. Finally she woke me clear up and said it was impossible
for her to sleep like this. Why didn't I go sleep in her former
room? She couldn't because of her allergy, she had to stay in
the foam rubber bed. So I moved into her room. And then I
knew that she was my equal, for most of the equal wives of
my friends lived like this.

Another night, I came home wanting very much to make
love to her. She had avoided my embrace for a long while.
She was always too nervous, or too tired, for the less she
worked the tireder she became; or she was busy, or simply
not in the mood. But tonight I would admit of no evasion.
She was beautiful and desirable, and I knew how well she
had once made love to me. Finally, I held her in my arms.
She knew I wanted her, and in a way as odd as mine she
loved me too. But there was no sensuous pressure of her body
against mine, no passion in her kiss. She put her arms about
my neck not to caress me but to hang like an albatross
against me. She pressed her head against my shoulder not for
amorous affection but to hide her face, to shelter it, in loneliness and fear and doubt. She did not resist me, or yield to
me, or respond to me, or try to avoid me. She only went
away and left me her body to do with as I pleased. And then
I knew that she was free, for most of the free wives of my
friends were like this with their husbands.

I had four choices, as I saw it: divorce her, have her psy-

choanalyzed, kill her, or return her to slavery. I was strongly
tempted to kill her, but I was an optimist, I thought she was
salvageable. Besides, who would do my housework for me? I
made her a slave again.

It is a wise provision of the law that says no slave may be
completely manumitted. Even substantial manumission provides for a five-year probationary period. Sandra had not
passed probation. I had the necessary papers drawn up, told
her, an hour before the men came, what was happening, and
had her sent to the FSB Rehabilitation School in Colorado
for a month.

She came back with the ring in her ear, saying sir to me,
and the very first night she washed my feet. Furthermore, she
made love better than she had done for a year. I thought we
were to be happy again, and for a week we seemed to be. But
the machines are still there to do most of the work, and she
still has her allergy. She does what a slave is supposed to do,
but it is an effort, she has to will it; it exhausts her.

One evening six months ago, I came home to find no dinner cooking, no foot bath waiting for me, no sign of Sandra
in her room. I found her lying on my bed reading *McCall's*
and smoking with a jewel-studded holder I had given her
when she was my wife. She flicked an ash onto the rug when
I entered the room, waved a languorous Hi! at me, and kept
on reading. I had my choice; she had clearly set it up for me.
I hesitated only a moment. I went down to the basement
where I had stowed away the three-thonged lash which had
been provided along with the manual of instructions when I
first bought her, and beat her on the bed where she lay.

I think I was more upset by the beating than Sandra was.
But I knew I had had to do it. I knew I had neglected my
duty as a master not to have done it long ago. I think now
that all this trouble could have been averted if formerly I had
only kept a firm hand, that is to say, had beaten her when
she had risen too presumptuously. For the truth is, Sandra is
happiest as a slave. That beating did her good, it kept her in
place, and she knew where she stood. It is no doubt all right
to free exceptional slaves, but not one like Sandra who is
happiest when hoping, when wheedling and pleasing, when
held to her place.

But the beatings I should have given her formerly would
simply have hurt; she would simply have avoided getting
them. Now, I am not so sure.

For she repeated the offense, exactly, within a month, and

I repeated the punishment. It wasn't so bad for me the second time. She began seeing just how far she could go before I would bring out the lash. She cooked more and more badly till I gave her a warning one evening. When I had finished speaking, she sank to the floor, pressed her forehead against my foot, looked at me, and said, "Your wish is my command." The irony was all in the act and words, if irony there was, for there was none in the voice or face. The truth was, as she discovered the next evening when she served me corned beef hash and raw carrots for dinner, my lash is her command. She seems happier, in a way, after these distasteful blow-ups, comes to my bed voluntarily and with the welts still on her back, does her work well, hums sometimes. Yet she falls back into her old stubborn mood, again and again. There seems to be nothing else for me to do but beat her. The FSB manual supports me. Yet I find it repugnant, and it cannot be good for Sandra's skin. I had to lash her a week ago, and already, from the dirt she is allowing to collect on the living room rug, it looks as though I'll have to do it again. This was not what I had wanted. Of course, I have learned how to make the lash perform for me, how to make it sting without really damaging, how to make nine blows lighter than three. But it seems a pity to have to resort to this, when it was all quite unnecessary. It's my own fault of course; I lacked the training, the matter-of-fact experience of being a master, and I did not set about my duties as a master so conscientiously as I should have. I know all this, but knowing it doesn't help matters a bit. Sometimes I think I should have killed her, it would have been better for both of us; but then she will do some little act of spontaneous love, as now bringing me a cup of hot chocolate and kissing me lightly on the back of the neck, which makes me glad to have her around. Yet tomorrow I shall have to beat her again. This is not what I had wanted, and it cannot be what she wants, not really. We were uneasy and felt something lacking when she was a slave before, though we were happy too. We were altogether miserable when she was free. Yet this is not what either of us had ever wanted, though we are both of us doing what we must.

Debut

Kristin Hunter

"Hold *still*, Judy," Mrs. Simmons said around the spray of
pins that protruded dangerously from her mouth. She gave
the thirtieth tug to the tight sash at the waist of the dress.
"Now walk over there and turn around slowly."

The dress, Judy's first long one, was white organdy over
taffeta, with spaghetti straps that bared her round brown
shoulders and a floating skirt and a wide sash that cascaded
in a butterfly effect behind. It was a dream, but Judy was sick
and tired of the endless fittings she had endured so that she
might wear it at the Debutantes' Ball. Her thoughts leaped
ahead to the Ball itself ...

"*Slowly*, I said!" Mrs. Simmons' dark, angular face was always grim, but now it was screwed into an expression resem-
bling a prune. Judy, starting nervously, began to revolve by
moving her feet an inch at a time.

Her mother watched her critically. "No, it's still not right.
I'll just have to rip out that waistline seam again."

"Oh, Mother!" Judy's impatience slipped out at last. "Nobody's going to notice all those little details."

"They will too. They'll be watching you every minute,
hoping to see something wrong. You've got to be the *best*.
Can't you get that through your head?" Mrs. Simmons gave a
sigh of despair. "You better start noticin' 'all those little details' yourself. I can't do it for you all your life. Now turn
around and stand up straight."

"Oh, Mother," Judy said, close to tears from being made
to turn and pose while her feet itched to be dancing, "I can't
stand it any more!"

"You can't stand it, huh? How do you think *I* feel?" Mrs.
Simmons said in her harshest tone.

Judy was immediately ashamed, remembering the weeks
her mother had spent at the sewing machine, pricking her already tattered fingers with needles and pins, and the great
weight of sacrifice that had been borne on Mrs. Simmons'

420

shoulders for the past two years so that Judy might bare hers at the Ball.

"All right, take it off," her mother said. "I'm going to take it up the street to Mrs. Luby and let her help me. It's got to be right or I won't let you leave the house."

"Can't we just leave it the way it is, Mother?" Judy pleaded without hope of success. "I think it's perfect."

"You would," Mrs. Simmons said tartly as she folded the dress and prepared to bear it out of the room. "Sometimes I think I'll never get it through your head. You got to look just right and act just right. That Rose Griffin and those other girls can afford to be careless, maybe, but you can't. You're gonna be the darkest, poorest one there."

Judy shivered in her new lace strapless bra and her old, childish knit snuggies. "You make it sound like a battle I'm going to instead of just a dance."

"It is a battle," her mother said firmly. "It starts tonight and it goes on for the rest of your life. The battle to hold your head up and get someplace and be somebody. We've done all we can for you, your father and I. Now you've got to start fighting some on your own." She gave Judy a slight smile; her voice softened a little. "You'll do all right, don't worry. Try and get some rest this afternoon. Just don't mess up your hair."

"All right, Mother," Judy said listlessly.

She did not really think her father had much to do with anything that happened to her. It was her mother who had ingratiated her way into the Gay Charmers two years ago, taking all sorts of humiliation from the better-dressed, better-off, lighter-skinned women, humbly making and mending their dresses, fixing food for their meetings, addressing more mail and selling more tickets than anyone else. The club had put it off as long as they could, but finally they had to admit Mrs. Simmons to membership because she worked so hard. And that meant, of course, that Judy would be on the list for this year's Ball.

Her father, a quiet carpenter who had given up any other ambitions years ago, did not think much of Negro society or his wife's fierce determination to launch Judy into it. "Just keep clean and be decent," he would say. "That's all anybody has to do."

Her mother always answered, "If that's all *I* did we'd still be on relief," and he would shut up with shame over the years when he had been laid off repeatedly and her days' work and sewing had kept them going. Now he had steady work but she refused to quit, as if she expected it to end at any moment. The intense energy that burned in Mrs. Simmons' large dark eyes had scorched her features into permanent irony. She worked day and night and spent her spare time scheming and planning. Whatever her personal ambitions had been, Judy knew she blamed Mr. Simmons for their failure; now all her schemes revolved around their only child.

Judy went to her mother's window and watched her stride down the street with the dress until she was hidden by the high brick wall that went around two sides of their house. Then she returned to her own room. She did not get dressed because she was afraid of pulling a sweater over her hair—her mother would notice the difference even if it looked all right to Judy—and because she was afraid that doing anything, even getting dressed, might precipitate her into the battle. She drew a stool up to her window and looked out. She had no real view, but she liked her room. The wall hid the crowded tenement houses beyond the alley, and from its cracks and bumps and depressions she could construct any imaginary landscape she chose. It was how she had spent most of the free hours of her dreamy adolescence.

"Hey, can I go?"

It was the voice of an invisible boy in the alley. As another boy chuckled, Judy recognized the familiar ritual; if you said yes, they said, "Can I go with you?" It had been tried on her dozens of times. She always walked past, head in the air, as if she had not heard. Her mother said that was the only thing to do; if they knew she was a lady, they wouldn't dare bother her. But this time a girl's voice, cool and assured, answered.

"If you think you're big enough," it said.

It was Lucy Mae Watkins; Judy could picture her standing there in a tight dress with bright, brazen eyes.

"I'm big enough to give you a baby," the boy answered.

Judy would die if a boy ever spoke to her like that, but she knew Lucy Mae could handle it. Lucy Mae could handle all the boys, even if they ganged up on her, because she had been born knowing something other girls had to learn.

"Aw, you ain't big enough to give me a shoe-shine," she told him.

"Come here and I'll show you how big I am," the boy said.

"Yeah, Lucy Mae, what's happenin'?" another boy said. "Come here and tell us."

Lucy Mae laughed. "What I'm puttin' down is too strong for little boys like you."

"Come here a minute, baby," the first boy said. "I got a cigarette for you."

"Aw, I ain't studyin' your cigarettes," Lucy Mae answered. But her voice was closer, directly below Judy. There were the sounds of a scuffle and Lucy Mae's muffled laughter. When she spoke her voice sounded raw and cross. "Come on now, boy. Cut it out and give me the damn cigarette." There was more scuffling, and the sharp crack of a slap, and then Lucy Mae said, "Cut it out, I said. Just for that I'm gonna take 'em all." The clack of high heels rang down the sidewalk with a boy's clumsy shoes in pursuit.

Judy realized that there were three of them down there. "Let her go, Buster," one said. "You can't catch her now."

"Aw, hell, man, she took the whole damn pack," the one called Buster complained.

"That'll learn you!" Lucy Mae's voice mocked from down the street. "Don't mess with nothin' you can't handle."

"Hey, Lucy Mae. Hey, I heard Rudy Grant already gave you a baby," a second boy called out.

"Yeah. Is that true, Lucy Mae?" the youngest one yelled.

There was no answer. She must be a block away by now.

For a moment the hidden boys were silent; then one of them guffawed directly below Judy, and the other two joined in the secret male laughter that was oddly high-pitched and feminine.

"Aw man, I don't know what you all laughin' about," Buster finally grumbled. "That girl took all my cigarettes. You got some, Leroy?"

"Naw," the second boy said.

"What we gonna do? I ain't got but fifteen cent. Hell, man, I want more than a feel for a pack of cigarettes." There was an unpleasant whine in Buster's voice. "Hell, for a pack of cigarettes I want a bitch to come across."

"She will next time, man," the boy called Leroy said.

"She better," Buster said. "You know she better. If she pass by here again, we gonna jump her, you hear?"

"Sure, man," Leroy said. "The three of us can grab her easy."

"Then we can all three of us have some fun. Oh, *yeah*, man," the youngest boy said. He sounded as if he might be about fourteen.

Leroy said, "We oughta get Roland and J.T. too. For a whole pack of cigarettes she oughta treat all five of us."

"Aw, man, why tell Roland and J.T.?" the youngest voice whined. "They ain't in it. Them was *our* cigarettes."

"They was *my* cigarettes, you mean," Buster said with authority. "You guys better quit it before I decide to cut you out."

"Oh, man, don't do that. We with you. You know that."

"Sure Buster, we your aces, man."

"All right, that's better." There was a minute of silence.

Then, "What we gonna do with the girl, Buster?" the youngest one wanted to know.

"When she come back we gonna jump the bitch, man. We gonna jump her and grab her. Then we gonna turn her every way but loose." He went on, spinning a crude fantasy that got wilder each time he retold it, until it became so secretive that their voices dropped to a low indistinct murmur punctuated by guffaws. Now and then Judy could distinguish the word "girl" or the other word they used for it; these words always produced the loudest guffaws of all. She shook off her fear with the thought that Lucy Mae was too smart to pass there again today. She had heard them at their dirty talk in the alley before and had always been successful in ignoring it; it had nothing to do with her, the wall protected her from their kind. All the ugliness was on their side of it, and this side was hers to fill with beauty.

She turned on her radio to shut them out completely and began to weave her tapestry to its music. More for practice than anything else, she started by picturing the maps of the places to which she intended to travel, then went on to the faces of her friends. Rose Griffin's sharp, Indian profile appeared on the wall. Her coloring was like an Indian's too and her hair was straight and black and glossy. Judy's hair, naturally none of these things, had been "done" four days ago so that tonight it would be "old" enough to have a gloss as natural-looking as Rose's. But Rose, despite her handsome looks, was silly; her voice broke constantly into high-pitched giggles and she became even sillier and more nervous around boys.

Judy was not sure that she knew how to act around boys either. The sisters kept boys and girls apart at the Catholic high school where her parents sent her to keep her away from low-class kids. But she felt that she knew a secret: tonight, in that dress, with her hair in a sophisticated upsweep, she would be transformed into a poised princess. Tonight all the college boys her mother described so eagerly would rush to dance with her, and then from somewhere *the boy* would appear. She did not know his name; she neither knew nor cared whether he went to college, but she imagined that he would be as dark as she was, and that there would be awe and diffidence in his manner as he bent to kiss her hand . . .

A waltz swelled from the radio; the wall, turning blue in deepening twilight, came alive with whirling figures. Judy rose and began to go through the steps she had rehearsed for so many weeks. She swirled with a practiced smile on her face, holding an imaginary skirt at her side; turned, dipped, and flicked on her bedside lamp without missing a fraction of the beat. Faster and faster she danced with her imaginary partner, to an inner music that was better than the sounds on the radio. She was "coming out," and tonight the world would discover what it had been waiting for all these years.

"Aw git it, baby." She ignored it as she would ignore the crowds that lined the streets to watch her pass on her way to the Ball.

"Aw, do your number." She waltzed on, safe and secure on her side of the wall.

"Can I come up there and do it with you?"

At this she stopped, paralyzed. Somehow they had come over the wall or around it and into her room.

"Man, I sure like the view from here," the youngest boy said. "How come we never tried this view before?"

She came to life, ran quickly to the lamp and turned it off, but not before Buster said, "Yeah, and the back view is fine, too."

"Aw, she turned off the light," a voice complained.

"Put it on again, baby, we don't mean no harm."

"Let us see you dance some more. I bet you can really do it."

"Yeah, I bet she can shimmy on down."

"You know it man."

"Come on down here, baby," Buster's voice urged softly, dangerously. "I got a cigarette for you."

"Yeah, and he got something else for you, too."

Judy, flattened against her closet door, gradually lost her urge to scream. She realized that she was shivering in her underwear. Taking a deep breath, she opened the closet door and found her robe. She thought of going to the window and yelling down, "You don't have anything I want. Do you understand?" But she had more important things to do.

Wrapping her hair in a protective plastic, she ran a full steaming tub and dumped in half a bottle of her mother's favorite cologne. At first she scrubbed herself furiously, irritating her skin. But finally she stopped, knowing she would never be able to get cleaner than this again. She could not wash away the thing they considered dirty, the thing that made them pronounce "girl" in the same way as the other four-letter words they wrote on the wall in the alley; it was part of her, just as it was part of her mother and Rose Griffin and Lucy Mae. She relaxed then because it was true that the boys in the alley did not have a thing she wanted. She had what they wanted, and the knowledge replaced her shame with a strange, calm feeling of power.

After her bath she splashed on more cologne and spent forty minutes on her makeup, erasing and retracing her eyebrows six times until she was satisfied. She went to her mother's room then and found the dress, finished and freshly pressed, on its hanger.

When Mrs. Simmons came upstairs to help her daughter she found her sitting on the bench before the vanity mirror as if it were a throne. She looked young and arrogant and beautiful and perfect and cold.

"Why, you're dressed already," Mrs. Simmons said in surprise. While she stared, Judy rose with perfect, icy grace and glided to the center of the room. She stood there motionless as a mannequin.

"I want you to fix the hem, Mother," she directed. "It's still uneven in back."

Her mother went down obediently on her knees muttering, "It looks all right to me." She put in a couple of pins. "That better?"

"Yes," Judy said with a brief glance at the mirror. "You'll have to sew it on me, Mother. I can't take it off now. I'd ruin my hair."

Mrs. Simmons went to fetch her sewing things, returned and surveyed her daughter. "You sure did a good job on yourself, I must say," she admitted grudgingly. "Can't find a thing to complain about. You'll look as good as anybody there."

"Of course, Mother," Judy said as Mrs. Simmons knelt and sewed. "I don't know what you were so worried about." Her secret feeling of confidence had returned, stronger than ever, but the evening ahead was no longer a vague girlish fantasy she had pictured on the wall; it had hard, clear outlines leading up to a definite goal. She would be the belle of the Ball because she knew more than Rose Griffin and her silly friends; more than her mother, more, even than Lucy Mae, because she knew better than to settle for a mere pack of cigarettes.

"There," her mother said, breaking the thread. She got up. "I never expected to get you ready this early. Ernest Lee won't be here for another hour."

"That silly Ernest Lee," Judy said, with a new contempt in her young voice. Until tonight she had been pleased by the thought of going to the dance with Ernest Lee; he was nice, she felt comfortable with him, and he might even be the awe-struck boy of her dream. He was a dark, serious neighborhood boy who could not afford to go to college; Mrs. Simmons had reluctantly selected him to take Judy to the dance because all the Gay Charmers' sons were spoken for. Now, with an undertone of excitement, Judy said, "I'm going to ditch him after the dance, Mother. You'll see. I'm going to come home with one of the college boys."

"It's very nice, Ernest Lee," she told him an hour later when he handed her the white orchid, "but it's rather small. I'm going to wear it on my wrist, if you don't mind." And then, dazzling him with a smile of sweetest cruelty, she stepped back and waited while he fumbled with the door.

"You know, Edward, I'm not worried about her any more," Mrs. Simmons said to her husband after the children were gone. Her voice became harsh and grating. "Put down that paper and listen to me! Aren't you interested in your child?—That's better," she said as he complied meekly. "I was saying, I do believe she's learned what I've been trying to teach her, after all."

Raymond's Run

Toni Cade Bambara

I don't have much work to do around the house like some girls. My mother does that. And I don't have to earn my pocket money by hustling; George runs errands for the big boys and sells Christmas cards. And anything else that's got to get done, my father does. All I have to do in life is mind my brother Raymond, which is enough.

Sometimes I slip and say my little brother Raymond. But as any fool can see he's much bigger and he's older too. But a lot of people call him my little brother cause he needs looking after cause he's not quite right. And a lot of smart mouths got lots to say about that too, especially when George was minding him. But now, if anybody has anything to say to Raymond, anything to say about his big head, they have to come by me. And I don't play the dozens or believe in standing around with somebody in my face doing a lot of talking. I much rather just knock you down and take my chances even if I am a little girl with skinny arms and a squeaky voice, which is how I got the name Squeaky. And if things get too rough, I run. And as anybody can tell you, I'm the fastest thing on two feet.

There is no track meet that I don't win the first place medal. I used to win the twenty-yard dash when I was a little kid in kindergarten. Nowadays, it's the fifty-yard dash. And tomorrow I'm subject to run the quarter-meter relay all by myself and come in first, second, and third. The big kids call me Mercury cause I'm the swiftest thing in the neighborhood. Everybody knows that—except two people who know better, my father and me. He can beat me to Amsterdam Avenue with me having a two fire-hydrant headstart and him running with his hands in his pockets and whistling. But that's private information. Cause you can imagine some thirty-five-year-old man stuffing himself into PAL shorts to race little kids? So as far as everyone's concerned, I'm the fastest and that goes for Gretchen, too, who has put out the tale that she is going to win the first-place medal this year. Ridiculous. In the second place, she's got short legs. In the third place, she's got freckles. In the first place, no one can beat me and that's all there is to it.

I'm standing on the corner admiring the weather and about to take a stroll down Broadway so I can practice my breathing exercises, and I've got Raymond walking on the inside close to the buildings, cause he's subject to fits of fantasy and starts thinking he's a circus performer and that the curb is a tightrope strung high in the air. And sometimes after a rain he likes to step down off his tightrope right into the gutter and slosh around getting his shoes and cuffs wet. Then I get hit when I get home. Or sometimes if you don't watch him he'll dash across traffic to the island in the middle of Broadway and give the pigeons a fit. Then I have to go behind him apologizing to all the old people sitting around trying to get some sun and getting all upset with the pigeons fluttering around them, scattering their newspapers and upsetting the waxpaper lunches in their laps. So I keep Raymond on the inside of me, and he plays like he's driving a stage coach which is O.K. by me so long as he doesn't run me over or interrupt my breathing exercises, which I have to do on account of I'm serious about my running, and I don't care who knows it.

Now some people like to act like things come easy to them, won't let on that they practice. Not me. I'll high-prance down 34th Street like a rodeo pony to keep my knees strong even if it does get my mother uptight so that she walks ahead like she's not with me, don't know me, is all by herself on a shopping trip, and I am somebody else's crazy child. Now you take Cynthia Procter for instance. She's just the opposite. If there's a test tomorrow, she'll say something like, "Oh, I guess I'll play handball this afternoon and watch television tonight," just to let you know she ain't thinking about the test. Or like last week when she won the spelling bee for the millionth time, "A good thing you got 'receive,' Squeaky, cause I would have got it wrong. I completely forgot about the spelling bee." And she'll clutch the lace on her blouse like it was a narrow escape. Oh, brother. But of course when I pass her house on my early morning trots around the block, she is practicing the scales on the piano over and over and over and over. Then in music class she always lets herself get bumped around so she falls accidently on purpose onto the piano stool and is so surprised to find herself sitting there that she decides just for fun to try out the ole keys. And what do you know—Chopin's waltzes just spring out of her fingertips and she's the most surprised thing in the world. A regular prodigy. I could kill people like that. I stay up all night studying the words for the spelling bee. And you can see me any time of day practicing running. I never walk if I can trot, and shame on Raymond if he can't keep up. But of course he does, cause if he hangs back someone's liable to walk up to him and get smart, or take his allowance from him, or ask him where he got that great big pumpkin head. People are so stupid sometimes.

So I'm strolling down Broadway breathing out and breathing in on counts of seven, which is my lucky number, and here comes Gretchen and her sidekicks: Mary Louise, who used to be a friend of mine when she first moved to Harlem from Baltimore and got beat up by everybody till I took up for her on account of her mother and my mother used to sing in the same choir when they were young girls, but people ain't grateful, so now she hangs out with the new girl Gretchen and talks about me like a dog; and Rosie, who is as fat as I am skinny and has a big mouth where Raymond is concerned and is too stupid to know that there is not a big deal of difference between herself and Raymond and that she can't afford to throw stones. So they are steady coming up Broadway and I see right away that it's going to be one of those Dodge City scenes cause the street ain't that big and they're close to the buildings just as we are. First I think I'll step into the candy store and look over the new comics and let them pass. But that's chicken and I've got a reputation to consider. So then I think I'll just walk straight on through them or even over them if necessary. But as they get to me, they slow down. I'm ready to fight, cause like I said I don't feature a whole lot of chit-chat, I much prefer to just knock you down right from the jump and save everybody a lotta precious time.

"You signing up for the May Day races?" smiles Mary Louise, only it's not a smile at all. A dumb question like that doesn't deserve an answer. Besides, there's just me and Gretchen standing there really, so no use wasting my breath talking to shadows.

"I don't think you're going to win this time," says Rosie, trying to signify with her hands on her hips all salty, completely forgetting that I have whupped her behind many times for less salt than that.

"I always win cause I'm the best," I say straight at Gretchen who is, as far as I'm concerned, the only one talking in this ventriloquist-dummy routine. Gretchen smiles, but it's not a smile, and I'm thinking that girls never really smile at each other because they don't know how and don't want to know how and there's probably no one to teach us how, cause grown-up girls don't know either. Then they all look at Raymond who has just brought his mule team to a standstill. And they're about to see what trouble they can get into through him.

"What grade you in now, Raymond?"

"You got anything to say to my brother, you say it to me, Mary Louise Williams of Raggedy Town, Baltimore."

"What are you, his mother?" sasses Rosie.

"That's right, Fatso. And the next word out of anybody and I'll be *their* mother too." So they just stand there and Gretchen shifts from one leg to the other and so do they. Then Gretchen puts her hands on her hips and is about to say something with her freckle-face self but doesn't. Then she walks around me looking me up and down but keeps walking up Broadway, and her sidekicks follow her. So me and Raymond smile at each other and he says, "Gidyap" to his team and I continue with my breathing exercises, strolling down Broadway toward the ice man on 145th with not a care in the world cause I am Miss Quicksilver herself.

I take my time getting to the park on May Day because the track meet is the last thing on the program. The biggest thing on the program is the May Pole dancing, which I can do without, thank you, even if my mother thinks it's a shame I don't take part and act like a girl for a change. You'd think my mother'd be grateful not to have to make me a white organdy dress with a big satin sash and buy me new white baby-doll shoes that can't be taken out of the box till the big day. You'd think she'd be glad her daughter ain't out there prancing around a May Pole getting the new clothes all dirty and sweaty and trying to act like a fairy or a flower or whatever you're supposed to be when you should be trying to be yourself, whatever that is, which is, as far as I am concerned, a poor Black girl who really can't afford to buy shoes and a new dress you only wear once a lifetime cause it won't fit next year.

I was once a strawberry in a Hansel and Gretel pageant when I was in nursery school and didn't have no better sense than to dance on tiptoe with my arms in a circle over my

head doing umbrella steps and being a perfect fool just so my
mother and father could come dressed up and clap. You'd
think they'd know better than to encourage that kind of nonsense. I am not a strawberry. I do not dance on my toes. I
run. That is what I am all about. So I always come late to
the May Day program, just in time to get my number pinned
on and lay in the grass till they announce the fifty-yard dash.

I put Raymond in the little swings, which is a tight squeeze
this year and will be impossible next year. Then I look
around for Mr. Pearson, who pins the numbers on. I'm really
looking for Gretchen if you want to know the truth, but she's
not around. The park is jam-packed. Parents in hats and cor-
sages and breast-pocket handkerchiefs peeking up. Kids in
white dresses and light-blue suits. The parkees unfolding
chairs and chasing the rowdy kids from Lenox as if they had
no right to be there. The big guys with their caps on back-
wards, leaning against the fence swirling the basketballs on
the tips of their fingers, waiting for all these crazy people to
clear out the park so they can play. Most of the kids in my
class are carrying bass drums and glockenspiels and flutes.
You'd think they'd put in a few bongos or something for real
like that.

Then here comes Mr. Pearson with his clipboard and his
cards and pencils and whistles and safety pins and fifty million other things he's always dropping all over the place with
his clumsy self. He sticks out in a crowd because he's on
stilts. We used to call him Jack and the Beanstalk to get him
mad. But I'm the only one that can outrun him and get away,
and I'm too grown for that silliness now.

"Well, Squeaky," he says, checking my name off the list
and handing me number seven and two pins. And I'm thinking he's got no right to call me Squeaky, if I can't call him
Beanstalk.

"Hazel Elizabeth Deborah Parker," I correct him and tell
him to write it down on his board.

"Well, Hazel Elizabeth Deborah Parker, going to give
someone else a break this year?" I squint at him real hard to
see if he is seriously thinking I should lose the race on purpose just to give someone else a break. "Only six girls running this time," he continues, shaking his head sadly like it's
my fault all of New York didn't turn out in sneakers. "That
new girl should give you a run for your money." He looks
around the park for Gretchen like a periscope in a submarine

movie. "Wouldn't it be a nice gesture if you were . . . to ahhh . . ."

I give him such a look he couldn't finish putting that idea into words. Grownups got a lot of nerve sometimes. I pin number seven to myself and stomp away, I'm so burnt. And I go straight for the track and stretch out on the grass while the band winds up with "Oh, the Monkey Wrapped His Tail Around the Flag Pole," which my teacher calls by some other name. The man on the loudspeaker is calling everyone over to the track and I'm on my back looking at the sky, trying to pretend I'm in the country, but I can't, because even grass in the city feels hard as sidewalk, and there's just no pretending you are anywhere but in a "concrete jungle" as my grandfather says.

The twenty-yard dash takes all of two minutes cause most of the little kids don't know no better than to run off the track or run the wrong way or run smack into the fence and fall down and cry. One little kid, though, has got the good sense to run straight for the white ribbon up ahead so he wins. Then the second-graders line up for the thirty-yard dash and I don't even bother to turn my head to watch cause Raphael Perez always wins. He wins before he even begins by psyching the runners, telling them they're going to trip on their shoelaces and fall on their faces or lose their shorts or something, which he doesn't really have to do since he is very fast, almost as fast as I am. After that is the forty-yard dash which I use to run when I was in first grade. Raymond is hollering from the swings cause he knows I'm about to do my thing cause the man on the loudspeaker has just announced the fifty-yard dash, although he might just as well be giving a recipe for angel food cake cause you can hardly make out what he's sayin for the static. I get up and slip off my sweat pants and then I see Gretchen standing at the starting line, kicking her legs out like a pro. Then as I get into place I see that ole Raymond is on line on the other side of the fence, bending down with his fingers on the ground just like he knew what he was doing. I was going to yell at him but then I didn't. It burns up your energy to holler.

Every time, just before I take off in a race, I always feel like I'm in a dream, the kind of dream you have when you're sick with fever and feel all hot and weightless. I dream I'm flying over a sandy beach in the early morning sun, kissing the leaves of the trees as I fly by. And there's always the smell of apples, just like in the country when I was little and

used to think I was a choo-choo train, running through the
fields of corn and chugging up the hill to the orchard. And
all the time I'm dreaming this, I get lighter and lighter until
I'm flying over the beach again, getting blown through the
sky like a feather that weighs nothing at all. But once I
spread my fingers in the dirt and crouch over the Get on
Your Mark, the dream goes and I am solid again and am
telling myself, Squeaky you must win, you must win, you are
the fastest thing in the world, you can even beat your father
up Amsterdam if you really try. And then I feel my weight
coming back just behind my knees then down to my feet then
into the earth and the pistol shot explodes in my blood and I
am off and weightless again, flying past the other runners, my
arms pumping up and down and the whole world is quiet except for the crunch as I zoom over the gravel in the track. I
glance to my left and there is no one. To the right, a blurred
Gretchen, who's got her chin jutting out as if it would win
the race all by itself. And on the other side of the fence is
Raymond with his arms down to his side and the palms
tucked up behind him, running in his very own style, and it's
the first time I ever saw that and I almost stop to watch my
brother Raymond on his first run. But the white ribbon is
bouncing toward me and I tear past it, racing into the distance till my feet with a mind of their own start digging up
footfuls of dirt and brake me short. Then all the kids standing on the side pile on me, banging me on the back and slapping my head with their May Day programs, for I have won
again and everybody on 151st Street can walk tall for another year.

"In first place . . ." the man on the loudspeaker is clear as
a bell now. But then he pauses and the loudspeaker starts to
whine. Then static. And I lean down to catch my breath and
here comes Gretchen walking back, for she's overshot the finish line too, huffing and puffing with her hands on her hips
taking it slow, breathing in steady time like a real pro and I
sort of like her a little for the first time. "In first place . . ."
and then three or four voices get all mixed up on the loudspeaker and I dig my sneaker into the grass and stare at
Gretchen who's staring back, we both wondering just who did
win. I can hear old Beanstalk arguing with the man on the
loudspeaker and then a few others running their mouths
about what the stopwatches say. Then I hear Raymond
yanking at the fence to call me and I wave to shush him, but
he keeps rattling the fence like a gorilla in a cage like in

them gorilla movies, but then like a dancer or something he starts climbing up nice and easy but very fast. And it occurs to me, watching how smoothly he climbs hand over hand and remembering how he looked running with his arms down to his side and with the wind pulling his mouth back and his teeth showing and all, it occurred to me that Raymond would make a very fine runner. Doesn't he always keep up with me on my trots? And he surely knows how to breathe in counts of seven cause he's always doing it at the dinner table, which drives my brother George up the wall. And I'm smiling to beat the band cause if I've lost this race, or if me and Gretchen tied, or even if I've won, I can always retire as a runner and begin a whole new career as a coach with Raymond as my champion. After all, with a little more study I can beat Cynthia and her phony self at the spelling bee. And if I bugged my mother, I could get piano lessons and become a star. And I have a big rep as the baddest thing around. And I've got a roomful of ribbons and medals and awards. But what has Raymond got to call his own?

So I stand there with my new plans, laughing out loud by this time as Raymond jumps down from the fence and runs over with his teeth showing and his arms down to the side, which no one before him has quite mastered as a running style. And by the time he comes over I'm jumping up and down so glad to see him—my brother Raymond, a great runner in the family tradition. But of course everyone thinks I'm jumping up and down because the men on the loudspeaker have finally gotten themselves together and compared notes and are announcing "In first place—Miss Hazel Elizabeth Deborah Parker." (Dig that.) "In second place—Miss Gretchen P. Lewis." And I look over at Gretchen wondering what the "P" stands for. And I smile. Cause she's good, no doubt about it. Maybe she'd like to help me coach Raymond; she obviously is serious about running, as any fool can see. And she nods to congratulate me and then she smiles. And I smile. We stand there with this big smile of respect between us. It's about as real a smile as girls can do for each other, considering we don't practice real smiling every day, you know, cause maybe we too busy being flowers or fairies or strawberries instead of something honest and worthy of respect . . . you know . . . like being people.

Biographical Notes

SHERWOOD ANDERSON (1876–1941)

Anderson, early in his life, feared that he might turn out like his father, Irwin, a jovial, theatrical raconteur who failed miserably to provide for his wife and family. To make up for his father's lack of ambition and money, the young Anderson worked energetically at a series of menial jobs which included delivery boy, farmhand, newsboy, factory employee, stablehand, and warehouse workman. At the age of thirty he had settled down to a conventional existence as a middle-class businessman, but during the next few years the writing which he had been doing in his spare time became increasingly important to him. The tension between the demands of his job and the need to devote himself to writing, which more and more preoccupied him, contributed to a nervous breakdown at the age of thirty-six. He left Ohio for Chicago to take a job there as an advertising copywriter, hoping it would provide financial support while allowing the time he needed for his literary career. His first novel, *Windy McPherson's Son*, appeared in 1916, and his first collection of tales, *Winesburg, Ohio*, followed three years later. Best known as a short story writer, he published three other collections: *The Triumph of the Egg* (1921), *Horses and Men* (1923), and *Death in the Woods and Other Stories* (1933).

TONI CADE BAMBARA b. 1939

Currently a Writer-in-Residence at Spelman College in Atlanta, Georgia, Bambara describes herself as "a community organizer, educator, parent, writer, and apprentice filmmaker." In preparation for an institute on children's film, television, and radio, she has been making films with neighborhood children and collaborating with some of them on a collection called *Chirrensay*, a "talking" picture book which is also a critique of educational programs for the young. An alumna of Queens College and the City University of New York, Bambara has taught at Rutgers, City College, Duke University, and Atlanta University. Her early work was published under the name Toni Cade. She added "Bambara," a maternal family name, as a tribute to the elders of the Bambara people of the Sudan. In addition to editing two anthologies, *The Black Woman* (1970), and *Tales and Stories for Black Folks* (1971), and writing numerous critical articles, she is the author of two collections of short stories, *Gorilla, My Love* (1972) and *The Seabirds Are Still Alive* (1977).

DOROTHY CANFIELD [FISHER] (1879–1958)

In 1904, Canfield received a Ph.D. in comparative literature at Columbia University, having written a dissertation on *Corneille and Racine in England*. While a graduate student at the Sorbonne, she studied languages, eventually becoming proficient in French, German, Italian, Spanish, and Danish. Always involved in educational theory, she observed the new pedagogical practices of Dr. Maria Montessori during a trip to Rome in 1912 and subsequently wrote two books explaining the Montessori method to Americans. During the First World War, Canfield moved to Europe with her husband and their two children so that they might perform relief services for the war effort. She edited a magazine for soldiers, arranged for the production of books and magazines for the blind, ran a commissary for the American Ambulance Field Service, and in the Basque country where she lived in 1918, helped refugees and organized children's homes. Back in America, she returned to her farm near Arlington, Vermont, which had long been in the Canfield family and at which she did virtually all of her writing. Among her novels are *The Squirrel Cage* (1912), *The Bent Twig* (1915), and *Rough-Hewn* (1922); among her short story collections are *Hillsboro People* (1915) and *The Real Motive* (1916).

ALICE CHILDRESS b. 1920

Born in South Carolina, but a long-time resident of New York, Childress is both an actress and playwright as well as a writer of fiction. Her play *Trouble in Mind* won the *Village Voice* Obie Award for the best original off-Broadway play in 1956, and in 1969 *Wine in the Wilderness* was produced on television by Channel WGBH in Boston. She directed and acted in the American Negro Theater over a period of twelve years and edited *Black Scenes: Collection of Scenes from Plays Written by Black People about Black Experience* (1971), published the same year in a paperback edition titled *Black Scenes*. Among her other works are a collection of sketches, *Like One of the Family: Conversations from a Domestic's Life* (1956); two one-act plays, *Moy's* and *String* (1971); and a book for children, *A Hero Ain't Nothin' But a Sandwich* (1973).

KATE CHOPIN (1851–1904)

In 1879, Chopin, her husband, Oscar, and five sons moved from New Orleans to Cloutierville, a small town in Louisiana where she gave birth to the last of her children, her daughter Lelia. Occupied with family concerns, she had never written a single word for publication, and her literary career, which was to begin when she was thirty-eight years old, was still a decade away. After the death of Oscar, she returned to her native St. Louis, and several years later, in 1889, two of her stories and a poem appeared. The following year, her first novel, *At Fault*, was published, and within a short period of time she had established herself as a short story writer of national reputation. Most of her stories were collected in two volumes, *Bayou Folk* (1894) and *A Night in Acadie* (1897). Amid a storm of abuse from literary critics, her masterpiece, the novel *The Awakening*, was published in 1899. Only recently has this novel achieved the recognition it has long deserved.

THEODORE DREISER (1871–1945)

Son of a stern German Catholic father and an affectionate Mennonite mother, Dreiser, who was born in Terre Haute, Indiana, recalled among his earliest impressions his overwhelming pity at the sight of the holes in his mother's badly worn shoes. Himself a "have-not," he felt the enormous temptations of American materialist society, having, as a young man, withheld money from his employer in order to buy the overcoat he desperately wanted. Dreiser's advanced education consisted of a single year at the University of Indiana, which was financed by Mildred Fielding, a high school teacher who believed he had great potential. Essentially, he developed as a writer through studying on his own such theorists as Huxley, Tyndall, and Spencer, and through practical experience as a reporter for newspapers in St. Louis, Chicago, Pittsburgh, and New York. His first novel, *Sister Carrie* (1900), received virtually no distribution since the publisher, Doubleday, Page and Co., after signing a contract with Dreiser, developed reservations about the novel's morality. Among the novels subsequently published were *Jennie Gerhardt* (1911), *The Financier*

(1912), *The Titan* (1914), *An American Tragedy* (1925), which was filmed in 1951 as *A Place in the Sun,* and *The Bulwark* (1946).

GEORGE P. ELLIOTT b. 1918

A professor of English in the writing program at Syracuse University since 1963, Elliott is the author of poetry, essays, literary criticism, and fiction. He has taught at Cornell University, Barnard College, the Writer's Workshop of the University of Iowa, and the University of California at Berkeley. Among his awards are a *Hudson Review* fellowship for fiction and both Guggenheim and Ford Foundation fellowships. His novels include *Parktilden Village* (1958), *David Knudsen* (1962), *In the World* (1965), and *Muriel* (1972). *Among the Dangs* (1961) and *An Hour of Last Things* (1968) are two collections of his short stories. According to Mr. Elliott, he has recently been working on a novel "about a young black woman who is defining herself against a middle-aged white woman."

WILLIAM FAULKNER (1897–1962)

Although he had already published a volume of verse and two novels, when he wrote *As I Lay Dying* in the summer of 1929, Faulkner was supporting himself stoking coal on the night shift at the power plant of his home town, Oxford, Mississippi. That year, which brought publication of two novels, *The Sound and the Fury* and *Sartoris,* also marked Faulkner's discovery that he had merely begun to explore the riches of Yoknapatawpha County, the archetypal Southern cosmos within his own mind. During brief periods in the 1930s and 1940s he went to Hollywood as a scriptwriter, working on the movie versions of Hemingway's *To Have and Have Not* and Raymond Chandler's *The Big Sleep* among others, but he always considered these trips financially motivated interludes away from Oxford. Among his other novels are *Light in August* (1932), *Absalom, Absalom!* (1936), *The Hamlet* (1940), *A Fable* (1954), and *The Reivers* (1962). He was awarded the Nobel Prize for literature in 1950.

MARY WILKINS FREEMAN (1852–1930)

In 1877, at the age of twenty-five, Mary E. Wilkins accompanied her parents, who had suffered financial losses, in moving into the home of Thomas Pickman Tyler, where Mary's mother, Eleanor, had accepted the job of housekeeper. Mary, the only one of four Wilkins children to survive into adulthood, had tried teaching for a year and had long been attempting to sell her poems and stories. Not until 1881 (the year after her mother's death), did Freeman succeed in selling any of her writing. Among almost forty volumes of her work which were subsequently published are the novels *Jane Field* (1893), *Pembroke* (1894), and *The Shoulders of Atlas* (1908), as well as collections of her short stories: *A Humble Romance and Other Stories* (1887), *A New England Nun and Other Stories* (1891), and *Six Trees* (1903). When she married Dr. Charles Freeman in 1902, she left New England to become a resident of Metuchen, New Jersey.

HAMLIN GARLAND (1860–1940)

Both in a small Wisconsin village to which his father had moved the family from Maine, Garland learned early about the brutalizing toil and poverty experienced by the unsuccessful seekers after "the American Dream." At the age of twenty-four, he left the Midwest for Boston where, essentially, he educated himself through extensive reading at the Boston Public Library. Ironically, the scenes which triggered his literary imagination and provided the material for his first tales were those of the harsh and dull farm life he encountered when he visited his family out West in 1887. His early stories were collected in *Main-Travelled Roads* (1891). This volume was expanded in 1910, when Garland included in the revised edition the stories of two other books: *Prairie Folk* (1893) and *Wayside Courtships* (1897). His most vital fiction reflects his desire for social and political reforms to help the struggling farm and working families he knew so well as a boy. Among his other works are *A Little Norsk* (1892), *Rose of Dutcher's Coolly* (1895), *Hesper* (1903), and the autobiographical narrative *A Son of the Middle Border* (1917).

CHARLOTTE PERKINS GILMAN (1860–1935)

Since the only time Gilman's mother, Mary Perkins, would reveal her overwhelming love and tenderness for her young daughter was when she believed Charlotte to be asleep, the affection-starved child did her best to remain awake until her mother came to her bed, "even using pins to prevent dropping off." "Then," writes Gilman in her autobiography, "how carefully I pretended to be sound asleep, and how rapturously I enjoyed being gathered into her arms, held close and kissed." Mrs. Perkins, an abandoned wife who was suffering pathetically from a lack of love, hoped that if she denied all signs of affection to Charlotte, the child would never need nor long for them. This "inoculation" against love was, of course, an utter failure. But, as with her mother's marriage, Charlotte's first marriage, to Charles Stetson, proved to have traumatic effects. At the age of thirty, Gilman had been divorced and had moved to California where she faced the most difficult years of her life. An ardent feminist, she supported herself by lecturing on socialism and on the status of women, teaching school, running a boarding house, editing newspapers, and writing. Among her works on social and feminist issues are *Women and Economics* (1898), *Concerning Children* (1900), *Human Work* (1904), and *The Man-made World; or Our Androcentric Culture* (1911). Her autobiography, *The Living of Charlotte Perkins Gilman*, appeared in 1935.

JOANNE GREENBERG b. 1932

Greenberg, a registered "Interpreter of the Deaf," teaches sign language in Colorado, and has written a novel on this subject entitled *In This Sign* (1970). She is also the author of three other novels, *The King's Persons* (1963), *The Monday Voices* (1965), and *I Never Promised You a Rose Garden* (1964). The latter, which was published under the pseudonym "Hannah Green," was made into a film in 1977. In it, Greenberg dramatized the return to sanity of a sensitive sixteen-year-old girl who had escaped into her own mad world in order to avoid the pain of the real one. She is also the author of two collections of short stories, *Summering* (1966) and *Rites of Passage* (1972). A graduate of American University in Washington, D.C., and the University of London, she is involved in teaching elementary school children about the history and structure of the English language.

ERNEST HEMINGWAY (1899–1961)

In the spring of 1919, Hemingway addressed the students at Oak Park High in Illinois, the school from which he had been graduated slightly less than two years earlier. But the young hero who described his war experiences to this school assembly felt, no doubt, that there was a lifetime of experience separating him from these boys and girls. In that short span of time, he had been a reporter for the *Kansas City Star*, covering violent and dramatic stories for the paper, had driven a Red Cross ambulance on the Italian Front, had been seriously wounded in both legs, and had fallen "wildly" in love with Agnes von Kurowsky, a nurse in Milan. During the 1920s, he supported himself in Paris as a newspaper correspondent, publishing his first volume, *Three Stories and Ten Poems*, in 1923. Two years later, he added nine stories and numerous miniature sketches to the original three stories to form *In Our Time* a volume which received critical acclaim for originality of technique and attitude. Among his best-known novels are *The Sun Also Rises* (1926), the work which established his reputation, *A Farewell to Arms* (1929), *To Have and Have Not* (1937), *For Whom the Bell Tolls* (1940), and *The Old Man and the Sea* (1952). His short story collections include *Men Without Women* (1927) and *Winner Take Nothing* (1933). In 1954 he won the Nobel Prize for literature.

KRISTIN HUNTER b. 1931

In recent years Hunter has been teaching creative writing at her alma mater, the University of Pennsylvania. Now a resident of New Jersey, she has worked as a columnist for the Philadelphia edition of the *Pittsburgh Courier*, as an advertising copywriter, and as Information Officer for the City of Philadelphia. Her article "Pray for Barbara's Baby" was selected for the Sigma Delta Chi Best Magazine Reporting of 1968 Award, and she has won a *Chicago Tribune* Book World Prize (1973). Her television play, *Minority of One*, received a Fund for the Republic Prize in 1955 and was produced on the CBS network in 1956. Among her books are three for young readers: *The Soul Brothers and Sister Lou* (1968), *Boss Cat* (1971), and *Guest in the Promised Land* (1973), which was nominated for a National Book Award. In addition to publishing poems, short stories, and articles in numerous magazines, she is the author of three novels: *God Bless the Child* (1964), *The Landlord* (1966; filmed in 1970), and *The Survivors* (1975). Her latest novel, *The Lakestown Rebellion*, will appear early in 1978.

RONA JAFFE b. 1932

Shortly after her graduation from Radcliffe College, Jaffe became an editor for a major New York publishing company. There she not only received a very low salary but, because of her youth, was relegated to a back room in order to avoid insulting the sensibilities of the writers whose work she edited. She was considered too young for the job "and a girl at that." Jaffe began her career as an author with the sale of a short story to *Seventeen*. Encouraged by an editor at Simon and Schuster, she wrote *The Best of Everything* (1958), which became a best seller and was made into a film in 1959. Among her other books are *Mr. Right Is Dead*

(1965), *Fame Game* (1969), *The Other Woman* (1972), *Family Secrets* (1975), and *The Last Chance* (1976), a novel which, according to its author, is concerned with "change and choice" as well as with "meaningless violence."

SARAH ORNE JEWETT (1849–1909)

At nineteen, under a pseudonym, Jewett published her first short story, "Jenny Garrow's Lovers," thus embarking on a long and successful career as an author. Although she was graduated from Berwick Academy, the strongest educational influence in her life was her father, Dr. Theodore Herman Jewett, a country physician. Traveling with her father about South Berwick, Maine, as he visited his patients, the young girl absorbed a great many impressions of human nature and became as well a perceptive observer of the New England seacoast and countryside. To a large extent, these experiences informed her vision as she began to write fresh and vivid short stories of rural American life. Among her works are: *Deephaven* (1877), *Country By-Ways* (1881), *A Country Doctor* (1884), *A Marsh Island* (1885), *A White Heron and Other Stories* (1886), and *The Queen's Twin and Other Stories* (1899). Her most famous and most representative work is *The Country of the Pointed Firs* (1896).

WRIGHT MORRIS b. 1910

Born in Central City, Nebraska, Morris has been a professor at California State University since 1962. He has complemented a successful literary career through an intense interest in photography, and been awarded Guggenheim fellowships for his work in both disciplines. A number of his books present both verbal and pictorial images, among them: *The Inhabitants* (1946), *The Home Place* (1948), and *God's Country and My People* (1968). His other works include *Man and Boy* (1951), *Love Among the Cannibals* (1957), *Fire Sermon* (1971), and *The Fork River Space Project* (1977). The University of Nebraska, presently publishers of over a dozen of Morris's novels, recently issued *Conversations with Wright Morris*.

JOYCE CAROL OATES b. 1938

One of the most prolific contemporary writers, Oates continues to teach English full time at the University of Windsor in Ontario,

Canada. Born in Lockport, New York, where she attended a one-room elementary schoolhouse, she was graduated from Syracuse University and received a master's degree in English from the University of Wisconsin. Oates, who has a compulsion to draw faces (and believes she may have already drawn several million faces in her lifetime), has indicated that she does not "write" her fiction while seated at the typewriter, but goes to the machine to write about the characters, their histories and behavior, after she has created and lived with them in her thoughts over a period of time. Among her novels are: *With Shuddering Fall* (1964), *Expensive People* (1968), *them* (1969), which won the National Book Award, *Wonderland* (1971), and *The Assassins* (1975). *The Wheel of Love* (1970) and *Marriages and Infidelities* (1972) are two of her numerous collections of short stories.

TILLIE OLSEN b. 1913

"Tell Me a Riddle," the title story of a volume of four of Olsen's tales, won the O. Henry Award for the best American short story in 1961. Currently a resident of San Francisco, she edited Rebecca Harding Davis's *Life in the Iron Mills* (1972) and published a novel *Yonnondio: From the Thirties* (1974). The title refers to the fact that the manuscript for this novel was rediscovered by Olsen almost forty years after she had been forced to set it aside for lack of time to complete it. In a poignant feminist essay, "Silences: When Women Don't Write," (*Harper's*, October, 1965), Olsen discusses the creative drive as well as the particular difficulties women experience in responding to it. Olsen, who has taught at Amherst College, Stanford University, and the University of Massachusetts at Boston, currently has a Guggenheim fellowship and is at work on a novel.

KATHERINE ANNE PORTER b. 1890

Born in Indian Creek, Texas, Porter is a distant cousin of William Sidney Porter (O. Henry) and the great-great-great granddaughter of Jonathan Boone, the younger brother of Daniel Boone. She supported herself as a newspaper reporter, ghost writer, and magazine writer both before and after traveling to Mexico in 1920 to study art. In 1930, a collection entitled *Flowering Judas and Other Stories* appeared, but not until five years later did the volume achieve its final form with the addition of four other tales. In 1931, she was awarded a Guggenheim fellowship and returned to Mexico. Later that year, she sailed for Europe, and this trip to Germany provided some of the background

materials for her only novel, *Ship of Fools* (1962). *Pale Horse,
Pale Rider* (1939) and *The Leaning Tower and Other Stories* are
collections of her tales, while *The Days Before* (1952) is a volume of essays and literary criticism.

J. F. POWERS b. 1917

In 1943 *Accent* published "Lions, Harts, Leaping Does," a short
story which Powers had written while working in a Chicago
bookstore. Selected for the volume *O. Henry Prize Stories* the following year, the story brought its author national recognition.
Prior to this success, Powers, who went to work in the middle of
the Depression, was employed as a department store clerk, door-
to-door insurance salesman, and chauffeur. A graduate of Quincy
College Academy, he has taught courses in writing at St. John's
University in Collegeville, Minnesota, Marquette University, the
University of Michigan, and Smith College. He has received Guggenheim and Rockefeller-*Kenyon Review* fellowships, and was
awarded the National Book Award for his first novel, *Morte d'Ur-
ban*, in 1963. *Prince of Darkness and Other Stories* (1947), *The
Presence of Grace* (1956), and *Look How the Fish Live* (1975)
are collections of his stories.

SHIRLEY SCHOONOVER b. 1936

Born in Biwabik, a Finnish-American community in Minnesota,
Schoonover now lives in Missouri, where she is at work on a
novel. She describes this work, *Flowers for Leah*, as the story of a
woman who has a heart attack in her fortieth year, and who must
struggle with a disintegrating marriage and an academic career.
Currently, she is also writing haiku which are being set to music
by composer Warren Benson and will be performed at Lincoln
Center. Two of her short stories were selected for inclusion in O.
Henry Award Prize Stories collections: "The Star Blanket" in
1962, and "Old and Country Tale" in 1964. Her novels include
Mountain of Water, nominated for a Pulitzer Prize in 1966, and
Sam's Song (1969).

RICHARD SHERMAN (1906–1962)

At Harvard, Sherman headed the editorial board of the *Crimson*
as well as writing for the *Advocate*. Upon graduation in 1928, he
wrote for *The Forum* and later *Vanity Fair*, becoming a free-
lance writer in 1935. In addition to publishing numerous stories,

he wrote four novels: *To Mary with Love* (1936), a best seller about the Twenties, which was made into a movie; *The Unready Heart* (1944), written in and about London while he was in the army; *The Bright Promise* (1947); and *The Kindred Spirit* (1951). Prior to the Second World War, he was a scriptwriter in Hollywood and worked on the screen plays of *To Mary with Love, The Story of Vernon and Irene Castle,* and *For Me and My Gal,* among others. Born in Bancroft, Iowa, and raised in Montana, he spent the last decade of his life in New York City.

JEAN STAFFORD (1915–1979)

Born in Covina, California, Stafford is the daughter of John Richard Stafford, who wrote Western stories under the pseudonym Jack Wonder or, occasionally, Ben Delight, and published one novel, *When Cattle Kingdom Fell,* under his own name. Although she has returned to the West only briefly, Stafford asserts that her "roots remain in the semi-fictitious town of Adams, Colorado, although the rest of me may abide in the South or the Midwest or New England or New York." She received a B.A. and an M.A. from the University of Colorado in 1936 and subsequently has taught at Stevens College and been a fellow at the Wesleyan University Center for Advanced Studies as well as a Guggenheim fellow and recipient of a Rockefeller Foundation grant. Frequently a contributor of stories and articles to magazines such as the *New Yorker* and *Harper's,* Stafford won the O. Henry Memorial Award for the best short story of 1955 for "In the Zoo." Among her novels are: *Boston Adventure* (1944), *The Mountain Lion* (1947), and *The Catherine Wheel* (1952). In 1970, she won the Pulitzer Prize for *The Collected Stories of Jean Stafford,* which contains, among others, stories previously published in *Children Are Bored on Sunday* (1953) and *Bad Characters* (1964).

JOHN STEINBECK (1902–1968)

Raised in the congenial atmosphere of the Salinas Valley of California, Steinbeck began early to absorb the sights and sounds of the country as well as the experiences of a wide range of working people. He attended Stanford University intermittently over a period of five years (without getting a degree) and had a series of jobs such as ranch hand, surveyor, road worker, deck hand on a freighter, hod carrier, and cotton picker. This physical work brought him into close contact with the laborers and farmers whose lives and problems inspired his fiction. His first work to attract popular attention was *Tortilla Flat* (1935), which humorously depicted the world of the Monterey *paisanos* (Mexican-Americans). Among his best-known novels are *In Dubious Battle* (1936); *Of Mice and Men* (1937), which was published as a dramatization as well in 1940; *The Grapes of Wrath* (1939), which won a Pulitzer Prize and was made into a film the following year, and *The Winter of Our Discontent* (1961). He published only two collections of stories: *The Pastures of Heaven* (1932) and *The Long Valley* (1938). In 1962, he was awarded the Nobel Prize for literature.

JOHN UPDIKE b. 1932

At the age of twenty-two, Updike had graduated *summa cum laude* from Harvard, won a fellowship to the Ruskin School of Drawing and Fine Art in Oxford, England, sold his first short story, "Friends from Philadelphia," to the *New Yorker* and been offered a job on the magazine's staff for the following year. No young writer could have wished for a more auspicious beginning of a creative career. In the little over two decades since that first success, Updike has published three volumes of poetry, seven novels, six volumes of short stories, two collections of essays, a play, and four books for children. Among his best-known novels are *Rabbit, Run* (1960); *The Centaur* (1963), which won the National Book Award; *Couples* (1968); *Rabbit Redux* (1971), and *A Month of Sundays* (1975). His short story collections include *Pigeon Feathers* (1962) and *Museums and Women and Other Stories* (1972).

ANNE WARNER [FRENCH] (1869–1913)

Born in St. Paul, Minnesota, Warner could trace her family roots to English settlers of Massachusetts in the 1630s. Educated at home by a clever, widely read mother and a French tutor, she found in the household of her scholarly lawyer father a congenial atmosphere for literary development. Married in 1888 to a businessman twenty-five years her senior, she began her literary career with the publication of *An American Ancestry* (1894), a genealogical account which she wrote for her son Charles after an infant daughter had died in 1892. Among her works are *His Story, Their Letters* (1902); *A Woman's Will* and *Susan Clegg and Her Friend Mrs. Lathrop* (1904); *The Rejuvenation of Aunt Mary* (1905); *Susan Clegg and Her Neighbors' Affairs* (1906); a collection of short stories, *An Original Gentleman* (1908), and *Susan Clegg and Her Love Affairs*, published posthumously in 1916.

JESSAMYN WEST b. 1907

At the age of twenty-nine, only weeks away from taking her oral exams for a doctorate in English, West discovered that she was suffering from an acute case of tuberculosis. Although the doctors believed she had little chance of survival, she emerged after a lengthy battle for her life to demonstrate new energy and a determination to do the writing which she had been postponing before her illness. In 1939, she published her first short story, "99.6," which deals with sanitarium life. The Friendly Persuasion, a series of sketches about a Quaker family during the Civil War, appeared in 1945, and West was co-author of the screenplay when this highly successful work was made into a film in 1956. Among her other works are The Witch Diggers (1951), Cress Delahanty (1953), South of the Angels (1960), Leafy Rivers (1967), Except for Me and Thee: A Companion to the Friendly Persuasion (1969), and two collections of stories: Love, Death, and the Ladies' Drill Team (1955) and Crimson Ramblers of the World, Farewell (1970).

EDITH WHARTON (1862–1937)

At the age of twenty-four, with her marriage to Edward Wharton only a few days away, Edith Jones timidly approached her mother, Lucretia, to ask for any information which would relieve her bewilderment and anxiety about her impending sexual union. Lucretia Jones termed the request ridiculous and accused her daughter of pretending to be stupid because certainly young Edith had seen enough statues and pictures to have realized that men and women are made differently. This was the extent of the sex education supplied to the bride-to-be. A member of a wealthy and socially prominent New York family, Edith appeared to be accepting a rather conventional role as a society matron in marrying Wharton. Her first full-length volume, The Decoration of Houses (1897), was much in keeping with this image since it was an elegant nonfiction work, written in collaboration with the architect Ogden Codman, and essentially addressed to wealthy collectors of art. Only after Wharton began to recover from a mental breakdown in 1898 did she come to recognize that she gained health and vitality as she worked, once again, as a writer of fiction. Thus, she completed several stories for her first collection, The Greater Inclination which appeared in 1899. Increasingly, she turned to her art, and although she certainly never thought of her writing as social protest, she might well be described as "a feminist surprised." Among her best-known novels are *The House of Mirth* (1905), *Ethan Frome* (1911), *The Custom of the Country* (1913), *The Age of Innocence* (1920), which was awarded a Pulitzer Prize the following year, and *Hudson River Bracketed* (1929).

WILLIAM CARLOS WILLIAMS (1883–1963)

Principally thought of as a major American poet, Williams published over thirty volumes of poetry, including a five-volume epic poem titled *Paterson*. At the University of Pennsylvania, where he was a medical student between 1902 and 1906, he met and became a close friend of two other young poets, Ezra Pound and H.D. (Hilda Doolittle), and later became an advocate for the group of poets known as "Imagists." Surprisingly, Williams was able to pursue an active literary career while maintaining his medical practice, becoming a well-loved and respected physician in Rutherford, New Jersey. Several editions of his collected poems have been published as well as volumes of fiction such as *The Great American* (1923), *The Knife of the Times and Other Stories* (1932), *White Mule* (1937), *Life Along the Passaic River* (1938), and *Make Light of It* (1950).

Anthologies You'll Want to Read